A STOLEN MOMENT

Why did she let her heart rule her head?

She did not knock on the sagging door, which stood slightly ajar. Pushing it open, she stepped inside and released the black-and-white spotted hounds, letting them find their own warm place in front of the fire.

Sarah was struck anew with Nathan's handsomeness. Casually dressed in Wellingtons, tight fawn breeches, and a collarless shirt, he sat in the lone chair, his feet stretched toward the dancing flames, his head lolled back against the high back of the chair. He was asleep.

When Sarah cleared her throat, he jumped to his feet. "What kept you?" He took her small hands into his large ones, kissing them and then holding them tightly. "I've been waiting for hours."

"I had not intended to come—"

Lord Chesterson's tender smile stopped her. "I had not intended to ask you, dear Sarah, but I could not help myself. Stolen moments are better than no moments at all . . ."

ZEBRA REGENCIES
ARE
THE TALK OF THE TON!

A REFORMED RAKE   (4499, $3.99)
by Jeanne Savery

After governess Harriet Cole helped her young charge flee to France—and the designs of a despicable suitor, more trouble soon arrived in the person of a London rake. Sir Frederick Carrington insisted on providing safe escort back to England. Harriet deemed Carrington more dangerous than any band of brigands, but secretly relished matching wits with him. But after being taken in his arms for a tender kiss, she found herself wondering— *could* a lady find love with an irresistible rogue?

A SCANDALOUS PROPOSAL   (4504, $4.99)
by Teresa DesJardien

After only two weeks into the London season, Lady Pamela Premington has already received her first offer of marriage. If only it hadn't come from the *ton's* most notorious rake, Lord Marchmont. Pamela had already set her sights on the distinguished Lieutenant Penford, who had the heroism and honor that made him the ideal match. Now she had to keep from falling under the spell of the seductive Lord so she could pursue the man more worthy of her love. Or was he?

A LADY'S CHAMPION   (4535, $3.99)
by Janice Bennett

Miss Daphne, art mistress of the Selwood Academy for Young Ladies, greeted the notion of ghosts haunting the academy with skepticism. However, to avoid rumors frightening off students, she found herself turning to Mr. Adrian Carstairs, sent by her uncle to be her "protector" against the "ghosts." Although, Daphne would accept no interference in her life, she *would* accept aid in exposing any spectral spirits. What she never expected was for Adrian to expose the secret wishes of her hidden heart . . .

CHARITY'S GAMBIT   (4537, $3.99)
by Marcy Stewart

Charity Abercrombie reluctantly embarks on a London season in hopes of making a suitable match. However she cannot forget the mysterious Dominic Castille—and the kiss they shared—when he fell from a tree as she strolled through the woods. Charity does not know that the dark and dashing captain harbors a dangerous secret that will ensnare them both in its web—leaving Charity to risk certain ruin and losing the man she so passionately loves . . .

Available wherever paperbacks are sold, or order direct from the Publisher. Send cover price plus 50¢ per copy for mailing and handling to Penguin USA, P.O. Box 999, c/o Dept. 17109, Bergenfield, NJ 07621. Residents of New York and Tennessee must include sales tax. DO NOT SEND CASH.

Lady Sarah's Fancy
Irene Loyd Black

ZEBRA BOOKS
KENSINGTON PUBLISHING CORP.

To My Sister Dee
with Love

ZEBRA BOOKS are published by

Kensington Publishing Corp.
850 Third Avenue
New York, NY 10022

First Printing: November, 1994

Printed in the United States of America

Chapter One

Lady Sarah Templeton stood on the second-story loggia of Templeton Hall and looked out over the Hudson River, listening to its constant throbbing, its splashing against the tree-lined banks. A soft fall breeze whipped at her blue skirt and lifted her auburn hair from her nape, cooling her flushed face. Her small hands were balled into fists, and inside one of those fists was a crumpled missive.

Sarah's mind went back to the time when her father, Lord Templeton plopped her down onto the plank floor of an abandoned house and said to her and to her brother Hoggie, who was eight years to her three, "We are in the Colonies, in Dutchess County. The river behind us is the Hudson. This will be called Templeton Hall on the Hudson . . ."

The seventeen years had passed quickly for Sarah, and now she was going home. A servant had placed the missive in the silver salver in the upstairs central room. Sarah had found it when she quit the small dining room where the family ate breakfast, served from a sideboard by servants dressed in proper livery.

Laboriously Sarah smoothed the crumpled paper and read the unbelievable words again, for the tenth time: *"Dear Lady Sarah, I pray that you will return to Merrymount to live."*

That was all, except: *Lady Lillian Merriwether, Merrymount, Rockingham, Northamptonshire, England.*

"What a strange message, so short, so blunt," Sarah said to the wind. It was the first word from her Aunt Lillian in seventeen years. Even at Christmastime.

The feeling that Merrymount was her home was a secret which Sarah carried in her heart, never sharing it with anyone, not even her father, whom she adored.

Nonetheless, Hogarth Templeton, before his death, had sensed her restlessness and expressed his resentment: " 'Tis in your past, and that is that." As a child, she had begged to hear about Merrymount and had been re-buffed.

So Sarah knew only what came to her in flashes of seventeen-year-old memories: rooms thickly carpeted, windows dressed in red velvet, a portrait of a beautiful woman over a black marble fireplace, a moat filled with flowers.

Guilt covered Sarah like a mantle. She had no right to feel the way she did, for America had been good to the Templetons. Surrounded by six hundred acres of rich river-bottom land, the once-abandoned house was now a mansion by anyone's standards.

Thick carpets kept out the winter cold that once seeped through the cracks of the plank floors. Two wings had been added, and a third story had been built to house the servants. Fine furnishings had been shipped from over-seas, then up the Hudson to Templeton Hall. Famous paintings hung on the walls.

Sarah sucked in a deep breath, exhaling slowly. Winter was just ahead. She felt it in the air. In the distance, a white egret dove into the river for its morning fish, then, spreading its wings, disappeared into the mist. A foghorn blasted the silence.

Sarah turned away from the river and, reaching inside her bosom, retrieved a clean handkerchief and wiped at the tears that had reached her chin. The worst part was ahead; she must needs tell Hoggie that she was leaving Templeton Hall. She dreaded it with the dread of the damned.

For an unpleasant moment Sarah let her mind dwell on the brother she had never understood. A love-hate relationship existed between them, and she regretted it immensely. Hoggie's name suits him well, she thought, for he hogged everything in sight.

Now that their father was dead, Hoggie owned Templeton Hall, the land, and, in a way, he owned her. As in England, the law of primogeniture stood in the Templeton household, just as if the family had never migrated to America. The oldest son inherited, and his siblings were left in his care until they married. Sarah and her half sister, Angeline, were expected to marry a fine gentleman with his own six hundred acres of land.

But even though Sarah had had many suitors, she had no inclination toward marrying. She had opted instead to attend school in upstate New York, where she had learned etiquette, dance, how to flutter her fan in the proper fashion, how to smile at a man without seeming forward, all things a gel needed to know about landing a proper husband.

As an afterthought, so it seemed to Sarah, reading and writing skills had been added to the curriculum, as were humanities and sums.

After finishing school, turning her back on a social season in New York City, where she could have mingled with the Astors, Sarah had come home to teach in a small school in Hyde Park.

Now, leaving the loggia, Sarah went into the upstairs central room which separated six bedroom suites, each with its own bath, sitting room, and dressing room. Stopping in the middle of the central room, she stood perfectly still, postponing, she knew, the confrontation with Hoggie. She let her mind settle on the exquisite room. Huge sofas and overstuffed chairs caught the sun, which cast shadows onto silk-covered walls and the colorful Aubus-son carpet. At the far end of the room was a stairway, with wide, carved balustrades, which led downward to the first floor. With desultory steps she started her descent, deter-mination showing in the set of her chin, while butterflies played hopscotch in her stomach.

She found Hoggie in the library, a room filled with shelves of leatherbound books. Hoggie did not read, with the exception of the *Dutchess County Weekly*, which he held high in front of his face. He sat behind a huge mahogany desk. When Sarah entered, he did not look up or speak.

Sarah quickly noted that, as always, her brother was dressed to the nines, an impeccably tailored black coat, a white shirt with stiff collar points, and gray breeches over black leather boots, which had been highly polished by a houseboy.

Sarah said in a very pleasant, businesslike voice, "Hog-gie, I must needs speak with you about an important matter."

No answer, only the rustling of paper as he turned a page.

Unlike their father, who was a gentle man, Hoggie was cruel and thoughtless. Sarah knew this more than anyone. When they were children, he had drowned a puppy, laughing with pleasure while she, screaming and crying, rode his back and pounded his head with her fists. At half his size she had not stopped him.

Now she longed to slap the paper away from his face and demand that he hear her out. But one did not de-mand from Hoggie. When he was angry those heavy lids could close over glittering slits of onyx. She went to sit in a red leather chair flanking the fireplace. And waited.

He can't hold the demme paper in front of his face forever.

Or could he?

Sarah tried to recall everything she had heard about her Aunt Lillian, and about Merrymount. A feeling of nostalgia came over her, for it was in this room her father had told her and Hoggie that this was to be their new home. As a child of three, Sarah had not understood the anger in Hogarth Templeton's voice, but when she was five, the knowledge came to her in a strange, unexpected way.

She was sitting on the floor, her head resting on her dear papa's bony knee, when he broke his silence about Merrymount and spoke of his leaving England: "Merrymount sits on a high ridge." A long silence, and then, "The place should have been mine. I worked it all the years I was married to your mother. We prospered, she called it *our* home, and then when she was gone, that was no longer true. I owned no part of it." He stopped to grimace and to spit in the spittoon beside his chair.

"But why?" Sarah had asked.

"Being the oldest child of Lord Merriwether, the fifth earl of Chesterson, your mother inherited Merrymount upon his death. There was no son, and the entailed part of the estates and the title went to a distant cousin, Nathan Adams. The will specified that after your mother's death Merrymount would go to your Aunt Lillian, your mother's younger sister. I stayed on, but after three years of trying to get along with her, I left and brought you and Hoggie to America. Thank God I had a little nest egg to purchase some land . . ."

He rubbed a rough hand against Sarah's thick curls and patted her head gently before reaching down and lifting her onto his lap, pressing her cheek with his. She could feel his sadness, and now remembered it well, most especially his next words: "You are like your mother, little Sarah."

His voice was choked. "With your auburn curls and dark green eyes, the same infectious smile. And you'll be tall like her . . ."

It was not often that Hogarth Templeton spoke of Sarah's mother, and after that particular time, he never, never spoke of Merrymount.

Sarah blushed with embarrassment as she remembered the precociousness of her solution: "Why did you not marry Aunt Lillian?" she had asked. "Then we could have all lived at Merrymount the same as before Mama went away."

"Never," her father had said, vehemence in his voice. "I think that is what the old maid, ape-leader they call them in England, wanted. She was an odd one, eccentric as an attic ghost, not like your mother at all."

He had gone silent after that, and a few months later he married Wanna White Eagle, a beautiful half-Iroquois Indian girl who had come to work at Templeton Hall as a housemaid. Rejected by her people because of her mixed blood, she had, years before Hogarth Templeton had migrated to America, left the reservation and sought a life elsewhere. Once she had confided in Sarah that she had come to the Hudson Valley looking for her white father, but had not found him.

Wanna had made Sarah's lonely father extremely happy until a flu epidemic took her, leaving precious Angeline, who was now five and ten years. Sarah had become her surrogate mother.

The gilt clock on the mantel struck ten times, and Sarah suddenly realized she had been reminiscing for more than ten minutes while waiting for Hoggie to speak. But he had not removed the paper from in front of his face.

Another page turned; he pushed his chair back and brought his booted feet up to rest on top of the desk. His loud sigh spilled out into the room.

Willing him to speak, Sarah glared at him through the paper, which anyone could read in five minutes. Dutchess County did not afford a lot of news. Stubbornness kept her from addressing him again.

Another five minutes passed, with the speed of a turtle crossing the road. The sound of the ticking clock filled the great gaping silence. Finally Sarah stood, turned toward a window, and looked out, letting her simmering anger cool. Once again she heard paper rustling, and then there was Hoggie's voice speaking in a disinterested manner. "The weather is nice today. Is it not, Sister Sarah?"

She waited a moment to respond so that she could steady her voice. "Yes, the weather is nice. I love the fall of the year, but that is not the subject I came here to address, Hoggie. I have some very important news."

He raised a brow. "Very important news? Is somebody's wife expecting her sixth child? Or her tenth?"

Hoggie had been married five years, but no child had been born to the union. Nor was there likely to be. Mayhap by his mistress, Sarah thought, if he could not find a doctor to solve the careless woman's mistake. It would never be Hoggie's mistake. Nothing ever was.

Sarah ignored her brother's sarcasm. "The post brought a missive from Aunt Lillian Merriwether. She wants me to come live with her at Merrymount."

Hoggie's feet hit the floor with a resounding thud. He half-rose from his seat, but then sat back down. His face was red with instant anger; from under hooded slits his dark eyes glared at her. Sarah cringed. Invisibly, she hoped.

"Aunt Lillian, the thief who stole Merrymount," he said in a loud, scolding voice. "And it is your wont to live with her?"

"According to Papa, she inherited Merrymount."

"It should have been his . . . then mine," argued Hoggie, pausing, and then, "I forbid you to go."

"How can you forbid me to go? Have you forgotten that I have seen twenty summers?"

"Twenty summers does not make you smart. And what do you propose to live on in your dear old England? I hear that Prinny is quite a spendthrift, pushing his peasants to the limit for taxes, while he waits for his mad papa to die and make him king. Do not forget that I inherited Templeton Hall and all the land—"

"Papa's will clearly states that Angeline and I are to be taken care of from the income from the Templeton land and that when we marry, we are to be dowered."

A huge laugh belched up from Hoggie's throat. "How will you collect? 'Tis a long way across that mighty ocean. And as far as that little half-breed Papa begat with his Indian squaw, she'll never see a penny from Templeton land. Let her go back to the heathens from whence her mother came. I hear those young bucks are quite lusty."

Sarah, her green eyes flashing, instantly moved to stand in front of the desk. "Don't you dare speak disrespectfully of our sister. She is a beautiful child, inside and out. You should be half as good."

Leaning back, Hoggie once again hid his smirking face behind the *Dutchess County Weekly*. "She can't stay here, except as a servant, as her mother was—"

Sarah's anger robbed her of reasoning. She was conscious only of a stab of unreality as she ripped the newspaper from her brother and, drawing her hand back, started to strike with all her might. Suddenly, as if someone touched her, she dropped her hand to her side. She would not let him bring her down to his level. She was a lady foremost; her dear papa had taught her that. Thinking to leave, she turned her back to him, but not before seeing his sardonic smile. His eyes were awash with delight at his ability to rile her to anger.

As Sarah rushed across the room, her brother called after her, "Should you be foolish enough to return to England and your precious Merrymount, you will no longer be welcome at Templeton Hall. Best you stay here and wed Sam Schuyler. He's got land, and he's been wanting to court you."

Sarah's answer was silence. She closed the door between them. What Hoggie had said was true. Sam had come calling several times, and once or twice they had sat together at the small church where they went on Sunday, but she would never wed Sam. Her heart had no yearning for him, not like she yearned for Merrymount.

Outside the door, servants bustled about, going in and out of the small receiving room, the large parlor, the grand formal dining room. When Sarah ran past them, they looked the other way, pretending they had not heard, but she knew that they had. Upon reaching the upstairs central room, which she had left only a short time ago, she encountered Mary Ellen, Hoggie's wife. She opened her arms to Sarah. They hugged affectionately.

"Oh, sister," exclaimed Mary Ellen. "I could not help but hear Hoggie's threat. What does it all mean? And what of sweet Angeline? I pray that she did not hear his hateful words."

Mary Ellen was a frail woman. Still just a child, Sarah thought. When she had come to Templeton Hall, she had been full of happy expectations of children and a contented family. But the years married to Hoggie had taken their toll, and now Mary Ellen's wren-brown hair was faded and unkempt, and sadness emanated from her hazel eyes. Still, when she smiled, she was, in Sarah's opinion, quite pretty. Cowed by Hoggie like a dog that had been kicked once too often, she seldom smiled.

"I received a missive inviting me to come to England and live at Merrymount," Sarah said. "Hoggie says I will go without means, but I will find a way, and I will take Angeline with me. I would not send her back to her mother's people. They turned Wanna out because she was a half-breed. They would do the same with Angeline. And I cannot leave her here to suffer Hoggie's mistreatment."

Sarah refused to release the hot tears that burned her eyes. It was time to plan, not cry, she told herself, heading to her room. Mary Ellen trailed behind, pleading, "Take me with you, Sarah. Please."

Sarah turned to look at her. "You can't mean that,

Mary Ellen. You're married to Hoggie. He's your husband."

"That is the problem. I love Hoggie, but I don't want to be married to him."

They were in the small sitting room adjoining Sarah's bedchamber, a pretty room with deep chairs covered in peach-colored silk. A bright fire burned in the fireplace.

"Sit down, Mary Ellen, and tell me of what you speak. I know Hoggie's faults, but you say you love him—"

"I should not have mentioned that at this time, when you are all upset with him. Things are difficult enough for you."

"Balderdash! Your troubles are my troubles. You know you are more than a sister-in-law to me."

Mary Ellen sat in pensive silence, and Sarah insisted, "You can tell me anything, Mary Ellen. Let us speak of this, and then I will think about how I am going to get to Merrymount with Angeline. Heaven knows that Aunt Lillian may not welcome her when she learns she has Indian blood."

Angeline, because of her ancestry, had not been allowed to attend public school, nor would a private school take her. Sarah had taught her at home.

"My problems with Hoggie are simple," Mary Ellen said. "Besides his overbearing ways, I want children; Hoggie doesn't. When I told him I would have a child whether or not he wanted one, he left my bed and took a mistress—then bragged about it. I see no reason to continue living together without that part of married life."

A sigh, a long pause, and then from trembling lips, "A baby would mean so much to me, Sarah. Mayhap I would not care then if he went to another's bed."

Sarah reached and took Mary Ellen's hand, felt the shaking, the dampness. She knew how difficult it was for her sister-in-law to speak of such matters. It was expected of women to suffer in silence. "Mary Ellen, how would you live if you left Hoggie? Would your parents let you return home?"

"They do not believe in divorce, and they would think me foolish and accuse me of disgracing them. Hoggie is so prominent in the community. Mama would tell me to look the other way. Like she has with Papa all these years. If I could go to England with you—"

"Listen to me, Mary Ellen. I have some savings from teaching that will pay passage for two, but not for three. I have a capital idea, though. Take my teaching job and save with all your might. It will keep you busy, and later, if things cannot be worked out with you and Hoggie, mayhap you can come to Merrymount. I'll talk with Aunt Lillian . . ."

Mary Ellen's face instantly brightened. She sat silent, and Sarah continued, "But first I must needs find a way to make Hoggie comply with the dictates of Papa's will. We can't go to Aunt Lillian as poor relations."

"Sarah, are you sure of what you are doing? England is a big place, and not very kind. The caste system is practiced in the worst way. There's the poorest of the poor and the richest of the rich, and never shall the twain meet. It's like an invisible line drawn between the East and the West End of London, with the nobility and aristocrats occupying the whole of the West End. Mayfair, they call it. Here, in this prosperous community, you help make up the upper orders, but there—"

"I care not for that, and I've never been more sure of anything in my life." Sarah's voice dropped an octave. "I belong at Merrymount."

She was facing John Jay Elwood, a tall, thin man who was her late father's man of law. He wore a black coat, white neck cloth, which, Sarah noticed, was spotted with coffee stains.

Spread on the desk that separated them were sheets of her father's last will and testament.

"I just want you to remind Hoggie that I am entitled to support, no matter where I live. I've pored over every word of the will, and nowhere does it say that I am required to live at Templeton Hall to receive that support. And the same for Angeline. I intend to take her with me."

When John Jay did not answer, Sarah repeated, "It does not say I can't go to England to live or that I am required to marry someone to gain support. You should know! You drew up the will for Papa, John Jay, and you know as well as I do that Papa would turn over in his grave if he knew Hoggie was acting this way."

John Jay leaned back in his chair and stroked his neatly clipped white whiskers. He then ran his long fingers through gray locks while eying Sarah over wire-rimmed spectacles that rested halfway down his long aquiline nose.

She stared back at him. Her back hurt from sitting so straight in the chair, while bone-softening fatigue threatened to engulf her. The past week at Templeton Hall had been very tiring and very unsettling.

"You were your father's favorite, all right," the solicitor said at last. "I tried to talk him into writing the will in another way, making his own arrangements for you and Angeline, dividing the land. But he was too English. He believed wholeheartedly that the oldest son should inherit, and that that son was the head of the family, taking his dead father's place and caring for the womenfolk as he would. I don't think he dreamed that Hoggie would be so stingy."

"Stingy! That's an understatement. For a week now we have battled daily over his duty, and he still says not a cent if I return to Merrymount. I guess Papa forgot that Hoggie was not raised in England, under English laws."

John Jay whistled through his teeth. What a formidable woman Sarah was. He had never seen her in this state, angry as a wet hen caught in a rainstorm. And how pretty she was. The prettiest girl in Dutchess County. Smart, too, and, as evidenced right now, stubborn as a mule. He smiled at her, tried for levity with a funny tale, and she just sat there, stone-faced, that little chin set in an obdurate line that would scare the devil out of a normal man.

Sarah stood and donned a coat with a beaver collar, and a hat of the same dark brown fur, which she pulled down over her auburn curls.

John Jay looked out the window. The weather was trying to turn nasty. He saw Sarah's rig, a small one-squab buggy and a handsome black horse hitched to a post in front of his office.

He promised, "I will talk with Hoggie—"

"Talk won't do any good. Just tell him I will sue to break the will. And don't forget to include Angeline. I'll sue as her guardian."

The lawyer shook his head. "Miss Sarah, Hoggie has far too many political friends. He rubs well with every judge in the county. Even in Washington. And 'tis a shame. I'm afraid we will have to settle for what I can pry out of him."

Sarah knew that Hoggie aspired for a high political office, that he spent considerable time courting all politicians, even President Monroe himself. Both had attended the College of William and Mary, giving them a common bond.

"Well, don't let him know that we'll settle."

The lawyer chuckled. "I've been practicing law a long time, Miss Sarah. I will give it my best, but I just thought it incumbent upon myself to inform you of my full doubt of the outcome. I pray that I am wrong."

"One can only do what one can do," she said.

Opening her portmanteau, she took out some bills and a small slip of paper. "There's one other thing, two in fact. Please obtain permission for Angeline to go to England. I don't think it necessary for you to tell the authorities that she's one-quarter Indian. She's been raised American. And we will need two passages. I plan to leave a week from today, if there's a ship sailing. And if you will send Aunt Lillian a missive, advising her of the time of our arrival, so that she can have someone dockside to transport us to Merrymount, I would certainly appreciate that, too.

"But don't tell her there's two of us. I think it best that she not know that Angeline is coming."

She handed him the bills and the slip of paper. " 'Tis luck that I have money for two fares; it's support I'm needing . . . until I become established."

"You won't be working there, surely. The upper orders look down their noses at anyone who toils for a living, even if they are as rich as Croesus. One must inherit."

"Well, I've inherited . . . if only I can get it. And don't forget to write to Aunt Lillian. I've already written my intent of coming to Merrymount, but since the fares had not been purchased, I could not tell her which ship I would be on. Besides, it will appear much more important to Aunt Lillian coming from the Templeton family's solicitor.

"And be sure to call her Lady Lillian Merriwether. I've read that a title is very important in England."

"I will take care of it for you, Miss Sarah."

The man of law followed Sarah to the door. He bade her goodbye and again assured her that he was on her side and that he would immediately contact Hoggie. It had begun to rain, a cold mist.

"Sarah," he called after her, "do you think it wise to take your sister? 'Tis banded about that she believes in Indian ways, calling up spirits of those passed on."

"Good," Sarah answered succinctly. "Mayhap she can call Papa back and he can change his will."

John Jay laughed at Sarah's sassy answer.

Sarah, however, did not laugh, for she did not think what she had said was funny, nor did she believe one

could call spirits back after they had left this earth, but if
Angeline wanted to believe that, and found comfort in
doing so, she saw no harm in it.

"John Jay," she said, "Hoggie hates Angeline. I can't
leave her at Templeton Hall. He would send her away or
make a servant out of her. 'Tis not worth thinking on."

No reply came from John Jay, just a cluck of his tongue.

Sarah turned away, patted her black horse's neck in
passing, and, raising her parasol, started walking up the
small incline that led to the white-steepled church, sitting
amid old and new tombstones. The mound of earth that
covered Hogarth Templeton's grave was still fresh, a
faded brown. He was alone. They would not allow Angeline's mother to be buried in a white-man's cemetery.
Tears came to Sarah's eyes. It was so unfair.

She murmured sadly to herself, "I must needs tell Papa
goodbye."

John Jay watched as Sarah walked resolutely away, her
back straight as an arrow, her head held high. In his
mind's eye he could see the stubborn set of her chin. As
he watched, she pushed at the hair that rested on her
neck. She was headed for the graveyard. Moments
passed, and then she was out of his sight.

The man of law stepped back and closed the door, and
as he did so, a strange feeling of foreboding came over
him like a strong puff of wind. Oddly chilled, goose bumps
prickled his skin.

The feeling left as quickly as it had come. His white
brows drew together in bafflement, but he knew at that
moment, and he did not know how he knew, that Merrymount would not be as Sarah Templeton expected. He
pondered, examined his feelings, asked where this feeling
came from, with no answer. He wanted to go after her.

And say what? he asked himself. That he'd had a premonition of something not just right? She would think he

had corkscrews for brains. He sighed, the only sound in
the room, and the silence remained total until he began
sharpening a quill with a knife he took from his pocket.
Sitting at his cluttered desk, he then penned a missive to
Lady Lillian Merriwether, Merrymount, Rockingham in
Northamptonshire, England. He would leave the name of
the ship and the approximate date of arrival blank until
he could purchase the tickets.

Chapter Two

Sarah and Angeline spent Christmas aboard the *Boston Queen*, and now, at last, they were docked at the East India Dock in the shadow of London. The crossing had been uneventful but long, so it seemed to Sarah, so anxious was she to reach Merrymount.

"There you are, miss," a white-clad sailor said as he lowered the copper-bound trunk he carried aloft down onto the teeming dock.

Sarah noticed that some of the passengers, the finely dressed ones, had their own footman to carry their luggage. His task completed, the sailor quickly walked away. She called her thanks after him, but in the din of moving feet and passengers squealing delight at seeing some kinfolk or other, she doubted if he heard her. Coaches, some grand, some not so grand, lined the quay along the dock.

Passengers rushed to the coaches. Sarah and Angeline had no choice but to wait; they had not a clue as to which of the conveyances was from Merrymount. Most surely it would be crested, Sarah mused, the fifth earl of Chesterson having been Aunt Lillian's father.

Crested coaches, titles, royalty, and even the gentry meant very little to Sarah, for though her own father was an earl, things of that nature were seldom, if ever, mentioned in Templeton Hall. She knew only what she had read.

Angeline said, "We are of the nobility, Sarah, and now that we are in England, we must curtsy to one another and call each other Lady Sarah and Lady Angeline." She stepped back and gave a quick bob, laughing as she did so, nearly falling over her feet. "I guess I need more practice."

Amused, Sarah agreed with her. "But you need not curtsy to me, Angeline. In America we never thought about our courtesy titles. I feel that I am more American than English."

Smiling and showing her pretty white teeth, Angeline said, "I am more American than you. The Indians were there first. I'm a native American. You were a transplant. Now we're both transplants."

When Sarah told Angeline that she was leaving Templeton Hall to live in England, at a place called Merrymount, she had enquired of Angeline if she wanted to return to her mother's people, then added, "For of a certainty I cannot leave you at Templeton Hall."

Angeline had answered without pause, "Why would I want to return to Mama's people? They cared not for her because her skin was more fair than theirs. You have always been so kind to me . . . and to my mother, although she was only your stepmother."

"I loved Wanna. She was a good woman. She made Papa very happy," answered Sarah.

Angeline shuddered perceptively. "But Hoggie hated Mama, just as he hates me." Tears filled her dark eyes. "Sister, please take me with you."

So it had worked out well, Sarah now thought, praying that Lady Lillian Merriwether would welcome the beautiful girl into her home. The prayer was in earnest, for Sarah was worried.

Dismissing that train of thought, Sarah looked around the dock, thinking that she would see someone who reminded her of her own mother. Surely Aunt Lillian and her sister resembled each other. *You peagoose, the only thing you know about your mother is a three-year-old's memory of a portrait of a beautiful woman hanging over a black marble mantel.*

No one on the dock resembled her memory of the portrait.

Someone would come soon, Sarah mused, and the wait would give her a chance to savor her first glimpse of London. She sniffed. There was a strange odor, and fog as thick as soup hovered over the magnificent brick warehouses that lined the Thames. The January wind was very strong and very cold.

Sarah didn't mind the stench, or the murky fog, even the cold. Soon she would be at Merrymount, far away from the chimney pots and the raw sewage. No doubt the country air would smell fresh and clean. A huge lump formed in her throat. Swallowing hard was to no avail, and tears of happiness welled up into her eyes. She was going home to Merrymount.

Sarah laughed when a wizened little cockney man hawked gossip about the Prince Regent's latest love. People pushed past each other to pay a shilling for a lampoon with a picture of Prinny on it. It was a strange sight.

Cargo handlers were loading and unloading the ships anchored in the harbor. Cheaply dressed girls flaunted their bodies at the workers, and at the sailors piling off the ships.

Flower girls pushed their carts onto the dock, holding out their little hands, begging for something to buy a piece of bread. Sarah's sympathy was great for those who suffered that which was unknown to her. She had never been hungry in her life, except when she, as a child, was made to wait until others were seated at the table before she could dive into her food. She held tightly to her reticule, which housed the meager pounds the Templeton solicitor had extracted from her brother Hoggie. Even though she wanted so much to help the pitiful little girl out, she did not dare buy a flower. She still smarted over the small amount Hoggie had allowed her.

"Hundred pounds now, a small stipend monthly for Sarah, nothing for Angeline," Hoggie had said. And he had many times in the weeks before their departure reminded Sarah if she left Templeton Hall for Merrymount she would not be permitted to return.

So Sarah had welcomed the day of departure, her only sorrow being that of leaving Mary Ellen, who had been tearful when they parted.

But it had been settled that she would take Sarah's place at the school, and it seemed to Sarah that even before they left Mary Ellen had changed for the better. Mayhap pride that she was doing something useful and was of value to someone brought about the change. Sarah prayed it to be so.

"I will come to England," Mary Ellen said as she gave Sarah and Angeline a last hug.

Sarah, hugging her back with deep affection, had not encouraged her to leave Templeton Hall, for it was not her bent to interfere in a marriage. She simply said, "We will miss you, Mary Ellen, and I shall write often."

Standing on the London dock, Sarah cautioned herself not to harken to the past. Everything would be wonderful when she reached Merrymount. Her eyes searched the dock, wondering where someone from Merrymount might be.

By now considerable time had passed since Sarah, Angeline, and their trunk had been deposited onto the dock, and a dull worry had set in. Nonetheless, Sarah, not wanting Angeline to know her growing concern, smiled brightly and asked, "Isn't this exciting, Angeline?"

"It would be if my feet didn't hurt." Angeline sat on the trunk and kicked off her half boots, showing heavy woolen stockings. Sarah laughed. It was not easy to get shoes on Angeline. To keep them on was even more difficult. She allowed a moment to study her sister, whose developing breasts pushed against the berry-wine wool shift she wore. A long, fur-lined cape did not hide hips that flared like those of a woman's. Her hair was black and long; her doe-shaped eyes, framed with long black lashes, reminded Sarah of black walnuts when wet with rain.

Right before my eyes, Angeline has developed into a beautiful woman, thought Sarah.

This train of thought shocked Sarah. She had always thought of Angeline as her *little* sister, although Sarah was only five years older. How had Angeline changed so quickly?

Sarah recalled that a certain mystique had always surrounded Angeline, like a rosebud enveloped in a mist. She revealed only what she wanted others to see. Wanna, Angeline's mother, had been that way.

Without ever having taken a lesson, she was a masterful harpist, playing haunting tunes of unknown origin. She spoke with great feeling and with blunt truthfulness. And she smiled often, which, in Sarah's opinion, added to her charm. As Sarah looked long at Angeline, she thought, as she had many times before, that her sister looked like an Indian princess.

Today, Angeline's black hair hung down her back in one long braid. Her face was one of ethereal beauty. Around her neck were many strands of colorful stones— rubies, emeralds, and pearls—given to her mother by their father, Hogarth Templeton.

Since Wanna's death, there had hardly been a day that Angeline had not worn the strands of beads, and once she had confided to Sarah that they made her feel close to her mama.

Sarah sat down beside Angeline on the trunk. The crowd had thinned. Most of the *Boston Queen*'s passengers were gone. Out of the corner of her eye, Sarah caught a glimpse of two small children waiting with a woman who wore a black dress with a white collar.

The children's clothes were similar. Both had sailor collars, but the girl wore white pantalettes that showed beneath her heavy coat, while the little boy wore knee breeches and white stockings. His small legs surely must be cold, thought Sarah, for his coat stopped at his knees.

It was by now getting quite late in the day, and the woman was pacing back and forth in front of the children, lifting her lorgnette often and looking at her watch, which hung from a chain attached to her black dress.

Sarah heard hoofbeats and the grinding of carriage wheels. Suddenly a carriage came into sight, stopping quickly near the dock. From the box, a man alighted and walked hurriedly from the carriage. He was tall and well-formed, and Sarah quickly noted that he wore a powdered wig. A huge greatcoat hung carelessly around his shoulders, as if the cold wind was no threat to his powerful body.

For a moment Sarah thought he was coming to claim her and Angeline, but that hope was soon shattered by the children's screams of delight. "Papa, Papa, we thought you would never come!"

Bending over, the man gathered the children into his arms, lifted them up, and gave each a kiss, laughing with them. He spoke to the woman, and then they turned and started walking toward the coach the man had just left. A gold crest was emblazoned on the panels, two dragons facing each other in a fighting stance.

Hitched to the crested coach were four restive horses, stomping the hard-packed earth and flaring their nostrils.

After opening the door and depositing the children onto the squabs, then helping the woman—by now Sarah had decided she was the children's nanny—in to sit opposite them, the man climbed up onto the box, took the ribbons from a boy who was holding them, handed him a coin, and gave the horses office to go. Which they did with gusto, their hooves gaining a certain rhythm as they moved out of Sarah's hearing and out of sight.

She wondered why such a grand coach did not have a coachman as the other waiting coaches had, even those not sporting a gold crest.

There was an empty quietness after the carriage left, a sort of loneliness that Sarah did not like.

Why did someone not come for them?

A gray darkness had settled over the dock.

Angeline said, "I saw those children on ship. They are twins, and they have been visiting their grandparents in Philadelphia. They were very friendly, but the nanny didn't like them talking to strangers."

"I can understand why," Sarah said, thinking they were so adorable that someone might want to steal them.

Once again Sarah heard the pounding of hooves, the sound of grinding carriage wheels. She turned and stared with great anticipation. *The Merriwether coach at last. I wonder what has delayed it.*

But it was not the Merriwether coach.

As Sarah watched, the man with the powdered wig jumped down off the box of his halted coach and headed in the direction of Sarah and Angeline, his stride as fast and as purposeful as when he had hurried toward his children.

Almost immediately he was standing in front of Sarah and Angeline, bowing gracefully from the waist. "I am Nathan Adams. I do not mean to be forward, but I could not help but notice that the two of you were waiting for someone to come for you. May I give you a ride somewhere? My children's nanny is with me, we would be properly chaperoned."

Sarah jumped to her feet, curtsied the best she could, and offered her hand, which he took, bending over it and brushing it with his lips.

Angeline mimicked Sarah, and he kissed her hand as well.

Sarah said, "You are most kind, but someone will soon come for us, and should we leave they would not know what happened to us. I feel that we should wait. They are coming from the country."

"It will soon be quite dark—"

"They will be here soon, I am sure. My aunt knows of our arrival. Something has delayed her . . ."

He bowed again. "I will take my leave, then. I pray someone will come for you soon." His eyes traversed the setting. "It is dangerous here, especially for two beautiful damsels—"

Sarah spoke quickly. "We are not afraid."

"This is not America," he said, and then he told them goodbye again, turned on his heels, and left, looking back only once before sprightly gaining his box on the waiting coach. Sarah listened again to the sound of turning wheels and the clop-clop of horses' hooves until she could no longer hear them, again feeling lost in the crowd of sailors and dock workers and the women roaming the dock.

"Are you touched in the head, Sarah?" Angeline asked. "We should have gone with him."

"Where? We have no place to go. Did you notice that he asked if he could take us *somewhere*. He certainly did not mean to take us home with him."

"That would have been a capital idea," Angeline retorted, her dark eyes laughing in a teasing way.

Sarah teased back, "Did you think his lordship handsome? I fear he's slightly old for you."

"Oh, he certainly was handsome, broad-shouldered, straight. I wanted so much to see his face, but the wig hid all but his smile. And I wasn't thinking of a beau for myself, but for you. I think mayhap you will marry him."

"Peagoose. He's married, with children. Besides, I won't have you matching me up with every Englishman who comes along. I remember your thinking I should let Sam Schuyler court me. My bent is to get to Merrymount as fast as I can."

Just then a charley stepped out of his black box and called out the time and the weather, telling them loud and clear what they already knew—that it was cold.

Angeline grabbed Sarah's arm and huddled close to her.

Forcing a tiny laugh, Sarah told her, " 'Tis only a London charley, calling out the time and weather. He will do that all night long, every hour. But he's there to help should someone accost us. I find that comforting." She put her arm around Angeline, feeling her warmth and her fright.

"How do you know so much?" Angeline asked.

"I've read a lot about London. Their ways seem peculiar because they are so different from ours. I suspect we will come to accept them."

"Not sitting here on this trunk."

Sarah crossed herself and murmured to the Higher Power a plea for guidance. She could not believe that no one had met them, that they were actually sitting on their trunk in the middle of a strange dock. No longer could she think of a legitimate excuse for Lady Lillian Merriwether's neglect. Why had the woman written the missive, asking her to come to Merrymount, and then neglect her in this manner?

Mayhap Aunt Lillian has died. The missive was written over ten weeks ago.

Her disquiet growing, Sarah stood and began pacing. Even through her thick woolen coat the wind was extremely sharp now that the sun was gone. She felt drained. The excitement of at last arriving in London and the disappointment of being left waiting for someone to fetch them had filled her with tremendous weariness. And she was ravenous.

A drunken sailor and a pock-faced lightskirt staggered near where Sarah was pacing. "Da ye want a fella?" he asked, pushing his woman of the night to laughter.

Sarah did not answer, and when they had passed on, she addressed her sister, "Well, we can't sit here all night. We have no choice but to hire a hackney and find lodging."

What kind of lodging? She had little money.

"We should have gone with the powdered wig," piped

up Angeline. Seeing the distraught look on Sarah's face, she jumped up and hugged her. "Don't worry, sister, I was only funning. We'll be safe, and tomorrow is another day."

Sarah hugged her tightly, and they clung together, neither crying for the sake of the other.

As they stood thus, Sarah saw over Angeline's shoulder the kind captain of the *Boston Queen*. Like a great wave, relief swept over her. If the Lord Savior had been walking toward them, He would not have been more welcome. On the way over, on the *Boston Queen*, she had several times engaged in conversation with Captain Barksdale and had found him very concerned for his passengers.

Now, drawing nearer, his voice was kind when he said, "I've been watching you girls. No one has come, eh?"

Sarah said, "I'm sure there's been a misunderstanding."

The captain shook his head, making a clucking sound with his tongue. "Every arrival I pray that this will not happen, but it always does, either side of the ocean. Someone is always left waiting."

Sarah talked through her tears. "Someone from Merrymount was supposed to meet us. Most likely our date of arrival was incorrectly written. Our solicitor—"

Captain Barksdale knew this was not the case. With the uncertainty of sailing conditions, no exact date was ever given for a ship's arrival. Those expecting friends and relatives to arrive on a ship came as many as five mornings consecutively to see if the ship had arrived in the night. "Come," he said, "I will take you back aboard and feed you. You must be starving. And I'm sure your warm bunks will afford a good night's rest." Turning to a passing sailor, he asked that he take the trunk back aboard the *Boston Queen*.

"Aye, Captain," the skinny sailor said, having no trouble heaving the trunk to his shoulder.

Sarah said, "We are most appreciative, Captain Barks-dale—"

" 'Tis my job. And it is a great pleasure. I'm in luck. Usually I get a cross old hen who takes her anger out on me." His laugh was jovial. He turned and started toward the tender that would return them to the *Boston Queen*.

Holding tightly to Angeline's hand, Sarah looked out over the harbor. Opposite the warehouses the Thames was spotted with wharfs, ships anchored to them. The tall masts and bare spars looked like giant crosses against the dull sky.

The euphoria of being here, in England, returned to Sarah, and her weariness and tears evaporated with a swift slash of the cold wind. Her steps were suddenly quick and lively as they approached the tender. "Come on, Angeline," she said. "Tomorrow, for sure, Aunt Lillian, or someone from Merrymount, will come."

Angeline did not answer. She lifted her eyes and prayed that it be so.

Once back aboard the *Boston Queen* they supped on fine fare at the captain's table, which was closeted in a tiny little room which was very comfortable and private. And it was warm, Sarah noticed. A steward brought roast beef, stewed kidneys, cabbage, a delicious pudding, and lots of hot coffee. It was difficult for Sarah not to stuff herself, and she noticed that Angeline was eating as if she were half-starved to death.

Captain Barksdale had already eaten, but he sat at the table with them and sipped wine. He said, "There are larger compartments available for you tonight, now that the ship is empty of passengers, but I thought you might be more comfortable in familiar surroundings."

"That's very thoughtful," Sarah told him. "And I do want to pay you—"

"I would not think of it."

The captain looked at Sarah, seeing a shockingly beautiful woman who held on to her reticule as if it stood between her and death. Not once on the way over had he seen her without the small bag, keeping it close to her body, sometimes holding it with both hands. He'd wager that she had no more than a few pounds, and most likely the money was secured to the bag's bottom with a huge pin. He asked, "Who is this relative who failed to meet you?"

"My aunt, Lady Lillian Merriwether. Have you heard of her? Her home is Merrymount, near Rockingham."

The captain laughed to lighten the ambiance. "I'm afraid not. I've never lived in England. Boston is my home. But I've read of Merrymount. It was used as a fortress in William the Conqueror's reign. I'm a great history buff."

"Oh! I am glad to hear that," said Sarah, and then she told the captain about having been born at Merrymount and leaving when she was three. "But I always felt that I belonged there. 'Tis my ancestral home. My mother inherited Merrymount when her father, the fifth earl of Chesterson, died. It was not entailed. Then, when Mama died, Merrymount went to Aunt Lillian, her sister. My father moved to America and would never talk to me about the place. He did say once that he did not rub well with Aunt Lillian, and that after my mother died, it was not his home to enjoy."

"Then you know nothing about what has transpired since you left there many years ago?" the captain asked, concerned.

"Seventeen years ago. Only that Aunt Lillian is still alive. She never wrote, not until I received the missive asking that I come live at Merrymount. Papa remarried after going to America, and Angeline is from that union."

" 'Tis strange that your aunt never wrote until now," he commented. "But I'm sure you will be very happy at Merrymount. I understand it's one of the grandest old manor houses left in England. And if you are not happy, you can always return to America. The *Boston Queen* sails across three times a year."

Sarah sipped her coffee, thoughtful before she spoke. "Oh, but I can't go back to Templeton Hall. My brother cut me off completely when I left, with a hundred pounds and a small monthly stipend."

"Your brother sounds like a nice chap," the captain retorted sarcastically.

"He hated Aunt Lillian more than my Papa did. Neither would talk about her. I just don't know much about her at all."

"You'll know soon. If no one comes to fetch you tomorrow, I suggest you take public transport. Mail coaches go to Rockingham. There, a hackney or a wagon and oxen can be engaged to take you to Merrymount.

"I keep a coach and four here in London; I will deliver you to the Swan with Two Necks. That is where public transportation, and the mail coaches as well, depart London. The Post Office is directly across, in Lombard Street."

"Public transport won't be necessary, Captain Barksdale," Sarah said. "I'm certain someone from Merrymount will come on the morrow."

Chapter Three

"I knew the old crow wasn't coming for us," said Angeline.

"You knew no such thing," retorted Sarah. "I was just sure someone would come."

"I know, Sarah. You are entirely too trusting."

Captain Barksdale quickly interceded: "Now, there's no point in arguing on who was right and who was wrong. We'll soon right the situation."

"I'm sorry, Angeline," Sarah said. "Most likely Lady Lillian is an old crow. I was wrong to trust her. I should have known that something was queer when she hadn't written in seventeen years, and then such a short missive. If I had not been so anxious to return to Merrymount . . ."

It was approaching five o'clock in the morning, and the three of them were in Captain Barksdale's coach on their way to the Swans with Two Necks. A coachman, wearing a tricorn and a coat of many layers, was on the box, cracking a whip over the backs of four handsome bays. The sound rang out into the dawn.

Inside the coach, lanterns burned for light, and heated bricks warmed the passengers' feet. Even so, Sarah had never been so cold in her life. She looked across at the captain, who had been kinder to her, and to Angeline, than any man she had ever known, with the exception of her dear papa.

Suddenly Sarah wanted so much to be back at Templeton Hall with her father. But that was impossible. Her
papa was gone. For a moment she was overtaken by grief.
Her shoulders shook and a dry sob escaped her throat.
She was scared. But the feeling passed quickly, and resolutely she straightened, lifted her head, and set her chin in
the stubborn line her papa used to tease her about.

" 'Tis the future I should be thinking about," she said,
so low that it drew no one's attention. The future. She
only wished she knew more what to expect. Again the
thought struck that her Aunt Lillian might be dead.

It did not bear thinking on, so Sarah focused her
thoughts onto the kind captain. With his beaver pulled
down to cover his ears and with his greatcoat collar
turned up, he looked as if he had no neck at all. She gave
him a smile. He smiled back and reached across to pat her
hand. "I have two daughters back in Boston. I see so little
of them."

"That accounts for your understanding our plight,"
Sarah said.

"That is so," he said, and then he added, "I'm certain
your aunt will explain why you were not met at the dock
when you reach Merrymount."

He prayed this was so. Yesterday, he had made enquiries, and what he had learned made him very apprehensive. According to *on-dits*, Merrymount had been boarded
up for ever so long. If the oldest of the girls, Sarah, was
not so mature, he would insist upon taking them back to
America straight away, paying the passage himself.

And then take the fare out of Hoggie Templeton's hide.

Sarah sat quietly, watching the creeping dawn, listening to the grinding of the carriage wheels. The crack of
the whip resounded into the quietness. Smoke curled
from chimney pots, and candles suddenly appeared in
windows. People were leaving their homes for work.

Angeline's words broke into Sarah's solitude. "I shall
gladly wring the old crow's long, black neck. Imagine! Left

freezing on a strange dock for two whole days, and people falling all over us. I've never heard words like those cargo handlers used."

"I should have given up sooner, Angeline," Sarah said. "But let's not speak of Aunt Lillian again until we hear what she has to say for herself."

"That's fine with me. Old crows are not my favorite subject, especially this early in the morning."

Angeline sat forward on the squabs and pointed to a man riding aloft in a chair. "That man should be whipped with new leather, making those poor men carry him. Is he too lazy to walk?"

Captain Barksdale leaned forward, seeing a rotund man sitting in a chair which was being carried between two poles resting on two small men's shoulders. "The two men carrying the fat man are grateful for the work," the captain explained. "No doubt the passenger is of the nobility and spent the night at the gaming tables. Now he is on his way home."

This did not satisfy Angeline. "Why can he not walk home?"

"Then the men would be out a fare. Taking a chair is proper transportation for the upper orders in London. If you spend much time in Town, no doubt you will see the Prince Regent riding aloft quite often, and I am told that a chair is the dandy Beau Brummell's favorite way to get about London. He loves looking down onto his peers."

"And who is Beau Brummell?" asked Angeline.

"London's most infamous dandy," answered Captain Barksdale.

And so it went, Angeline asking questions and the captain answering, Sarah listening.

"You'll be a Londoner before you know it," the captain told Angeline, and she disputed that wholeheartedly. She would stay in the country, if they ever found Aunt Lillian.

Sarah sometimes smiled at the banter. By now they were far away from the dock and were riding on cobbled streets. Gaslights, hanging from outstretched arms attached to iron posts, shone dimly through the fog. She had read that the posts and arms had been forged from cannons used during the recent Napoleonic war.

Sarah was anxious to reach the Swan with Two Necks. How long it seemed since she had left the New York harbor. Pressing her face to the coach's glass window, she peered at the street signs. The fog was a detriment. Then, without warning, she felt the coach jerk and gain great speed. Puzzled, she started to ask why, but Captain Barksdale spoke before she could make the enquiry. "We're nearing the center of town. Our destination is not far off. I made arrangements late yesterday for you to take a mail coach, which is much faster than public transport. It will take you as far as Rockingham, and a hackney can be had to take you to Merrymount."

"I cannot thank you enough . . ."

The coach swerved and threw Sarah against Angeline. She looked out, seeing horses, horses, horses. Some were with riders, and others were hitched to coaches, the conveyances big, small, opulent, and plain. The opulent coaches had powdered coachmen with tricorns and French gloves, and traveled as if they were going to a fire. The kind captain explained that the bollards, which stood at street corners, had been put there to stop the equipages from wheeling off the street and running the pedestrians down.

Sarah grabbed a rope and held on for dear life.

Angeline, thinking it great fun, squealed and said that she was glad the old crow hadn't met them at the dock.

This brought only a light reprimand from Sarah. "Please, dear, refrain from calling her an old crow. Remember, we must needs live with the woman."

Captain Barksdale swayed with the moving carriage. To him it was no more frightening than being in rough waters aboard the *Boston Queen*. "This road is the main artery to the turnpikes out of town. Most of these people have country homes, and they are hell-bent on reaching them as fast as they can."

"I don't blame them a whit. If I lived in London, I would be in a big hurry to get out of here," declared Angeline.

"You've only seen the East End. The upper orders live in the West End in fine town houses, and there's shops like you've never seen. Goods of all sort can be bought. On Bond Street especially, and every man worth his weight vies to own the best horse and the most impressive equipage the trade has to offer. And he dearly loves to show off what he owns. There's gentlemen's clubs, for men only, where men gamble and socialize. The best food is served—"

"Don't they work?" asked Angeline.

"There's a great gulf between those who have and those who have not," explained the captain. "Those who have inherited wealth and a title are not supposed to toil for a living. Those who have made a fortune in the trades are not accepted into the social world of the *ton.*"

Sarah said, "Is that what my brother Hoggie was referring to when he said England was known for its caste system? And Papa's man of law spoke of the separation of classes."

"In a way, though not exactly like it is practiced in India. As time goes on, you will learn the ways—"

"I think anyone who does not work is lazy," Angeline said.

Captain Barksdale chuckled.

By now they were on Lad Lane, and ahead of them coaches were arriving and leaving, all piled high with passengers and luggage. One had a coop of white leghorn chickens on its top. Across from the Swan with Two Necks, drawn up in double file outside the Post Office, were black-and-maroon mail coaches, with scarlet wheels and the royal coat of arms emblazoned on the doors. Sarah counted twenty-seven coaches.

"You will travel on Number 10," the captain said. "After getting the morning mail, it will pull into the yard to gather passengers. I only hope it is not too crowded for your comfort."

"I pray that we will not have to ride outside," said Angeline. "Look at those poor people there, riding on top, one man sitting on top of a trunk. He will freeze to death."

"He's dressed for the journey," Captain Barksdale assured her. "The coachman, if he has a kind heart, will stop and let the passengers exchange places with those inside when it appears they might freeze."

Their coach pulled inside the courtyard of the travel station, where half-awake travelers were piling out of the second- and third-floor galleries, pulling on their boots, and taking their places on the outgoing coaches. Cold and bleary-eyed travelers from the night coaches untangled their limbs and hastened into the coffee room. The smell that drifted out the door set Sarah's taste buds to watering. They had eaten breakfast on the *Boston Queen,* but now that seemed hours back.

As if he could read Sarah's mind, Captain Barksdale took his big round watch from his coat pocket and checked the time. "I'll ask that a repast be prepared for you. That will take less time than going inside. The mail coach will be here momentarily, and I don't want you to miss it."

He was gone only a few minutes. Sarah and Angeline stood huddled against the building, shivering. Angeline pulled her fur-lined cape close around her and then put her arm around Sarah to give her warmth from her body. A coach bounded by, so close one could reach out and touch the passengers. Quickly Sarah took a second look. Inside were the twins she had seen the first night they had arrived at the London dock. The nanny's head, sporting her snow-white platter cap, was visible above the little heads of blond curls.

"Look," Sarah said.

"I see them," answered Angeline. "I wonder where the powdered wig is? And I wonder where they are going? Public transport doesn't seem the thing for them."

Sarah was quiet for a moment before saying, "One never knows what is going on with other people. I would have thought the children would be riding in their father's crested carriage."

That was all the time they had to discuss the powdered wig's children and the nanny. So much had happened that neither could remember his name. Captain Barksdale returned with food wrapped in a newspaper and handed it to Sarah. "I do hope you have a pleasant journey and that you find Merrymount as you've dreamed all these years it would be. I should be very disappointed if you don't write."

Earlier he had given Sarah his London address, which he said was a room at a boarding house he used when he was in London for as much as a fortnight.

"Thank you again for your concern, and I do promise to write," Sarah said, holding tight to the warm food.

Angeline gave him a big hug, and he laughed, even though his eyes were swimming in tears he couldn't hide. In a gruff voice, he said, "Here's Number Ten."

A guard, dressed in scarlet livery, stood on the boot of the mail coach, one foot resting on the top of the locked mailbox. A workman heaved the Templeton trunk atop the coach and strapped it down. As Sarah and Angeline, with the captain's aid, climbed in to sit with the other passengers on the squabs, the guard blew his long brass horn to clear the way, and quickly Captain Barksdale pressed a five-pound note into Sarah's palm.

"No," she said, but he did not listen. Turning, he was soon lost in the crowd.

The horn blowing snapped the four horses to attention. Ahead, coaches pulled aside to let them pass. The horses reared, flared their nostrils, flailed their forelegs in the air, and plunged forward. After that, all Sarah could hear was thunder-beating hooves hitting the cobbled street and an occasional crack of the coachman's whip. She marveled at the expert way the coachman handled the bays. This was the last leg of the journey, and she did not want a mishap. She looked out and saw that the sun was rising over London. Soon she would see Merrymount.

From two kilometers away, Sarah caught her first glimpse of her ancestral home. She caught her breath, for, sitting like a great giant atop a tree-covered ridge, it seemed the most magnificent dwelling she had ever seen, with its crenelated roof towering skyward.

"Years ago 'twas fortified," said the man driving the wagon. "Situated high like thet, the men on the roof, with their arrows pointed in every direction, could see fer miles and miles. Specially if the enemy wuz trying to slip in by boat on the River Welland. Or through the valley on the other side."

"Was it ever attacked?" Sarah asked.

"Not thet I know. But that wuz years back, during King William's time. The manor house has been restored many times, starting with the first earl of Chesterson, and I think it be needing it again, except there ain't no more earls. It will be taking a miracle to bring it back to its former grandness."

Sarah did not ask what he meant by that. She would wait and ask Aunt Lillian. She had so much to ask Aunt Lillian.

When they had reached the small village of Rockingham, Angeline had insisted upon engaging a wagon drawn by an ox to take them to Merrymount, claiming it would be great fun to see the "old crow's" eyes when they arrived in such manner. Since a wagon and ox was by far cheaper than hiring a hackney, it was not difficult for Sarah to acquiesce to Angeline's wish. Now, she was

sorry. The only protection from the snow that had begun
to fall was a tattered blanket furnished by the driver.

He was wrapped from head to toe in a heavy greatcoat,
long boots, gloves, and a red cap pulled down to his eyes.
"Ye shoulda knowed how cold it would be," he said
unsympathetically.

"Is it this cold here all the time?" asked Sarah.

"Nope, only when a blizzard blows in. We git maybe
two a year."

Sitting beside the driver on the buckboard, Sarah and
Angeline huddled closer together and pulled the blanket
higher to cover their faces. Only their eyes showed below
their fur hats. The wagon began to climb upward, and
when they came to a clearing, Merrymount was visible to
Sarah. The wagon groaned and squeaked.

Angeline whispered to Sarah, "I believe the wheels
need greasing. I just hope we don't lose one before we get
there."

"Hush," Sarah said. "We have enough to be concerned about without worrying about losing a wheel."

"Eh? What was that," the driver asked.

"Nothing," Sarah assured him.

Angeline giggled.

Time passed interminably slow.

Then at last they were at the top of the ridge. The land
was flat, acres and acres of it; the trees had been cleared
away, and in the center of the flat land was Merrymount,
a backdrop for the fiercely falling snow. Sarah sucked in
her breath.

The beauty of the place affected Angeline not at all.
"Do they call this place Flat Top?"

" 'Tis a ridge, nothing more; a good place for a fortified
house. The other side of the ridge slopes into a valley of
rich soil, with a stream running through it. Used to produce crops but not now. Not since the drought started.
Bet they be glad to see this snow. Any kind of moisture is
better than none at all."

Sarah didn't hear the last part. She smiled. He had said there was a stream. She remembered the prettiest blue stream . . . a three-year-old *could* remember.

The wagon rolled closer to the house, and Sarah gasped. Windows were covered with boards, and the chimney pots were void of smoke. A huge gatehouse with a portcullis—huge iron grating suspended by chains and cornered between grooves—stood between them and the house, but there was no sign of a bailey wall that protected a fortified house.

Sarah told herself that centuries had passed since the wall was needed. But why the portcullis? She had no recollection of that at all. Just the moat, and it was filled with tangled weeds, not with flowers as she remembered.

" 'Tis deserted," she said under her breath. She wiped at the tears that were instantly on her cheeks. How could a dream be so quickly destroyed?

" 'Tis banded about that the old woman has turned into a recluse," the wagon driver said, pulling on the reins and stopping the oxen, whose warm breath was fogging out into the cold. "Mayhap you should return to town."

Snow had banked around huge closed doors.

"Aunt Lillian invited me to Merrymount, and this is where I plan to stay," said Sarah in a steely voice. She jumped down off the wagon and asked, "Driver, would you please unload our trunk?"

"But, sister, how can we get into the house if there's nobody home? Surely the door is locked."

"If that is the case, we will climb through a window—I see the lower ones are not boarded up. We certainly can't stay out here in the snow, and we certainly can't return to Templeton Hall. Hoggie made that clear enough."

"Mayhap we could find the kind captain if we returned to London. We could find work. You're an excellent teacher, and I can work with my hands. I'm quite handy—"

"No." Sarah's words were spoken with much more

certainty than she felt. But she could not in her most
far-fetched dreams consider leaving Merrymount. Where
Aunt Lillian was, she did not know and, at the moment,
did not care. Turning to the wagon driver, she handed
him a coin. Seeing his difficulty with the big trunk, she
helped him tug it to the ground. It was much too heavy
for them to carry to the house. She would unpack a small
amount at a time and tote it in after she had been in the
house long enough to get warm. She yanked at her fur
hat, but it would not cover more of her face. A gloved
hand held her reticule tightly.

"Come on, Angeline," said Sarah. "We can't stand out
here in the cold."

Hand in hand they started walking, almost running,
toward the house. A narrow wooden bridge allowed passage over the moat. Behind them the wagon was departing, its wheels creaking.

Angeline looked back over her shoulder. "Sister,
should we let him go? What will happen if we can't get
into the house?"

"We *will* get in the house. We've come too far . . ."

Just then a spotted hound dog, as big as a donkey, so
it seemed to Sarah, cleared the corner of the house, followed by a mate as big, or bigger, than the first one.

"Cain, Abel," a voice called.

The dogs bounded toward Sarah and Angeline. A
woman came into view. She wore a wide-brimmed,
floppy, gypsy hat that showed only a portion of her face,
huge thick gloves, a fur coat that reached her ankles, and
heavy boots. As the distance narrowed between them,
Sarah could see that in spots the fur was worn. But that
did not alter the fact that the coat had at one time been
very grand.

"Cain, Abel," the woman scolded, and when the dogs
quieted, coming back to dance around her, she said in a
highly cultured voice, "I'm so glad you are here, Lady
Sarah. And I can say that it's about time. I've been ex-

pecting you for five days now. I'm Lady Lillian Merriwether, your Aunt Lillian."

If Angeline had not curtsied, Sarah would not have
thought of it. She dipped slightly—for manners' sake—
but she was in no mood to accept the proffered hand.

"What do you mean, you've been expecting me for five
days? Why did you not send someone to meet us or, better
yet, come yourself? Do you realize what a struggle we've
had reaching Merrymount?"

She looked at her Aunt Lillian's face. She had a long
neck like a crow, quite a long nose, and a disarming smile.

"I would have loved to come to London, Lady Sarah,
but I was much too busy taking care of Cain and Abel."
Lady Lillian patted the hound with a black nose and gave
a little laugh.

Sarah was not in the mood for levity and did not
respond. She stared at the old woman.

Angeline stood behind Sarah, and Lady Lillian, seemingly noticing her for the first time, said, "I see you have
brought your abigail. That is good."

"Angeline is not my abigail—"

"Come in, do come in. 'Tis very cold out here, but I
can't promise much better inside. There's hot cider. I
shall be ever so glad for this blizzard to break."

Sarah, with Angeline trailing, followed her Aunt Lillian
through a side door and into a large room which appeared to have once been a formal receiving room. There
was still a quiet elegance about it, fine threadbare furnishings, a worn Aubusson rug, and a marble fireplace.
Sarah's quick eye noted the empty space above the mantel and wondered if that was where her mother's portrait
used to hang. She thought not; the red velvet window
coverings were missing.

The coals in the grate were gray, too burned out to
produce smoke, Sarah thought. Hanging over the grate,
a black iron kettle emitted the wonderful smell of hot

cider. A white cloth covered a nearby tea table on which were china cups, saucers, and a silver ladle.

Sarah went to sit in a chair, motioning for Angeline to do the same.

Cain and Abel found their places close to the hearth and, stretching their long, spotted bodies, rested their heads on their huge front paws.

Lady Lillian ladled the cider into cups and served Sarah and Angeline. "The apple crop was good this year, even though the apples were very small due to the drought. I'm sorry I can't offer you tea."

"Thank you," Sarah said graciously.

Angeline declared, "We're Americans. We prefer cider."

Lady Lillian, still wearing her fur coat and her big hat, poured a cup of cider for herself and went to sit in a deep chair near the burned-out fire. Obviously the chair was her favorite, for the once-plush upholstery seemed to hug her thin body. She said to Sarah, "You look exactly like your mother. She was the pretty one."

It pleased Sarah to hear that she looked like her mother. Her papa had once told her that. "I don't remember her."

"Of course you don't. She died when you were born. I was devastated to lose her, but I was ever so fond of you." Lady Lillian shook her head. "Now, that Hoggie. He was a different story. He called me ape-leader because I wasn't married, and then said I was so ugly no man would have me."

"That sounds like my brother," Sarah said. "Kindness personified." The cider had warmed her. She stood and removed her coat and hat, Angeline following her lead. Lady Lillian picked up a small silver bell and rang it delicately. An elderly woman, dressed in faded, rustling bombazine, came to take the coats and hats. Lady Lillian introduced her as Mrs. Hilda Armstrong.

"This is my precious niece from America, Lady Sarah Templeton," said Lady Lillian.

The old woman dipped.

Sarah acknowledged the introduction, and then turned to Angeline. "And this is my sister——"

Lady Lillian's mouth flew open. "Your sister! Why . . . why, I don't understand. You don't look a thing alike."

" 'Tis simple. Papa married an Iroquois Indian, and Angeline was born of that union.

"Well, I never. I thought Indians were savages. How could he do that to you——"

Sarah stopped her with succinct words. "Wanna was a wonderful stepmother, and *Lady* Angeline is as dear to me as if she were born to my own mother.

"Angeline, I'm sorry to be speaking of you as if you were not here, but I feel that this is something that must needs be discussed right away."

"And, Lady Lillian, I brought Angeline because Papa is dead. She is my charge, and if she is not welcome at Merrymount and is not to be treated as my equal, then we shall return to America at the quickest possible sailing."

Angeline looked at her askance, and Sarah knew why. She was bluffing. If Aunt Lillian turned them out, they would have to go sit on their trunk in the snow. They had no place to go.

The threat did not sit well with Lady Lillian; her answer came quickly. Too quickly, Sarah thought. "Of course she can stay at Merrymount. But I warn you, others will look askance on that dark skin. We English are a bunch of snobs." She forced a smile.

"I'm sorry I called you an old crow when you didn't meet our ship," said Angeline, thinking no more of the old woman than she thought of her.

Lady Lillian laughed. "You're a sassy one, like your sister. Lady Sarah kicked me in the face when she was one year old. I had no doubt that she would find her way to Merrymount."

She paused for a moment, then continued, "I simply did not have the means to travel to London. The crested carriage has not been out of the carriage house for three years, and I would not think of going into London in anything less."

Pity swelled Sarah's heart. The room was suddenly warm. She went and hugged her aunt and smiled when the old woman said, "Hogarth didn't have the sense of a widgeon, didn't know a good thing when he saw it. He could have had Merrymount had he not been so stubborn. I offered it to him on a platter."

Sarah remembered her papa saying something about Lady Lillian wanting to marry him. Hiding a smile, she asked, "Were *you* served up on that platter?"

"I certainly was. But he said I was too stubborn. Stubborn, ha! He was the one who was stubborn."

"Is that why you never wrote all those years, Aunt Lillian?"

A blush showed on Lady Lillian's face. "I had my pride."

Sarah was glad she had come, however difficult the journey had been. Now, suddenly, she had a past and would soon be privy to it. But all that could wait, she told herself, except the one question inside of her that was bursting to come out. "Why, Aunt Lillian, did you invite me to Merrymount? You knew nothing of Papa's death. The timing—"

"No, I didn't know he was dead, God rest his soul. The timing was right. I felt it here." She put her hand over her heart.

"Felt what?" asked Sarah.

"That you could save Merrymount. Blunt, that is what is needed. As a proper Englishman would say, 'At the moment, I'm short in the pockets.' But he would never lose his pride or his belief that things would get better."

Sarah automatically hugged her reticule that held her earthly wealth, one hundred pounds from Hoggie and what was left of the five-pound note from Captain Barksdale. She couldn't save a flea.

"Don't look so startled," said Lady Lillian. "I'm seldom wrong when I get these feelings."

"What feelings?"

"I just told you, the feeling that you could save Merrymount."

"Aunt Lillian, I can't save Merrymount. I'm poverty-stricken—"

"With your looks, dear child, you will never be poverty-stricken."

Sarah glanced at Angeline, who was doing a poor job of hiding a smile.

This was entirely too delicate for the young girl's ears, thought Sarah, but she did not know how to adroitly change the subject. "Aunt Lillian, you can't be speaking about . . . about what I am thinking. Do you plan a courtesan's life for me? Well, I—"

A big laugh spilled out into the room. "No, child. Although I hear tell courtesans fare right well with the men of the upper orders. And you would have no trouble there. But I have other plans. Very exciting plans. We'll speak of them on the morrow."

As if that dismissed the subject, Lady Lillian picked up the silver bell and rang it again, and when Hilda came, Lady Lillian told her to have John Wesley bring the trunk in out of the snow.

"He can use Caesar to pull the sled. When they get as far as the back door, you can unpack and carry the things to the room just across the hall. The girls will sleep there. It will be warmer than upstairs, and lighter."

"Yes, m'lady," Hilda said, bobbing.

After the maid had left, the room was quiet. Sarah was glad; she needed time to think. Surely Aunt Lillian had windmills in her head to send all the way to America for her to save Merrymount. From what? From whom? She looked beyond the window; night had descended upon Merrymount. Snow was falling through the moonlight. On the morrow, Lady Lillian would be asked numerous questions when the two of them were away from Angeline's delicate ears.

Chapter Four

The next morning Lady Lillian opened her mouth, pointed at her throat, and squeaked. She had the worst case of sore throat Sarah had ever seen. All the way down, her gullet was as red as a beet. And little wonder, Sarah thought. During the night a glass of water began freezing beside her bed.

And she'd had no business out in the blizzard walking those ugly hounds, Sarah concluded. She stood beside Lady Lillian's bed, wondering what to do. There was a fireplace in her bedchamber, but no fire.

"There's no coal for a fire," Hilda said when Sarah rang for her. "Me and the mister—John Wesley—sleep in the kitchen, close to the stove, though it furnishes precious little heat after a short while has passed. But we manage with heavy quilts and by sleeping close together." She gave a shy grin. "We ain't done that in years."

"Something good out of something bad," Sarah said, turning to Lady Lillian, who was snuggled under heavy quilts and still shivering. "We'll move your bed into the room where there's a fire."

Hilda left to fetch John Wesley, and he and Sarah moved the narrow bed into the room where a small fire burned. She tucked a down comforter around the old woman and put hot bricks, wrapped in a blanket, to her

feet. Hot chicken broth, along with the hot cider, soothed
her red throat. But it did not stop her fretting.

"You lie still and for heaven's sake stop trying to talk,"
Sarah scolded. "The blizzard has blown itself out, and the
sun is shining. The worst is over. But you must needs give
your poor throat rest."

Hilda, who had been trying to help, turned to leave the
room. "I think there's a wee bit of devil's brew left. I'll mix
it with rock candy . . ."

No doubt the devil's brew would stop Lady Lillian's
fretting, Sarah thought. She did not know about the rock
candy.

Winter sunshine shone through the window. Outside,
tree branches, heavy with snow, were still. A certain
peacefulness came over Sarah, and for the first time she
wondered if there was anything to reincarnation, if truly
she had lived at Merrymount in another life. She stopped
the thought right there. She had been taught that to even
think such thoughts was sinful.

Sarah wanted more than anything to go exploring,
inside and outside the huge manor house. So far she had
seen only the room where Aunt Lillian had brought them,
which Sarah thought of as the Warm Room, the small
bedchamber which she and Angeline had slept, Lady
Lillian's bedchamber, and the basement kitchen, where
last night's supper of mutton and this morning's breakfast
of porridge were served at a long plank table that had
been moved close to the fire.

"I've never eaten in the kitchen," Angeline told Hilda.

Hilda laughed and assured her that not too many seasons back no one at Merrymount ate in the kitchen.
"Even the help had their own dining room. And the
butler, the lofty old soul, had his own private place to
dine."

"Where did they all go?" asked Angeline.

Hilda flung out her arms, her wrinkled face and soft
brown eyes alight with anger. "Gone to a rich household

somewhere, I suppose. When the crops failed and there was no money to pay, they deserted Lady Lillian like rats leaving a sinking ship. Me and the mister felt our duty to stay . . . even without pay."

She paused before adding, "And, too, we be getting up in years. We didn't want to make a change."

"I'm glad you stayed," Sarah said. "What would Aunt Lillian have done without you both?"

"She would have sent for you sooner," piped up Angeline.

Sarah, ignoring Angeline's chipper, though possibly astute, remark, turned her thoughts back to what she would do this day. It would be impossible to talk with Lady Lillian, to ask her all the questions she had planned to ask. The sunshine looked so inviting, and she did not feel it prudent to go prowling over the big house without the old woman's permission. The house being so large, she would need a guide. The outside won. She would see the other side of the ridge, mayhap find the stream she remembered.

Excusing herself, she left Angeline and Hilda commiserating and went to her room, dressing in the warmest clothes she could find: a pair of Hoggie's woolen breeches and a sweater with a hood. The extra warm clothes had been packed at the last minute, and Sarah could not remember whatever had possessed her to take up the meager space in the trunk to bring them. Now, she was glad that she had. The winter sunshine did not fool her: she knew that it was terribly cold outside even without the strong wind of yesterday.

Woolen stockings and boots with small heels were pulled on, and lastly she donned a full-length, fleece-lined red mantle. And then gloves. She laughed at her reflection in the looking glass. She was as round as a barrel.

She left the house. Hilda would tend Lady Lillian.

It had not taken Sarah long to form a very concise opinion of Lady Lillian Merriwether. She was a thorough-

bred, not a black crow, and very strongly opinionated.
Very spoiled, very selfish.

Leaving by the side door through which she had entered Merrymount, Sarah walked swiftly until she came to
the stables, seemingly deserted with the exception of a
lone black horse romping around a fenced lot. John Wesley was there, holding high a leather bridle, which the
horse was obviously taking great delight in ignoring.

"He will come when he's tired of romping," John Wesley said when he saw Sarah.

"Are you going into town?" she asked.

"No. I be hitching him to the sled and going to chop
wood. Helps warm the house and saves what little coal we
have."

"Good luck," Sarah said.

She left the man and horse playing their game and was
quickly on a footpath through a thicket of trees. The
ground was still flat, but before long she was on the side
of the ridge and moving downward. Coming to a clearing,
she stopped and shaded her eyes with her hand. Below
was the valley.

She walked on and on, enjoying herself immensely
while imagining her dear papa overseeing crops growing
on the land, her mother visiting the tenants and taking
care of their needs. A tear trickled down her cheek. She
swiped at it with the back of her gloved hand and prayed
that come spring, seed would sprout and the land would
again produce abundant crops.

If the rains would come. Mayhap that was what Aunt
Lillian had meant when she said Sarah could save Merrymount.

Sarah laughed. Was the old woman addled? She,
Sarah, couldn't make it rain. Suddenly the terrain leveled
again, and the ground was almost as flat as the top of the
ridge that held Merrymount. In the distance she could see
a farm pond, sunshine glinting off the ice, She squinted.

A figure was dipping and spinning, bending low, skating backward.

For a long while, Sarah stood and watched. As a child she had skated on the frozen ponds that dotted Templeton land, wearing boots with narrow heels like the ones she wore this day.

Sarah could not help herself; leaving the path, she started running toward the pond and the stranger who was having so much fun. The air was cold to her face, a tree limb grabbed at the hood of her sweater, pulling it back from her head, letting her auburn curls fall loose against her shoulders.

Sarah laughed when her boot heel first touched the ice, for suddenly she was a child again, wanting to compete with the stranger, clearly, at closer scrutiny, a man. She would best him. At a glimpse she could see that he was tall and broad-shouldered, and his blond head was uncovered, as if he did not feel the cold at all. His coat, which came only to his slim hips, was red-and-black Scottish plaid. The legs of his tight-fitting breeches fit into long boots to which were attached ice skates.

He stopped and stared at her.

Sarah started moving, lightly, gracefully over the ice, her red cape billowing out from her. She felt happy, light and free, and gay. She could not remember experiencing such elation. Only vaguely was she aware that the man was still standing and staring at her. That was not what she wanted; she wanted to match her skills against his. She would never tell him that she had been named ice skating champion of Dutchess County before she had seen two and ten summers.

"Come on," she called to him, "I will race you."

A smile, but not a word from the stranger, and then the race began, back and forth across the pond. They circled the pond twice, and it was a huge pond.

He was the first to slow to catch a breath, but she was

the one who lost her balance and toppled into him, taking him to the hard ice with her.

Their limbs tangled, and they laughed.

At last he asked, "Where did you come from? I think I am alone, and then I look up and there's a beautiful girl with beautiful whiskey-colored curls . . ."

He was smiling.

Sarah was enjoying the mystique of the meeting. She did not want to tell him she was from Merrymount, for there was bound to be questions. "I came around the ridge. I enjoyed your show for a full ten minutes before I decided to join you."

"And best me. None of my friends skate on ice, and quite frankly, they think I am bacon-brained for indulging myself. They claim that I will break a limb or catch my death."

Still feeling mysterious, Sarah raked her unruly hair back with a gloved hand and said, "I've been skating since I was five years old."

"Where?"

"Wherever I come upon a frozen pond."

"Do you meet many strangers? Do you tell them your name?"

"Never."

They were by now sitting up, their shoulders touching, and the feeling that washed over Sarah was so shockingly exhilarating that she felt sure it was part of the euphoria of being at Merrymount, of skating and feeling like a child again. There was no other reason for the feeling. She had never felt anything before when a man touched her. Well, no man had ever touched her, except Sam Schuyler, and that was quite by accident. He had apologized profusely. This stranger did not seem to be apologetic in any way. She scooted, putting minute space between their shoulders.

"Don't move away," he said. "Your shoulder was keep-

ing me warm. Should I become chilled and catch my
death, my friends will blame you."

He has the most engaging smile, thought Sarah. His eyes
were positively riveting. Feeling herself blush, she feared
she was acting like a schoolgirl, instead of a schoolmarm.
"How can they blame me when they don't know me?"
she asked.

"Nor do I. Will you please tell me your name?"

"No."

"Then I shall speak of you as the mysterious girl with
whiskey curls who came around the bend of the ridge to
skate with me." He took her chin in his hand and turned
her face to his. "You have lovely eyes . . . and your
lips . . ."

He brushed her lips with his.

She jerked back. "Why did you do that?"

He laughed. "Because I had the most uncontrollable
desire to do so. And because you would not tell me your
name."

Sarah felt herself shudder. A strange warmth suddenly
flooded her body, and she would have gasped had she not
swallowed the sound. She had broken all rules of propriety. One did not kiss a stranger; not even in America were
such brazen actions condoned. But she hadn't kissed him.
He had kissed her, and she had the feeling that she could
not have stopped him had she tried.

The fact that he had kissed her did not disturb Sarah
as much as the heat that it had stirred inside of her. She
had read Byron's book of poems that spoke of such feelings, thinking them risqué to say the least. And now,
sitting there on ice, beside a perfect stranger, she was
having those very same titillating feelings Lord Byron had
described. It was beyond bearing.

Sarah, thinking she was turning into a hussy, jumped
up and skated skillfully away from temptation.

She wanted him to kiss her again.

* * *

Nathan Adams, Lord Chesterson, watched Sarah disappear into the snow-covered trees, and even then, he sat for a long while until his lower extremities reminded him that he was sitting on ice. Small wonder, he thought, that the ice had not melted beneath him, letting him sink into oblivion beneath the frozen surface. Never had his body suffered such a shock from a frivolous kiss.

Suffered was not quite the word, he told himself. In truth, it was a most pleasant feeling, one he had not experienced in some time. His heart beat in his throat, and his loins ached with desire.

Quite a normal feeling for a man of thirty, but . . .

He looked again toward the woods. She was gone. He removed his skates and got to his feet. Holding them by their leather straps, he flung them over his shoulder and walked in the opposite direction from that which she had gone.

He wondered if she were staring at him from behind a tree.

He wished he had grabbed her and kissed her again.

A man, a decent man, would have done exactly as he had done, let her go, he thought.

For once, Nathan wished he were not decent. The ridge curved, and soon he was on the other side and in sight of Copthorne, his home. It was small compared to Merrymount sitting stately on top of the ridge. He had never craved the big house. He had craved the land which went with it, mostly because it ran with his land, which had been awarded to him by a fluke of nature. With the land had come a title, the sixth earl of Chesterson.

Nathan had heard that the rich land, and Merrymount as well, would soon be on the market, due to nonpayment of taxes. Much to his chagrin, he did not have the blunt with which to purchase it. For years his expenses had been much more than his income, and now, after three years of drought, he was up the River Tick.

It was not Nathan Adams's nature to dwell on something over which he had no control, and when he entered his house, he was again thinking of the girl with whiskey curls, the skating whiz, and smiling to himself.

His brother's wife, Georgena, looked up when he entered the kitchen. "You look like a cat that just caught a mouse."

Nathan laughed. "I caught one, but she got away. Had the most beautiful whiskey-colored curls."

"*She* got away, and you're smiling?"

Georgena was a plump little thing, with straight brown hair and brown eyes that sparked when she talked. She was a true friend of Nathan's, his confidante, and many times he had felt that had he not had her he would be in Bedlam. During his late wife's lingering illness, Georgena had come every day to offer her support, and three years back, when Naneen had died, Georgena and William had moved into Copthorne. Childless, they adored the seven-year-old twins.

Georgena poured two cups of coffee and offered one to Nathan. "Do you have time to sit a spell? Laura and Larry are with the tutor."

Nathan followed her into a cozy room off the kitchen. When he had moved into Copthorne, he had had the kitchen moved from the musty, cold basement, saying that not even servants should have to work in depressing surroundings.

The chairs and sofas in the morning room were done in bright yellow linen, dotted with red cabbage roses and bright green leaves. Sunshine cut a swath across the black-and-white tile floor. The crackling fire in the fireplace warmed and cheered Nathan.

"Tell me about the mouse," Georgena said after they were seated. "It's been a long time, Nathan. As William and I have been telling you, you need a wife."

Nathan laughed. "Hold on. I've only met the girl, and I don't know her name." He paused. "At first I thought she was an apparition, a figment of my imagination, and then she began skating . . . without skates. The most gorgeous curls fell to her shoulders . . . her mantle, bright red, billowed out from her like wings, and even under a thick sweater and heavy breeches, I could detect a well-formed figure."

"Breeches!" exclaimed Georgena.

"I don't think she's from the upper orders. Mayhap that's why she wouldn't tell me her name. Most likely she's a maid from one of the houses around here." He sat pensive for a moment. "But her voice was well-modulated. And on second thought, she didn't speak like a maid, and, for some strange reason, I felt that I had heard that voice before. A ridiculous thought."

"Was it English?"

"Yes, but different."

Georgena looked at her brother-in-law and felt pity. He had lost his dear Naneen, and her illness had taken every pound he could lay his hands to, and then came the drought. The many doctors he had taken his wife to had failed to diagnose the illness.

Georgena remembered too well watching Naneen die in Nathan's arms. To her knowledge, he had not looked at a woman since. Mayhap an occasional trip to a woman of the night to relieve his manly need, but he kept no mistress. And he had shown no interest in finding a wife for himself or a mother for the twins.

Copthorne, the twins, and taking care of his constituents' needs by serving in the House of Lords had seemed enough. Now, his hazel eyes were sparkling with life, and the Cheshire-cat smile had not left his handsome face.

But a girl who would wear breeches! And skating on farm ponds is hardly the thing . . .

Just then William came in. He was not as large a man as his brother, nor as handsome, but he had the same disposition: serious, but fun-loving, caring and kind. He went to Georgena and bent to give her a peck on the forehead. Then, slapping Nathan's shoulder affectionately, he said, "Fustian! 'Tis cold as blazes out there."

"And the sunshine gives the appearance of warmth," Georgena said. She was anxious to share the news about Nathan's skating adventure with her husband. They kept no secrets from each other and had often spoken of Nathan's need for a helpmeet, even though it would mean they would no longer be needed to care for the twins.

Nathan stood to greet his brother. "The moisture from the snow came at a good time for the winter wheat."

"Yes . . . yes, it did. I only wish there had been more of it," said William. "It turned too cold too quickly."

"Seems those beautiful black clouds are void of moisture."

Georgena was well-aware that "her" men could talk of rain, or the lack of it, and crops all day. She intentionally intruded. "William, you must hear of Nathan's wonderful experience. Go ahead, Nathan, tell him about the girl who could outskate you but refused to tell you her name. While you're doing that, I will get William a cup of coffee."

"The devil take me!" said William. "I don't believe *anyone* can best you skating, and I do wish you would give it up. You're going to break a limb."

This brought a chuckle from Nathan. How many times had he heard that? "She was a pretty little thing . . ."

Taking his seat again, he sipped the coffee and told his brother everything that had happened, except about the desire that filled his loins when their shoulders touched. Nor did he tell William how he had lost control and kissed her. Although the kiss was hardly a kiss, his lips still burned from it. In his mind's eye he could see her back as she disappeared into the trees, the whiskey curls resting on her squared shoulders, the determined way she walked.

I must be losing my mind. It was such a brief encounter.

"Shall we send a sleuth out to look for her?" William asked teasingly, grinning at Nathan over the rim of his cup. "For a long time, Georgena and I have prayed that you would find the right girl—"

Nathan answered quickly. "No. I shall not look for her. She did not wish to see me again, or she would have told me her name."

Sarah walked through the woods as fast as her legs would take her. She swore at herself, for her face still burned from embarrassment. She supposed it was embarrassment, but what was making the rest of her body feel as if it were on fire? "Oh, dear God, please give me a sign that the stranger didn't sense the way I felt. I could not bear it."

The prayer was not meant to be sacrilegious; she just needed someone to talk with. But mayhap God was not the one from whom she should seek answers about physical desire. She was not totally ignorant of the needs with which one was born. And she had seen farm animals mate.

Sarah did not feel like an animal; she felt like . . . she couldn't bring herself to say the word. She walked on, looking for the creek that had stayed in her memory. The sound of voices came through the trees, and she recognized one as Angeline's.

Calling to her, Sarah walked in the direction of their voices when Angeline said, "We're over here. I'm helping John Wesley cut wood to supplement the coal."

"She's good hep, too," said John Wesley.

The trees thinned, and Sarah stopped and stared. Angeline had an ax and was chopping at a tree. John Wesley was cutting the trunk of a felled tree and piling the logs on a sled. The black horse that had been romping in the exercise lot was hitched to the sled. When Sarah approached, he flung his head in the air and snorted.

"Angeline," Sarah scolded, "you will chop your leg off."

Angeline stopped her chopping and turned to look at Sarah. "Where have you been?"

"I found the most wonderful farm pond and went skating."

She did not mention the stranger. At five and ten summers, Angeline was entirely too young to know of such things. Sarah asked John Wesley, "Where is the creek that runs through Merrymount land? I was looking for it when I came upon the pond."

"'Tis about two kilometers to the west. Runs the other direction. Mighty cold to be walking thet far."

Now that her body had cooled, the cold was beginning to penetrate Sarah's woolen clothes. She pulled the hood up over her head and held it close to her cheeks. "I think I agree with you, and mayhap I shall return to the house and check on Aunt Lillian. I didn't tell her I was leaving."

"Hilda done told her that you left, but she didn't say where you wuz going because she didn't know."

Angeline, resuming her chopping, brought the ax down hard on the trunk of the tree. A huge chip flew through the air and missed hitting Sarah by an inch. "You could help us chop wood."

Sarah laughed. "I think I'll pass. You're a good wood chopper, Angeline. Where did you learn?"

"It just comes natural with her, I can tell," said John Wesley.

Sarah said goodbye and turned toward the path the sled had made. The climb to the top of the ridge took much more effort than walking down had taken, and when she finally reached the top, she was winded and fatigued. Of course the strenuous skating could be the cause of her fatigue, she mused.

And the wonderful excitement. She supposed the aftermath of that could leave one feeling drained. Stopping and standing still for a moment, she drew several deep breaths. Her body had calmed, but her lips still felt the thrill of the stranger's lips. Reaching up, she touched her mouth with the tips of her fingers, feeling wonderfully wicked.

Sarah tried to push the thoughts from her mind and walked on toward the house. Without the wind it was quiet and peaceful. And then, out of the quietness, she heard a chicken squawking. Looking around, she saw beyond the stables a chicken yard. Hilda was holding a black-and-white hen, its wings flapping furiously. With every flap, the squawking grew louder.

"Liked to have never caught her," Hilda said when she saw Sarah. "Chased her all over the place."

"Why did you want to catch her?"

"To eat, of course. Were it not for the chickens John Wesley raises, and the sheep, most likely all of us would be by now in the poor house, or starved to death." She inclined her head toward a flat-topped building a goodly ways away. Through the open door Sarah saw sheep bundled together against the cold. A small outbuilding held the chickens. Closely woven wire formed a containment yard.

"Hilda, is that why Aunt Lillian sent for me? Did she think *I* could keep you from starving to death?" Sarah asked.

"She didn't tell me any sech thing. But Lady Lillian has good reason for anything she does." Hilda shook the flapping, squawking hen and told her to be quiet or she would chop her head off now instead of later, and then, looking Sarah straight in the face, she asked, "What did m'lady tell you?"

"That she sent for me so that I could save Merrymount."

"Most likely she feels thet way. No doubt she plans on finding you a rich husband. Lord knows something has to be done, and she gave up on finding a rich husband for herself many moons ago."

Chapter Five

Angeline drew back the ax and whacked at the tree trunk with all her strength. She swore in the Iroquois language, and John Wesley was quick to ask her what she had said. She laughed. "Just some choice words I learned from my mother, but only when she thought she was alone and when she was angry with someone . . . like Hoggie."

"Who's Hoggie?" John Wesley asked.

"My half brother, though I claim no kin to him. He was mean to Mama because she was Indian, and he was mean to me. Of course he was such a sneak, he only said ugly things to us when Papa was not around. And Mama would never tell on him."

"He'll git his just due," predicted John Wesley, bobbing his head in an affirmative manner.

"I don't know, John Wesley. Seems like the good ones are the ones who never win. Take Sarah. She's the dearest person on this earth, and Hoggie turned her away from Templeton Hall with a mere pittance and told her she could never come back. And me, too. Me, without a penny."

"God will punish him, just wait and see."

"Sometimes I talk to Mama's Spirits, but I don't think they will do anything because I have hatred in my heart."

"Spirits . . . you mean you talk to God?"

"I don't know whether there's a difference or not. Mama always said the Spirits of those gone would take care of me."

John Wesley scratched his head. "Your ladyship, if I wuz you, I wouldn't be talking about stuff like that. Hereabouts people believe in witches, and they mayhap take you for one."

This brought laughter from Angeline. "A witch I'm not. They sell their souls to the devil and fly through the air on broomsticks in the night, so I've heard. Had I been like that, I would have swooped down and flogged Hoggie good and proper." She whacked at the tree trunk again, hard, as if she were hitting Hoggie.

After that they worked without talking until John Wesley declared that Caesar, the black horse, could not pull more than what was on the sled.

The restive horse snorted and flung his head. John Wesley went over and rubbed his neck and told him they would be going soon and that he would feed him when they returned to the stable.

"What do you feed him? Did not the corn and wheat burn up in the drought?"

"Turnips. And an occasional apple. There wuz some rain after it wuz too late for the crops, so we planted acres and acres of turnips. We gathered them before the ground froze and put them in the root cellar."

"Who's we?" Angeline asked. "You and Hilda? Did Lady Lillian help?"

"No, her ladyship, as poor stricken as she is, is still a lady of quality. And my Hilda would have her no other way. She loves bobbing to her lady. And I have to admit, I like it, too. 'Tis an honor to serve the nobility, even them thet can't pay their taxes."

Angeline did not understand that at all. In America you were either rich, middling rich, or poor. Every man, no matter his financial circumstances, if he were an honorable man, could be addressed as "Mister" if he so desired.

She concluded there was a lot to learn about the English ways, and then she went back to the subject of who planted the turnips. *We* had to be more than one. She asked the second time: "Who planted the turnips?"

"There's two tenants left. Had no place to go, so they stayed on. They raise some food by carrying water from the creek to water a garden. Of course each year brings hope. No one could believe that for three years straight there would be so little rainfall, sometimes only a few huge drops would come out of hovering black clouds. There's always heavy mist in the mornings, then hot sun the rest of the day."

Angeline pulled her cape close around her to keep out the cold, sharper now that she had stopped chopping. "There will be lots of rain next year, John Wesley. I promise."

"You promise? How could you promise—"

"I'll tell you if you promise not to tell."

"You got my word."

"Mama showed me how to do the rain dance her people did."

John Wesley's eye got big. "I told you thet was frowned on in these parts. People are scared to death of witches, and of ghosts. Ever old house in England has its own ghost, but people shy away from them." After a long pause: "I guess England's ghosts are what you call the spirits of those passed. People hereabouts just might think yer calling them up . . . and they might hang you."

"Well, all I can say is they shouldn't be so judgmental, the bad shape they are in. Somebody needs to pray for rain."

John Wesley cracked the whip over Caesar's back and gave the eager horse office to go. He glanced worriedly at Angeline, as pretty as any girl in England, he'd wager, with lovely brown skin and chocolate brown eyes, and he sure would hate to see her hanged for being a witch. *A rain dance! Talking to Spirits!*

"I'll be careful, John Wesley. I won't let anyone see me doing the rain dance. But something must needs be done if Merrymount is to be saved. Poor Lady Lillian, she would die should she lose that old place, though I don't know what she wants with it, all boarded up the way it is."

"It don't bear thinking on," John Wesley said. "I pray that another year brings more than turnips and a few dried-up apples."

And I'll starve to death if I have to eat turnips, thought Angeline. She looked at Caesar pityingly and vowed that this day he should have an apple for being such a good horse and helping gather wood.

Lady Lillian's sore throat lasted three days. Sarah didn't believe the whiskey and rock candy had helped a whit, but it had kept her from fretting so much. This day she insisted she be allowed out of bed.

For three days Sarah had thought of little else other than the plight of Lady Lillian, and the thinking had brought one conclusion—mayhap she could manage to fall in love with a rich man. Love was the sticky part. Never would she make a marriage of convenience. She had heard of such marriages. The wife was nothing more than chattel. And why not? The husband, probably old and fat, had bought her, had he not?

So Sarah had her plan set in stone; she would tell Lady Lillian that she would marry a man deep in his pockets *only* if she fell in love with said rich man.

With that settled, Sarah had spent the three days of silence from Lady Lillian thinking about the stranger on the pond, his laughing hazel-gray eyes, his engaging smile that seemed so genuine, his deep English voice. She wondered where he had attended school, what he did for a living. He could even be married. At night he pranced through her dreams, loving her, wanting her, making her want him.

After such a dream, Sarah's face burned with embarrassment, even shame, when she thought about the heat his touch sent through her body, the way her lips quivered under his kiss.

Was it just a light brushing, or had he kissed her with lingering passion?

Her dreams held out for the lingering passion.

"Oh, dear God," she prayed, "please don't ever let me see the man again, and please, please don't let him know what his touch did to me. He would think . . . no, not think . . . he would know what kind of girl I am."

The prayer came from Sarah's lips but not from her heart. The very next day she found herself sneaking through the woods and peering toward the pond. The stranger was nowhere to be seen. As far as she could see, the valley was as empty as yesterday's dream. She went to find the creek she remembered and was ecstatic when she stood on its banks, as if she had found an old friend.

The spring-fed stream wound through rich black soil dry and cracked from the lack of rain. A thawing had set the water free, letting it move languorously downstream to empty into River Welland.

Sarah regretted there would be no more skating on the pond until there was another blizzard and hard freeze. She could hardly hope for that, she told herself, returning to the manor house, and, at the moment, wanting nothing more than for Lady Lillian to be well enough to converse with her.

Sarah was delighted to find her aunt wrapped in a wool blanket and sitting in her chair in the warm room. Sarah sat opposite her.

The older woman looked chipper and alert, and Sarah was relieved, for she had no notion of approaching the subject of how they would save Merrymount from tax collectors in a light manner. She was not accustomed to

other people planning her life, and she wanted answers,
for she was as serious as she had ever been in her life.

"Aunt Lillian, we must needs talk."

"Why, of course, dear child," Lady Lillian said in a
squeaky voice. "What a shame that I was forced to bed
soon after your arrival. And I was counting on us getting
on with our plans immediately."

"What plans?" Sarah asked, feeling her banked anger
edging toward the top of the dam. She said succinctly, "If
you are planning to have me marry a rich man to save
Merrymount, the answer is an unequivocal *no*. Not unless
I fall in love with him. I am sorry you are in such a bad
way financially, and I will work my fingers to the bone to
help you save Merrymount, but I will not sell myself to the
highest bidder."

Sarah took a deep breath.

Lady Lillian did not speak. Her eyes were on Sarah,
studying her, and not smiling.

Sarah watched as a tear trickled down one side of Lady
Lillian's thin face.

She wants to make me feel guilty. Sarah sighed. Wood
burned in the fireplace, and hot cider bubbled in the iron
kettle, filling the room with its delicious smells. Sarah
waited.

At last Lady Lillian spoke. "Lady Sarah, my dear niece,
there is a lesson here that you might learn. Time and
experience have been my teachers. You are much too
young to have learned from time, and I doubt that your
experiences have been that many, or that harsh. One
should never say what one will not do until all facts have
been presented."

Sarah lifted her chin. "Nothing can make me do it. I've
always dreamed of someday being happily married to a
man I love, having children, making a home—"

"Balderdash! That's romantic tomfoolery. In England,
one marries for convenience, for position, and, yes, for
money. Save your love for a lover—"

"Aunt Lillian! I can't believe my ears. Are you suggesting that I marry some rich old gaffer, then take a lover?"

Lady Lillian did not immediately answer, as if she were measuring her words. Then, at last, "Your mother married for love, a lord who did not have a feather to fly with. Our father was the earl of Chesterson, and when he died, all the entailed properties went to a distant cousin. It was expected that we marry men with their own fortunes. Fortunately Merrymount was not entailed, else Alice and Hogarth would have lived among the lower orders. That's what I mean by time and experience bringing their own lessons."

Sarah could not help herself, she had to say it. "By your own admission you wanted to marry Papa after Mama died."

Lady Lillian lifted her head slightly. "That was long after I was on the shelf. I had wanted to marry a titled man with wealth, but he never came along." Her eyes were focused on Sarah's face. "Had I married Hogarth, it would have been a marriage of convenience. I knew in my heart that I could not maintain this big house with hired tenants. A place like Merrymount must needs be loved, and managed well."

She paused, sighed deeply, then went on. "Your mother loved Merrymount; I love it; and I knew that when you saw it, you would love it, too."

Sarah's eyes became misty. "I repeat, Aunt Lillian, I will not sell myself to the highest bidder, not unless I love the man and he loves me. How I feel about Merrymount has nothing to do with that."

"Lady Sarah, please do what is right. With your looks, men, rich and poor, will be at your feet."

Sarah set her chin in a stubborn line. "I doubt that."

"Darling Sarah, England's ways are different from those in America. I was willing to marry your father to save Merrymount."

She spoke as if it would have been a great sacrifice to

have married Sarah's father, and Sarah resented it. She pulled herself up straight. "My father was a very handsome titled man."

"What does that mean when one does not have a—"

"I know. A feather to fly with."

Sarah could understand why her father had refused to take Merrymount and its land if his sister-in-law came with the bargain. Lady Lillian Merriwether was a very forceful woman, and most likely she would have lorded it over him that Merrymount belonged to *her*. Sarah saw the hidden pain that quivered on Lady Lillian's words, the anxiety and worry that registered on her furrowed brow.

Still, I cannot do it.

Sarah rose from her chair and went and hugged her aunt in all sincerity. "We will put our heads together and come up with a plan to pay the taxes on Merrymount. 'Tis not the end of the world, Aunt Lillian. One big crop—"

"You don't understand . . ." The old woman's voice broke completely, and she began to sob. She hugged Sarah, holding her for a long time, and then she cleared her throat and managed in a hoarse whisper, "Come with me."

Sarah followed Lady Lillian out into the hallway. A cold draft met them head-on. "Aunt Lillian, you will catch your death. Get back into the room with heat. Your throat—"

"What matter my throat if I lose Merrymount?"

Sarah grabbed Lady Lillian's arm. "That is ridiculous. I told you we would scheme and plan. I won't desert you. There has to be a way."

The old woman jerked her arm free. "I will show you Merrymount, and then I will tell you the whole of it. There's more . . ."

Their hurried steps took them first into a huge room, at least fifty by a hundred feet, Sarah concluded.

"This was the beginning of Merrymount," said Lady

Lillian informatively. "Knights slept here. You were here when you were a child. We played Go and Find, which meant I would hide and you would come and find me. Usually I hid behind one of the big corner pillars."

Sarah did not recall this part of Merrymount. A huge fireplace, large enough to roast a small cow, was against one wall. Her eyes went immediately to the portrait above the marble mantel, hoping to see her mother's picture which she so vividly remembered. Instead, old King Henry, dressed in his finery, glared down at her. Ancestral portraits hung judiciously on the high walls.

Lady Lillian continued, "In your mother's time, wonderful *ton* dances were held here, with dancing until dawn, and then the hunt would begin, after a huge breakfast served in the hunt room."

Here, Sarah noticed, all the furniture was well-preserved, faded perhaps, but not worn like in the room where Lady Lillian basically lived.

'Tis like a shrine to the past, Sarah thought as they walked through a very formal receiving room, through a withdrawing room, all windows boarded up. Another door opened into a dining room, which, Sarah calculated, would seat more than one hundred.

At last they came to the most beautiful room Sarah had ever seen, and the feeling of nostalgia was so strong that her breath came in ragged spurts. Her booted feet sank deeply into plush carpet; red velvet draperies hung at the windows. Just as she remembered. There was a fireplace with a black marble mantel.

Sarah started running to the far wall, toward her mother's portrait. It was in shadows, for there was no light, except that which seeped around the boards over the windows. Through streaming tears she was indeed an exact copy of her mother, the same auburn curls, the same green eyes . . . and the same smile. A mother's smile.

Sarah swallowed past the lump in her throat. This . . . this portrait was the only mother she had ever known.

Was this what had drawn her back to Merrymount? A child's search for her mother?

Wanna had been a wonderful stepmother, but there was a difference. Sarah had not been born of Wanna's body, the same blood did not flow through their veins.

Sarah did not speak.

"She was the most beautiful woman in England," Lady Lillian said. "She could have had any man in the world. Even the Prince of Wales, later King George III, took a fancy for her. She turned her back on all of them . . . for your father."

"I am glad she did," Sarah said, gazing at the portrait and returning the wonderful smile. "That is my wont, Aunt Lillian, to marry a man whom I love. I suppose we can pray that he will be rich."

Lady Lillian started to cry. Forgetting about her own feelings, Sarah patted and soothed the old woman. "Don't cry, Aunt Lillian. We'll think of something. Something short of my marrying for money will work. I'm sure of that. We just haven't given this enough thought."

"But you just don't understand—"

"I understand perfectly," Sarah said, guiding Lady Lillian back out into the great hall. She would see the rest of Merrymount another time.

Lady Lillian was persistent. "You don't understand the whole of it."

"Would you please explain the whole of it, Aunt Lillian? What more could there be other than overdue taxes?"

For a moment Sarah thought about petitioning Hoggie for funds, but that thought vanished as quickly as it had materialized. The cold was penetrating her warm clothes. She feared Aunt Lillian would suffer a setback. She wanted to go back and stare at her mother's portrait, feel the love of her smile. She wanted to be a child again, cuddled in her mother's arms.

Lady Lillian's words pulled Sarah from her own needs.

"Lady Sarah, the whole of it is that besides the back taxes, I have borrowed from the money lenders in London, and they are threatening to send me to debtor's prison."

The old woman's sobs resounded in the big open space of the great hall. Sarah's first inclination was to say, "How ridiculous!" She could not believe what she was hearing.

The sobbing grew louder. Lady Lillian pulled a tattered lace handkerchief from her bosom and blew into it.

Sarah could not bear it; she pleaded, "Don't cry, Aunt Lillian. I cannot forebear your going to debtor's prison. One does what one must needs do. I'll marry a man for his money . . . if such a man can be found . . . and . . . and he is willing."

"Will you give me your word?" asked Lady Lillian.

"Yes, Aunt Lillian, I give my word that I will somehow save Merrymount from the tax collectors and you from debtor's prison." Then Sarah did something she had never done, being a Methodist. She crossed herself. At the moment it seemed the proper thing to do.

Chapter Six

Since Sarah had never been in love, she did not immediately feel a great loss from having promised Lady Lillian she would search out and wed a man who had wealth enough to keep the aging woman out of debtor's prison and to keep Merrymount from being sold to the highest bidder. Lady Lillian had said that gentlemen of the *ton* would be falling at her feet. If that indeed was truth, then mayhap she would be lucky enough to fall in love with a gentleman with considerable wealth.

Sarah's next question to herself was how she would meet these wealthy gentlemen. Lady Lillian lived in her own little world, with Hilda and John Wesley. Sarah suspected that pride kept her from making morning calls as she, Sarah, understood the upper orders did. The post had not brought invitations to social events in the area. When Sarah spoke with Angeline about this, she received a quick answer: "You met Sam at church. Anyone can go there, rich or poor."

"You have such a logical mind," Sarah said, and immediately began making plans to attend church services in Rockingham come Sunday next.

Lady Lillian thought it a capital idea but objected strenuously to going herself.

"You must needs go, Aunt Lillian," argued Sarah. "It would not appear seemly for two strange girls to suddenly appear at church unchaperoned. Everyone would wonder where we came from."

"I don't have a new gown. You and Angeline go. Every head will turn—"

Before Sarah could answer, the distressed look disappeared from Lady Lillian's countenance, and her eyes began to twinkle. "I have a capital idea. A lady of quality always has an abigail to accompany her. 'Tis beyond the pale to go out unchaperoned. Oh, this will work deliciously. You, Sarah, will enter the church, dressed to the nines, with Angeline walking a bit behind you. 'Tis the thing with the *ton,* to have an abigail."

"I will do no such thing," said Sarah. "Angeline will be introduced to everyone as my sister, which she is. I can't imagine your suggesting such a thing, Aunt Lillian. 'Tis too ridiculous to ponder."

"But I don't mind."

Sarah turned to see Angeline standing in the doorway, her black hair hanging down her back in a thick braid, her kind brown eyes twinkling with amusement. "I love a charade," she said, smiling, showing white teeth.

"I will not allow it," Sarah declared vehemently.

But in the end Sarah lost the argument, even after she had threatened to throttle Angeline for siding with Lady Lillian.

But for sure the old woman was going to church even if she, Sarah, had to drag her, she told both of them, and quickly one of Lady Lillian's faded gowns was dyed a deep purple.

Sarah found in a closet a cache of old fur muffs, which she ripped apart and trimmed a cape of good fabric for Lady Lillian to wear. Another muff was cleaned and brushed for her hands, and Angeline designed a wonderful Gypsy hat from used felt, adding purple plumes purchased from a vendor who made weekly stops at Merrymount.

Sarah would wear her coat trimmed in beaver and her

beaver hat, and Angeline would wear her long red cape over one of Hilda's black bombazine dresses.

"No, that's too fine," argued Lady Lillian. "A coat borrowed from Hilda will do just fine."

'Tis too ridiculous for words, thought Sarah.

No one was more excited than Angeline when Sunday at last came. The weather was fair, and the coldness had abated to chilly but not drastically cold.

"I bound you will catch every eye there, male and female," Angeline said to Sarah.

There was a fondness in Angeline's voice that made a lump come to Sarah's throat. She said, "I doubt that. Besides, I only need one husband . . . if he's willing and able to save Merrymount."

"Now don't go saying you're looking for a rich husband," chimed in Lady Lillian.

Come Sunday, the gig was crowded with the three of them on one seat, but they managed, with Lady Lillian holding the ribbons, expertly cracking the whip over Caesar's back.

The black horse had been rubbed down by John Wesley, and his coat shone in the winter sunlight. Sarah listened to his hooves going clip-clop on the hard-packed ground while wishing she were skating on the pond with the handsome stranger.

He has such a ready smile.

Remembering brought a surge of happiness into Sarah's otherwise confused world. Never in her imagination did she think on going to church to find a rich husband. She did not understand her feelings. When she thought of the stranger, her breasts throbbed, an unfamiliar feeling; she blamed the hardening of her nipples on the cold weather. Her cheeks were burning hot.

At Copthorne, Lord Chesterson creased his white cravat to perfection, then slipped on his blue superfine coat.

His unruly blond hair was pomaded to no avail. It still curled down to touch his shoulders. He whistled a merry tune and allowed a smile to crease his well-chiseled face. It was good to be home with his children. He loved the atmosphere his sister-in-law and brother brought to Copthorne. Love and warmth filled every room, and squeals of laughter from the twins often shook the rafters.

There was even a dog and cat, Melvin and Bathsheba, most often stretched out in front of the fire, waiting for someone to fill their food and drink bowls. Never would Melvin think of chasing a rabbit for food, nor would Bathsheba think of catching a mouse.

Perfectly worthless, but very, very lovable, his lordship thought, the smile lingering. Everything around him bespoke of the perfect family, perfect harmony, perfect happiness.

But it isn't perfect, Chesterson thought. Of late he had found himself lonely more than happy. When Naneen had died, he was devastated with grief and mourned for a long time. Now, he wanted a helpmeet; a wife. He wanted to fall in love.

His lordship supposed that accounted for his springy mood this day as he dressed for church. A little extra care had been taken with his appearance, for he had learned from John Wesley of Merrymount that the girl with the whiskey curls, who had bested him at skating, had recently arrived at Merrymount . . . from America. She wasn't a maid as he had first thought. Her being American, he was sure, accounted for her strange accent.

Lady Lillian just may have her niece at church today, and any gentleman worth his salt can arrange a proper introduction.

The excitement Nathan felt when he and the American skated together returned. He remembered too well how she'd made him feel a man again, how his blood had raced through his veins, hot, hot, hot with desire. Standing before the long looking glass, he gave an elegant leg and laughed. "I'm so happy to meet you at last, Lady . . ."

Lady what? He still did not know her name. The delicious feeling of wanting again engulfed his loins, and he had to delay leaving his dressing room until it had subsided, lest it show through his skintight fawn breeches.

When he did venture out into the blue-and-gold withdrawing room, William looked up from his chair beside the fireplace and smiled. "You look chipper, Nathan. Anything new in your life?"

Chesterson smiled and went to sit in the chair that flanked the opposite side of the fireplace. He took a huge round watch from his waistcoat pocket and looked at it. "The children are being dressed for church. Will you and Georgena come along?"

William gave a wicked smile. "Thanks, but I think Georgie and I will take advantage of some time alone."

Nathan laughed. "You're a lucky man."

"I count my blessings every day," said William.

How his lordship envied his brother. The servants, which consisted of a housekeeper-cook and a nanny for the twins, always had Sunday off. Nathan thought of how Copthorne once was staffed with competent help. He prayed that time would soon come again. From his waistcoat pocket, he brought out an enameled snuffbox and took two big whiffs. He often smoked a pipe, but not when he was with his family. Only when he was alone in his cabin.

The fire in the fireplace crackled and popped. He felt its warmth. Melvin and Bathsheba were contentedly stretched out in front of the fire.

After a long moment of silence, William raised a brow and asked, "Have you heard any more about the girl you met while skating?"

"Yes, I was delighted to hear from Lady Merriwether's houseman, John Wesley, that she is the old woman's niece from America. A schoolmarm, John Wesley said. That accounts for her proper speech, although not sounding much like a genuine Englishwoman."

" 'Tis not a requirement. I hear they have quite good schools there. Have you made your way to the top of the ridge? I would have let no grass grow under my feet—"

Nathan, smiling, said quickly, "I've no doubt of that. I remember when you were paying your addresses to Georgena. But I prefer the subtle approach . . . should she be at church."

William threw his head back and laughed. "So that's your sudden interest in church. I was hoping that a guilty conscious from some delicious sin was taking you there for repentance."

"I regret infinitely that that is not the case. I enjoy a good sermon, and I'm not past confessing my sins. It's just that my time is limited."

"When you are too busy to sin, in the way which men sin, that is, you are too busy," said William teasingly.

Just then the twins, Laura and Larry, followed by Georgena, bounced into the room. "Papa, Papa," they squealed as they ran and climbed onto his lap.

Laughing, he hugged them both. They were dressed in their sailor clothes, the ones they had been wearing when he met them dockside when they returned from their visit to their maternal grandparents. "You're both mighty prettily dressed," he said, sending with his eyes his thanks to Georgena, who had gone to stand beside her husband's chair, placing her hand on his shoulder.

"But I'm prettier than Larry, Papa," piped up Laura. "Girls are prettier than boys." She bounced down off Nathan's lap and twirled around. Her long skirt flared, showing white pantalettes and black patent slippers.

"Girls can be pretty, if that's their silly wont," said Larry. "I prefer to be handsome. Like Papa."

Nathan swallowed past a lump in his throat. He waited for Laura to say she was pretty like her mama, but she didn't. He wondered if she had forgotten or had refrained from using the reference out of pity for him. Oftentimes he had told them how much he missed their mother. He wanted them to know that he had loved her with all his heart and that they had been born of that love.

He placed Larry on the floor, rose to his full six-foot height, took each twin by the hand, and said, "Well, you're both pretty and handsome enough to please me. Just make sure you act as pretty as you look. I will have none of that stretching your neck and looking around when the vicar is speaking, like the last time we attended church."

"I'll be better than Larry," promised Laura, holding tight to her father's hand.

"She's always saying that, Papa. I'll show you today. I'll act proper just like you teached us."

"Taught us," Nathan corrected, after which he turned to Georgena and thanked her for dressing the children so well.

"As you know, Nathan, 'tis my pleasure to help out. As much as I wish you to find a helpmeet, I dread the time when I will no longer be needed to care for the children. I missed them terribly when they were visiting their grandparents in Philadelphia."

Nathan went to her and kissed her cheek. "You and William will always be needed in my life. Nothing will change that. I just pray the time will soon come when you will not have to do chores that should be done by servants. Spend this day with your adoring husband. Stay out of the kitchen. I shall see that the children are fed."

Smothering laughter, William said, "Mayhap you can finagle an invitation to Merrymount for lunch."

Nathan chuckled. "That's a capital idea. I'll see if I can arrange it."

"What are you two talking about?" Georgena asked. "You know that Lady Lillian hasn't been seen out of that big house for a year or more. Why do you think she will be at church?"

Nathan gave his brother a wink. "You explain . . . *after* I've removed four *big* ears."

His lordship could not imagine anything worse than listening to the twins explaining to Lady Lillian Merriwether's niece *why* he had this day come to church.

Chapter Seven

They gained Rockingham much faster with the high-stepping black horse at the tongue of the carriage than with the oxen laboriously pulling the wagon. And, thought Sarah, the weather this day was much nicer, a sunny winter day with snow in the air. She pulled in a deep breath. She had been right about one thing; the air smelled much sweeter in Northamptonshire than in London.

Remembering the two days she and Angeline had waited for someone to fetch them, and their ultimate rescue by the kind Captain Barksdale, made her grimace. She was not entirely over her anger with her aunt. It was then that she had begun to think that returning to Merrymount would not be as she had envisioned. Now, unbelievably, she was on her way to church in search of a rich husband. It did not bear thinking on.

Lady Lillian pulled the black horse to a quick stop in front of the church, and Sarah looked about, thinking that the edifice, absent a steeple, was not particularly pleasing to one's eye. Lichen grew up the walls of tan brick turned a spotted brown with age. Weeds and grass grew around the ancient tombstones in the graveyard, in which the church sat in its center. She was glad that her mother was buried in the Merriwether plot on Merriwether land.

As yet Sarah had not visited her mother's grave. She

had, however, many times gone to stare up at her mother's portrait, to feel the closeness, to bask in the love that emanated from her beautiful green eyes. At times it seemed to Sarah that she would reach out and touch her.

Wanting to know more of the life her mother and her dear dead papa had lived, Sarah had explored the part of the big manor house not shown to her by Lady Lillian. One could get lost in rooms, all most exquisite, but cold and dark.

As Sarah had moved from room to room, she envisioned the whole of the manor house coming to life with glamorously dressed guests filling the great hall, and, as Lady Lillian had mentioned, hunts for the men after a big breakfast served by liveried help.

Sarah's ruminations ceased when Angeline leaned over to her and whispered, "Do you see a handsome man who looks as if he might be rich?"

"Who says he has to be handsome?" asked Lady Lillian.

A boy came to take the ribbons and to help them alight the chaise. A sound reached Sarah's ears, the rushing of River Welland. She saw thatch-roofed cottages stretching down the hill toward the valley below.

"Don't be a slowpoke," Lady Lillian said, drawing Sarah's attention. They alighted from the chaise, then walked briskly toward the entrance of the church, Lady Lillian a step ahead, Sarah and Angeline following.

Angeline forgot that she was to walk behind Sarah, and Lady Lillian stopped to say, "An abigail walks behind her lady."

Angeline giggled, and Sarah, for the tenth time that morning, said, "This is ridiculous."

And for the tenth time Lady Lillian ignored Sarah's words.

With her head held proudly high, Lady Lillian marched down the middle aisle toward the front of the church, looking neither right nor left until she stopped at

a pew with a copper plate bearing the name Merriwether.
A young lad sat there. Bending, she whispered loudly that
he must needs move. Which he did posthaste, grumbling,
"The pew is always empty, 'cept today when 'tis my wont
to sit in it."

Sarah was mortified, and she could feel her face grow
hot. She looked around to see who was watching and
listening, and found everyone's slightly widened eyes staring at them, obviously surprised to see the reclusive Lady
Lillian at church, and even more surprised to see that she
was accompanied by a stranger and her abigail, dressed
in an old, too-short coat.

Sarah quickly turned from the crowd to stare at the
stained-glass windows through which the winter sun
shone. And then she heard a little voice whispering
loudly, "Papa, Papa, there's the ladies from the ship. The
grown-up woman and the beautiful Indian girl from
America that Nanny Bothwell didn't want us to talk to."

A masculine voice shushed, and when Sarah turned her
head, she was looking into the face of the stranger from
the pond. He smiled. She wanted to die.

"The powdered wig," whispered Angeline, and then
not too quietly, "Mayhap he's the rich husband you are
looking for."

Sarah wanted to die some more. Quickly taking her
seat, she found it impossible to concentrate on what the
vicar was saying. Something about sinning, she was sure,
which made her feel all the more wicked for the sinful
feelings she'd had when the stranger had kissed her. She
didn't know why those kinds of feelings were sinful, except
surely anything that delightful had to be bad for one's
soul. She couldn't stop herself from surreptitiously steal-
ing quick glances across the aisle.

Each time the twins were stretching their necks and
grinning at her, and at Angeline. The stranger was smiling at her. Was no one listening to the vicar?

At last the benediction was being said. She would leave

as soon as the last word was uttered. This was not the place to come looking for a rich husband. Letting her eyes wander over the congregation, she did not see a man who looked as if he had a quid to his name.

Unless the stranger was rich.

"That's Nathan Adams, the sixth earl of Chesterson," Lady Lillian said, and then she added sternly, "Best to cut him. He's poor as a church mouse."

"The sixth earl of Chesterson? You mean the distant cousin who inherited the entailed estates when Grandpapa Merriwether died?" asked Sarah.

"The one and same."

"He's of the nobility," piped up Angeline.

Lady Lillian gave a speaking frown. "Abigails do not speak unless spoken to. Can't you play your part?"

Before Angeline could answer, Lady Lillian turned her attention to Sarah. "He's titled, but not a feather to fly with. The drought has done him in as it has the rest of us. And, too, he had a sick wife for ever so long. I hear he spent a fortune on her illness, and she still died. Poor man."

"Well, that proves he's kind, and I think he's handsome, and I think Sarah should meet him," said Angeline defiantly, and when Lady Lillian sent her another frown, Angeline informed her, "I don't want to be an abigail if I can't talk. You didn't tell me I must needs pretend to be deaf and dumb."

"Servants don't converse with their betters," Lady Lillian said authoritatively.

"This is ridiculous," Sarah said again.

They were now outside the church, and Sarah saw Lord Adams walking toward her, the twins ahead of him and headed straight for Angeline.

"Hmph! Wouldn't you know, here Lord Chesterson comes," complained Lady Lillian. She did not smile, Sarah noted, when the earl took her hand and bent over it.

"Pleased to see you out, Lady Lillian. Would it be too bold of me to ask for a proper introduction to your companion? Your niece, I believe."

His eyes were on Sarah, and before she could stop him, he had dropped Lady Lillian's hand and was holding hers, sending that wonderfully strange feeling all the way up her arm, onto her neck, and then over the whole of her. He kissed the back of her hand. "We meet again," he said. "Mayhap this time I can know your name."

He turned to look at Lady Lillian, and when she made no attempt to tell him her niece's name, he said to her, "Lady Lillian, would you be so kind as to formally present your niece, so that I might know her name."

"Lord Chesterson, I present Lady Sarah Templeton," said Lady Lillian, with very little effort to disguise her displeasure.

Chesterson, his hazel-gray eyes twinkling with laughter, gave a fancy leg, and before Sarah could put her hand behind her, he had it in his hand. Bending his blond head, he kissed it again, and when Sarah tried to jerk her hand away from his firm grasp, he held it tighter than before. His smile was disarming.

"Sarah. What a lovely name, as lovely as the girl who wears it. Have you been skating again? But that wasn't the first time we met. While the poor vicar was trying to deliver his message, my children were reminding me that you were on the *Boston Queen,* and I recalled then that you and the pretty dark-complexioned girl were waiting on the dock—"

"That's her abigail," said Lady Lillian.

"Oh, Aunt Lillian, end the charade," said Sarah. "She is not my abigail." Sarah turned to Chesterson. "That's Lady Angeline. She's my sister, and she gets her dark complexion from her Indian mother, who was my stepmother. In America."

Chesterson's eyes darted from first Sarah and then to her Aunt Lillian. He sensed cross purposes here. He was glad to know that Sarah, if she were going to be his wife, was not the deceitful type. And then he remembered his earlier assumption that any man worth his salt would manage an introduction to said girl, which he had done. Now, did not the same thing apply about finagling an afternoon with her?

She's even prettier than when we were on the pond.

Nathan felt his heart racing. He could not allow failure. Looking at the twins and the Indian girl—did Lady Sarah call her Angeline?—he had what he thought was a capital idea and said quickly, "The twins have taken such a liking to your sister, Lady Sarah, would it be too forward of me to suggest that the twins ride with Lady Angeline and Lady Lillian, and that you ride with me? I have always wanted to know more about America—"

This was not so. He had visited his late wife's parents in Philadelphia. For a moment the earl felt a twinge of guilt for the lie. A desperate man does desperate things, he told himself, resolving not to let Sarah get away. He *had* to know more about this American niece of Lady Lillian.

"Our chaise is too small for an extra passenger," said Lady Lillian, looking expectantly at Sarah, who spoke up and agreed with her aunt. No decent woman would stand on sacred ground and shiver when a man held her hand, she thought, even though the hand-holding was against her will. No, it would never do. She would *not* ride in the carriage with Nathan Adams.

But she did. Angeline volunteered to hold one of the twins on her lap. And she further said, "Sister, everyone is gone, but I didn't see a rich man in the whole of them. They all looked as if they were in need of a square meal."

Lady Lillian cleared her throat to signal Angeline to keep quiet, and, in truth, the old woman was most happy to acquiesce to his lordship's riding arrangement just to get Angeline away from him before she informed him that she would die if she had to eat another turnip.

The girl is impossible, thought Lady Lillian, and not smiling.

Determined to carry out his plan, Nathan quickly took Sarah's arm and guided her to his crested carriage. He let down the step and helped her inside, and then went to speak to the coachman on the box. "Don't bother putting the bays to the bits. I'm in no hurry to reach Merrymount."

The coachman winked and gave a knowing smile.

After replacing the step, the earl sprightly swung himself up to sit by Sarah. He was glad that in the country he kept a coachman, mostly for his sister-in-law's sake. In town he drove his own coach. To cut expenses.

He sat close to Sarah, his thigh rubbing hers, even though she had scooted as deeply into the corner as she could possibly get. "You will push out the side of the carriage if you keep moving away from me," he said. "I didn't realize that you were so shy. You should not be, you know, dear Sarah, since we are to be married."

"Are you all about in the attic?"

His smile turned to laughter. "I knew that would get some response. What's wrong? You don't appear the quiet type. Skating on the pond—"

"That does not signify."

"What do you mean, it doesn't signify? We were two strangers having a lovely time skating on a frozen pond. And you bested me. Now that we have been properly introduced, you have turned into an ice maiden."

"We were strangers. That's why that meeting doesn't signify. And we're still strangers, so please don't start that nonsense about us getting married."

"Why? Are you spoken for back in America?"

This was a great concern for his lordship. If she should be promised, then it would be against propriety for him to seek to pay his addresses. The thought made him weak. In England when a girl was spoken for, she was the same as married.

Sarah seized the opportunity to rid herself of this disturbing man. "Yes, my affianced is Sam Schuyler in Hyde Park, New York, not too far from Templeton Hall on the Hudson, my home."

"Then why in the world are you at Merrymount? Should you not be at home with your love?" His voice was sharp with disappointment.

"Aunt Lillian sent a missive inviting me to come to Merrymount. I was born at Merrymount and left when I was three. I thought it wise that I satisfy the yearning to see my birthplace before I settled with a husband."

That's part truth, thought Sarah.

"Then I only imagined that you enjoyed our kiss. An affianced girl would not deliberately let another man kiss her."

"I did not let you kiss me. You did it before I could stop you. I assure you I am an honorable woman, true and faithful to the man of my heart."

This was true, thought Sarah. She would be true to the man of her heart should there ever be one. Certainly it was not Sam Schuyler, who had kissed her once on the cheek and then apologized profusely for doing so.

They rode along in silence, she thinking everything settled. Her heart had stopped its pounding. Had not Lady Lillian said that Nathan Adams was as poor as a church mouse? He could never save Merrymount from the Crown's tax collectors and Lady Lillian from the money lenders.

Nathan was thinking on what to do next. It had started out as a tease, his saying they were to be married. Now, his heart refused to accept that she would never be his wife. *The gods have decreed it.*

His lordship inwardly scoffed at such a thought. He did not believe in fate. Or did he? He looked at her, studied her beautiful face, probed the depths of her green eyes so like the sea at eventide. He wanted to kiss her again. And again. For a moment on a frozen pond, she had brought his dead body back to life and had flamed anew the fire he thought squelched forever. Was that love or need?

Mayhap both, he thought, reaching to take her hand. Having learned from experience, he clasped it tightly so that she could not jerk it away.

So they rode thus to the top of the ridge, where, looming ahead of them, Merrymount stood, its windows boarded up, the chimney pots empty of smoke, the peaks in its crenelated roof melting into the sky.

The driver stopped in front of the portcullis and gatehouse. His lordship helped Sarah from the carriage and held her arm as they walked across the narrow bridge that bulged up over the moat. "You need not come in," said Sarah, and Nathan quickly answered, "I must needs collect my children."

The spotted hounds, Cain and Abel, came running to meet them, and when they neared the house, the twins and Angeline burst out the door, the twins calling, "Papa, can we stay for lunch? Lady Angeline said that their cook could prepare the most delicious turnips."

Sarah wanted to throttle Angeline.

"Of course," Nathan answered, mentally crossing himself for the turn of events, and then he added, "If we are invited."

"I have already issued the invitation," said Angeline, avoiding Sarah's blazing eyes.

"That is most kind of you, Lady Angeline, and I accept most graciously," said Nathan.

Inside the house, Lady Lillian looked as if she were going to take to her bed, and Sarah, knowing it was from embarrassment, sought to put her at ease. "Lord Chesterson thinks it is a capital idea that you had the foresight to board up the windows before the terrible blizzard. He told me he could hardly keep coal to warm his house, and it is not nearly as huge as Merrymount."

She avoided his lordship's eyes, for he had said no such thing. But she did not care. He had practically forced

himself upon them for the afternoon, and he could eat
turnips in the basement kitchen with the rest of them.

As it turned out, the meal consisted of more than turnips. Hilda, as if she had expected guests, mayhap the rich
man they were looking for, had prepared a wonderful pot
of chicken and dumplings. Not that there was much left
of the hen she had killed, but the broth was wonderful,
and Lord Chesterson, Sarah noticed, ate as if he were
near starving.

The twins thought it great fun to eat in the kitchen and
many times said so while they were ladling food into their
little mouths. Each time they were cautioned by their
father not to talk when they were eating.

"I'm afraid I'm not much of a disciplinarian," he said
when Angeline and the twins had departed the table,
saying they were going to explore the big house.

Lady Lillian had excused herself, saying she would
repair to her bed for an afternoon nap.

"I'm afraid I have lost control of Angeline as well," said
Sarah when she and his lordship were sitting across the
table from each other, sipping hot cider. "Since arriving
at Merrymount, she does not follow instructions at all."

"Such as not serving as your abigail."

"That was Aunt Lillian's idea. I objected strenuously,
but she said that any lady of quality, whatever that means,
has her own abigail. I had my own lady's maid in America, but I could not afford passage to bring her with me."

"I understand Lady Lillian's thinking. She wants you to
be accepted into society so that you can make a good
marriage and save Merrymount."

Sarah almost rose out of her cane-bottom chair. "How
did you know—"

Nathan laughed. "'Tis not difficult to recognize the
obvious. It is banded about that Merrymount is to be sold
for past-due taxes; there's no coal to heat the place. So she
sent for her beautiful niece."

"For a stranger, you certainly know a lot about Aunt Lillian's business."

"My land runs with the Merriwether land. I would like to buy it when it comes up for sale, but I'm afraid I'm short in the pockets."

"Aunt Lillian said you were as poor as a church mouse."

"And that accounts for my cool reception this day from her."

"I'm afraid so."

"Do you feel that way? Have you not enjoyed my company?"

"That does not signify," answered Sarah quickly.

Too quickly. For Nathan knew immediately that she *had* enjoyed his company, even though she could not bring herself to admit it. For a moment he felt downcast, but only for a moment. He was not ready to concede failure. More time was needed. He must needs win her heart. No doubt she had won his, and a smitten heart was very lonely in solitude. Looking over the rim of his cup, he gave her his most charming smile. "You were lying about being affianced to some jackanapes in America, were you not?"

Sarah had completely forgotten that tale and reminded herself that lying never worked for her. She silently vowed that she would, from this day forward, tell the truth to this man. It was as if he could read her mind. Embarrassed, she sought to make amends. "I thought if I told you I was spoken for, you would not continue with that nonsense about marrying me. Even though I knew you were just funning—"

"Oh, but I wasn't funning, lovely Sarah. With all my heart, I wish you to be my wife."

Sarah looked at him. His eyes were soft and caring. The laughter was gone, and the usual smile was absent from his sensuous mouth. Her heart started pounding, and she wanted to tell him she felt the same way, that his kiss still burned on her lips, that his touch sent her whole body into spasms of the most wonderful feelings. Instead she said, " 'Tis impossible, my lord. I gave Aunt Lillian my word that I would make a proper marriage . . . to save Merrymount."

Nathan looked at Sarah, unbelieving. His voice bespoke his anger. "What does she need with this huge house? She never entertains as the nobility is expected to do. She's even stopped receiving morning callers. Let the tax collectors have Merrymount."

"There's more to it than Merrymount," Sarah said in a low voice. "My aunt is in danger of going to debtor's prison. She's borrowed from the money lenders in London . . ."

Chapter Eight

The next morning Sarah awakened to the sound of snow driving against the window. She looked out. In the distance tree limbs looked like splintered crystals. The room was extremely cold. Sometime in the night Angeline had moved onto the narrow bed with her and was now lying as close as possible for body warmth.

Sarah smiled, and her vision was dimmed by tears. Angeline, half child, half woman, each unafraid as long as Sarah was near.

Easing away from her sister, Sarah slipped out of bed, gasping when her bare feet hit the floor. The cold had seeped through the worn carpet. Quickly she donned Hoggie's wool breeches and sweater, then slipped woolen stockings and leather boots onto her feet. With a gentle shake, she awakened Angeline.

"'Tis time to get up, Angeline. Breakfast will be cold."

Angeline stretched and yawned. "Were it not for Hoggie being so mean, I would wish that we were back at Templeton Hall."

"Wishing would not make it so. Not only do we not have passage, we would not be welcome there should we go. So let's not waste time on wishful thinking. Hurry, dress quickly, and you will not feel the cold. Hilda's hot porridge will warm you in no time."

While Angeline dressed, Sarah stood in front of the gilt

mirror, which certainly looked out of place in the sparse room, and brushed her dark red-brown curls until they shone like copper. *Like new penny,* she thought.

Money! Oh, if only she had blunt. She thought of Lord Chesterson's impossible proposal and smiled. Of course he did not mean it, but it was flattering to hear him say that she would be his wife. She did not understand men, especially Lord Chesterson, who had begun talking about marrying her almost before he knew her name.

"He's a great tease," she said sotto voce.

Nonetheless, Sarah held close to her heart the feeling that came over her when she thought of his lordship. It was her secret. Not even Angeline would know. And, of course, Lord Chesterson must never know.

"What did you say, sister?" Angeline asked.

"Putting futile thoughts in words."

"Like what?"

"Just wondering aloud about how we could make enough money to pay the taxes on Merrymount and to pay the money lenders in London. I do not wish to go rich husband hunting. What if I don't meet such a man?"

"Certainly not at church, if yesterday proved to be the best around," replied Angeline, dressing hurriedly. "Too bad Lord Chesterson doesn't have a feather to fly with. Or, to speak properly, teacher, should I say a feather with which to fly? He's so handsome."

Sarah ignored the part about proper speech. She had taught Angeline well, and the girl knew her grammar perfectly well. "I suspect," Sarah said, "his lordship has all of London at his feet. He's a great flirt, which shows he has had lots of practice."

"I think he's smitten with you, and I think I shall help him in his pursuit. I would be most delighted to have him for a brother-in-law."

"And what about Merrymount . . . and Lady Lillian? Could you bear to see this grand old house go on the auction block, or, even worse, see Lady Lillian go to debtor's prison? You know about the prison ships anchored off England's shores, I am sure. Or they might even send her to Australia. I hear that is done, also."

"She's your aunt, not mine," retorted Angeline. Giving Sarah a mischievous smile, she continued, "That old woman will never go to debtor's prison. She will talk her way out of it somehow. They would probably turn her loose just to keep from hearing what she has to say. I tell you, sister, Lady Lillian has windmills in her head. Can you imagine her wanting me to be your abigail?"

"I believe you were in total agreement to that, over my objections."

"That's true. I just wanted to help, and then I forgot to play the role." Angeline giggled. "I failed my first test in my effort to help you find that rich husband."

Both now dressed, Angeline's black hair braided into a thick plait which hung down her back and Sarah's hair tied back with a riband, they left the cold room and sought the warmth of the drawing room. Sarah noticed that Angeline, even in her heavy woolen clothing, wore the long strands of beads, a gift from Wanna, her Indian mother. Somehow they made the girl appear elegantly dressed.

"Lady Lillian did not seem too upset with me," said Angeline, still on the edge of laughter.

"Most likely her mind was moving ahead to our next step in this preposterous plan."

Sarah soon learned that this was true. As soon as breakfast was served and eaten, with practically no conversation, Lady Lillian rose from her chair and announced that they must needs talk and that that talk would take place in the warm drawing room.

Sarah looked to see if it were still snowing and grimaced when she saw that it was. Not that she minded another blizzard, if only the wood Angeline and John Wesley had cut would last. A pitiful amount of coal remained in the bin.

"There's no other way," Lady Lillian said as soon as she seated herself in the chair which had become molded to her thin frame. Her hair had been perfectly coiffured. Either by Hilda or herself, thought Sarah, noting that Lady Lillian wore the purple gown that had been dyed for her church-going.

Papa said she was eccentric, thought Sarah, as she took her place in the chair on the opposite side of the fireplace. The old woman sat quietly and waited, her hands crossed demurely in her lap.

Angeline sat cross-legged on the floor, holding Abel's head in her lap. Cain stretched out nearby. Angeline stroked their long necks while giving no indication that she was hearing what her elders were saying.

"There's no suitable husband in Northamptonshire; that was in evidence at church yesterday," said Lady Lillian. "The drought has left the men with nothing to manage in the country, so they've all gone. Most likely into London, to the gaming tables, and we must needs follow."

"And do what?" Angeline asked. "Sell flowers on the streets for bread to eat? Where would we live? And besides, why would Sarah want to marry a man she had to drag from a gaming table?"

"Don't be impertinent, child," retorted Lady Lillian. Then, addressing Sarah, she said with almost religious solemnity, "The Season starts in mid April. We shall have you come out, and that way you are sure to catch a rich husband."

Sarah looked long at Lady Lillian, wondering if she realized the absurdity of what she had just said. One did not come out in society without means. "As Angeline said, do I sell flowers on the streets and pray that a rich gentleman of the upper orders will ask me to become leg-shackled to him, offering me his wealth as a betrothal present? Aunt Lillian, that is ludicrous."

Lady Lillian unabashedly continued, "That is why I am

putting forth this plan. I was awake half the night . . . but that's beside the point. If you are as smart in the head as I think you to be, you will think of a way to raise the blunt to finance a come-out. Surely you brought some assets with you, mayhap some jewelry we can borrow on?"

"I brought no jewelry. I had none, for I've never cared for anything more than a jeweled comb for my hair. I have my mother's pearls which Papa gave me—"

"There's a wonderful man in Corby, you know, the industrial town famous for its ironstone. Mr. Gunningham offers more than fair prices. All of the family jewels have gone to him when I was desperate for blunt. I have been most satisfied with his generosity."

Sarah did not have the least interest in this Mr. Gunningham who would gladly pay a fair price for her mother's pearls. "How much money would be needed?" she asked, more from curiosity than from interest.

"At least two thousand pounds. And we will have to be frugal with that. But there must needs be beautiful gowns, a fashionable place in Mayfair, and there will be the ball which I will give in your honor. An impressive staff—a butler, of course, in fine livery. A handsome carriage and horses can be rented from Tattersall's. One must needs make morning calls, and there's the five o'clock squeeze in Hyde Park. They tell me that even the courtesans go shopping for a new protector there." She gave a deep sigh. "To snare a rich husband, a girl must needs give the appearance of inherited wealth. With Merrymount as your ancestral home . . ."

Sarah shook her head. "'Tis out of the question. Mama's pearls, which I would not part with for the world, would bring less than a hundred pounds in the best market."

Just then Angeline pushed herself up and left the room. Cain and Abel followed behind her. Sarah thought nothing of it and, in truth, was ready to leave herself. The

things on Lady Lillian's mind would not bear thinking on.
Two thousand pounds, indeed!

"She will be a problem in London," Lady Lillian said.
"Who?"

"Lady Angeline, of course. I think it best that we leave
her at Merrymount with Hilda and John Wesley. We
can't pass her off as a servant. We witnessed that yesterday. And mark my word, questions will be asked. Your
heritage will come into question. The *ton* believes in pure
blood."

Sarah felt herself bristle. Through the window she saw
precious Angeline romping in the fast-falling snow with
Cain and Abel. How could Lady Lillian be so unfeeling?

Sarah set her jaw and spoke emphatically, "We shall do
no such thing. If I go to London, Angeline goes. And I'm
not sure that either of us will make it."

When Lady Lillian started to speak, Sarah shushed her,
saying, "I fear, dear aunt, that if a rich husband is to be
found for me, you must needs come up with a more
plausible plan than the one just presented."

"Don't give up so easily, Lady Sarah. I believe things
happen that are willed to happen. And mayhap you can
think of something better. Lord Chesterson, for instance.
Have you thought of asking him for help?"

Sarah lifted a dark eyebrow askance, almost smiling.
"Ask Chesterson to help me find a rich husband?"

"Well, you don't have to tell him that it's a rich husband you're seeking. He could be most helpful in your
getting introduced to the right people . . . men."

Sarah let the subject drop lest she say too much. She
would not tell her aunt that she had already told Lord
Chesterson that she must needs make a convenient marriage. She rose to her feet. She would not think on what
she had told his lordship or what he had said to her. It
rankled her sensitivities to have been put in the position
of trying to save Merrymount, and Lady Lillian, in the
way her aunt had suggested. And it hurt terribly to know

that was why she had been invited to Merrymount. Not
wishing to delve deeper into the subject, Sarah said again,
this time under her breath, "Two thousand pounds! The
woman is daft."

"I have some missives to write," Sarah said aloud, and
she quickly quit the room and went to her cold bedchamber, where she stuffed a few shillings into her pocket for
postage, and then, taking quill and paper in hand, found
her way to the warm kitchen, which she found spotlessly
clean and vacant. Over the fire in the grate, a black kettle
emitted the smell of boiling turnips.

In her missive to John Jay, the Templetons' solicitor,
Sarah wrote briefly about the voyage over, saying only
that they had reached England safely. She made no mention of the dire straits in which she had found Merrymount. What was the use? He could not help, and
besides, most likely by the time a return reply reached her
the tax collectors would have come and the money lenders, as well.

To Captain Barksdale she simply thanked him again
for his kindness. She left much unsaid and hoped that this
was not unfair. He had been genuinely concerned about
her and Angeline, and she did not want to add to that
concern by telling him about the boarded-up windows
and the unpaid taxes.

To Mary Ellen, Sarah poured out her heart:

> My dearest sister-in-law:
> Merrymount is a beautiful place, high on a ridge
> and very impressive to those on the outside. Inside
> it is cold, and there's no coal with which to heat it.
> A drought has devastated the community, and Lady
> Lillian, being a woman who has lived off the land
> others worked, has fared poorly from the drought,
> and she has come up with many unworkable plans
> to save Merrymount. Though the plans makes no

sense at all, she tells me that I must find their solutions.

I know you will keep this confidential, Mary Ellen, for I could not forebear Hoggie's gloating. Something will be done. But I know not what.

I wish you were here, dearest Mary Ellen. Something has happened to me which I do not understand. I have met the most handsome gentleman— English, of course—Lord Chesterson, and when he touches me it is like my flesh is on fire, and my heart pounds so that I find myself tongue-tied. I think I am developing a *tendre* for him, but I find that too silly for words. And it cannot be love, for he is a stranger. I am ashamed of these feelings . . .

And so the letter went, two pages in Sarah's lovely script. As she sealed the missive, she thought that if only Angeline were older, mayhap she could confide in her. It would help. Mary Ellen, having been in love, even if that love had been killed by Hoggie's selfishness, would understand.

Sarah donned her heavy coat and went to find John Wesley to see if he might be going into Rockingham. If so, she would ask him if he would please post her letters. Most likely he would go if the snow let up. At the moment, that did not seem a possibility. She had never seen snow fall so fast and so furiously, as if the heavens were dutybound to turn the whole world white. The distant trees looked like statues, their outstretched arms covered with white feathers.

She found John Wesley and Angeline, and Cain and Abel, in the stables. They were rubbing and shining a handsome carriage bearing the Merriwether crest. It was the first time Sarah had seen it. She thought it very pretty and very grand.

"I keep it covered for protection," John Wesley said to

Sarah. "And the door is always locked. Lady Lillian's notion, as if someone would steal it."

"Why isn't it used?" enquired Angeline.

"No cattle to pull it. Once it was pulled by four seventeen-hand chestnuts, with gold-and-black trappings. But they wuz sold, just like everything else that wuz loose." John Wesley shook his head gravely. "A matter of time and we'll all be gone from Merrymount. She can't hold on much longer. And one of these days poor Caesar will call it quits." He inclined his gray head toward the lot where the black horse was romping and sniffing the snow.

"This snow should bring enough moisture for early spring grass," said Sarah. She gave the letters to John Wesley. "Would you be so kind as to post these for me, should you be going to Rockingham?"

"Reckon Lady Angeline and me will be traveling over to Corby as soon as the snow lets up. I'll mail them there."

Sarah left the stables. It was not until later that she wondered why they were going to Corby. Deciding that it was not her duty to know everything that was going on at Merrymount, she walked on through the woods, taking the same footpath she had taken before, knowing that she was headed for the pond. Common sense told her that only when the temperature dropped sufficiently would the pond freeze deeply enough to accommodate skaters. Reaching up with a gloved hand, she wiped away huge snowflakes that had lodged on her long dark eyelashes.

At Copthorne Nathan stood and watched the snow bank in the courtyard below the window. He did not see the beauty of it, for his mind was thick with memories of the Sunday past and of the short time on the pond when he had felt so young, so gay, so happy. This day, the oldness had crept back into him. He felt as if life had been sucked from him. Saving Merrymount called for blunt, which he did not have.

"I must needs make a convenient marriage," Sarah had said, and the words had cut into his heart like a stake. He hardly slept that night. Now, he castigated himself for rushing things, by talking so soon about marriage. Like a schoolboy, he told himself. But would waiting have made a difference? Lady Sarah had already given her word to her Aunt Lillian. When he had first teased her about becoming his wife, it was only that, teasing. He had even suspected it was desire alone that had made her so attractive to him. That was understandable. He had been a widower for three years, and no mistress. Not that he hadn't desired one, but he simply could not afford one.

But, Nathan reasoned, it wasn't just desire that had driven him to this state; he was desperately in love with the whiskey-haired girl. He closed his eyes, saw her wide smile, her green eyes twinkling with laughter. God had made her for him.

His lordship laughed then, cynically. If God had been so kind, then why was it impossible for him to have what the Supreme Being had meant for him to have?

He could picture her at Copthorne and in London among his peers. He yearned to hold her in his arms throughout the long lonely nights, to confide in her his innermost thoughts, to hear her laughter in the mornings.

He wanted . . .

"The devil take me," he said aloud, and heard laughter behind him. In the thick of his roundaboutations, he had forgotten where he was, certainly not in London where he was alone much of the time. He turned with a sense of utter hopelessness and greeted his sister-in-law. "Why are you laughing, Georgena?"

"I think 'tis the first time I've heard you talking to yourself. I'd much rather hear your laughter."

"I have nothing much to laugh about," Nathan replied.

"What's troubling you, Nathan?"

Nathan thought plump Georgena very pretty, with her soft brown eyes and a wide smile that bespoke kindness.

This day she wore an attractive gown of puce velvet. He commented on it. "Your gown, 'tis very pretty."

"It is very warm, and why are you changing the subject? What's wrong, Nathan? It will help to talk."

Nathan went to lean toward the fire, holding his hands to the flames, gazing into them with fixed eyes. He did not know where to begin. To put his feelings into words, and he had no objection to doing this with Georgena, would seem so youthful, and he was three times ten, a father, a widower.

But did that make a difference to one's heart? At last he said, "She cannot marry me."

Georgena's brow raised visibly. "Who?"

Nathan did not answer. He breathed into the silence.

"Do you mean Lady Lillian's niece from America?" asked Georgena. "I knew you were hoping to see her at church this Sunday past and that you had managed an invitation to Merrymount to lunch . . . but, Nathan! You've not already asked her to marry you?"

"Oh, but I have. At first I was teasing her about becoming my wife. And then I found I meant it with all my heart. And for some inexplicable reason, I felt the urgency to get things settled. So I proposed to her in Merrymount's basement kitchen, over cups of hot cider."

Georgena clucked. "You know *that* is not the thing. You were supposed to have asked Lady Lillian's permission to pay your addresses—"

"Hang the *thing*. In matters of the heart, social strictures fade into the background. At least they did with me. I just felt it, and I blurted it out."

Georgena sank down into a chair, crushing the skirt of her velvet dress, which flowed full and free from under her full bosom. "And what did she say? Was she not as anxious as you? I cannot imagine . . . unless she is promised to someone in America . . ."

Remembering Sarah's ruse brought a smile to Nathan's otherwise somber face. "At first that is what she said, that she was promised to Sam Someone-or-other, but, in truth, she is a terrible liar. Guilt was all over her face, and in her wonderful green eyes. That led me to persist in my suit until she told me the awful truth."

Georgena's eyes grew big in her round face. "What? That she's already married?" That could be the worst of things, she thought, her anxiety growing.

Nathan hesitated. He knew without doubt that he could trust his sister-in-law not to impart to anyone what he was about to tell her, but somehow he felt that he must needs extract a promise of secrecy from her before going further with the information. He wanted to tell her. He wanted to spill it out of himself onto someone else. Then hopefully the pain would lessen. "Georgena," he began, "please do not feel put off if I ask for your complete loyalty on what I am about to tell you. Should the truth be bandied about, it would be impossible for Lady Sarah to carry through with her promise. No man of the upper orders, especially one with blunt, will marry her if he knows the whole of it."

"Nathan, you are talking in circles. Lady Sarah's promise? What promise? Of course I will not tell it, except to William, who, as you know, is as secretive as I am. We do not indulge in *on-dits.*"

The painful words poured from his lordship's lips. "Lady Sarah has given her word to Lady Lillian that she will make a marriage of convenience . . . to save Merrymount from the tax collectors . . . and Lady Lillian from debtor's prison."

Georgena leaned back in her chair, rolled her eyes toward the ceiling, before asking, "Nathan, are you sure it is not your need for female companionship that has driven you to such an extreme as to believe you are in love with a girl you've just met? Most especially in love with a girl who tells she must needs make a convenient marriage. She has rocks in her head."

"Don't think I haven't mulled this over and over in my

mind. I have fought these feelings with all my strength. To no avail. I bound that I would be happier living with Lady Sarah in the unconventional way than I would be with another woman in—"

His lordship stopped there. His words were pushing the bounds of propriety, even to one's sister-in-law, who was more like a blood sister. "To hear Lady Sarah's laughter is heaven, to see that wonderful smile across the table brings a lump to my throat. Even when her eyes are misty with sadness, as they were when she spoke of her duty to her Aunt Lillian, I am filled with warmth that has nothing to do with passion."

The word slipped out; he had not meant to say it.

Georgena, a married woman who was passionately in love with her husband, thought nothing of discussing the delicate subject with her brother-in-law. What bothered her was that he should feel so strongly about a woman he could not have. She had fallen instantly in love with William, but he had had the means to claim her for his wife. "Is there not some way, Nathan, that you can borrow the money and pay the taxes on Merrymount? Surely we will not have another year of drought, and Lady Lillian could repay you—"

"Don't think I haven't thought of that, but, as you know, Copthorne and its land are entailed. I cannot borrow on the estate, and there's nothing else."

For a moment Nathan let himself remember when his coffers were brimming, before Naneen's lingering illness. He was not sorry, for he had loved his wife.

But not the way I love Lady Sarah.

Suddenly engulfed with guilt, Nathan swore under his breath. But he could not help the way he felt about Lady Sarah, and he did not intend to waste time fighting that which he could not help. There had to be a solution. Another thought entered his mind. He would aid and abet his love in marrying a man deep in the pockets, and then, after she had produced an heir for the lucky man,

he, Nathan, would take her as his mistress. That was
perfectly acceptable in London society. He felt his face
grow hot with shame for the thought.

"I fail to find too much sympathy for Lady Sarah," said
Georgena, breaking the long silence. "Could it be that she
is not in love with you and that she is using any convenient
excuse for not marrying you? I know that is painful for
you to hear, but you must needs explore every possibility,
Nathan."

"I've thought of that, but I know it isn't so. One can
tell. On the pond, when she ran away, she was running
from herself. The kiss, slight though it was, was like a
spark from a banked furnace. The kiss awakened a longing in her soul, just as it did in mine."

Georgena straightened. "Well, then you must have the
girl. But before we start to plan, let me say that I think
Lady Lillian is mighty selfish. Imagine, her asking her
dear niece to marry someone she does not love just to save
that big old monstrous house that has been going down
hill since Hogarth Templeton left it. Seventeen years
ago."

"I, too, feel that Sarah is being made the sacrificial
lamb to satisfy the old woman's pride. What does she
need with Merrymount? She never has elegant balls or
receives morning callers. And since there is no coal for
heat, they live in a few sparse rooms."

"Why did you not enquire of Lady Sarah about the
necessity in the old lady living there? Why should *she* have
to save the place? It should be sold to someone who will
make use of it, restore it to its former grandeur—"

"Lady Sarah says 'tis her duty to save Merrymount,
and she would not listen to argument. Lady Lillian is her
dead mother's sister. I suspect that, in a moment of uncontrollable sympathy, Lady Sarah made this promise
and is reluctant to go back on her word. But this is only
suspicion. Lady Sarah did not say that."

" 'Tis strange, if you ask me," Georgena said.

They sat for awhile, she looking out at the snow, he staring into the fire. "Nathan," Georgena at last said, "as soon as the weather clears, I shall call at Merrymount. I would very much like to meet your Lady Sarah."

Later, Georgena expressed her grave doubts to her husband. "William, your brother is smitten, and I, for one, think 'tis his extreme loneliness. He's practically lived the life of a monk since Naneen's death. Mayhap we should entertain and invite eligible girls—"

William shook his head. "Nathan would not tolerate our interference. I suggest you make friends with this Lady Sarah, for I am certain that, since Nathan has his mind set, she will someday be your sister-in-law."

"Of course you are right, William."

"Dearest, Nathan knows his own mind, and I doubt that you or I or the gods themselves could change it under any circumstances."

Georgena breathed a deep sigh. "Well, he certainly seems to have his mind and his heart set. I suppose we'll just have to wait and see. I do hope Nathan doesn't get hurt. He's had enough of that."

"I know, dear. Give things a chance to work out. For now, we're alone, are we not?" Smiling, he reached out his long arms.

Georgena went to him, received a warm kiss, and then, pulling away, said, "William, *that* will come later, but now I must needs send a missive to Merrymount, asking permission to call."

Chapter Nine

"I will not take less than a thousand pounds," Angeline said to Mr. Gunningham, the jeweler in Corby. Spread on the counter in front of her were her ruby and emerald beads.

The jeweler laughed so hard that his slight body shook.

Angeline stared unabashedly into his dark eyes. He wore thick glasses with delicate silver frames; his dark moustache was gray-sprinkled, and his high collar points looked as if they might be digging into his drooping jowls that wiggled like jelly. His head was bald and pink.

Angeline could not forebear the laughter.

"What you have here, Mr. Gunningham," she said, "are genuine rubies and emeralds which once belonged to an Indian princess . . . from America. My grandmother."

The smirking laughter subsided, and Gunningham turned his gaze to the beads. His fingers moved over them with delicate authority. From a table behind him, he took a jeweler's eyeglass and held it to his eye.

"Indian princess, eh?" Meticulously, while Angeline waited, hardly able to breathe, he examined each emerald and each ruby, and there were many of them. "Ah, here's a nick in one of the rubies."

Angeline did not answer. For all she knew they were made of glass. She only knew that they had belonged to her mother, who had one day given them to her, saying,

"Angeline, keep these always, and when you pray, clasp them tightly in your hands, and the Spirits will hear you."

"They are Indian prayer beads," she told him, "which makes them of special value." Another thought came to her. "Only the royalty of the tribes were permitted to wear them."

When Gunningham failed to reply, Angeline added, "Indian gods take no notice of a nick in a stone, or even two nicks."

Tears pushed at her eyes, but she refused to give them freedom. Only for Sarah would she part with the precious gift from her dear Wanna, who never had riches to offer, just bountiful love.

"And Sarah is the same, so full of love," she said to herself so quietly that it did not gain the jeweler's attention.

Dear, dear Sarah, Angeline thought, growing impatient. The pain in her heart would go away when she had the thousand pounds in her hands. She watched as Mr. Gunningham left his stool and moved to stand in the doorway of his tiny little shop, lit only by flickering candles. He was frowning. Angeline feared he had found another nick.

But the jeweler was not looking for another nick. In truth, he had never seen anything so perfectly perfect as the emeralds and rubies he held in his hand. A treasure trove, but he did not want the girl to know of his certainty. He had no doubt she was Indian. Her skin was dark enough. He smiled at her story about Indian royalty. Everyone who came in his shop had such a story to tell about the jewels they wanted to sell.

While continuing to examine the beads intently, Gunningham said off-handedly, "So you're from America. An Indian princess. I didn't know they had royalty among the Indians there. I hear tell they are savages."

Angeline felt herself bristle. "I'm sure that a lot of stories about America are bandied about in England, and most likely not nice stories since we fought and won our independence from England not too far back. But one must not believe everything one hears. I'm considerably proud of my Indian heritage."

Why doesn't he give me the thousand pounds and be done with it?

"I will make you a fine offer of one hundred pounds—"

"One hundred pounds! Give me my jewels. I will take them into London. And to think Lady Lillian Merriwether said you were a fair man." Angeline grabbed for her beads, only to have them moved from her reach.

"Not so fast," said Gunningham. "I didn't know you were from Merrymount . . . yet, I had heard Lady Lillian's niece had come visiting from America." Removing his eyeglass, he bent his head and stared over the top of his wire-rimmed glasses at Angeline. "You're not that niece?"

"No. I am half sister to Lady Lillian's niece. But Lady Lillian is quite fond of me, and she will take offense at your behavior, should I tell her."

Angeline wished that were true, but Lady Lillian had made it quite plain that she only tolerated Sarah's sister because Sarah demanded that she do so. Lifting her chin, Angeline continued staring at the jeweler. Her small hands were balled into fists, which she hid behind her so the jeweler would not see them trembling.

Mr. Gunningham repaired to his stool behind the counter, still holding tightly to the precious jewels so that the haughty girl could not gain possession of them. He would buy them, but the trick was to get them as cheaply as possible. He licked his lips as he imagined the price he could demand, especially after he had created a fake certificate of their origin. "Imagine owning jewels that had once belonged to an American Indian princess," the ladies of the *ton* would say, as they laid out their husband's blunt for them.

The thought excited Gunningham so that he could hardly contain himself and thought for a moment he might wet his breeches. "Two hundred pounds," he said, nonchalantly. "That is my best offer."

"Five hundred pounds, and that is my *last* offer," said Angeline. It was far short of the two thousand pounds Lady Lillian had said a come-out for Sarah would cost, but mayhap she could think of something else to sell. She shook her head; she had nothing else of value. And then an idea came to her. She blurted out, "Five hundred pounds . . . on one condition."

Gunningham's eyes became slits behind his glasses. "What condition?" he asked quickly. The girl was smarter than he had thought.

"That I can hold them in my hands for a little while, just to say goodbye . . . and to say a little prayer."

"Whatever for? Do you really believe some Indian god would hear you?"

"Mayhap you should practice talking to *your* Supreme Being more often, Mr. Gunningham. Might help you be a better person, more fair in your business dealings."

Reluctantly the jeweler handed over the jewels. "A bargain is a bargain, miss. And you can have them only for a minute. So make your prayer short. I have more important business to tend to." Under his breath, he said, "Imagine, an Indian praying."

Angeline, holding the strands of beads lovingly, turned her back and, one by one, kissed each jewel. Even though her eyes were closed tightly, tears seeped from under her long lashes and wet her cheeks. Her heart full to bursting, she whispered the prayer to Wanna's spirit, asking for guidance on how to gain the rest of the money for Sarah's come-out, and she asked that her mother understand why she was parting with the precious gift.

Hearing Mr. Gunningham clearing his throat, she turned and handed him her only worldly possession and, without a word, grabbed the notes he held in his hand and rushed from the shop. Only when she had reached the street did she stop and count them: five-hundred pounds.

Quickly she stuffed the blunt into her coat pocket and made her way to where Caesar and John Wesley were waiting. Her tears had dried on her cheeks, but the pain had not left her heart. With difficulty, she managed a smile. "I'm sorry I took so long. I pray you didn't near freeze to death."

"I be dressed warm," John Wesley said as he took her hand and helped her into the equipage, then wrapped a blanket around her. "Put your feet on the bricks, Lady Angeline. Mayhap they still have some heat to them."

Angeline did not feel the cold. Her heart was pounding in her chest; she had prayed for guidance, and she still did not have a clue as to how to raise the rest of the blunt for Sarah's come-out. She looked down at her bosom and felt naked. Tears started again, but she bit her lower lip and thought of the pain so that the tears would stop. She said to John Wesley, "How long does it take for a prayer to be answered?"

"I don't pray very often, Lady Angeline, and sometimes I get an answer, and sometimes I don't. I suppose it depends on whether or not the good Lord wants me to have what I ask for. And sometimes the Lord works in mysterious ways."

Angeline didn't answer. She became pensive. She had prayed, but she knew that her faith was weak. And mostly she had asked Wanna's forgiveness for parting with the beads. Mayhap the Spirits did not want her to have what she had asked for. She should have held out for a thousand pounds. How foolish she had been. Five-hundred pounds would only pay for a quarter of a come-out for Sarah.

The high-stepping horse galloped over the road speedily. The clop-clopping hooves resounded in Angeline's ears. It was no longer snowing, but the undulating hillocks were white against the blue sky.

At last they came to the top of the ridge; Angeline saw Cain and Abel galloping out to meet the chaise.

"Thanks, John Wesley, for taking me to Corby," Angeline said, and then she jumped down and ran to meet the hounds. She would romp in the snow with them before telling Sarah what she had done.

But that time did not immediately come. Lady Lillian was always about, so it seemed to Angeline. And Hilda was underfoot, bobbing and asking her ladyship if there was something her lady wanted.

It was after a supper of mutton and turnips when Angeline and Sarah were in their cold bedchamber, shivering, getting ready for bed, that the opportunity presented itself. Angeline feared that Sarah would cry, and sure enough she did as Angeline explained in minute detail her business transaction with Gunningham, the *fair* jeweler.

"The old gaffer refused one cent more. I asked for a thousand pounds."

Sarah hugged her sister devotedly. "Why did you not talk this over with me, Angeline?" Her voice was low and barely audible.

"You would have stopped me," answered Angeline.

"Yes, I would have. Those beads were as important to you as saving Merrymount is to Aunt Lillian."

"Is your heart really in this scheme of finding a rich husband?" asked Angeline. "Why—"

"Only because Lady Lillian is my mother's sister. I can't explain . . . I gave my word."

"You don't have to explain, sister," said Angeline. "If that is your wont, then we must needs think of a way to have your come-out with five-hundred pounds."

Chapter Ten

During the time Angeline impatiently waited for some sign from the Spirits that they had heard her prayers, Georgena Adams, along with the twins, Larry and Laura, called at Merrymount. Angeline romped in the snow with them, and Cain and Abel did their part by jumping on the twins and by running after snowballs they threw. The threesome built a beautiful snowman, which they named Beau Brummell after the London dandy.

The twins laughed with glee when Angeline creased a piece of white sheet and made a cravat for the Beau.

"Oh, if only we had a black beaver for his head," said Larry, and Laura said she thought the snowman was a girl and needed a pretty bonnet.

After the visit, Sarah told Angeline that Lord Chesterson's sister-in-law had called only out of curiosity, not from friendship. "I am bound that she thinks something might come of Nathan's and my friendship, which is not a friendship at all . . . just because we skated on the pond together."

"But he did insist upon your riding in the carriage with him when we left the church, without his children," Angeline replied. "That proved he wanted to be alone with you. And later you sat unchaperoned in the kitchen with him. Did he say he loved you? I'll wager he stole a kiss."

Sarah could not help but laugh at her sister's romantic

imagination. Was it Angeline's rampant romantic thoughts, or was the girl wise beyond her years? She, Sarah, had not told anyone about his lordship's proposal of marriage. Nor had she mentioned the kiss the very first time they met, even before he knew her name.

"We talked of a lot of things," she said to Angeline. "I told him that I must needs make a marriage of convenience, and he was taken aback. As was his sister-in-law. Much to Lady Lillian's chagrin, Lord Chesterson had already told Georgena. Without delay Lady Lillian swore her to secrecy, saying a marriage of convenience would be impossible if the *ton* knew I was looking for a man with means to save Merrymount."

Angeline's brown eyes widened. "Lord Chesterson didn't! Of course he did. You just said so. Oh, sister, he's in love with you. Can't you tell? He would not be talking on such a personal matter to anybody if it was not his wont to marry you himself."

Sarah smiled at Angeline. "Georgena Adams does not feel sympathy about Lady Lillian's plan to save Merrymount and herself. It seems Georgena and William married for love and they have been blissfully happy."

"And neither do I feel sympathy," said Angeline, "not for Lady Lillian. It's just that *you* feel you should do this thing."

The conversation had taken place the week past, and now it was Sunday again and the three of them, Sarah, Angeline, and Lady Lillian, were on their way to church, crowded into the chaise meant for two passengers, with Lady Lillian again holding the ribbons. The black horse flung his head and snorted, stepping high, clip-clopping down the hard surfaced road.

Sarah felt light in spirit because most likely she would see Nathan when they arrived at the ugly church. She drew a deep breath and sucked in sharp country air. Remnants of snow filled the corries and crevices of the hillocks, but she was not unpleasantly cold. She wore her warm coat trimmed in beaver, and her beaver hat. Their feet rested on bricks that John Wesley had heated.

As Lady Lillian pulled Caesar to a stop in front of the church, Sarah's eyes moved furtively over the crowd of milling people. She scolded herself for her disappointment when she did not see his lordship's blond head.

But Sarah did not have long to think on her disappointment, for right away Georgena and William Adams and Nathan's rambunctious children came to greet them.

"What a divine hat," Georgena said to Lady Lillian, and then she introduced her husband William. He generously let down the step and helped them to the ground.

"I'm very happy indeed to be meeting Lady Lillian's relatives from America," William said.

Sarah could feel his eyes studying her. She thought he favored Nathan in looks, but not nearly as handsome. She said to him, "Lord Chesterson speaks highly of you, Mr. Adams."

"William, please. Mr. Adams makes me feel old." He gave a soft laugh, and then said, "Nathan tells me he is quite taken with you, Lady Sarah. Georgena and I are enormously pleased. It has been a long time since he has taken notice of any girl. And him three years a widower."

Before Sarah could respond—if she had known what to say—Lady Lillian let her voice be heard. "If Lord Chesterson is taken with Sarah, I fear he's bound for disappointment. Sarah will have a come-out in London when the Season starts. I'm sure she will have her pick of suitors. Gentlemen with means. Is that not every girl's wont?"

Sarah was embarrassed and not just a little angry. She did not like being discussed as if she were merchandise for sale.

Is not that what I am, a piece of merchandise, if I go through with this preposterous plan?

The thought sent Sarah's spirits plummeting, and she was glad when they were inside the church. She marched down the center aisle, looking neither right nor left, feel-

ing every eye on her back. The vicar's words did not lift
her spirits. Could he not speak on something other than
sin?

This day Sarah felt very sinful for the feelings Chesterson had aroused in her. But that was beyond her strength;
it was not of her doing, she argued, and the vicar prosed
on.

Angeline bent her head to Sarah and whispered, "I
have the answer."

"The answer to what?" Sarah whispered back.

"My prayer has been answered. I know how to increase
the five-hundred pounds to two thousand pounds. I knew
Mama would tell me how."

Lady Lillian jabbed Sarah in the ribs and whispered for
her and Angeline to be quiet. After that, Sarah listened to
the vicar, remembering not a word of it, and back at
Merrymount, she, as quickly after lunch as possible,
guided Angeline into their bedchamber and asked,
"Angeline, what were you talking about in church? I
suggest you take the money back and retrieve your
beads—"

"Oh, Sarah, you simply have no faith. Mama told me
the jewels were blessed, and if I would hold them and pray
to the Spirits, my prayer would be answered. And that is
exactly what happened. Today in church it came to me.
Do you recall that when we met up with Georgena and
William Adams her remark about Lady Lillian's beautiful
hat? Well, that is the answer. We shall make Gypsy hats
and sell them."

Sarah stared at her, open-mouthed. "I don't get your
meaning."

"Peagoose," exclaimed Angeline, "I made Lady Lillian's hat, and mayhap you did not notice that women
were taken with it: they positively stared as she walked
down the aisle, and after church, too. All with envy."

"So you are suggesting that you make hats and sell
them to the women of the church?"

Angeline laughed. "Nothing as simple as that. It would take forever to increase our capital that way. Besides, I doubt that any two of the churchwomen could afford such a hat. Think big, sister. We'll start a hat company, give it a Parisian name. I read that anything Parisian is ever so popular in London."

Sarah was astounded at such a grandiose plan, and at the young girl's business acumen. Angeline, however, was not smart in the ways of the *ton*, Sarah decided. Did she not know that tradesmen were not welcome in high society? And *what* would the *ton* think of trades*women?* They would run in the opposite direction.

Not wanting to dampen Angeline's enthusiasm, Sarah listened with half interest while Angeline said, "Don't you see, sister, we will get someone to sell the hats for us, calling on all the wonderful shops in London, Bath, Brighton—all the places that high society frequents." She paused for a moment. "No one will know that it is *our* company. I know that we don't know a thing about London or society, but mayhap Lord Chesterson will help us in that area."

"Angeline, you have windmills in your head. Even Lady Lillian suggested that we use his lordship for connections. 'Tis out of the question. He's quite a busy man, being a member of Parliament."

And if he is serious about wanting to marry me himself, would he help bring about a come-out that would most likely take me away from him? If one can believe what Lady Lillian says, I'll be snatched up by the rich man of my choice.

"We can ask," said Angeline. "I wager he will help all that he can. He's such a kind man. That's what one does when one is in love, help with anything his beloved desires."

"Even to find a rich husband?" Sarah shook her head and smiled at her sister. She was so beautiful, and so innocent.

Sarah sat for a long moment. The idea of a hat business

had begun to seem slightly plausible. Angeline had proven her talent; the hat she had made for Lady Lillian was an eye-catcher.

But asking Nathan for help. Never!

Angeline went on planning. "We can buy the plumes and other trimmings from the vendor, and we can invest a few pounds in copies of French fashion magazines. There should be pictures aplenty—"

"Let me think on it, Angeline," said Sarah. "But don't mention it to Lady Lillian. As she has proven, she's a tittle-tattle and can't keep her mouth shut about anything. I can see why Papa went all the way to America to get away from her."

"I don't see why she wants to save this big old house anyway," complained Angeline. "And I want it understood that I am not helping her with the money from Mama's beads." She paused, then added, "I would do anything for you, Sarah."

"I know that you would, dearest Angeline. 'Tis a matter of pride, I suppose, with Aunt Lillian, to keep the house. It has been in the Merriwether family for over a century."

"Then she should have found a rich husband for herself. Not put it off on you."

"Angeline, I see nothing to be gained from more discussion on *why* Lady Lillian is the way she is or what her wonts are. I have given her my word. Have you forgotten that she is in danger of going to debtor's prison? I don't think even you would want that. I could not bear it. She's Mama's sister."

Angeline was quiet after that, and Sarah decided to go for a walk, either to the pond or to the creek that flowed through the Merriwether land. Winter sunshine cut a swath across the room. She said to Angeline, "I'm going for a walk in the woods. May I borrow your red cape?"

"Of course, Sarah."

"Won't you come along?

Pray, let her refuse.

"I think not," the young girl answered. "I will repair to the kitchen and sketch beautiful hats."

Taking parchment and quill, Angeline left, and Sarah changed from her church clothes to a walking dress, and then changed that one for another, and then another. She did not want to be *too* dressed up should she see his lordship. He would know that she was hoping to see him. Her heart beat fast in her throat as she envisioned his wonderful smile, his kind, well-modulated English voice.

At last Sarah decided on a walking dress of gray wool, rather plain, a low neckline, and falling from under her bosom to her ankles. Her half-boots were red, to match the cape she had borrowed from Angeline. A gray wool scarf with fringe covered her auburn curls that fell to her shoulders.

Remembering that Nathan had said her curls were the color of whiskey, she smiled into the looking glass and saw the laughter in her green eyes. "As long as I alone know how he makes my heart sing, I will keep on sinning," she said to the empty room, giving out a light laugh. Suddenly she was happy. She quit the room and went into the yard. Taking the same footpath she had taken before, she was soon into the woods and thought to cut westward and head for the stream.

She did not know why, just that she felt drawn to do so.

After walking for quite some time, Sarah realized she had gone full circle and was totally lost. She came to a clearing and looked up to get the direction of the sun. Again, she started off. Merrymount was to her back, and should she walk long enough, she would come to the edge of the ridge, which dropped down into the valley.

Smelling smoke, she went in the direction of the scent, and before going very far, she saw a small cabin with gray smoke curling up from its lone chimney pot. The cabin teetered on the edge of the sloping hillock.

Sarah cautiously approached and gave a soft knock on

the sagging door. A voice invited her in. Nathan's. Her breath caught in her throat. Easing the door open, she could not help but smile. Even though he was a stranger, she felt as if she had known him always. His words startled her: "I knew you would come."

Sarah laughed. "Are you a mind reader?"

"No, but I was willing that you would come. The Good Book says that if you cast your bread upon the water, it will return to you threefold. So I thought if I cast my thoughts upon the wind, it would bring you here."

"I believe the Good Book is speaking of good deeds, not a rendezvous in a cabin."

Sarah walked into the warm cabin and looked around. Nathan was dressed in buckskin breeches and waistcoat. His shirt was collarless. He was sitting in an old rocking chair with faded cushions.

His lordship gave Sarah his charming smile. In his hand was an unlit pipe, which he immediately attempted to light by dragging a lucifer across the hearth. While he pulled on the pipe's stem with quick puffs, the fire on the grate sparked and popped, sending out warmth. On the floor was a faded rug, worn thin from years of wear.

Still unable to believe she was actually in a cabin with a man, Sarah looked at him bemusedly, half-smiling.

Laying down his pipe, which failed to respond to his effort to light it, he stood and came to remove her cape and the scarf that covered her head. He laid them in the chair that held his coat.

"Ah, those whiskey curls. Let them go free." Boldly he touched Sarah's hair. And then he turned Sarah to him and kissed her. Not a quick kiss like on the pond, but deep and hungry.

Sarah's mind whirled for a moment before she gained the good sense to push him from her. "Sir, you are breaking propriety, being so forward."

"And you broke propriety by coming to a man's cabin without a chaperon."

"I was merely curious. I saw the smoke—"

Nathan's laughter filled the small room. "You came because you could not help yourself. I wanted to see you so badly you could feel my yearning. I believe in that, don't you?"

"Believe in what?"

They were still standing in the middle of the floor staring at each other. The room was mostly in shadows, shut in by trees that held the winter light. All around them, the air hung still and silent as Sarah waited for him to speak.

At last, his lordship said, "I believe when two people love each other, words are unnecessary. They know what the other is feeling."

"Have you lost your mind, Nathan Adams? I'm not in love with you. You are a stranger—"

"We have never been strangers. This was meant to be. God made you for me and me for you, at this particular time in our lives."

Sarah could not believe what she was hearing. Was Nathan daft? Just because they enjoyed a kiss . . .

"Nathan, you know that I must needs make a marriage of convenience. I thought to be honest with you. You are talking nonsense."

As if she hadn't spoken, or because she had, he again took her in his arms, this time holding her so tightly against his long, lean body that she could not push him away. "I learn quickly," he said, smiling down into her eyes before he kissed her as if he sought food for his starving soul.

It was not Sarah's wont to push him away. She forgot the vicar's words. Slowly her arms crept upward until they circled Nathan's neck, and she gave her lips to him gladly, parting them when his tongue persisted. Never had she felt that something was so right. His trembling arms were like braces of steel as they held her to him. Heat, now familiar and delicious, flooded her body, growing with his lordship's strong need that burned its way into her being. Her breasts throbbed with sweet pain against his broad chest.

Sarah, at twice times ten, was not a slowtop. Knowing that she was in deep, deep trouble, it was with all the effort she could muster that she ended the kiss and stepped back. And his lordship, as if he realized they were overstepping their limits of control, let her go with obvious reluctance. His face was a mask of solemnity, infectious laughter no longer lit his gray eyes, now somber and serious.

As Sarah stood before him, her soul feeling naked, she knew she could not let this happen. She could not fall in love with this man.

Nathan started to speak, "I'm—"

"Don't say you're sorry, please." Sarah was remembering Sam Schuyler of Hyde Park, his quick apology for a light kiss on her cheek. She could believe that Sam was genuinely sorry, but not Nathan. He had poured his soul into hers. She did not want him to be sorry.

"Not for the kiss," he said, "but that I almost lost control. I would not harm you for the world, precious Sarah."

She forced a little laugh, and her next words invaded the stillness that held the room in its grip. "I believe 'tis the girl who is to call stop, which I did. Although not soon enough. We should not have been kissing like that. Nature of animals is—"

"It was not the nature of two animals. Love was in that kiss, and wanting, as two people who are in love want."

"Nathan, you are talking lunacy. We've slightly met. I wish that we could be friends, get to know each other—"

"That's a capital idea. As long as I can steal a kiss now and then. I'm not in any great rush." It was a lie, but he sought to calm her fears.

When laughter returned to his lordship's countenance, Sarah was glad. For a moment she had been frightened.

If he had wanted to kiss her again, she would have let him. And this time she might not have found the strength to stop him from taking her as his own. Over his lordship's shoulder, she spied an easel with a painting resting on it. "Do you paint?" she asked, glad to change the subject.

"Not seriously. 'Tis an outlet, a guard against loneliness. If I were a serious painter, I would need more light than this cabin affords."

Sarah walked closer to the painting. The half-bent woman resembled her.

" 'Tis not a good likeness," he said. "I painted it from memory, the time we skated together."

"I've wanted another blizzard, one that would freeze the pond hard enough for skating."

Nathan gave a light laugh. "I, too. I would like another go at outskating you."

They went to sit, she in the rocking chair and he on a bench directly in front of her. Holding her hand in his, he looked at her and smiled.

"What are you smiling about?"

"I can see you years from now, sitting by the fire, those whiskey curls white, a shawl around your shoulders, while we talk about our children . . . and their children."

"Nathan! I will have no more of that talk. If we can't be just friends, then we will be nothing at all." She started to rise, only to be stayed by his big hand.

"Now I really am sorry. Please stay. We will just talk."

"And not about being white-headed and talking about *our* grandchildren. I've told you that I intend to make a marriage of convenience, and that is that. Nothing will deter me. I've given Aunt Lillian my word. And I was taught by Papa that a person's word is law."

Afraid that he would drive Sarah from the cottage, his lordship did not say what he wanted to say, that Lady Lillian would drive any man from Merrymount, just as she had driven Hogarth Templeton to America. The place had been sinking since the day the good man had

left. No, he did not think Lady Lillian Merriwether deserved the loyalty which her niece was willing to give. No
doubt the old woman had extracted Lady Sarah's word
when the girl was the most vulnerable.

Nathan had no notion of giving up on winning Lady
Sarah. He would bide his time. He asked, "How do you
like my little hideaway? Hunters used to use it. There's a
small kitchen, and another room with a bed. I understand
that years ago hunters who were actually hunting for food
used it."

"I think it is wonderfully private. Do you stay here
. . . or just visit on occasion?

"I stay over at times, though not often. I come here and
paint, but mostly I come to think. That's what I was doing
today, thinking about you, willing you to come."

Sarah withdrew her hand from his. "I must needs tell
you about the Gypsy hat business . . . ."

Chapter Eleven

"Are you daft?" said plump Georgena Adams to Nathan, who had just returned to Copthorne from the cabin in the woods. It was quite late, for he had lingered after Sarah had taken her leave, thinking on all that she had told him and savoring that lovely moment when a kiss had brought them so close that he had felt as one with her. He had thought on what to do, and then explained his plan to Georgena

Chesterson smiled. No, he wasn't daft; he was in love. Through the window he saw fireflies, their orange tails blinking, flitting about in the deepening twilight.

"Well, are you or are you not?"

"What?" Chesterson asked.

"I asked if you are daft." Georgena retorted.

Lord Chesterson looked at his brother William, winked, then asked of Georgena, "Why do you say that? Do I look daft?"

"You say you love Lady Sarah—"

"That is true, from the moment of first laying eyes on her."

"Then why, in the name of good sense, are you willing to help her with a come-out into London society so that she can find a rich husband?"

"How else can I keep an eye on her?" he asked. "How

can I save her from herself? I not only promised my assistance but yours as well, Georgena."

"My assistance?" she sputtered.

William looked on, laughing. He had heard exchanges like this before between his wife and his brother. They were the closest of friends, and he, William, was grateful for that.

"Yes, Georgena, you are to assist in marketing the Gypsy hats that Lady Angeline will make; I will afford the ladies handsome horses to pull the Merriwether crested carriage, and they will live in my London town house with me. It's in excellent location, and a good location is a must if one is to appear rich."

"You don't have enough servants to appear rich," Georgena argued, "and besides, it would not look proper for them to share your lodgings. Remember, the *ton* is very strict with their rules."

"I will say that I am very interested in seeing my very wealthy cousin launched into society."

"You are a cousin . . . of sorts," said William.

"Of sorts is right. Only a smidgen of Lady Sarah's grandfather's blood runs through my veins, hardly enough to inherit the earldom when he died. But they could find no one else, no male heir other than me." He looked at Georgena. "The hat business is to afford blunt for other aspects of this charade."

Nathan left the mantel on which he had been leaning and went to sit in a comfortable chair of red leather. Georgena and William were already sitting. His lordship could feel their closeness, and he envied them. The ambiance in the room was wonderful, he thought, looking about. Lit tapers cast circles of yellow light on the rich carpet and on the old elegant furnishings. The family dog and cat were in their place near the fire; the children in the nursery with their nanny.

Home, his lordship mused, and in his opinion, fine

enough for His Majesty, old King George, or the Prince
Regent, who loved everything grand.

Nathan stretched his long legs toward the fire burning
brightly in the grate.

Sarah should be here with me.

He said aloud, "You know, Georgena and William,
that I plan to marry Lady Sarah, and quickly. I'm not a
patient man."

"It seems to me that you've been quite patient," said
William. "Three years have passed—"

Georgena spoke up, enquiring at length about the hat
business and how she was to help. Nathan explained to
her that she could help by taking Angeline into the prominent towns of England and establishing a market for the
hats.

Looking pityingly at her brother-in-law, Georgena exclaimed, " 'Tis a terrible plan, but I will do whatever you
want me to do, Nathan. However, when Lady Sarah ups
and marries some nabob who can pay the debts against
Merrymount, do not come to me for sympathy. I think
you are all about in the attic."

Nathan became pensive. Mayhap his sister-in-law was
right, but he had to have time with Lady Sarah. She was
not one to give her heart easily, and it was up to him to
make her see the folly of saving Merrymount. "What do
you think, William?" he asked of his brother. "Am I daft?
I have no doubt that should I leave Lady Sarah to her
own volition, she will be married to some scoundrel in no
time. With her in my own house, I can prevent that from
happening."

"It seems a capital idea to me," William said. "I'm
intrigued by this hat business. Did you say Lady Angeline
has only seen five and ten summers?"

"According to Sarah, her sister is very talented. She's
part American Indian and has strong intuition, believes in
asking Spirits for guidance, and she strongly believes this

hat business will be a great success. She sold her mother's beads for blunt to capitalize the business."

William frowned. "What about Lady Sarah being involved? Society will certainly condemn—"

"No one is to know. The company will have a Parisian name and a blind address. I wish I had the blunt to buy Merrymount."

"Would you actually want that big old manor house?" asked William. "Unless one wishes to live for society alone and have hunts and balls—in other words live the kind of life you've always detested—it seems that Merrymount would be a burden around one's neck."

For a long moment Nathan was quiet, and the quietness spread out into the room. Then, as if talking to himself, he said, "I would do anything to win Sarah for my wife."

Upon leaving Nathan's cabin, Sarah walked slowly through the woods, making her way back to the footpath that would take her back to Merrymount. He heart beat in her throat; yet, it felt heavy in her soul. She had wanted to stay longer with Nathan but did not trust herself to do so. His slightest touch seared her flesh and started her trembling. Even now, her body was warm from his touch. Only the chill wind against her cheeks rooted her to reality. She must needs do what she had to do.

Then she tossed her head angrily and asked herself why she had stopped the kiss. Why had she not, in the heat of passion . . . and love, given herself to him? As he had wanted, as she had wanted.

Hot blood suffused her face; it felt as if it were on fire. How could she think such worldly thoughts? A woman was supposed to stay pure for the man she married, and even if by chance she should marry Nathan, and there was little chance of that, she should be a virgin on their wedding night.

"Why?" she asked aloud. "Who made that rule?" She laughed ruefully. "Of course it would be a man . . ."

Sarah felt foolish walking along talking to herself, but suddenly she realized what was happening. For the first time in her life she was having independent thoughts. Her thoughts, not someone else's. And she wondered again why a woman should be a virgin when she married when it was a well-known fact that men kept mistresses.

Did not a woman have the same needs, the same feelings as a man? If she were to keep herself pure for her husband, should he not keep himself pure for her? She wondered where Nathan would go for relief, then laughed. Courtesans were used for that, and light skirts, though he did not seem the light-skirt type.

Demme, it was not fair.

Sarah knew the answer: society was all powerful, and society was ruled by men. She kicked a stone from her path and swore silently. The warm stirring in her lower extremities abated, but the questions did not leave her thoughts, and when she remembered Nathan's sensuous lips on hers—and she could hardly forget for a moment—she wanted to turn and run back to him. "Let someone else save Merrymount for Lady Lillian," she said, and then Sarah thought about her dead mama. Would Alice Templeton think her daughter selfish?

Since coming to Merrymount, Sarah had spent considerable time conversing with her mother's portrait that hung over the handsome mantel, but she had not been to her mother's grave. She held a three-year-old's memory of going to the graveyard with her father to say goodbye when they departed England for America.

The feelings of that day suddenly came back strongly to Sarah. She had not felt that her mother was in the cold ground on which she and her father were kneeling. Her mother was back at the manor house, held firmly and always by an elaborate gilt frame over a black marble mantel.

That day, Sarah and Hogarth Templeton had left the graveyard quickly, returning to the house. Where, Sarah remembered, a warm fire burned brightly in the grate and the beautiful woman smiled down at her little girl so lovingly. Sarah had asked Hogarth Templeton to lift her up and let her touch the woman's face, and he had.

This day, Sarah decided, she would once again visit her mother's grave. Mayhap her mother's spirit would offer guidance.

It didn't.

Sarah left the graveyard feeling much as she had felt when she had left it when she was three, empty. Her own thoughts of independence from social moors—of making a *marriage de convenance* to save Merrymount, of giving up kissing Lord Chesterson forever—was more than she could forebear. She headed back toward the manor house, asking herself why Lady Lillian needed so very much to keep Merrymount, except to assuage her pride?

Sarah concluded that the old woman did not want to admit that she had, all those years ago, been wrong in driving Hogarth Templeton away.

The decision came slowly as Sarah walked slowly. She would not, could not, make a marriage of convenience to save Merrymount. Having made that one important decision, all other unanswered questions left Sarah's mind, and she felt a wonderful uplifting of spirit of a euphoric nature. In front of her, Cain and Abel were loping to meet her.

Upon closer scrutiny Sarah saw also a rich black carriage-and-six pulling away from the portcullis, headed toward the road that led to Rockingham. Sitting on the box was a fat coachman wearing a multilayered coat and a tricorn. One of his hands held the ribbons, the other a long leather whip, which he cracked over the horses' backs, the sound resounding into the quietness of the ridge. A highly liveried footman rode the back.

Shielding her eyes from the lowering sun, Sarah

strained to see who was inside the carriage. It appeared to hold two large men, both wearing black high-crowned beavers and sitting tall and straight. An ominous feeling suddenly engulfed Sarah, and she began to run, the hounds dancing along beside her.

Pushing the side door of the manor house open, she practically fell into the Warm Room.

Lady Lillian, her wrinkled face as white as a freshly washed sheet, was lying on the floor.

Angeline was looking down at her. When Sarah entered, Angeline said, "She's simply having a spell of the vapors. I'm certain that she'll wake up in a minute. I heard her fall and came . . ."

"She looks dead to me," said Sarah. "Get the vinaigrette and ring for Hilda."

By the time Hilda and John Wesley had joined them, Lady Lillian was letting out little moans and slapping at the vinaigrette. She pushed herself up into a sitting position and opened her eyes, which, Sarah noted, held a wild look, as if she did not know where she was or who the people around her were.

"Aunt Lillian!" Sarah exclaimed. She was on her knees, shaking the old woman's shoulders. "What happened?"

Lady Lillian reached to embrace Sarah, saying, "Oh Alice, I knew you would come back. Why did you leave me and go to America? That must have been an awful place, filled with savages."

Sarah, looking at Hilda and John Wesley, shook her head. "Could you help me lift her onto her bed, John Wesley?"

"I want to sit in my chair while we talk," said Lady Lillian. "There's so many *on-dits* that we must needs discuss. You've been gone ever so long." She patted Sarah's cheek. "Alice, you are as beautiful as ever."

With John Wesley's help, Sarah lifted the old woman into the chair. After she seemed comfortable, Sarah

draped a wool afghan around her thin shoulders, then
asked John Wesley to fetch the doctor.

Then there was nothing to do but wait and listen to
Lady Lillian's mad ravings. The time passed slowly for
Sarah. For once Angeline was quiet. She held the hounds'
heads in her lap and stroked them. Not even when the
little man in a black coat came, his hair tied in a pigtail,
did she utter a word.

"Shock," the doctor quickly diagnosed as he poured
into a spoon a dose of laudanum and forced it between
Lady Lillian's clenched teeth.

Sarah could not stop the tears that pushed at her eyes.

Angeline moved closer and put her arm around Sarah's
shoulder, comforting her. Sarah reached for her sister's
hand and held it tightly. This could not be happening.

The doctor shook his head, peered at his patient
through his quizzing glass, and said, "Her ladyship has
had a terrible shock. Keep her quiet and pray that her
senses will come back to her."

"But what if that doesn't happen?" asked Sarah worriedly.

"Then she will just have to go to Bedlam. Happens all
the time. Especially at her age. Something just snaps."

Sarah found herself wanting to slap the uncaring doctor. Could he not see the poor woman's despair? She
asked, "Is there not something we can do, other than
wait?"

"I fear not. Just wait. She most likely prefers the world
she's in now better than the one she just left."

"Alice," Lady Lillian said, "come sit beside me. I'm so
glad you've come home."

Sarah sat beside her, patting her hand, smiling wanly.
Had it been only today that she had gone to Lord Chesterson's cabin? It all seemed years past, and she was glad
when the laudanum began its work and Lady Lillian
started to doze.

"Aunt Lillian," Sarah said, "we must needs get you into bed before you fall out of your chair."

It was only moments before Lady Lillian was fast asleep.

"Will she need supper?" Hilda asked.

"I think not to disturb her," Sarah answered, and the maid, her eyes red from crying, bobbed and left.

Angeline rose from her place by the fire. "Sister, I have something to show you."

Sarah looked at her quizzically. "Then come with me into our bedchamber. Mayhap it won't be too cold." She still wore her heavy coat and brown beaver hat.

In the bedchamber Angeline lit candles and pulled back the window coverings to let in what was left of the day's light. Waving her hand, she said to Sarah, "Look at my afternoon's work. I hope you are duly impressed."

Sarah's eyes widened in disbelief. Words would not come, for before her, spread on Angeline's narrow bed, were gorgeous drawings of Gypsy hats, each different from the other.

"Twenty-six," said Angeline, grinning proudly.

"Angeline, I can't believe you did these; they are wonderful. Where are the fashion magazines—"

"I didn't have fashion magazines. They just came out of my head. Coming over on the *Boston Queen,* I saw several women wearing the wide-brimmed hats, and I embellished on what I remembered."

Caught up in the excitement of Angeline's wonderful accomplishment, Sarah had forgotten her resolve not to have a come-out to search for a rich husband. "Angeline, this day I resolved that to dupe some nabob in to marrying me to save Merrymount would be most unfair to him."

"I've thought all along that it was a farrago of nonsense, that you should not be the sacrificial lamb. Lady Lillian . . ."

She paused pensively for a moment, and Sarah looked

at her questioning. "What is it, Angeline? There's something you are not telling me."

"Those men threatened Lady Lillian, scared her to death."

"Oh, dear merciful God," exclaimed Sarah. "I had completely forgotten to enquire as to their business at Merrymount. I saw them leaving. What do you mean, Angeline? Did they threaten Lady Lillian? Were you there? Did you hear?"

"I heard, but Lady Lillian didn't know I was listening. I crept up from the kitchen when John Wesley came in and said there was a carriage out front."

"And? Angeline, stop stalling. Did they come about the overdue taxes on Merrymount?"

"No. They came to tell the old woman that she was going to debtor's prison."

Chapter Twelve

Wrapped in a down quilt, Sarah sat beside Lady Lillian's bed throughout the night, holding her bony hand and soothing her when she stirred. Hilda had sat with her while Sarah and Angeline went to the basement kitchen for supper. They had waited on themselves, and only once did Angeline break the engulfing silence, saying in a very unsympathetic voice, "The old crow will have her way if she has to go mad to do it."

"Angeline," Sarah had scolded, but not harshly. It was Angeline's right to mistrust the old woman, but Sarah did not believe that Lady Lillian was putting on an act. There was one thing for certain, thought Sarah as they sat in the warm kitchen, Providence had decreed that she make a marriage of convenience, and quickly. The resolve she had made while returning from Nathan's cabin, and from her mother's grave, vanished in the wake of the visit from the money lenders and the terrible thing that followed. Now, sitting beside Lady Lillian's bed, thoughts tumbled through Sarah's mind.

I can forebear Mama's sister having to leave Merrymount; I can see where it might be for the best, but I can't allow her to go to debtor's prison. Sarah watched through the window as streaks of orange appeared on the horizon, outlining the winter-black trees, their barren limbs laden with snow. A damp mist rose up from the ground.

The night had been long, and the Warm Room had become cold, even though John Wesley had come to stoke the fire and add wood that he and Angeline had cut.

Shivering, Sarah pulled the quilt closer around her and leaned forward to see if her aunt was breathing normally, relieved to find that she was. All night long her loud snoring had chortled through the room but had now abated to barely audible wheezing, which escaped through her thin lips, making them tremble in a pitiful way. Sarah prayed for the old woman to wake up and be her normal, irascible self. Anything was better than this.

The sound of the door opening caused Sarah to turn. Hilda stood in the doorway, holding a silver tray with a china cup and saucer, from which steam curled up into the chilled room. "I'm fetching you hot cider, m'lady." She looked anxiously at Lady Lillian. "I'll gladly go fer a cup fer her if she would only wake. Do you suppose she will sleep like this forever?"

"I don't think so, Hilda. I think the doctor gave her a huge dose of laudanum. When that wears off . . ."

Sarah took the cup of cider and sipped. "This is wonderful, Hilda. Thank you. You and John Wesley are so thoughtful. He stoked the fire throughout the night."

"Yes, I know. He's terribly worried about her ladyship. I don't know what we'd do should she . . . you know . . . pass on, or if she ends up in Bedlam."

"Being mad doesn't kill anyone, Hilda. And I don't believe for a moment that Aunt Lillian is permanently ill. I think the doctor exaggerates, although he was right when he said she was in shock. That is believable."

Hilda crossed herself. "I pray so," she said, worry pouring from her old faded eyes. Sarah felt her heart squeeze tightly in her chest, and before she could stop herself, she was saying, "Hilda, don't worry about yourself and John Wesley. Lady Angeline and I will take care of you."

The words had just come out, and Sarah knew instantly that she had made another promise which she mayhap could not keep. How could two poverty-stricken orphans from America add the responsibility of aging servants to that of saving Merrymount from the Crown's tax collectors and Lady Lillian from the money lenders?

Sarah could not scold herself, for she had reacted to the circumstances no differently than her father, Hogarth Templeton, would have. She remembered vividly his many kindnesses to the people who worked at Templeton Hall and his loving protectiveness of Wanna, his Indian wife. Even though the good man was gone, his strength, wisdom, and love were folded in and around her heart. And Angeline was so much like him, but more fierce in her outspokenness.

How different things at Merrymount were than what she had fancied, thought Sarah. She let out a quivering sigh, and then took a big gulp of hot cider. Her thoughts went back to Templeton Hall, the many years she had yearned to return to Merrymount. Now, only the portrait of her mother seemed real. The house was cold, and the moat had grown wild with weeds. She wanted so much for spring to come so that she and Angeline and John Wesley could clear the ground and plant flowers. She would *make* her dream come true.

But Sarah knew that this could not happen, for she would be in London looking for a rich husband. She drank the last of the cider and handed the cup back to Hilda, who bobbed and again glanced worriedly at Lady Lillian before quitting the room.

A low moan came from the bed, and Sarah quickly stood and bent over Lady Lillian, letting the quilt slip down to puddle at her feet. She still wore the clothes she had worn to Nathan's cabin, the gray wool walking dress. Her auburn curls were loose from the riband, and when she bent over Lady Lillian, they fell around her face.

The moan was only an indication that Lady Lillian had woken from the drugged sleep. She looked at Sarah and smiled normally. Sarah was elated until Lady Lillian asked, "Alice, why are you up so early? And you're already dressed."

Sarah's disappointment grew with the realization that the old woman had simply escaped from that which she could not forbear back to a happier time.

"I've been here all night, Aunt Lillian," Sarah said. "You gave us quite a fright. And I'm not Alice; I am Alice's daughter . . . from America. I'm Sarah Templeton."

Lady Lillian pushed herself up onto her elbows and stared at Sarah. "Why do you want to fun me, Alice? How could you have a daughter when you aren't even married. Papa would frown . . ."

Sarah, tears pushing their way onto her cheeks, turned and saw Angeline standing behind her. She was dressed in a long slim dress of red wool, her hair in a long black braid. Only her brown eyes showed that she, too, had not slept well. They were circled with shades of red, as if she might have cried in the night. Sarah greeted her with a forced smile.

"Sister, let me sit with her—"

"No one need sit with me. I shall be out and about in a few minutes. Ring the bell and have a servant bring my breakfast."

She was her irascible self, all right, thought Sarah. She told her, "You may sit in the chair, and your breakfast will be brought, but, Aunt Lillian, you are not going to be up and about until you set your thinking straight." She said again, this time more emphatically, "I am not your sister Alice; I am Sarah Templeton, Alice's daughter, your niece from America."

Bewilderment showed in Lady Lillian's aging countenance.

Sarah nodded to Angeline to ring the bell, and when Hilda came, the breakfast of porridge and mutton was quickly brought, and the old woman began eating ravenously.

"Would you stay with her while Lady Angeline and I go belowstairs for our breakfast?" asked Sarah.

"I don't need anyone to stay with me, Alice."

Lady Lillian's words were ignored. "Of course I will sit with her, Lady Sarah," said the maid as she bobbed. "But 'tis not right that you and Lady Angeline help yerselves."

"Stuff!" piped up Angeline. "In America women are not so helpless, and we are not bowed to all the time. You're going to wear your legs out bobbing up and down, Hilda."

Hilda managed a smile. "Oh, Lady Angeline, you are a card."

"That, she is," said Sarah, smiling at her sister.

When Lady Lillian was ensconced in her chair and the fire had been stoked, Sarah took Angeline's hand and they headed to the basement kitchen for their own breakfast, and to talk. As they were leaving, Sarah heard her old aunt say, "That Alice is just too busy for her own good, always has been."

"She's putting on," said Angeline as soon as they were out of the room.

"I don't think so, Angeline," said Sarah. "I just think the real world is too much for her and that she has escaped back to a happier time. Did you note that she spoke of when Alice was not married to our father. I'd wager the old woman never drew a happy breath after they married, Papa not being rich."

"She certainly does not understand love," replied Angeline. "Else she would not be bound that you marry for money. One's heart should be first consideration."

"Well, since I'm not in love—"

"Balderdash! Of course you are in love with Lord Chesterson. How could you not be, with him so in love with you?"

Sarah gave a mirthless laugh. "Angeline, you are incorrigible. What can I say that will convince you that you are wrong?"

"Nothing, for I know 'tis so. Chesterson is so smitten with you that he can't sleep nights. And you are a fool if you don't love him back."

By now they were in the kitchen, porridge and hot bread in front of them. Sarah was thoughtful for a long moment before saying, "One does what one has to do. I cannot see my mother's sister go to debtor's prison. That is the family loyalty I learned from our father, Angeline. 'Tis not what I choose, but what I must needs do."

Angeline lifted a dark eyebrow. "Aha! Then you admit that you are in love with Nathan Adams?"

"I admit no such thing, and I would appreciate your not talking about it. We will get on with your plan to make and sell hats while praying that 'tis not too late to pay the money lenders."

Needles and thread were gathered, and the work began in earnest on making the Gypsy hats; the French name Louiezon was chosen—because Georgena once had a friend by that name. A room at Merrymount was cleared and used as the workroom.

As Nathan had requested his sister-in-law to do, she came every day to Merrymount to offer her assistance. Sarah appreciated this, and she changed her mind about Georgena only being curious. Although Georgena did not approve of Sarah's future marriage of convenience, she was there to help Nathan in any way she could. *The same family loyalty as I feel for my family,* thought Sarah.

Labels were stitched in fancy script by hand, and handsome hatboxes were affixed with colorful ribbons, with "Louiezon Hats" brazenly showing.

After a business conference, the three, Angeline, Sarah, and Georgena, decided that it would be best to use Corby's post office to receive orders. They knew no one in that industrial city, unlike Rockingham, where the word was bound to get out.

Angeline, of course, was the designer. She also did much of the stitching. Sarah could only smile when the young girl dove into the work as if her life depended upon it. Angeline said more than once, "I'm certainly not doing this for the old crow, but for you, Sarah, because it is your wont."

The work on the hats progressed must faster than Sarah had expected, but it seemed that Lady Lillian had made no progress at all. She talked incessantly to "Alice." Hilda watched over her, while ringing her hands and praying that her ladyship be made whole soon. Then one day the money lenders returned. Hilda ran to fetch Sarah.

"You can't send a sick woman to debtor's prison," Sarah told them, and they laughed. The viler looking one of the two warned, "This will be our last call before we send the Bow Street runners for her. Charges will be filed . . ."

Sarah desperately tried to bargain for time. "Can you not take some of the rich furnishings from Merrymount?"

Lady Lillian would have a spell of the vapors when she learned of her offer, Sarah thought, but at the moment she did not care what the old woman would say.

Sarah's hopes were quickly put to rest with, "The tax collectors have a lien on Merrymount and all its furnishings. 'Twould not be legal to sell off those things."

"I have a strand of pearls . . ." Sarah saw a greedy glint appear in both the money lenders' eyes. One said, "That would buy you some time, nothing more."

"How much time?"

"One month."

Sarah quickly calculated; it would take at least two months to get the hat business established. "Three months," she said with alacrity, pulling herself up to her full height and setting her chin in the obdurate line.

The greedy men looked at each other, and the viler one said, "Aye, three months it will be—*after* I examine the pearls."

Sarah quit the room to fetch the pearls. Her hand shook uncontrollably when she shoved them in the direction of the repulsive one. "They're genuine, all right, and you can have them after you've signed a three-month extension to Lady Lillian's note."

"Let me examine them."

"Not until you've signed the extension," Sarah said, taking from her pocket a piece of parchment that she had thought to put there when she went to her bedchamber. Quickly she wrote the correct words on the paper and held it forth. "Both have to sign it, and should you try to cross me, I will send the Bow Street runners after *you.*"

After the agreement was signed, the awful man, whom the other called Luke, took the pearls. Sarah watched as his beady eyes turned to slits, and she thought she saw drool dripping from the corners of his mouth. Never had she wanted to tear into another person so much. "Three months," she said. "And don't come back to Merrymount; the money will be brought to your establishment in London."

Luke dropped the pearls into the pocket of his long-tailed coat. The smug look on his craggy face gave Sarah the shivers, and her anger grew, anger which she used to hold her tears in check until the door closed on their backsides.

With Georgena coming to Merrymount every day, it was inevitable that Lord Chesterson would hear of the pearl transaction, and he was overcome with anger at the men and with sympathy for his Lady Sarah. So straight away he called at Merrymount, asking to see Lady Sarah alone.

Hilda called Sarah to the Warm Room. Taking Lady Lillian's hand, the maid gently led the old woman from the chamber, saying consolingly, "We will go to the kitchen, yer ladyship."

When Nathan and Sarah were alone, his lordship scolded kindly, "You should have come to me, dear Sarah. I am not deep in the pockets, but I have not been reduced to penury. I would not have allowed you to give them your mother's pearls."

"Oh, Nathan, they were the most despicable of men, no heart and no soul. They would not listen to my promise to pay."

"Money lenders are not noted for their kindness, but what is done is done. Somehow I will regain the pearls for you. Now, we must needs talk of other things. Georgena tells me that most of your meals consist of mutton, chicken, and turnips."

"That is true, but spring will soon come, and wonderful things will be grown."

Nathan looked quite distressed. His gaze searched Sarah's face as he said, "Georgena also passed to me that you have no milk or butter. Do you not have a milk cow?"

Sarah was embarrassed that his lordship, or anyone for that matter, would know of such personal matters. She had spent much of the one-hundred pounds she had brought from America for sugar for the cider, salt pork to season the turnips, and for a small amount of coal. She had also paid the doctor who had come to call on Lady Lillian.

"We shall be just fine," she said defensively. "The hat business—"

"That will take time, too much time. I shall dispatch Copthorne's steward to Merrymount straight away with a milk cow, and a young yearling will be butchered and salted down so that you can have beef."

"I can't let you do that," protested Sarah, but thoughts of a haunch of roasted beef set her mind whirling. *He is a man of the first water,* she thought, giving her first smile since the day the money lenders had departed Merrymount.

Nathan smiled back at her as he reached to pull her

into his strong arms. "If you are to make a marriage of convenience, you must needs stay healthy."

And then he kissed her and held her as if he never intended to let her go. Which he didn't. There would be no marriage of convenience for his Lady Sarah, he silently vowed, not as long as there was breath in his throbbing body.

Chapter Thirteen

For the next three weeks Merrymount was at sixes and sevens from morning until night. Georgena Adams came every day from Copthorne to help cut, stitch, and shape. John Wesley fetched supplies, and Hilda watched after Lady Lillian as if her employer were a helpless child.

The older woman spent most of her time crouched before a window, looking out toward the gatehouse and portcullis, and beyond to the road that led to Rockingham, the road which the money lenders used when coming to Merrymount.

"They might come today," she would say, and Sarah's heart would hurt for the irascible, pitiful woman who looked at her blankly and called her Alice.

With the exception of Lady Lillian's uncertain condition, everything worked out well, Sarah thought later. The milk cow was brought from Copthorne, along with enough grain to last until the grass could green, and a yearling was butchered, salted, and delivered to Merrymount. That night a big haunch of beef had been roasted.

Sarah had never smelled or tasted anything so delicious, and when John Wesley went into Rockingham for more felt and other supplies, she took shillings from what was left of her one-hundred pounds and asked that he buy tea and coffee. By then she despaired at the thought of more apple cider, even though it did give out a pungent odor, making the big old house feel homey.

And then one day Lord Chesterson called at Merrymount to tell Sarah he would be going into London to sit in the House of Lords. "Is there anything I can do for you before I leave?" he asked.

"You've already been too kind," Sarah told him, and when he enquired about the hat business, a meeting was quickly called in the workroom with Angeline, Georgena, and Sarah present.

His lordship was shown the ten hats that had been made, all different, and then the hatboxes, of which Sarah was extraordinarily proud. It had been her idea that each Gypsy hat have its own black silk box, with a bright red silk ribbon for a bail. "Would it not be excellent advertising among the women of the *ton?*" she had asked. "From what I have learned, and knowing human nature, the ladies of quality vie to outdo one another."

Because of the extra cost, Angeline had been doubtful. But she acquiesced to Sarah's wishes when Sarah said, "What could be more beneficial to our cause than to have a duchess strolling down Bond Street, her abigail walking three steps behind her, swinging by a wide red silk ribbon a hatbox with 'Louiezon Hats' stitched in silver into the black silk? I'll wager that every lady of quality in London would be clamoring for a Gypsy hat. Because of the French name they will assume, without being told so, that the hats are from Paris."

Now Nathan looked admiringly at the hats, the boxes, and then into Sarah's eyes, losing himself in their green depths. Familiar warmth instantly traversed his body.

Georgena said, "Nathan, now that we have produced these beautiful hats, can you not advise us how and where to sell them? It's imperative that society not know that Lady Sarah is part owner of a hat business, else they would cut her. You rub with those who will buy them."

Nathan turned from Sarah so that he could think on

the business at hand. His gaze went from the handsome hats to the handsome boxes. No one spoke until at last he said, "Lady Arbuthnot would be the perfect lady of quality to use for promotion of the hats. Mayhap I could make her a gift of one. Her husband was a member of Lord Liverpool's government, and we rubbed well together. Since his death his widow gets around considerably, but not beyond the pale."

Without thinking, Sarah spoke quickly. "Does that mean you are her escort while she is getting around considerably?"

Nathan smiled, for he believed Sarah's quick reaction meant that she cared enough to be jealous. "On occasion I have been her ladyship's escort to small parties in private homes. Her year of mourning is in its last month, and she can soon go to the theater and to other social events where wearing a hat would be appropriate."

Georgena said, "I think it a capital idea, Nathan, for you to call on your friend with a Louiezon hat, a gift for her wounded heart."

Nathan, seeing the frown on Sarah's brow, thought that mayhap he could work his friendship with Lady Arbuthnot to his advantage, in addition to having her introduce the Louiezon Hats to London's ladies of quality. "Elizabeth is a lovely woman," he said, suppressing a grin.

Georgena, knowing Nathan as she did, quickly caught his intention. "Oh, Nathan, you are brilliant. After much coaxing from *your* Lady Arbuthnot, you can tell her that other hats can be ordered from our address in Corby, that a representative of the company resides nearby. I think a small white lie would do no harm. Do you not agree, Sarah?"

Sarah jerked her head around. "I'm sorry, Georgena, my mind was elsewhere. Do you remind repeating—"

"Not at all, dear Sarah, for it is such a wonderful plan."

Listening to Georgena again explain the plan, the

frown on Sarah's brow deepened. How could she prevent Nathan's using Lady Arbuthnot to further their cause of making money for her come-out. She was beginning to hate the word.

But, she mused, it would be prudent to wait until she and his lordship were alone to ask more questions, if she could enquire without his sensing her jealousy.

Georgena said, "Nathan, do you not think that I should call on the more fashionable shops in Brighton and in Bath, and leave one of our creations on consignment to be sold *only* to a member of the upper orders? Nothing would be more fatal than to have the hats too plentiful, making them common. We must needs price them out of the lower orders' reach."

"Do you think fifty pounds?" asked Angeline, quickly calculating how many hats they would have to sell to make the profit that would pay for the come-out. Some of the capital had been used for supplies.

"Not less than two hundred pounds for each hat," said his lordship. "Remember, due to Napoleon's hungry quest to conquer the Continent, anything from Paris is at a premium. These hats are for duchesses and for aristocrats' wives."

So the price was set. No more than twenty hats would be sold.

"Lady Lillian said that two thousand pounds will be adequate for the come-out. Money over that will assure Sarah an outstanding wardrobe," said Angeline, and Georgena began talking of sending for an excellent modiste to begin cutting and stitching.

Sarah did not share Angeline and Georgena's enthusiasm. She felt her heart plummet. Had Nathan been funning when he told her he loved her? Why was he going to so much effort to help her find a rich husband? Anger was in the look she gave his lordship as he walked closer to her and said in a resonant whisper, "Why the reproachful look, my love?"

"Don't call me your love—"

He gave her an engaging smile. "Meet me at the cabin tonight. I leave at first light on the morrow."

"I will not compromise myself—"

A low laugh flowed from his lordship. Leaning his head conspiratorially, he said, "My dear Lady Sarah, both of us have been compromised by the other, by our sheer need to touch, to talk, to kiss. And I cannot stop myself from wanting to hold you one more time. Can you deny me that? I'm certain your future husband will never know, should he care."

"And why would he not care?"

"Because you will never kiss him the way you kiss me. He will take your lack of feeling as inexperience, believing egotistically that you are his virginal bride."

"And so I shall be," retorted Sarah, lifting her chin slightly, more for show than for certainty, for she was not at all certain that, should she go to the cabin, her words would remain true. "I will not meet you, m'lord, so don't bother yourself to go."

"I shall be there," he said, and then he gave a fancy leg and left, black silk hatbox in hand.

Sarah watched his retreating back, her resolve firmly in place: she would not go to the cabin.

It was not until later, after having eaten a fine meal of beef, browned succulently and smothered with rich gravy, that Sarah found her resolve weakening. She and Angeline were in their bedchamber, and Angeline was sitting cross-legged, Indian fashion, in the middle of her narrow bed, and Sarah had taken the only chair the small room afforded. An infrequent fire burned in the fireplace, casting shadows onto the walls.

"What were you and Chesterson whispering about?" asked Angeline.

"Nothing of importance," retorted Sarah, and then she found herself telling Angeline the whole of it about her and Nathan. Suddenly it seemed that she must needs talk with someone besides herself about the situation. "He asked me to meet him at an ancient hunting cabin he frequents in the woods."

Angeline's answer came as no surprise to Sarah. "Oh, sister, that is about the most romantic thing I've ever heard. Of course you are going, and you will let him kiss you again and again. And I think you have something missing in your belfry if you don't marry him. He's in love with you."

Angeline's quick reply made Sarah laugh. "Angeline, do you not know anything about propriety? A lady would not permit such liberties. In truth, one should always have a chaperon."

"Stuff! That's some more strictures of the *ton*. But if you really need a chaperon, I shall be most happy to oblige." Angeline was smiling, showing beautiful white teeth.

"No," Sarah said, "if I go, I must needs go alone, and no one is to know."

Angeline left the bed and went to hug Sarah. "I will keep your secret, dear sister."

Tears clouded Sarah's eyes. She wanted so much to go, she could not deny that, but she was frightened. She remembered his lordship's kisses and how she had wanted him to keep on kissing her forever. Her body was not to be trusted. No, she would not go to the cabin tonight.

Sarah's heart, her whole being, told her otherwise.

If she did not go, when would she ask him about his special friend, Lady Arbuthnot? asked her logical mind.

Before Sarah could mention this to Angeline, her sister began again about the foolishness of a convenient marriage. "Why should you be trapped in a loveless marriage for Lady Lillian?" she asked.

"Mayhap I shall fall in love with a fine, rich gentleman from the upper orders," said Sarah. A few amorous kisses did not mean she was in love with Nathan Adams. After all, she had seen twenty summers, and his was her very first real kiss. Most certainly Sam Schuyler's peck on the cheek could not be called a kiss.

"Well, are you going?" asked Angeline, bringing the conversation back to romance, her favorite topic.

"I'm thinking on it."

"Thinking will only get you in trouble. Listen to your heart," advised the young girl. "I'll ring for John Wesley and ask that bathwater be readied for you in the kitchen. I'm sure that by now Hilda has finished the supper clean-up and is in the Warm Room watching over Lady Lillian, who, no doubt, is crouched by the window looking for the money lenders."

"Bathwater? Why should I bathe at this late hour?" Sarah walked to the window. " 'Tis growing dark."

"The bath is so that you will smell sweet for Lord Chesterson, and the hour is perfect. I declare, Sarah, do you not have *any* romance in your soul? Soon the moon will furnish light. I would not have you lost in the woods. Then for sure your secret would be out."

So it was decided, mostly by Angeline, that she would walk part way with Sarah. Cain and Abel should go, should Sarah meet a stranger.

This brought laughter from Sarah. "Most likely those ugly hounds would lick a stranger's hand."

Preparations were made, a quick bath, after which Sarah donned a walking dress of purple wool; delicate humming birds and butterflies had been embroidered on the sleeves. The decolletage was not excessively low, thought Sarah. Only a slight amount of white flesh showed.

Angeline dressed Sarah's hair, pulling the auburn curls back and tying them with a riband at her nape. "You are so beautiful, Sarah," she said. "If you were not my beloved sister, I would be frightfully jealous."

They laughed together, and the room, so it seemed to Sarah, was, for the first time since their arrival at Merrymount, filled with a degree of happiness.

They left by a back entry at the end of a long corridor. After leashing the hounds, they walked past the stables and sheep barn and were soon into the woods, following the footpath that led to the edge of the ridge.

Cain and Abel sniffed and pulled against their leashes, only to calm down when Angeline spoke crisply to them. The atmosphere was one of solemnity until Angeline laughingly scolded, "Sarah, will you please stop acting as if you are going to your execution."

" 'Tis just that I know I should not be meeting his lordship this way. 'Tis against propriety."

"Stuff. Propriety be hanged. In America—"

"But we're not in America, Angeline. We should learn English ways," countered Sarah, and then she added, "I may as well tell you the whole of it. When Nathan mentioned engaging the assistance of Lady Arbuthnot in promoting the Louiezon hats, I became extremely jealous."

"That only proves that you care about him, and if that were not so, I would not be encouraging this meeting. You and Nathan should spend time together, to know each other better. He's leaving tomorrow, and this is your last chance."

Sarah looked at her sister, thinking that what she had said was true. She, Sarah, knew very little about the sixth earl of Chesterson. The thought of his having a love interest in London and that he was going there on the morrow had set her heart to pounding. She had heard of girls being green with jealousy, and this was certainly true of her. It was a very uncomfortable feeling.

At the rim of the ridge, Sarah stopped and said to Angeline, "The cabin is in that direction." She pointed. "I can find my way now. You should turn back before we leave the footpath. Take Cain with you."

Angeline hugged Sarah. "The hounds will not be parted and would cause an awful ruckus should we try. 'Tis not far, and I am not afraid. I won't wait up for you, so stay as long as you like."

Sarah laughed. "You are quite a matchmaker, Angeline. I will not be long, but please don't wait up. Make sure the door isn't locked. I shall slip in and into bed in just a little while."

Sarah and the hounds left the footpath and went into the woods. The winter-stripped trees seemed to part for her. Below the valley was bright and beautiful. She listened to an owl hooting in the distance.

The dogs behaved nicely, not barking at the sounds, only occasionally straining to break loose and run.

Sarah did not hurry, for she wanted time to plan what she would say to Nathan when she asked about his London friend. Her jealousy continued to surprise her. Never had she experienced such a strong emotion, and she thought it quite unhealthy. She would be very nonchalant when she made the enquiry, she planned, and in her mind she listened to her own words when, tossing her head and looking the other way, she would say, "By the bye, Nathan, tell me about Lady Arbuthnot. Do you think she might be someone I should know as I make my debut into society? Mayhap she can assist me in choosing the right husband and warn me if a rake is showing interest. After all, I am from America, and we enter society differently there . . ."

The wind was cold to her face, but her brown coat and beaver hat kept her warm. She came to a small clearing. Ahead was the hunting cabin, light showing through a small square window. Gray smoke curled snakelike toward the sky. She smiled. Nathan had not paid mind to her declaration that she certainly would not this night meet him at the cabin. The smile turned to light laughter, for she strongly suspected that Nathan Adams cared little about propriety. Mayhap in Town he would acquiesce to society's strictures, but here on this remote hillock, who would know?

The thought was of considerable comfort to Sarah. *Still, 'tis totally foolish . . .*

Why did she let her heart rule her head?

She did not knock on the sagging door, which stood slightly ajar. Pushing it open, she stepped inside and released the black-and-white spotted hounds, letting them find their own warm place in front of the fire.

Sarah was immediately struck anew with Nathan's handsomeness. Casually dressed in Wellingtons, tight fawn breeches, and a collarless shirt, he sat in the lone chair, his feet stretched toward the dancing flames, his head lolled back against the high back of the chair. He was asleep.

When Sarah cleared her throat, he jumped to his feet. "What kept you?" He took her small hands into his large ones, kissing them and then holding them tightly. "I've been waiting for hours."

"I had not intended to come—"

Nathan's tender smile stopped her. "I had not intended to ask you, dear Sarah, but I could not help myself. Stolen moments are better than no moments at all. I so wanted to be with you before leaving for London. My life there is quite lonely, even when I'm busy with government duties."

His lordship's voice died in the silence of the room. He helped Sarah from her coat. Taking her beaver hat that she held out to him, he hung the hat and her coat on a coat tree that stood in the corner. The warmth of the room rushed over Sarah.

Looking around, she noted that the room was in shadows, lighted only with a candle and light from the blaze that burned briskly in the fireplace. The smell of brewed coffee wafted through the room. The ambiance was one of intimacy, not for casual conversation, Sarah thought, and she planned: *I'll wait a while to ask about Lady Arbuthnot.*

"I've made coffee," said his lordship. "And I brought scones and jelly from home." He paused and gave a laugh. "Nothing slips by Georgena. She came into the kitchen and asked where in the world I was taking scones. Of course she knew."

Before Sarah could comment, he had quit the room, returning shortly with a tray holding cups of steaming coffee, a plate of scones, and three different jellies, which he placed on a table covered with a white cloth. He inclined his head. "You sit in the chair. I'll take the bench."

Sarah sucked in the wonderful aroma. "I had a full supper, but this smells wonderful."

"It is wonderful, because we are sharing." He looked at Sarah, his eyes misty, as if loneliness reached down to rob his soul. Sarah took the cup he held forth, sipping the hot liquid while studying him over the cup's rim. "You miss being married, don't you, Nathan?"

"A man was meant to have a mate," he said. "Do you not miss belonging to someone?"

"I've never belonged to anyone. I'm very inexperienced where men are concerned." A pause, and then, "I can be nothing but truthful—I wanted very much to come here tonight, though I knew it was not proper."

That was not what Sarah had intended to say at all. Why did this man affect her in such a way? As he gave her a studied look, then a smile, her mind whirled.

Could I be in love?

Of course not.

He is a stranger.

I want him to kiss me . . . passionately.

Sarah drank from her cup, added jelly to a scone, ate it, and allowed only an occasionally glance into Nathan's eyes.

"Lady Sarah," he said, "I have asked for your hand in marriage, but I have nothing more than my love to offer you."

"If it were not for Aunt Lillian's debts, that would be enough. She . . . she told me that you were poor."

Reaching across the table, he took her free hand. "That

is true, in way of ready blunt. But things will get better. I expect tremendous crops this year. Four years of no rain is past reality for England. We've had three."

Quietness settled over the room, and then Nathan asked, "Do you love me, Sarah?"

"I don't know what love is, Nathan. As I told you, I wanted terribly to come here tonight. I had thought to ask you about Lady Arbuthnot—"

Nathan threw his blond head back and laughed. "I do hope you are jealous."

"Oh, no, 'tis not that."

Everything was going all wrong, thought Sarah. Why had she not enquired in the manner she had planned?

"There's nothing wrong in feeling jealousy if one is in love. I'd be terribly jealous if I thought you were interested in someone else."

"Then I must be in love with you, for I burned with this awful feeling when you called Lady Arbuthnot your 'special friend,' and your leaving for London on the morrow did not help. God's truth, I believe that feeling drove me here tonight."

Nathan rose from the bench and walked toward her. "I will be perfectly honest with you, my love. If I had not met you—and I call our meeting fate—I might have considered Elizabeth when her mourning came to an end. But now I can think of no one but you. I dream of you at night."

"Nathan," Sarah said in a quiet voice. "If fate brought us together, then why is it not possible that we be together? You are aware of my promise to Lady Lillian and of her madness."

"Yes, I am very much aware—"

Sarah swallowed a huge sob. Hot tears were instantly on her cheeks. "Nathan, I could not bear my mother's sister going to debtor's prison."

"Oh, my darling Sarah, don't despair. There just has to be a way."

He reached for Sarah and lifted her to her feet, putting his long arms around her and holding her so that she could hardly breathe. It felt so right, and she let her own arms move of their own volition to encircle his neck. His sensuous lips came down to claim hers, wiping out every niggling thought of what should be and should not be, what was against propriety and what was proper. A torrent of emotions flowed through her; all the feelings she had been fighting flooded her body in uncontrollable desire as each time Nathan captured her mouth with his own.

Slowly his tongue explored the inside of her mouth, tenderly caressing every nerve, and then he moved to press her neck with his lips and then the white flesh of her bosom. "Dear God," she heard him say, "no man ever loved a woman or wanted her more than I love and want you, sweet, sweet Sarah."

"And I love and want you," Sarah answered, wanting to push him away, but finding herself totally unable to do so. She felt his hand tremble as he touched her cheek; his hazel eyes were misty as they searched her soul.

Nathan looked away. God, she was beautiful tonight, and her words made uncontrollable passion rage through his throbbing loins, made his breath come in ragged spurts. He tasted her lips again and again.

I must needs make her mine tonight.

The thought shocked his lordship. He was an honorable man; she, a lady of quality. He had not come to the cabin with this in mind, far from it, but the future loomed so hopelessly. Mayhap this would be their only chance for true and complete happiness. If they could not have forever, they would steal this night.

Just this once, he silently promised, and then he lifted her into his arms and carried her to the small bedroom lighted only by moonlight that streamed through a small window.

"I love you," he whispered into the stillness

"I love you, too, Nathan," Sarah answered, and then they were on the soft bed, together.

Chapter Fourteen

Lord Chesterson did not leave Copthorne at first light. It was nearing that time before he finally dozed off to sleep. What he had done weighed heavily on his mind. Not that he would go back and undo it, for, God's truth, it was the most wonderful thing that ever had happened to him. But he could not help but worry about Lady Sarah. He had wronged her; they must needs marry. But how? He had not a feather to fly with, not in ready blunt, and he'd spent the night thinking upon where to come by it.

Pulling himself up in bed, he leaned his head of blond curls against the high headboard and looked out into the room, which was in shadows, Even though he wore a flannel nightshirt, he felt cold. Beyond the windows winter frost clung to the trees and to the brown-tipped grass. Last night upon returning, he had made a fire to warm the room, and the coals now lay gray and dead in the grate.

His lordship sighed deeply and wished that, just this once, he could ring for a servant to bring hot coffee. He thought back on the time when Copthorne was teeming with servants, and this only drove him deeper into the desponds. He cursed the drought that had dried up his crops, and he cursed his own weakness.

To make a lady of quality his without prospects for

marriage was not to be thought upon. Even worse was to think of that woman, whom he loved more than he loved life, marrying another man to save her aunt from prison. To have that man hold her as he had done was beyond bearing.

Nathan found himself praying while tears squeezed past his eyelids. He had not prayed, nor cried, since grieving for Naneen. Even at its worst, he had known that time would make the hurting better. Now time could only make the hurting worse.

Last night he had pleaded with Lady Sarah to marry him, saying, "We'll find a way to make things right for Lady Lillian." It was an empty promise, and she had known it. She cried and said that one did not shirk one's duty regardless of how much one wanted to fling a promise to the wind. Images of her sitting before the fire, in the lovely purple dress, her hair askew, tears sparking her beautiful green eyes, tortured his mind. He could feel her naked body against his, her breasts throbbing against his heaving chest, smell the sweet smell of lavender in her hair.

His lordship's own words echoed through his head: *This must not happen again.*

And it wouldn't. He slammed his fist against the feather mattress, swore aloud, actually taking God's name in vain, which he vehemently believed was wrong, and if he had not heard a knock on the door, he knew without doubt that he would have shook his fist toward the heavens and cried out in supplication that God bring rain, that God give him Lady Sarah for his wife . . .

Instead, his lordship called, "Enter," and the door was suddenly pushed open.

It was his brother William, standing there holding a cup of hot coffee with steam curling up into the chilly room. The wonderful aroma assaulted Nathan's nostrils.

"Are you ill, Nathan?" Williams asked. "You were

supposed to leave at first light." He held the cup out to his brother.

Nathan took the cup, feeling grateful, but before he could voice his thanks, William said, "Fustian, Nathan, you look like you've been used for a witch's broom-stick—"

"Nothing like that," Nathan answered, "but I did have a fitful night. It was first light before I finally fell sleep, and then it was sporadic." He drank from the cup and swore when he burned his tongue. "I feel foolish having you bring me coffee."

"I brought it because I wanted to. I knew there was something wrong, and I want to help." William took the chair nearest the bed and sat staring at Nathan. "Do you want to talk about it? Sometimes it helps."

"There's nothing new." Of course he was not going to tell his brother, or anyone else, what had actually happened in the cabin. "I've made no secret of wanting to marry Lady Sarah Templeton, and it becomes more hopeless every day. It's as if I am at Eton and in love for the first time. And I've seen thirty summers."

"Love is for any age, so don't feel foolish. I pray that rain will come—"

"And I, too. But the money lenders only gave Lady Sarah three months to produce the blunt Lady Lillian owes or they will press charges. They took Sarah's pearls that had belonged to her mother for the extension. I hope to buy those back. I have enough for that."

" 'Tis a kettle of fish the girls from America have gotten themselves into by coming to Merrymount."

"That's true, and I tend to agree with Lady Angeline. The old woman is selfish and self-centered. When Lord Templeton took his family to America, the old woman did not write to them, not even at Christmas, until she had run Merrymount so deeply into debt that she was desperate. 'Tis unfair to ask Lady Sarah to make a convenient marriage."

"I take it that Lady Sarah knows this but feels it her duty to save the place."

"She promised Lady Lillian . . . I suspect in a moment of sympathy. Now she feels she can't go back on her word. Says 'tis the way Hogarth Templeton brought her up. If you ask me, I believe that it stems from childhood memories of her mother, that it isn't Merrymount at all." Nathan took a huge gulp of coffee, it having cooled enough so that he could bear it, and then he said, "As I said, she has given Lady Lillian her word about this come-out and finding a rich husband. I must needs hold up under it all and help in any way that I can. It would be more bearable if I did not know that Lady Sarah loves me as much as I love her."

William gave his brother a quizzical look but did not comment. Some things were better left unsaid, he thought, as he looked pityingly at his brother. Lord Chesterson was of the first water, as honorable a man as he had ever known. William said, "If I can help, please let me know, though I am as short in the pockets as you are. When do you plan on departing for London, now that the morning is most gone? Mayhap tomorrow?"

Nathan sat his empty cup on the bedside table and swung his long legs over the side of the bed. "I will leave shortly, and I think I shall take the twins with me. For some reason I cannot bear being alone in that big town house. Their company will help. Would you ask Nanny Bothwell to prepare them to leave straight away, and we'll take their tutor. I would not have my little ones get behind in their learning."

"That's a capital idea, Nathan. Children are a comfort."

Nathan did not miss the sadness in William's voice. How William and Georgena wanted children. His lordship almost felt guilty when he took the twins away from them, even for a short while. William now stood in the doorway, and Nathan said to him, "Thanks, brother, for the coffee, and thanks for listening to a lovesick old fool."

"You are not an old fool, and pray, don't give up. Something may turn up. Miracles do happen. Mayhap the hat business will save Merrymount . . . and the old woman as well."

"That might happen if there were more time," said Nathan. "If the Gypsy hats sell well, other styles could be developed. Lady Angeline is quite talented, I understand. But three months is not quite long enough for the hat business to make enough profit to save that big old house from the tax collectors and Lady Lillian from the money lenders. How foolish the old woman has been."

"I agree about Lady Lillian," replied William. "Georgena thinks 'tis a sure thing for the hat business. I shall be helping her as much as I can, driving her to Bath and to Brighton to leave hats on consignment. Last evening she was trying to think of an excellent modiste to make Lady Sarah's wardrobe for her come-out."

"Demme the come-out," swore Nathan. "I cannot forbear some nabob pawing the woman I love. And should it come to marriage to one of those rakes, by God, I will take her as my mistress. 'Tis done all the time when the marriage is one of convenience.

William shook his head. "I pray that it will not come to that," he said. A long pensive pause, and then, "I will go now to inform Nanny Bothwell."

After William's departure, Chesterson sat on the side of the bed, thinking about his lovely Sarah, wondering if she, like he, had slept late. How did she feel? Angry with him? He did not think so. Somehow he felt that she had reached out desperately for love, a love stolen from her. She had been a virgin but had not cried out in pain, and she had given herself to him so completely. A man could tell.

If she had been sorry, he told himself, she would have said so. He had walked with her as far as the stables. Instead, she had let him kiss her as if the kiss had to last forever, and she had kissed him in kind. He had watched until she entered Merrymount, his heart aching with loneliness the moment she left his side.

Realizing he could not spend the rest of the day reliving last night, Nathan stopped his roundaboutation and dressed quickly in a Weston blue superfine coat, a tan waistcoat, and camel-colored breeches. Lastly, he folded a pristine white cravat around his neck and, for a giddy moment, wondered if the London dandy Beau Brummell would approve. Thinking thus was better than dwelling on his pain.

He would skip breakfast, he decided, for he knew his crested carriage was waiting. How he hated not to be prompt. And how he hated to put distance between himself and Lady Sarah. Mayhap that was the reason he had this day been laggardly. Again, he let himself imagine her in his bed, sleeping late, her beautiful auburn curls splayed out onto her pillow, the cover turned back to reveal the white flesh of her bosom showing through her thin muslin nightdress, and again passion filled him.

He would send her flowers. No, that did not seem appropriate; he would send her a missive, sealed, of course, and in it he would reassure her of his undying love. From his writing desk, he took parchment and scrawled words from his heart onto it and then sealed it with a glob of wax, into which he pressed his crested ring. He could not tear her from his mind; his heart ached. He cursed Lady Lillian and her debts.

Nathan's swearing was abruptly interrupted by the twins bursting into his room, each competing for the first words, "Papa, Papa, we're so glad we're going to Town with you."

His lordship knelt on one knee and held his darling children close as he silently thanked God for them. Finally he released them. Stepping back, Laura asked, "Are you sad, Papa? Your eyes are all misty."

* * *

At Merrymount, Sarah was listening to Angeline's persistent questioning. "How many times did he kiss you? You were gone a very long time—"

"You were not supposed to wait up," Sarah said evasively. She did not want to talk with Angeline or with anyone else. Her mind was on Nathan and last night, Very tactfully she suggested that Angeline let her be. "Go to the workshop, sister, and leave me for a while. I must needs gather my thoughts—"

"Are you thinking of calling the whole thing off?"

"Calling what off?" Sarah asked.

"Your come-out, peagoose. Now that you know Lord Chesterson is as much in love with you as you are with him, why have the come-out? You have no need of but one husband."

They were in their bedchamber; the hour for rising long past. Angeline had eaten breakfast and had returned to see what was keeping Sarah, who was still in bed, the covers pulled up under her chin.

Sarah's voice was heavy with sleep. "Scoot, Angeline. Do not make me cross. When I'm ready, I shall come to help you and Georgena with the hats."

"Hilda is keeping your porridge warm," said Angeline.

She reluctantly quit the room. *Without finding out a whit of what went on,* she thought. She had been petitioning Wanna's Spirit to please stop this madness of Sarah marrying for convenience. She impatiently wished the Spirit would answer.

Left alone, Sarah, too, searched for an answer. She loved Nathan with all her heart, and she was not sorry for what happened. She had stolen a few moments of happiness, no, not just happiness but total ecstasy and the overpowering feeling of belonging completely to someone she loved. She would never have that if she made a convenient marriage. She could still feel Nathan's close-

ness. Would God strike her dead if she said she was not
sorry? She prayed not. Tears clouded her eyes, for she
knew that never again would Nathan hold her as he had
held her last night. He had said, "This must needs never
happen again."

She prayed that having lain with Nathan, having
known his wonderful love, would make it easier to pro-
ceed with her search for a rich husband. She was certain
that there were many girls who had never had even one
blissful night to remember.

Sarah felt her heart lighten. She even smiled when she
remembered Nathan telling her that should she be forced
to marry some nabob that he would take her as his mistress. " 'Tis done all the time," he had said, his hazel eyes
serious, as was the set of his chin.

Of course he had not meant it. Time would take care
of the pain, last night would grow dim in both their
memories, and each would go on with the life fate had
dealt them.

Knowing she had lingered too long in bed, Sarah threw
off the covers and went to the washbasin, splashing cold
water onto her face. As she stared at her reflection in the
looking glass, she noted that she appeared the same as
before she went to the cabin.

Only her heart had changed, she told herself; it no
longer belonged to her. She had given it to Lord Chesterson. Hurrying to finish her toilette, she quickly brushed
her hair and tied it at the nape, and then she donned a
blue wool day dress over her white pantalettes, lastly
slipping on black half-boots over thick stockings.

When Sarah entered the kitchen, Hilda was standing
by the stove and stirring the porridge. She bobbed.
"M'lady, I hope yer had a pleasant sleep."

Sarah could not help but smile. She had not yet
become accustomed to Hilda bobbing every time she
entered the room. But the English maid had refused to
stop, and Sarah had stopped telling her that it was entirely

unnecessary. "Thank you, Hilda," she said, "and please, only a small helping of porridge. I'm not the least hungry, but fear I shall be if I don't eat something."

"Mayhap a little beef, left over from last evening. Will give you strength. Ye must have been tired—"

"I'm not lacking in strength, Hilda," said Sarah. "Nor was I overly tired when I slept late. I have several things on my mind, one of which I would like to discuss with you."

"Oh, m'lady, what have I not been doing to suit you? Just tell me and I promise to try harder." The fright in the old servant's eyes touched Sarah's heart. As Hilda had once said, they had nowhere to go should they leave Merrymount. Sarah watched as she ladled porridge into a bowl, then adding milk and wild honey. After placing the bowl on the table, Hilda brought hot coffee in a fine china cup.

" 'Tis not that, Hilda," Sarah said. "You and John Wesley should have no concern about losing your place at Merrymount. But I must needs speak with you about Lady Lillian—"

"John Wesley is with her now, if that's your concern. They be in the small parlor. Her ladyship hardly wants to leave there, being that it's the place she can see them coming, the money men, I mean."

Sarah sat down at the long table and began eating the porridge. It tasted delicious, and she found that she was hungry after all. "This is wonderful, Hilda. Now, about Lady Lillian. Do you think her condition has improved— her madness, I mean—since the day the money lenders came and threatened to file charges? Lady Angeline believes Aunt Lillian is pretending to be mad. I wanted to ask you, since you are with her while we are working on the hats most of the day."

"M'lady, that old woman is mad as a hatter, she is. I keep my eye right on her, and she is living in the past, calling you Alice and ranting about you marrying a man without a feather to fly with. To your face, she is loving and kind, but mind yer, she's mighty riled because Lord Templeton didn't have blunt."

"Were you here then, Hilda?"

"No. Me and the mister came after your mama was married to your papa. She loved that man so, but that didn't make any difference to Lady Lillian. Since she couldn't find a rich husband for herself, she wanted your mama to find one. And she's still blaming her. Of course she's not going to show her anger to yer face. She ain't that mad."

"So now she wants me to do what she could not coerce Mama to do."

"I guess so, whatever thet word means." Hilda shook her head. "Every night I petition the Lord above to bring back Lady Lillian's senses, and mayhap He will someday. But now I'd say that Lady Angeline's wrong. Lady Lillian ain't puttin' on. As I said, she's mad as a hatter, and she's scared out of her wits. One day in debtor's prison would finish the poor thing."

"Thank you for sharing your opinion with me, Hilda, and thank you for keeping breakfast warm. I'll try not to be so late in the future."

Hilda bobbed. "My pleasure, m'lady."

Sarah rose from her chair and quit the kitchen. She did not this day want to work on the hats since she did not want to hasten the day of her move into London. Ascending the stairs, she came to the long corridor that led to the front of the house and decided that she should stop by the Warm Room and speak with Lady Lillian. Mayhap something she would say would trigger the old woman's memory. And then Sarah wondered what difference it made whether Lady Lillian lived in the past or the present. Either was equally gloomy.

Sarah's sister-in-law, Mary Ellen, came to mind, and suddenly Sarah was overcome with homesickness. Looking back, even dealing with her selfish brother Hoggie, her life had been somewhat peaceful. *But had I not come to Merrymount, I would not have met Nathan.*

That did not bear thinking on, and Sarah continued down the corridor, coming to the right door and pushing it open. Lady Lillian was crouched in front of the window, and John Wesley was sitting in a chair watching her.

When Sarah entered, Lady Lillian jerked her head around and beamed a huge smile at her. "Alice, I'm glad you're here. You won't let them take me, will you? I never worry when you are near me." She stood and held out her arms.

"No one is going to take you, Aunt Lillian," said Sarah, giving the old woman a hug. Her aunt was dressed in black from head to foot, and it seemed to Sarah that she had aged years since that fateful visit from the money lenders.

Letting Lady Lillian hold her in her arms, sorrow filled Sarah's heart, sorrow for herself, sorrow for her mad aunt. Hilda was right; there was no improvement in Lady Lillian's condition. Turning away, Sarah hurried from the room.

But instead of going to the workroom to make hats as she knew she was expected to do, she roamed aimlessly through Merrymount's long corridors, the spacious halls, the many bedchambers and withdrawing rooms, the great hall, and finally, the room that held her mother's wonderful portrait.

As Sarah stood staring up at the likeness of her mother, so much like herself, she realized that this had been what had drawn her to Merrymount. Not the big house, as she had thought. She had never known what it was like to suckle her mother's breast, to be held tightly by loving arms, and to be kissed by warm lips when tucked into bed. But she had remembered this wonderful portrait, the wonderful smile so full of love. Merrymount had been a fancy; the portrait, a longing for something which life had denied her, a mother's love.

She smiled up at the picture, saying aloud, "I am the age, twenty summers, at which you chose the path you would take. I'm glad you chose Papa. But, Mama, I have no choice. I could never be happy with Nathan knowing that our love had sent your sister to debtor's prison, no matter how foolish the old woman has been. She can hardly be blamed for letting Merrymount slide forever from her grasp and for borrowing money she knew she could never repay, even if there was not a drought. A woman is not supposed to know how to manage an estate. It is a man's world."

Sarah drew comfort from having spoken the words, but the void in her heart, the hopelessness of her love for Lord Chesterson, did not lessen. Turning her back on the portrait, she went hurriedly to help with the hats, and she did not answer when Angeline, who was in the workroom alone, enquired as to where she had been.

"You're in a strange mood, sister," said Angeline. Raising a quizzical eyebrow, she added, "I've never seen you like this."

Her voice showed genuine concern, and Sarah knew this was so. "I'm sorry, Angeline. I do not mean to worry you, but there is something bearing on my mind, something I must needs think through by myself."

"I understand," the girl said. "I've teased you a lot about your letting Lord Chesterson kiss you, and I'm sorry. I should know that you will always give any decision you make serious thought."

"Sometimes thinking and wishing does not make it so," said Sarah. "What do you wish me to do, stitch or cut?"

"Stitch, I guess," Angeline answered. "Have you not noticed that Georgena is not working? A messenger from Copthorne came for her, and he brought a missive for you."

Surprised, Sarah quickly asked, "Is something wrong at Copthorne?" She reached for the letter that Angeline had taken from her pocket and now held in her hand. *Lady*

Sarah Templeton was scrawled across the front of the envelope.

"It seems that Lord Chesterson is taking the twins into Town with him, and he sent for Georgena to tell them goodbye," explained Angeline. "She seemed anxious when she left.

"Nathan says she is terribly fond of the twins. I wonder why he's taking them—"

"Most likely because he couldn't take you," answered Angeline with alacrity, directing a huge smile at Sarah.

"You do like to fun me, don't you, Angeline?" Sarah said, and then she walked to the far end of the sewing room, where a small fire burned in the fireplace, sending out warmth and the smell of wood burning. She ripped the seal and took out the parchment. "Dearest Lady Sarah, I am leaving Copthorne this day for London, but I leave my heart at Merrymount with you. Take good care of it, my dearest, for no man will ever love you as I love you, more today than yesterday."

He had signed it simply "Nathan."

The message was clear to Sarah. Between yesterday and today was their precious night in the cabin, their stolen happiness. As the fire in the sewing room sputtered and the flames danced merrily, she held the missive close to her heart.

Chapter Fifteen

Lord Chesterson's crested carriage tooled through the turnpike gate at Hyde Park Corner and soon thereafter came to an abrupt stop in front of Storm's End, his handsome town house.

Storm's End—he had always wondered where it got its name—was located two doors from Apsley House, the town home of the Duke of Wellington. The excellent property had come to him with his earldom, and he was thankful for it, with one regret: Storm's End, like his country estate, was entailed. He would gladly sell the property and pay Lady Lillian's debts if that were possible.

The two days on the road from Copthorne had not offered a solution to his problem of Lady Sarah being lost to him forever, and his mind had been on little else.

The driver pulled the carriage under the Corinthian portico with huge white columns. In one of Nathan's prosperous years, he had had the four-story brownstone refaced with the white stone from Bath. He wished now he had saved the blunt that it cost him. But Naneen had wanted the facade to be white, and he could hardly be sorry that he had done it for her.

There was a small courtyard, and in the back, cobbled mews for the cattle and carriages. *Before Lady Sarah arrives, I must needs engage a coachman and grooms,* planned Nathan, remembering the need for her appearing to be prosperous. This caused him to grimace. Lady Lillian had been right; he indeed was as poor as a church mouse.

No footman appeared to let down the step, but before Nathan could open the door and alight, Copthorne's coachman, Garrick, hopped down off the box to do the honors, bowing from the waist and offering a hand to the nanny.

Nathan, refusing help, alighted and lifted the twins out, kissing them on the forehead before setting their feet to the hard surface of the driveway. Their little bodies were pliant. Tired, Nathan supposed, feeling guilty for having brought them because he needed the comfort of their presence in the empty town house. "Nanny Bothwell will take you inside," his lordship said to them.

Taking a small hand in each of hers, Nanny Bothwell promised hot chocolate and sugar cookies as soon as they had bathed and changed into fresh clothes.

Frederick, the twins' tutor, a Frenchman who had come to England to live at the outbreak of the Napoleonic wars, was the last to leave the carriage, along with an armful of books and tablets. His black quizzing glass swung from the wide lapel of his frock coat. A man of few words, he nodded to his lordship and quickly disappeared into the house to find the room near the nursery that was kept for him. For three years, with the exception of the time the children went to America to visit their maternal grandparents, he had lived wherever they lived.

Lessons were three hours each day, two in the morning, and one in the afternoon. He was also their riding instructor.

He thought they were wonderful children, and he treasured his position; therefore, he prayed that the crops on the estate would be bountiful, that Lord Chesterson would once again be deep in the pockets. He had never known a more deserving man than his lordship, he often told God in supplication.

Left alone with the driver, Chesterson thanked the coachman for the way he had handled the ribbons and for the speed with which he had gained London. On the morrow Garrick would return to Copthorne, for he was needed there to drive Georgena. "She will be going to Brighton, and to Bath, shortly," said Nathan.

"She be a nice lady," Garrick said, "and Mr. Adams, he's of the first water. I do hope this year the spring rains come."

"And I, too," said Chesterson.

Garrick left then to take the horses to the stables. Excellent quarters, with provisions, were available for his overnight stay. On the morrow he would return to Copthorne by public transportation.

Nathan watched him go. The weather had held nice for the journey into town, but now it threatened snow. The sky was overcast and the air smelled of moisture. He turned to enter the house and felt loneliness engulf him. The long great hall seemed much too large, too empty, the winding stairway so wide and so grand. Lady Sarah should be descending to meet him, her lovely face awash with light from the huge chandelier with its glistening prisms . . .

"Demme, stop," he scolded. Taking the highly polished steps two at a time, he reached the landing and turned right, toward his library. There, he lit the fire that had been laid, then poured himself a drink and began to cogitate while staring at the struggling, crackling flames.

Someway, somehow, he must needs come up with the blunt to keep his Sarah off the Marriage Mart.

He thought of White's, the only gentlemen's club to which he belonged. Mayhap at the gaming tables luck would smile on him. Then his lordship remembered the Gypsy hat, in its black silk box, that he was to present to Lady Arbuthnot. Later, he would call on her. *But that will only promote Lady Sarah's come-out . . .*

Nonetheless, he had given his word, he told himself,

and later, when he called on his friend, she greeted him with great enthusiasm, and with, one might gather from her actions, great devotion.

Brazenly she kissed him on the cheek and told him her dreadful mourning was over, that she was ready to receive his addresses.

She was a tall, comely woman, giving a commanding appearance, with sparkling eyes and wheat-colored hair pulled up into a bundle of curls atop her head. Recalcitrant wisps framed her oval face. Each earlobe was adorned with a sparkling diamond earbob.

Worth a fortune, thought Nathan.

That she was ready to receive his addresses came as a surprise to his lordship; he had never asked to pay his addresses. But he had befriended her when she lost her husband, and he had never made it clear that he wanted only friendship. Now, it seemed, he was to pay for the error.

" 'Tis excellent to see you, madam," he said in a formal tone.

"Stuff! Why so formal? You have always called me Elizabeth. As I told you, the dreadful mourning for that dreadful husband is over."

"I was quite fond of his lordship," Nathan hurriedly replied. "We rubbed well together in our work in the Parliament, and I thought he was most generous with you. I'm surprised to hear you refer to him as dreadful."

"Oh, he was most generous. Why else do you think I stayed with the old gaffer? It was an arranged marriage, dreadful, dreadful, dreadful, but, yes, very lucrative. My pockets are very deep now that the estate is settled. I received all but the entailed part, which went to God knows who. Some cousin or other that carried the Arbuthnot name. A silly law, but I care not about that." She gave a most seductive smile. "If you were my husband, m'lord, you would be very rich."

Nathan was so taken aback by this behavior that he

almost laughed. He had come to solicit her help with promoting the Louiezon Hats, but if he should make her a gift of the one he'd left in the carriage, she would misinterpret his intentions.

What a coil!

Well, there was nothing for it. He must needs clear up the matter straight away. Should he let it go, he just might be trapped into an engagement from which he would have to cry off, and that would not appear proper with his constituents, nor his associates in London. In truth, he would be disgraced. Society would cut him.

And what would Lady Sarah think?

He cleared his throat and said, "Lady Arbuthnot, I am in no way anxious to marry. As you know, Naneen has not been gone—"

"Stuff! She's been gone three years, and I know you are in poor straits financially, and I have the blunt."

"I would never marry a woman for blunt. You know that. I believe love should have top priority." And then his voice became as firm as if he were speaking in Parliament. "I do not love you, my dear Elizabeth, and that is that. I do not want a marriage of convenience. I would like to keep your friendship, however."

Suddenly, his lordship wanted to turn and run.

Her ladyship laughed. The corners of her mouth turned impish. "I wager you will change your mind."

Before Nathan could answer, she stepped to the sideboard and poured brandy into a crystal glass and handed it to him, and then she poured herself one as if the conversation had never taken place. She smiled at him over the rim of the glass. "So, 'tis settled. You are not in the mood to marry at the moment, so we shall be friends, as before. As a friend, what can I do for you?"

Nathan did want to keep her as a friend, and he chose to believe she had been funning him about marriage. Sitting, she motioned to a handsome chair, and he went and sat down.

They were in an elegant receiving room on the first floor of her brownstone town house, located near Berkeley Square. The room, Nathan noted, was an excellent backdrop for her ladyship, very stylishly done in delicate mauve and pink, accented with pale green, colors that complemented her wheat-colored hair and ivory complexion.

"Would you stay for supper?" she asked.

"Thank you, no," Nathan said. "In truth, I came to ask a favor of you."

His lordship had decided that he would be nothing but straightforward with this woman. He would not make her a gift of the hat but would ask her outright if she would promote the Louiezon Hats with the *ton*.

After telling her about the Parisian-styled hats, he said, "The representative of the company can be reached through the post office in Corby. A percentage of the profit will be paid to you . . . and all you have to do is walk down Bond Street wearing the Gypsy hat, with your abigail carrying the handsome black silk hatbox.

" 'Twould be excellent advertisement, and I wager that every lady of quality in London would be clamoring for one. But I must warn you, the supply is limited. Only a few can be had by ordering from the representative in Corby."

"Oh, I must needs see the hat before I could make such an arrangement," said her ladyship, suddenly showing great interest. "What if I should look an ogre in it? I'm very particular about my appearance, now that I am husband-hunting."

Nathan rose and set down his brandy glass, still half-full, on the sideboard. Excusing himself, he went to his carriage. The box was in the boot. Hurriedly he retrieved it and returned to present it to her ladyship.

A big sigh filled the room when the lid was lifted to reveal the wide-brimmed hat with tall curly plumes of deep purple, gold, and deep green.

Nathan regretted that he had been prevented from making a gift of the hat to his friend, and when she appeared to be on the verge of the vapors, he reached to take her arm, then thought better of it. Quickly he dropped his hand to his side. "I take it that you are pleased, madam."

"Pleased! Oh, m'lord, 'tis the most gorgeous hat I have ever seen! Every milliner in Town will be clamoring to handle these things, especially since they are from Paris." She ran to a long, gilt-framed looking glass and placed the huge hat on her head.

The crown was high enough to accommodate the bundle of curls, Nathan noticed, and it showed her oval face to advantage. Again she let out a deep sigh. Resting his arm on the mantel, he watched with great interest. Having never considered her exactly beautiful, he thought the hat very becoming, and said so. "Will you agree to the business arrangement I presented?"

"Business arrangement! I do not need your paltry percentage. I must needs have three of these gorgeous creations. Whoever is the designer? What's the price? Never mind, I will pay—"

"Two hundred pounds each."

"Two hundred pounds? Are you daft? Oh, never mind. I keep forgetting how deep in the pockets my dear husband left me."

She turned to quit the room, but Nathan stopped her with, "The supply is limited. I fear you must needs be happy with the one you are wearing. And the only information you are to give out is that an order can be placed to Louiezon Hats, via the post office in Corby."

"Why the secrecy? I should think the company would be anxious for London trade. I'm sure any milliner in Town—"

"The worst thing that could happen is for the market to be flooded with Gypsy hats. And should a milliner try to copy the design, he or she would be promptly sued."

This had just occurred to Nathan, and he hoped a threat passed on by her ladyship would be sufficient. It would not do for Lady Angeline to apply for a patent, thus revealing that the hats had been made at Merrymount, Rockingham, in Northamptonshire, England.

The hat business with his friend finished, his lordship became anxious to leave. Her comportment had been quite unsettling; therefore, although she begged him to stay for a repast, as soon as she had passed the two hundred pound note to him, he begged to be excused. He received his greatcoat and top hat from the butler and left quickly, glad that her ladyship was so preoccupied with her new hat that she had, so it seemed, forgotten her pursuit of him as her next husband. Once outside, he took a great gulp of fresh air.

It had begun to snow, the sky was leaden, and twilight hovered over the city. The gaslights were being lighted by the lamplighter.

Nathan's black horse, hitched to a black tilbury, was tethered to a post outside Lady Arbuthnot's brownstone. His lordship rubbed the horse's neck while speaking gently and unloosening the leather wrapped around the post. Then he jumped into the tilbury and headed for White's. It was not so much that he wanted to gamble or even have a drink with a friend, but he wanted to see what had been going on in Town during his absence.

It was a known fact that one's club was headquarters for political goings-on, and it was for this reason that Nathan retained his membership. Two days hence, the House of Lords would convene, and he wanted to test the political climate.

Lord Chesterson was a member of the Tory Party, which had been intent on prosecuting the war with undiminished vigor, whereas the Whigs had been divided in their aims. His lordship was convinced that without Tory support, Wellington's army in the Peninsula might have failed and Napoleon might have never been defeated. As it was, the British and their allies were the masters of Europe.

But the war was behind them, Nathan told himself as he tooled toward St James's Street where White's was located.

Since the troublesome war had ended, his lordship had taken up the cause of unjust labor laws pertaining to children. It was unconscionable to him that a young boy could be whipped in order to force him to climb into a chimney. Sometimes the lad got stuck and had to be pulled down, losing part of his tender skin. And there was no law against this transgression.

It was not a popular cause, and not one the *ton* wished to acknowledge existed, but his lordship knew that it did, and he was determined to see that something was done about it. He thought of his own little children and thanked God that he had always been able to provide for them, though sometimes meagerly. He'd seen girls no older than Laura pushing flower carts, and he knew for a fact that girls, sometimes as young as four years, were allowed to work in factories on the East Side.

But the *ton* lived in Mayfair, the West Side. There were no factories there; therefore, they did not exist.

"Children should be in school," he said aloud, lifting the whip and cracking it over the black horse's back, listening then to the fast clop-clop of hooves against the cobbled street. The horse whinnied and snorted, throwing high his head, as if he knew he was showing his stuff. Lights appeared in windows of the handsome houses they passed.

I would not be going to White's if Lady Sarah were at Storm's End, thought Chesterson, and again his mind returned to Merrymount, and the future. How hopeless it was. The three months the money lenders had allowed Lady Lillian were flying by with lightning speed. The Gypsy hats would afford a come-out for Sarah, but it would not pay Lady Lillian's debts. The fact remained that Sarah must needs find a rich husband. "Dear, merciful God, provide a way to prevent that from happening," prayed Nathan, meaning it with all his heart. He brought the black horse to a stop in front of White's, and after giving the ribbons to a waiting boy, he shook the snow from his top hat and entered the grand club. How he wished he were in Northamptonshire in the old hunting cabin, with a single lighted candle and the flames from the fire casting shadows on a worn and faded rug.

With Lady Sarah.

Lord Chesterson felt a pricking at the back of his eyes. He thought of her lovely green eyes, trusting him so completely. He could feel the way her mouth softened when he kissed her, how silky her tongue had felt under his, the way her untutored body arched to meet his thrusts, and he swore under his breath. He could not, would not, let her belong to another man in that way. By all that was holy, God had given her to him.

"Good evening, m'lord," a voice said, and Chesterson found himself looking blankly at a liveried footman who was reaching to take his coat and top hat. He wasn't in the cabin with Lady Sarah; he was here, in a gentlemen's club whose stately grandeur would take one's breath away.

Chapter Sixteen

"I wonder if Lord Chesterson has seen Lady Arbuthnot?" Sarah said, more to herself than to Angeline. Standing before the looking glass while brushing her auburn curls, she studied her features. Since the night in the cabin with Nathan, she had become a stranger to herself. Until then her appearance was something she had taken for granted. Now it was very important. Never in her life had she been so cognizant of what others called her "beauty." Her face was round, and her green eyes *did* sparkle when she smiled.

Laughter bubbled up inside Sarah. She even had small ears.

"Are you jealous of Lady Arbuthnot?" asked Angeline.

"Of course not," Sarah said, knowing it was a lie. Jealousy was her constant companion, especially now that his lordship was in Town and she so far away at Merrymount. And she was quite angry. Why did doubt have to set in and keep her awake half the night? She should be thinking about the rich husband who would soon be a reality.

But the thought of thrusting herself onto the Marriage Mart sent Sarah's head spinning and her stomach churning. More and more of late she had fought to push the ugly thoughts from her mind, and more and more it was there for her to think about.

Angeline spoke. "Well, I'll wager every *ton* lady in Town is after him, and their mamas, too."

"You're a lot of help," retorted Sarah, giving one last brush to her hair before tying it back with a riband. She had promised to go ice fishing with Angeline. Another blizzard had blown in, and the pond was frozen solid. But she had no desire to go skating . . . without Lord Chesterson.

"Are you ever going to finish your toilette?" asked Angeline.

"I'm ready, but I think we are daft to be going ice fishing. Why not wait until summer to go fishing, when it is warm?"

"We may not be at Merrymount come summer," said Angeline, her tone sad.

"You like it here, don't you, Angeline?"

"I like the woods, the wonderful fresh air. I wish things were different. You had such high hopes when we left America."

Sarah was silent for a long moment. "I know, and I will admit to disappointment, but one can't give up."

"Yes, I know, sister, one has to do what one must do . . . like marry a nabob to save an old woman who thinks of no one but herself." The sarcasm was blatant in Angeline's words.

"Come on," said Sarah, trying to lighten the mood. "This day will be a happy day. Thank goodness that you and John Wesley did a lot of wood gathering before this blizzard came. I believe 'tis worse than the first one."

For three days they had been confined to the manor house, mostly in the Warm Room with a blazing fire, while the wind keened, sleet peppered the windows, and ice gathered on the tree limbs, making the world appear to be one big white ball. Beyond the ridge on which Merrymount sat, scudding mist clouds, in varying shades of gray, swelled up from the valley.

"I'm ready," Sarah told Angeline. "But first I must needs check on Lady Lillian."

Poor dear, she thought, when she saw her aunt crouched before the window, staring at the gatehouse and the portcullis. In a very low voice, almost a whisper, Sarah cautioned Hilda to keep a close eye on her. "She might wander out into the freezing weather."

Hilda bobbed. "I promise I won't let the poor dear out of my sight, m'lady.

Dressed in the warmest clothes they had, Sarah and Angeline then left the house and were soon on the footpath that led through the woods, both thankful that the strong wind had diminished its wrath.

Sarah had never been ice fishing. She remembered Angeline's mother taking her daughter, but they had never invited her, Sarah, along. She hadn't minded. She had sensed that it was a special time for mother and daughter. Sarah looked at Angeline and smiled. She had an ugly wool bonnet—probably a castoff of Hilda's, Sarah thought—pulled down as far as it would go around her face. Hanging down her back was the heavy plait of black hair. In her hands she carried two one-gallon pails in which there were strings attached to fish hooks and some awful-smelling bait. She had given Sarah a pick to carry, saying, "To chip the ice. I have extra string in my breeches' pocket. We'll string the fish until we are ready to—"

A flush of horror washed over Sarah's face. "Don't say it! I refuse to kill a fish."

Angeline laughed. "You would not survive long in the woods, should you get lost."

"I hope I'm never lost in the woods."

And so the conversation went. Since coming to Merymount, the bond between Sarah and her sister had been forged as never before, and Sarah was thankful for it. She missed Mary Ellen, her sister-in-law, and wondered again why she had not received a reply to her letter. It had been weeks since she had sent the missive. And she had not received the stipend from Hoggie. There were times, like now, with Nathan so far away, that Sarah felt utterly homesick for Templeton Hall. But not for her brother Hoggie.

If things at Merrymount were as I envisioned—

"But they are not, and that is that," Sarah said in a very low voice.

"Are you talking to yourself, sister? Why not share your thoughts with me? I'm a good listener."

"I was thinking about Templeton Hall. Do you ever feel homesick, Angeline?"

"Only for Mama and Papa, but never Hoggie. I'm much happier here with you. And with mad Lady Lillian. Mayhap we should get old King George out here with her. They would make a good pair, both mad as hatters."

"Angeline!" scolded Sarah, but laughing. "If you were truthful, you would admit fondness for our Aunt Lillian—"

"Your aunt, not mine." Angeline smiled. "I do feel a small attachment. Mama always said to never judge a man until you've walked a mile in his moccasins, and I've never walked in Lady Lillian's moccasins. It's just that I don't like what she is doing to you."

"I keep praying that something will happen."

"Like Lady Lillian wandering out into the cold and catching her death? Then they couldn't take her to prison. And the taxpayers could take Merrymount, and we could . . ."

Sarah only heard the part about Lady Lillian catching her death. Her voice was sharp. "Angeline, I will not have you talk that way. The Lord will not smile on you if you have a selfish heart."

"Stuff! He's already smiled on me aplenty when He made me your sister. Mama said that, and she just knew that He guided her to Templeton Hall when she was looking for work. She loved Papa dearly."

"I know she did, Angeline," said Sarah pensively.

By now they were at the pond, and Angeline was digging a hole in the ice which, Sarah thought, must be solid at least twelve inches down. She sat on one of the gallon pails, turned upside down, and when Angeline announced the hole ready for fishing, Sarah dangled a string with hook and bait on its end into the water. A short distance away, Angeline was making another hole.

She was only doing this silly thing to appease Angeline, Sarah told herself, wanting to hook a fish and get it over with.

"I'll just wager that Hilda can fry fish that will melt in your mouth," said Angeline.

"Will you not speak of fried fish—"

This amused Angeline. How tender-hearted Sarah was. Angeline was becoming more and more concerned about the coming days when Sarah would be in London. Already a modiste had come to Merrymount to measure for the gowns and other necessities Sarah would need for her come-out. And on Sarah's insistence, Angeline's measurements had been taken as well. Georgena had written the modiste and suggested she come to Merrymount, and when she came, Sarah was honest with her, saying, "We are anticipating money, but as of now, there is none with which to pay you."

"I will take my chances," the lady had said.

Sarah had not told her that they were depending on the Gypsy hats to finance the new wardrobe and other expenses as well.

"I wonder how Georgena and William are doing in Brighton and Bath. I do hope it is not this cold there." Angeline paused. "Sarah, I pray the hats sell."

"Of course they will, Angeline. They are so beautiful. You have wonderful talent."

"The time is drawing near when you'll be leaving for London, if the money comes in."

"What do you mean, when *I* will be leaving for London? You are going with me. Within a year or two, you will be having your come-out."

"No, I won't be going, Sarah. Before Lady Lillian lost her senses, she told you that I would be a hindrance."

"Balderdash! You are going with me to London. I would not think of going without you."

Just then Sarah felt a hard jerk on her string, and by instinct she held on tighter, feeling the fish flopping about in the water, and it was not until he settled that Sarah pulled the spotted fish through the hole. She felt her heart pounding.

Angeline squealed and came to take the hook from the fish's mouth. "Sarah, I'm sure you caught the winner, and I don't even have my hook in the water."

They fished for two hours until midafternoon, and Sarah did not even feel the cold. Time and again she pulled a fish from the water, and that night, no one enjoyed the fish supper more than she did. Husband-hunting was the last thing on her mind as she asked for a second helping of fish and more of the wonderful corn cakes Hilda had made.

But later, husband-hunting came back to Sarah with surprising force. Angeline had, because the room had turned so cold, crawled into the narrow bed with Sarah. Into the room's stillness, Angeline whispered, "I wager Lord Chesterson misses you as much as you miss him."

Sarah wanted to throttle her. "I doubt that," she said, "but let's not speak of it. We must needs get some sleep."

Angeline became quiet, and Sarah stared at the ceiling while she relived the night in the cabin. Tears made the darkness in the room darker. Angeline's even breathing indicated sleep, and the quietness in the room deepened.

How I wish I could be with Nathan forever, Sarah thought, forcing her eyes to close, willing sleep to come.

But when wishing did not make it so, Sarah slipped from the bed and went to the window, kneeling and looking out into the winter night. Stars sparkled in the velvet sky, and a half-moon shone down on the white earth. Looking to the heavens, a prayer formed in her heart, which she whispered out into the enveloping stillness, "Please, God, provide a way . . ."

A week passed before the post delivered missives from Mary Ellen and from John Jay Elwood, the Templeton solicitor. She was ecstatic when she saw a third missive, stamped in London. Although she was most anxious to read the news from America, she ran to her bedchamber and locked the door behind her. The last thing she needed was Angeline's questions about the missive from Lord Chesterson.

Throwing herself onto her narrow bed, Sarah ripped the waxed seal into which was indented the Chesterson crest and began reading:

> My dearest Sarah,
> I have become quite busy in London. Sitting in the House of Lords, often speaking my piece, is challenging, but I still have time to think of you. God's truth, my darling, you are never far from my thoughts. I pray each night for a solution to our problem, and I envision you doing the same. It seems that it will take intervention from a higher power if you are to become my wife, instead of my mistress.
> I am serious, my love, when I say that if a solution cannot be found to your aunt's indebtedness and you are forced to wed to save the old woman from prison, I will take you for my mistress, if you are willing. My love for you is undiminished by this thought, and I believe that in the sight of God you would be my true wife, for there should be no other reason for marriage other than love, of which my heart is overflowing for you.

I have done everything possible here, even going to the money lenders in Charges Street to borrow against what personal property I own. Regretfully I found that would not be nearly enough. Interest on the money Lady Lillian borrowed has grown by leaps and bounds. A good friend offered a loan. Again, that was far short.

When I went to Lady Lillian's lenders to enquire about the amount of the loan, I attempted to retrieve your pearls. The thieving scoundrels denied having them, said they had been sold, but would not say to whom. I regret this infinitely.

The time is drawing near when you will be in London. I think of this with great trepidation but also with the feeling of great happiness of having you in proximity, where I can touch your hand and look into those beautiful green eyes. I relive the time in the cabin . . .

The signature was a simple N.

Lying on her back, Sarah felt tears stinging her eyes and then suddenly they were spilling out to dampen the pillow beneath her head. Sentimental tears, she mused, for she was filled with happiness as she hugged the letter to her throbbing breast.

Somehow Nathan would find a way for them to marry. Sarah refused to think of the alternative.

Just then a knock resounded on the door. Sarah smiled. Who else could it be but Angeline? Quickly Sarah lifted the feather mattress and slipped Nathan's missive under it, and then she went to unlock the door.

"Why are you locked in?" the girl asked, not reproachfully. "Is something wrong, sister?"

"No. Quite the opposite. I received missives and wanted privacy when I read them."

"I'm sorry I intruded." Angeline turned to go.

"Oh, no, Angeline. Don't be a peagoose. I want you to

hear what Mary Ellen and the Templeton solicitor have
to say."

Angeline's face brightened. "At last a letter from Mary
Ellen. I hope she's left that selfish Hoggie." She hopped
onto her bed and sat cross-legged while Sarah, on the
opposite bed, read:

> Dearest Sisters,
> How far away you seem. But I will not dwell on
> that. Your missive was received with gratitude, and,
> Sarah, I hope Lady Lillian has stopped planning a
> convenient marriage for you. At least I can say that
> when I married, I was in love with Hoggie.
> Which brings me to my greatest news. I am *en-
> ceinte*. The baby, and I pray a boy, will be born nine
> months from the day the two of you departed Amer-
> ica. In my desolation, I seduced Hoggie. A bottle of
> good wine helped.
> I hope you do not think this trickery, Sarah, but
> you know how I want a child to love, and, too, since
> Hoggie has avowed to disinherit you and Angeline,
> I must needs produce an heir to the Templeton
> land.
> "Hoggie has announced for the Senate, and in
> private he talks incessantly of the Presidency when
> Monroe's term comes to an end. The President is
> often at Templeton Hall.

The letter went on about trivial things. It was only at
the end of the letter that Mary Ellen again mentioned
coming to Merrymount. She had enclosed a few dollars—
from her teaching salary—and this made Sarah very
weepy.

Dear, dear Mary Ellen, Sarah thought.

"I think Hoggie should be shot at sunrise," said Angeline, making Sarah laugh.

"You are always wanting to shoot someone, Angeline,

when in truth you wouldn't hurt a flea. I noticed you took the fish to John Wesley to have them dressed for cooking."

Angeline smiled. "Only because 'tis so messy cleaning fish."

Sarah opened the solicitor's letter and was relieved to see that it contained a ten-pound note, which, he explained, would be a semi-annual payment. Twenty pounds a year, she calculated, and thinking to herself that no matter how bad things were at Merrymount, she was glad she had left Templeton Hall. And she was especially glad she had brought Angeline.

The solicitor also expressed that he had welcomed the news that everything was wonderful at Merrymount. "The day that you were in my office, Sarah, I had an unexpected premonition that you would find things terribly wrong at Merrymount. I am so happy that I was wrong," he said, and then he had signed off with an apology for not having secured more assistance from Hoggie Templeton.

Sarah handed the money to Angeline. "When you and John Wesley go into Rockingham, buy staples for the kitchen. Hilda will give you the list. I noticed that she fixed corn cakes for breakfast, and lately there's been no scones with the tea. I'm sure she is out of flour."

"I have some of the money from my necklaces."

"That is the capital for your business."

"One must eat." Angeline paused. "Besides, if orders don't come in soon, we most likely will be eating Gypsy hats."

"You let me worry about that," said Sarah. She forced a smile, "You just keep busy worrying about who deserves to be shot at sunrise."

As Angeline rose to go, she said, " 'Tis wonderful news that Mary Ellen will soon have a baby."

"I couldn't be happier for her." Sarah, looking at her

sister, asked, "Angeline, do you know what *seduced* means?"

"Of course I do. I've seen female cats squat and moan when in heat. Of course the tomcat would come running to hop on her. That's a pretty good example of seduction. Except I'm sure Mary Ellen was more refined in her approach."

Sarah was amazed. It wasn't difficult to mother Angeline; the girl had learned the facts of life from watching farm animals mate.

Angeline continued: "I pray Mary Ellen's baby doesn't look or act like Hoggie." She crammed the ten-pound note into the bosom of her red wool dress that fell straight from her shoulders to the top of her half-boots. "I'll speak to Hilda now."

"I would appreciate it," said Sarah, anxious to be alone. After Angeline had quit the room, Sarah retrieved Nathan's letter from under the feather mattress and read it again. It was the sweetest letter she had ever received— well, it was the first love letter she had ever received—but it was wonderfully grand, she told herself, and then she thought of what was missing.

His lordship had not mentioned his special friend, Lady Arbuthnot, who was to help promote the Gypsy hats.

Chapter Seventeen

When another week had gone by and no orders had come in for the hats in the workroom, Sarah began to worry. After the weather had cleared, John Wesley and Angeline had gone to Corby three times making enquiries at the post office, coming back to report that the postmaster looked at Angeline as if she were queer in the head. "I ain't never heard of Louiezon Hats," he declared with great emphasis.

Georgena and William returned to Copthorne, reporting that the hats had been well-received in the fashionable shops they had called on in Brighton and Bath. They had left two on consignment.

But no orders had come in.

Sarah began to count the days left in the three-month extension the money lenders had given Lady Lillian, and she sank deeper into the desponds.

She wrote to Nathan, expressing her concern. She did not write of what was in her heart, that he was on her mind day and night. It would only make what she had to do worse, she rationalized, and spoke only of business. "My wardrobe is being made, and there is no blunt to pay the modiste. I was so sure the hats would sell . . ."

Angeline talked hardly at all. She spent much of her time in the workroom secretly poring over the Parisian magazines, *La Belle Assemblée* and *The Lady's Magazine*, and designing other hats. She had put her heart and soul into the Gypsy hats, and if they did not sell, then perhaps another design would.

She read the editorial comments: "High Life" and "Fashionable Chit-Chat," "Continental Notes." She found them amusing, but she could not believe that women of quality were actually wearing transparent muslin gowns. They must needs be light skirts of the first order, she decided, and she learned a new word, *plumassier,* which meant a man who furnished plumes and feathers for hats. She learned about the subscription balls on Wednesday evenings at Almack's, and she laughed when she read that the Duke of Wellington had been turned away from the exclusive temple of the *ton* because he was not wearing the proper attire. How could they do that to such a man of such high standing?

All of this was fascinating to Angeline; she wanted to learn more, and she began to be glad that Sarah wanted her to go to London, which, she decided, was a whole new world from Merrymount. His Grace, the Duke of Wellington, lived at Apsley House, the first large mansion at the beginning of the built-up area beyond the Hyde Park Corner Turnpike. She wondered where Lord Chesterson lived, and she wondered if she and Sarah would ever see that other world, which, as she read and reread the magazines, had become more and more fascinating to her. Why could she not open a millinery shop on Bond Street?

This thought made Angeline laugh sardonically. What made such an idea come into her head when those women of quality refused to buy her Gypsy hats? Every day her spirits sank lower. She even cried when she thought about Lady Lillian being carted off to debtor's prison, even though the old woman, being so self-centered, most likely deserved to go. And Angeline cried when she thought of Sarah having to marry for convenience. *What a coil!*

Only when Angeline was with Sarah did Angeline

smile. The days dragged by. The trips to Corby became less frequent.

And then one day, soon after breakfast, John Wesley went to Corby alone. Angeline refused to go, thinking, but not saying, that she could not forbear another sneering smile from the hateful postmaster. "No, there are no missives for Louiezon Hats," he would say, his thick gray eyebrow arched almost to the top of his forehead, while a smart smile showed his toothless gums. It made Angeline's stomach turn inside out.

"You go to Corby, John Wesley," she said. "I really don't feel like going."

So she spent the day in the workroom, designing more hats, even cutting and stitching a lovely turban which she understood the dowagers wore to balls held at Almack's Assembly Rooms.

Outside, the weather, although cold, was bright and sunny. Normally she would be romping with Cain and Abel, but this day she only wanted to be alone, and when Sarah came to the workroom, Angeline hid her sketches under the worn and tattered *La Belle Assemblée* and *The Lady's Magazine*. She did not want Sarah to know that she had given up on the Gypsy hats.

Sarah didn't notice, nor did she notice the worried frown on Angeline's brow. She had news of her own. "Angeline, I believe Lady Lillian's mind is returning to normal. Just now she called me Lady Sarah and asked if I was enjoying my stay at Merrymount. Her mind isn't completely clear, but there's definite improvement. She took the hounds out for a romp, with Hilda, of course. Hilda has been faithful in her care through this whole ordeal, and I'm grateful for that."

"Did you tell her that most likely your stay at Merrymount would be short-lived? Poor thing. If she's doomed to debtor's prison, it would almost be better if her mind would stay addled."

"Oh, Angeline, don't be so gloomy just because there

have been no orders for the hats. It takes time for a business to catch on."

"Time is not what we are blessed with," replied Angeline.

Sarah was quiet for a moment. She sat on a stool across the worktable from Angeline. At the end of the long table, lined up in perfect order, were the seventeen hats, left to be sold at two-hundred pounds each. *Mayhap they are overpriced.*

"Aren't you pleased with the news about Lady Lillian?" asked Sarah, who could see that to talk of the hats would only deepen Angeline's desponds. "I've been worried sick about her."

"Like I said, if the old woman's bound for debtor's prison . . ."

"Oh, Angeline, stop it. 'Tis not like you to be in the desponds. I look to you for hope. Orders for the hats will come."

"It has been weeks, and not one order has been received."

Sarah went to put her arms around Angeline, for the young girl had begun to sob. "I've failed you, Sarah," said Angeline. "I just thought the hats would sell."

"I wager that John Wesley will bring a fistful of orders when he returns. Now stop your sobbing and let's go for a repast. Hilda is frying more of our fish, and there's hot bread. We have a lot to be thankful for, Angeline."

Angeline acquiesced, but not joyfully. It was not until late in the afternoon that her mood brightened. A jubilant John Wesley bounded into the Warm Room, gave a half-bow, and then, smiling from ear to ear, handed five missives to Angeline, saying, "The old jackanapes weren't so high and mighty today, even asked me what a Louiezon Hat looked like. I told him they were only for the upper orders, a limited supply, and there was no reason for him to know."

Angeline squealed with delight. "Oh, I wish I had been

there. I would have given him the same kind of sneering smile he's been giving us."

"I finally told him they were Parisian hats, but I didn't tell him they were made right here at Merrymount. No need for him or anybody to know." The houseman was still wearing a big smile when he quit the room.

Angeline turned to give the orders to Sarah. "Here, sister, you open them. 'Tis beyond bearing."

Sarah was laughing, and Lady Lillian was looking on in puzzlement, her faded eyes filled with tears. " 'Tis orders for the Gypsy hats, Aunt Lillian," Sarah told her, as she ripped one envelope after another open. Four contained two-hundred pound notes, and the other, addressed in Nathan's handwriting, held the note from Lady Arbuthnot and a short missive from Nathan: "I did not make a gift of the hat to her ladyship. She was happy to pay the price, and she promised to help promote the Louiezon Hats. She is going on in society now, and I expect orders for the remaining hats to pour into the Corby post office."

In another vein, he had added, "I am readying my London residence for your arrival. Today I hired an excellent butler by the name of Gifford. I haven't forgotten that an appearance of considerable blunt is necessary for a successful come-out."

Other than the reference to Sarah's come-out, his lordship said nothing personal to Sarah, but she was so happy to see Angeline smiling that she refused to be concerned and dismissed it from her mind. For the moment. Later that night, after Angeline had stopped gleefully extolling the success of the Gypsy hats and had dropped off to sleep, Sarah retrieved Nathan's letter from under her feather mattress and read it again. She did not need to light a candle. A swath of moonlight cut across the room. She hardly needed that, for she knew the words by heart, and she felt tears fill her eyes when she came to the part that meant more to her than all the rest. Hugging the missive to her, she whispered into the night, "I relive the time in the cabin . . ."

The words comforted Sarah; Nathan loved her, she told herself, and soon she drifted off to sleep, only to dream of his lordship and Lady Arbuthnot riding in Hyde Park during what she had heard called, "the five o'clock squeeze," when all the pures and the impures went to see and be seen. In Sarah's dream, Lady Arbuthnot wore the Gypsy hat she had purchased from his lordship.

Since Chesterson had made it perfectly clear to Lady Arbuthnot that he was not interested in becoming leg-shackled to her, he felt comfortable in accepting her invitation to ride in the park at five o'clock. And, too, he had had a wearing day. For two hours he had debated in the House of Lords for the passage of a law to protect England's children from being forced to work as climbing boys, cleaning chimneys too narrow for their bodies and ruining their lungs by inhaling the black accumulation of soot that clung to the bricks. His mind and thoughts could bear a change. He longed for Sarah in such a painful way that at times he thought he must needs be losing his mind. In desperation, he even thought of marrying Lady Arbuthnot. Had she not offered him unlimited blunt if he would agree to marry her, thus putting him in the position of paying Lady Lillian's debts and possibly saving Merrymount from the Crown's tax collectors?

These desperate thoughts came to his lordship late at night when sleep evaded him. But in his waking hours he was ashamed. Nonetheless, the solution—if it could be called that—returned to him again and again.

It would save Lady Sarah from making a convenient marriage, he thought more than once, and he readily admitted that should he save her from making that convenient marriage, he would not be forced to suffer the agony of her belonging to another man in the Biblical sense. *That* he could not forbear. But could Lady Sarah forbear his belonging to Lady Arbuthnot in the Biblical sense?

God's truth, Nathan admitted, he was miserably in love.

"Why the gloom?" Lady Arbuthnot asked as the crested carriage tooled toward Hyde Park. She was dressed to the nines in a carriage dress only unlimited funds could buy, Nathan thought, noticing also that the purple silk matched the highest plume in her Gypsy hat.

It did not take long for the hat to draw the attention of the *ton* ladies. Even Harriett Wilson, the infamous demi-rep, enquired, "Where did you get the magnificent hat?"

" 'Tis a Louiezon," answered Lady Arbuthnot. "And they are not readily available. I had an inside source."

"You must tell me. I will pay any price."

But Lady Arbuthnot demurred, and later she told Nathan that she certainly did not want *that* woman to own a hat that faintly resembled the gorgeous hat she was wearing.

"But you must needs spread the word that a limited number of the Gypsy hats are available through a representative in Corby at two-hundred pounds each. The Louiezon Company is quite anxious to dispose of the available hats."

"I agree with you, Nathan, but I shall pick and choose those whom I wish to have one. Did you not say that no two are alike? I would die of mortification should there be another like mine."

"I assure you that yours was the prettiest of the lot. I picked it myself, knowing the colors which most become you."

"Oh, m'lord, how perfectly divine of you. I know I must be special to you, else why would you be bent on choosing the most handsome of the hats for poor little me? You can deny your feelings, if that is your wont, but I can see it there in your blazing hazel eyes. You are fond of me, and, trust me, that fondness will grow. I've been

thinking that mayhap a loan of considerable amount
would help you, since you are set against marriage—"

"I would not ask for a loan without knowing I could
repay—"

"Stuff! If you never repaid it, I would still have more
than I can spend in a lifetime. You must needs not forget
that my late husband was one of the wealthiest men in
England."

Chesterson felt a shiver run down his spine, or, as the
old saying went, he felt someone walk over his grave.
Clearly Lady Arbuthnot was trying to trap him into marriage. If he could not repay the loan, no doubt he would
be given the choice of marriage to her ladyship or debtor's
prison. His answer was quick. "One good crop will put
me deep in the pockets. A loan will not be necessary."

He then said a silent prayer that the rains would come
this year and that the crops would be bountiful.

Suddenly he wanted to be away from this woman. How
could he have ever thought of becoming leg-shackled to
her? Even to save Lady Sarah from making a convenient
marriage. There must needs be a better way. Leaning his
head out the window, he gave the driver office to turn the
carriage around and return her ladyship to her home.
The ride had served its purpose, he told himself. Enough
ton women had seen the Louiezon Gypsy hat. No doubt
the orders would be flowing in to the Corby post office.

Chapter Eighteen

When Lady Lillian did not come down for breakfast, Sarah went to her bedchamber, knocked lightly on the door, and when there was no answer, she opened the door and went quickly in. It was then that she knew the old woman had recovered completely from her madness. Propped up in bed, her face mud-packed, her graying hair in clay curlers, and a chin strap securely in place, she looked like a statue. Sarah smiled.

Since the last cold spell, the weather had turned considerably warmer, and Lady Lillian's bed had been moved from the Warm Room back to her bedchamber, which was a pleasant place, Sarah thought, even though the red window coverings were faded and the Turkish rug worn thin in places. A fire smoldered in the black marble fireplace.

Smothering laughter, Sarah stared at the old woman, who pointed to her face then shushed Sarah away by flinging a long, thin arm toward the door.

"I know when I am not wanted," Sarah said good-naturedly, thinking that no amount of mud-packing could alter the poor woman's aristocratic nose. Quitting the room, Sarah went to the workroom in search of Angeline. The girl was spending entirely too much time there and being very secretive about what she was doing.

She found Angeline sitting at the long worktable, bent

over a tablet of drawing paper. On her head was a purple turban with green and yellow plumes, which looked ludicrous with her too-large breeches and red sweater, which was also three sizes too large.

So engrossed was Angeline in what she was drawing that she did not hear Sarah enter the workroom. She looked up with a start when she heard Sarah's voice. "Angeline, why are you spending all your time hiding out here? The Gypsy hats have all long since gone. The modiste has been paid—"

"And more orders are coming in," said Angeline.

"Well, what do you think? Should more hats be made?"

"No," Angeline answered quickly. "Not until next year. As Lord Chesterson said, it is necessary to keep them scarce or we will find ourselves selling them for one-half of what we are charging. But I think other hats can be sold under the Louiezon label. Like this turban. From the *on-dits* I read, dowagers will be clamoring for something unusual to wear during the Season."

"Angeline, 'tis a capital idea, but I don't like your working so hard. You help John Wesley with the wood gathering, and I heard from Hilda that you even feed the sheep and gather the eggs from the henhouse."

"I like to help. I would like to be a farmer." Angeline looked at Sarah worriedly, and then in a rush said, "Sister, if you don't land that rich nabob, and Lady Lillian is carted off to debtor's prison, and Merrymount is sold for past-due taxes, you and I, and Hilda and John Wesley, will need something to fall back on. Even if you marry Lord Chesterson, and I pray that you will, he could not take on upkeep of two aging servants and his wife's sister. I'm only thinking ahead. The Gypsy hats sold so quickly, others will most likely do as well. I could not forbear Hilda and John Wesley, at their age, having no place to go."

Tears clouded Sarah's eyes. How kind of Angeline to think of Hilda and John Wesley. "Angeline, please do not plan on my marrying Lord Chesterson. You know I have given my word to Aunt Lillian that I will make a convenient marriage, and our Papa taught both of us to never go back on our word."

"He did that," Angeline said pensively, the frown on her brow deepening.

Sarah tried for levity. "Somewhere in London Town a rich man is waiting to be snared into my web. I will not think of those scurrilous money lenders sending my only aunt to debtor's prison." Sarah could not help the break in her voice, and she stopped for a moment before saying, "I've tried to stop thinking of Lord Chesterson, and I believe he is doing the same. His missives are very distant. He speaks only of his preparation for my come-out, which means he is prepared to launch me onto the Marriage Mart. His last intelligence mentioned obtaining vouchers for Almack's Assembly Rooms. Whatever that means."

"Oh, I know about Almack's," piped up Angeline. "The last time John Wesley and I went to Corby, I indulged myself with several back copies of *La Belle Assemblée*, and on the editorial page it tells all about Almack's Assembly Rooms in King Street, off St James's Street." She opened a yellowed copy of the magazine and read aloud: *"Here, a committee of seven high-born women rule with absolute authority, and they alone have the privilege of granting vouchers of admission to the subscription ball on Wednesday evenings, and no one is allowed in without their approval. The intrigue that goes on to obtain* entreé *to this temple of the* ton *occupies the time and energy of everyone . . ."*

"What a waste of energy," Sarah said. "In America . . ."

But she must stop thinking of how things were in America. And, too, mayhap in New York City's society there was a place such as Almack's, ruled by seven powerful women. She'd turned her back on a come-out into society there.

And I wish I could do the same here, she thought, pushing

herself up onto the worktable and taking the turban from Angeline's head and putting it on her own.

" 'Tis lovely," she said as she peered into a looking glass hanging on the wall for the purpose of trying on the Gypsy hats. Her auburn curls fell to her shoulders, and Sarah could not help remembering Nathan calling them whiskey curls. Tears misted her eyes, but she willed them away. She said again, "The turban is lovely."

"But much too old for you," said Angeline. "That is for Lady Lillian. I suppose she's told you that she cannot wait to chaperon you when you go to the routs and soirees."

"Oh, yes. Lately she's talked of little else, but 'tis much better than having her crouched beneath the windows watching for the arrival of the money lenders."

Sarah told Angeline about the mudpack and the chin strap, and Angeline hooted with laughter.

"And her hair was done in clay curlers," continued Sarah. "I don't think she was too happy about my finding her in such a state, but I was worried when she didn't come down for breakfast. Then when she didn't answer my knock on the door, I simply pushed the door open and went in." Sarah laughed. "The mudpack had rendered her speechless."

"She's fasting, also," said Angeline. "She plans on having a very girlish figure by the time we go into Town. Those were her words, not mine. And when the modiste measured her for gowns, she asked that a tad bit of padding be added to push her bosom up above the neckline."

The two sisters laughed until their sides hurt.

When the laughter had subsided, Angeline showed the sketches she had drawn for Sarah's hats. "One to match every gown, even two made of straw. *Those* were a challenge, but I think I have the straw woven into the shape I want. They will have wide brims, not stiff, but sort of floppy." She smiled her wide smile, showing beautiful white teeth, and said unabashedly, "Quite seductive."

Sarah let the seductive part pass. She had gotten used

to Angeline knowing more than a girl who had only seen
five and ten summers should know. "Where in the world
will I wear a wide-brimmed straw hat? And do you think
that rich nabob will care what kind of hat I am wearing?"

"Most certainly! And you will be the best-dressed lady
of quality in London, the envy of every *ton* woman who is
vying for a man. I pray that the modiste Georgena acquired is as good a seamstress as she is reputed to be. I
keep wondering if that is so, then why is she not in London plying her trade. That is where the blunt is, not here
in drought-stricken Northamptonshire."

"I hear she prefers to live in the country with her
husband and children," said Sarah, and then she added,
"That makes perfectly good sense to me. If circumstances
were different, I would want nothing more than to live in
the country with my husband and children."

There was a wistfulness in Sarah's voice that Angeline
could not miss, and it made her sad to the core of her
being. But she could not change things, she thought, as
she took up her needle and started stitching, and the
workroom became painfully quiet. Gone was the levity of
only a few moments before.

The silence grew louder, and then Cain and Abel
bounded into the workroom, followed by Georgena and
Madame Christina LaCross, the inexpensive modiste
Georgena had acquired. Two ladies in gray bombazine
followed, loaded down with finished gowns, pelisses, mantles, and shawls: everything for a complete wardrobe except hats and bonnets.

Angeline had made it clear when the measurements
were being taken for Sarah's wardrobe, and hers as well,
that she would create the hats for Sarah's head. So immediately she brought forth her sketches. On some she had
already cut the patterns.

"You are a genius," said the modiste as she viewed the
sketches. "I believe you and Lady Sarah will be the talk
of the *ton*."

"Lady Sarah will be the talk of the *ton*, but not I. Personally I think it is a monstrous way to catch a husband."

Georgena and the modiste laughed, and Georgena said that within another summer or so no man of the *ton* would be safe from Angeline, not with her looks. "I hear the routs are fun aplenty, and the dancing at Almack's is something for a young girl to dream about. Especially since the wife of the Russian Ambassador had introduced the waltz to London. They say it is very seductive, but I don't see how, since the two people dancing are forbidden to touch bodies." She stopped to laugh. "Lord Byron wrote a poem called 'The Waltz,' and now 'tis all the rage."

"I refuse to enjoy it," said Angeline. "Looking to snare a rich husband, indeed!"

Then and there, a plan began to form in Angeline's mind. *Sarah will NOT marry anyone other than the man she loves, Lord Chesterson. I will see to that.*

Angeline began matching the fabric she had bought to the gowns the modiste and her helpers had piled on the worktable, deciding which would go with the walking dresses, the carriage dresses, garden dresses, opera dresses, and on and on.

And in every color in the rainbow. Angeline examined the finished gowns. Every stitch was perfectly made, and every gown made to the patterns she, Angeline, had copied from the French magazines, all fit for the French Court.

"I must needs see them on you," said Madame La-Cross, a slight French accent to her voice. "And you, too, Miss Angeline. There's gowns for you . . . and for Lady Lillian. My girls and I worked night and day to get them finished in time for the Season."

Sarah cringed. Not about the dresses, but at how soon the Season would be upon them. But there was a quickening to her pulse. Soon she would see Lord Chesterson.

She wondered if he still prayed that something would happen to prevent her marrying someone rich. And if she did so, did he still plan on making her his mistress?

"Lady Sarah," said Georgena, pulling Sarah from her reverie. "I'm dying to see these gowns on you. Can't you work up a wee bit of enthusiasm—"

"I beg your forgiveness. My mind was wandering," Sarah answered. Taking the first dress off the top of the pile, a white muslin with delicate spring flowers, she went behind a dressing screen and began to change, glad when one of the girls in gray bombazine came to help her. There were tiny buttons to be buttoned and ribbons to be tied.

The girl pulled and straightened silently, but when everything was in place, she sighed deeply and said with great feeling, "You are so beautiful, m'lady. And the gowns . . . the *ton* ladies will think yer rich." She clucked and smiled. "This one shows a little ankle."

"And a lot of bosom," said Sarah, feeling her face flush with embarrassment as she looked down at the white flesh above the neckline. *What will Nathan think?*

The modeling went on and on. Sarah pranced and paraded around the room in the wonderful gowns, stopping to stare unbelieving into the looking glass. She had never seen such a wardrobe. Some of the pelisses were trimmed in satin.

The mantles, large rectangular pieces of lightweight fabric gathered at the neck, were worn over the day dresses when the weather was only a little cool. They sometimes matched the dress they covered.

Sarah was sure the wardrobe would cost the two thousand pounds they had allotted for the entire come-out.

And there were Kashmir shawls.

Sarah pushed thoughts of Nathan to the back of her mind and, as any young girl would, she told herself, let herself be caught up in the excitement that filled the room. The modiste was all smiles, as were her helpers, Georgena, and even Angeline.

The last, a full evening gown in white, had elegant ruffs of Brabant lace, emulating gowns worn during the Elizabethan era, although more elaborate, the skirt flaring to show more ankle when one danced the scandalous waltz.

"That will be your Almack's gown," said Angeline. "I read that they, both men and women, dress to the nines to go there."

"A gown for you to wear," said Madame LaCross, looking at Angeline and holding forth a gown of pale green. " 'Tis not styled as elaborately as your sister's, but you are younger. When you have your come-out, I shall take great joy in making your wardrobe. You are equally as pretty as Lady Sarah, but in a different way."

"I will never have a come-out," declared Angeline vehemently, "and if Lady Lillian had not—"

"Do I hear my name?"

Every eye turned to see Lady Lillian entering the room, the mudpack gone, replaced by rouge on her cheeks, lamp black on her brows, and berry juice on her lips.

Most likely the juice she had stored away the past summer, thought Sarah.

Tucked in Lady Lillian's upswept hair—Sarah was sure Hilda had done the honors—were red roses, faded from years past. She wore the dress that had been dyed purple for her to venture out to church in Rockingham.

"You look lovely," said Sarah, changing the subject, for she did not want Angeline to finish what she had started to say.

"Why, thank you, Lady Sarah," Lady Lillian said as she swept deeper into the room, obviously having forgotten that someone was talking about her when she entered. Or not caring. The dresses on the worktable caught her eye. She lifted her lorgnette, which was fastened to the shoulder of her gown by a chain, and peered. "Are these your new gowns, Lady Sarah? Faith, you will snare more than one rich man with these." She turned to the modiste and asked if her new gowns were finished. "Being of noble blood, I'll be expected to chaperon Lady Sarah, and I must needs dress accordingly."

"They are at the bottom of the pile," the modiste said. "And so are Lady Angeline's—"

"Angeline's?" exclaimed Lady Lillian. "I don't take your meaning. We cannot possibly allow her to go to Town for the Season. There'll be too many questions asked. Lady Sarah's heritage will come into question, and what on earth will we tell them? 'Twill ruin Lady Sarah's chances—"

"We'll tell them the truth," said Sarah, her anger instantly flaring. "I've told you before that either Angeline goes, or I will not go, and, Lady Lillian, mayhap in debtor's prison you will learn to be more sensitive to someone's feelings beside your own. Papa spoke the truth when he said you were an ingrate. Were it not for Angeline, none of us would be going to London, except to seek employment. Angeline started the Louiezon Hat Company while you were crouched beneath the window watching for the money lenders to come take you away."

Lady Lillian's mouth dropped open. Obviously she was not accustomed to such a set-down, thought Sarah. The old woman sputtered, and her face flushed redder than the berry juice on her lips. "I beg your forgiveness, Lady Sarah. Sometimes I do suffer from foot-in-mouth disease."

Before anyone could utter a word, the old woman quit the room without looking at her new gowns. When she was gone, Angeline burst out laughing. She came and hugged Sarah, saying, "I saw a little bit of Papa in you, sister. Kindness personified until someone pushes you to the edge, and then that Templeton temper flares."

"Oh, she makes me so angry. But yet, I find myself feeling extremely sorry for her. She's a true eccentric."

Sarah's temper dissipated quickly, and she asked Madame LaCross and her helpers to please not pass on what had transpired there in the workroom. "It will do little good to have a Season if it be known that I am poverty-stricken and my only purpose for being in Town is to snare a rich husband to save my old aunt."

The modiste and her helpers agreed, and they promised to be mum about what had happened, leaving after Angeline had modeled gowns whose necklines, so Angeline declared, were positively disgraceful.

Sarah sucked in her breath. "Angeline, you look like an Indian princess. I've never seen anyone so beautiful."

"Stuff!" Angeline answered. "Beauty is as beauty does, and sometimes I'm not beautiful. I get so angry at Lady Lillian."

After that, with things settled, Georgena, Angeline, and Sarah talked of the hats they would make before the Season started. Georgena reported that Nathan had sent word to William to furnish four of Copthorne's best horses to pull the Templeton crested carriage into London. He would send the twins and Nanny Bothwell home before the Season started, and the carriage bringing them would be used for luggage when those from Merrymount came into Town.

"I shall be so happy to see my precious children," Georgena said, longing in her voice.

No one answered, and quietness once again enveloped the room and those in it. Sarah looked away, letting her gaze rest on the ridge beyond the windows and beyond the ridge a sky made beautiful by the setting sun. Her heart was heavy beyond bearing. Nathan had planned it all, down to the last detail—the best horses from Copthorne were to pull the Merriwether crested carriage. She would be thrust onto the Marriage Mart in *ton* style. Warm tears dampened her cheeks. Why could she not stop hoping when there was no hope? she asked herself. For a fleeting moment she relived the time she and Nathan spent in the cabin, and then, excusing herself, she quit the room to go find Lady Lillian to assure her that she would not have to go to debtor's prison, that her, Sarah's, come-out had been planned . . . down to the last detail.

Chapter Nineteen

"Do you want me to be hanged for witchery?" Angeline said to John Wesley when he asked her to do an Indian rain dance. They were soon to repair to London for Sarah's come-out, and still the spring rains had not come. Worry showed on the old servant's wrinkled face.

He's scared, Angeline thought, looking pityingly at him. His faded eyes were sunk back into his head, as if he had not slept for a week.

"We won't let anyone know," he answered. "Just me and you will go into the woods, and you can do whatever yer people do when you need rain as much as we do. I tell yer, Lady Angeline, none of us can survive another year of drought. Not even Lord Chesterson and Copthorne."

Angeline wished for her beads her mama had given her. So many times she had held the beads in her hands and talked to Wanna's Spirit, like when she asked the Spirit to show the way to making money for Sarah's Season, and the idea of the hat business had come to her from nowhere. And what a success the hat business had been.

But the beads were gone.

"All right, John Wesley, but I confess to you that my faith is weak."

"Well, it won't hurt," he said. "We'll wait till nightfall."

"And I want your promise that you won't tell. I don't

want to be called a witch, and I certainly do not want to
be hanged."

"I promise, Miss Angeline. Not even Hilda will know.
Sometimes she gets carried away and talks too much, like
some women do." He gave Angeline a sly grin. "But not
you. I know you won't tell anyone that we prayed for
rain."

Angeline grinned. "Oh, so you are going to pray, too."

"I thought I would talk to my Anglican god while you
talk to your Indian god. That way we'll have everything
covered."

"A capital idea," Angeline said, smiling.

They parted then, Angeline promising to meet him at
the stables thirty minutes after darkness had descended.
As she walked back to the manor house, she looked up at
the gray-black clouds scudding across the sky and addressed them. "If you are holding rain, let it fall on this
parched earth."

Angeline crossed herself, although she had never done
such a thing before. But she had seen other people do it
and thought it might help, and she smiled when she saw
lightening streak across the sky. Most likely it had been
skipping around up there before now and she had not
noticed. She walked slowly, pondering, laughing when a
huge drop of rain struck her cheek. And then a sudden
downpour was drenching her.

Instead of running for shelter, Angeline stood and
looked up at the dark sky, letting the rain hit her face.
Laughter gurgled up from her throat, and she let out a
loud whoop and held her hands toward the sky. She heard
someone calling to her. "Lady Angeline, are you daft?
You will catch yer death."

Hilda stood in the back doorway, shaking her head.
She motioned for Angeline to come in out of the rain.

Angeline could barely hear her above the sound of the
rain pounding the thirsty earth. It was a glorious sound.
The heavy, dark clouds were the most beautiful things she

had ever seen. She wondered what John Wesley was thinking and could imagine the smile on his face.

" 'Tis a sudden spring shower. England is famous fer them," said the maid when Angeline finally darted into the house.

"I pray that it's more than a shower," said Angeline. She wiped the rain from her face and waited for her breathing to slow to normal.

Hilda scolded, "We just got Lady Lillian cured from her madness, and now yer acting strange." She bobbed.

"Oh, Hilda, stop your bobbing. Isn't the rain wonderful? Now John Wesley can stop worrying."

Hilda clucked, "Yer must needs change your clothes. What would happen if you came down with the croup and couldn't go into Town with Lady Sarah and Lady Lillian?"

"I would like that just fine," said Angeline. She had no desire to go to *ton* parties. God's truth, a case of the croup would be preferable, she thought, and her mind began planning how to pretend she had the croup even when she didn't have a cold.

Hilda's next statement changed Angeline's thinking. "Don't start your scheming, Lady Angeline. Yer must needs go to London to watch over Lady Sarah, not let her be taken by some nabob unworthy of her. Now, you run along, and I'll fetch water so yer can have a hot soak. I'll fetch some whiskey. That'll ward off a cold."

"You are a very smart woman, Hilda," said Angeline. She began walking down the long corridor, looking back once to say, "I promise I'll see that Sarah marries the right man."

And I'll make sure that man is Lord Chesterson.

In her bedchamber Angeline watched the huge raindrops sluice down the windowpanes, and when Sarah came into the room, Angeline grabbed her sister and danced round and round, hardly noticing the cold that was beginning to penetrate through her wet clothes. "Isn't it wonderful, Sarah?" Angeline asked.

"What?" Sarah enquired. She danced because Angeline was pulling her along and swinging her arms. "Angeline, what has come over you?"

"The rain, Sarah. Don't you see 'tis raining? Now the crops can grow, and I won't have to do the rain dance for John Wesley. He was so worried, and I was worried because he said country people believed in witches, and if it rained and they knew I had done the Indian rain dance, they might hang me for being a witch."

"Angeline, you are making no sense. Now stop this." Sarah lowered herself onto the side of her narrow bed and stared at gleeful Angeline, who was this day acting like a girl much younger than her five and ten summers.

Sarah was glad to see Angeline happy, and she was glad to see the rain, even though it had come too late to save her from the dreadful upcoming Season.

"We were to go into the woods," said Angeline, "so no one would know. I was to pray to my Indian god and John Wesley to his Anglican god."

Angeline was sitting cross-legged on her own bed. She pulled a quilt up over her shoulders, holding it tightly under her chin.

"Well, I'm glad you escaped being accused of witchcraft," Sarah said. "The rain is wonderful. I only wish it had come sooner, like three years ago. Mayhap Lady Lillian would not be so needful . . ."

Sarah's voice died to a whisper while rain pounded the side of the manor house and beat against the window. The wind keened in the eaves, filling the room with its sounds.

"Sister," Angeline said above the keening, "I'm sorry I've been difficult about going to the London parties with you. Hilda set me straight."

Sarah raised a quizzical eyebrow. "Hilda?"

"She said I must needs go along and make sure some

unscrupulous nabob didn't talk you into marrying him. And I think that's a capital idea, your being so trusting. I still don't see why you have to sacrifice your happiness for the old crow's . . ."

Just then there was a loud knock on the door, and Hilda's voice could be heard. "John Wesley is here with hot water for yer soak, Lady Angeline."

Before Angeline could answer, John Wesley entered the room, carrying two pails of steaming water. Hilda followed, carrying a tin tub. She placed it near the fireplace, and after John Wesley had emptied the water into it, he put several sticks of wood on the grate and struck a lucifer to it. "Don't want you to be cold, Lady Angeline." He gave a big grin and said, "I'm happy about this rain. Now yer won't have to fear the neighbors seeing yer doing what yer wuz afeard they would see you doing."

"And what was that?" Hilda wanted to know, putting her hands on her ample hips.

Angeline giggled, and John Wesley said, "Thet's for me and Lady Angeline to know." He winked at Angeline and left.

Hilda moved the dressing screen in front of the tub to afford Angeline privacy, and Angeline, after looking out and assuring herself that the rain had not stopped, quickly stripped and stepped into the hot water, not knowing until then how chilled she had become. The fire felt wonderful to her back, and the hot water quickly warmed her. She let out a huge sigh. There were moments when life could be positively delightful.

Hilda dropped a bar of homemade soap over the screen. "Here, scrub good while I fetch yer toddy."

Lady Sarah was watching this with interest, amused at how Hilda and John Wesley spoiled Angeline, and when Hilda returned with the hot toddy—warm water, sugar, and a tiny bit of whiskey—Sarah laughed aloud.

After Hilda had bobbed twice and left, Sarah said, "I can see why you prefer staying at Merrymount to going to London. Most likely the servants there will not be so kind."

"Why can Hilda and John Wesley not go to London?" Angeline asked, scrubbing until her skin began to sting.

"Someone has to stay at Merrymount should the tax collectors come and claim the property."

"Well, they won't be claiming Hilda and John Wesley."

"I asked John Wesley that if the tax collectors should come, could he plead Lady Lillian's case and promise them money after my Season in London." She paused and was quiet for a long moment. "I told him that if extra time was not granted that he and Hilda are to take Mama's portrait to Copthorne and go stay there themselves. The money lenders took Mama's pearls, but I refuse to let them have her portrait. I'll come to Copthorne for the portrait after I'm married."

The words wrenched Sarah's heart. She drew her knees up and rested her chin on them and ground her teeth together to keep from crying.

The pain in Sarah's voice did not go unnoticed by Angeline. "You will not be marrying anybody except Lord Chesterson. I promised Hilda—"

"How could you promise Hilda such a thing? You know the purpose of the dreadful come-out."

"I know, but I have concluded that 'twould be better for selfish Lady Lillian to spend some time in debtor's prison than for you to marry some unworthy nabob you don't love. In truth, a short stretch on a prison ship might humble the old crow."

"I told you, Angeline, that I will do my best to love my husband—"

"Only if he is Lord Chesterson. You can't love two men, and you're already in love with his lordship." Angeline took the towel Hilda had left and started rubbing her already red skin, and then she noticed a long flannel gown had been left hanging over the screen. She pulled it over her head and ran and jumped onto her bed, then settled her heavy braid of black hair down her back.

Sarah did not say more about marrying anyone. She would do what she had to do. Of late she had spent much of her time fighting the desponds, and to talk about what was ahead only reminded her of Nathan's missives and how distant they had become. How could she hope when he seemed to have given up? And she could not stop herself from imagining him being with Lady Arbuthnot. She hated being jealous more than anything in the world.

Hilda returned with a supper tray of beef stew and warm milk. "Yer get under the covers, Lady Angeline. You must needs not be sick. Do you remember yer promise?" The maid bobbed, rustling her faded bombazine.

"Yes, Hilda, I remember the promise." Angeline scrambled to get under the covers. Hilda put pillows to her back and pulled the worn coverlet up under her neck. And then she stood guard until Angeline had drained the glass.

"Hilda, did you and John Wesley not have children?" asked Sarah.

"We had one wee one, but she died a babe. My heart has never stopped hurting."

"You are so kind. 'Tis a pity you didn't have a gaggle of children to spoil."

"Well, the Lord gave us her ladyship. I fear we've spoiled her something terrible, for she is a mite selfish."

"A *mite* selfish!" Angeline almost choked on the hot stew. "She's the most—"

"Angeline," said Sarah, " 'tis best left unsaid what you are about to say."

"I know how Lady Angeline feels, and 'tis true enough," said Hilda. "But me and the mister love her ladyship and feel honored to have served her all these years." The maid smiled, bobbed, then quit the room.

When Angeline and Sarah were alone, Angeline giggled and said between spoonfuls of the stew, "I think I might get used to being waited upon."

Sarah laughed. "You mean become a true lady of quality?"

Merriment sparkled in Angeline's dark eyes. "That will be the day, sister." Angeline turned to look out the window at the downpour of rain. "This is not a spring shower, 'tis a genuine rain. I hope it rains until River Welland tops its banks, like the Hudson so many times did when we were in America."

"Do you miss home?" asked Sarah.

"Only if Papa and Mama could be there. I'm happy to be here with you, watching it rain."

Sarah rose from the bed. "Well, I don't have a maid to bring my supper, so I'll repair to the kitchen and see if Hilda saved some mutton stew. Thank the good Lord we no longer have to survive on turnips." She walked to the door and turned back. "Mayhap it will rain until we depart Merrymount. The sky shows no sign of clearing."

"I pray so, Sarah," said Angeline sleepily.

And rain it did, for three days. Angeline did not catch her death as Hilda had feared, but many times during those rainy days she wished she could escape into the woods, for Lady Lillian took it upon herself to teach Sarah how to go on in London society. Angeline could not endure it.

"This is a courtly curtsy," Lady Lillian would say, dipping gracefully, holding her head just so. Never mind, Angeline thought, that Sarah had been trained in upstate New York on how to flutter a fan; Lady Lillian was sure it was not as refined as the way English ladies of quality comported themselves.

Angeline wanted to spit, and Sarah was not too happy with the instructions. It was when Lady Lillian said, "A lady of the _ton_ never, never snaps her fingers, no matter how much she is agitated or how quickly she wants something done," that Sarah exploded.

"Balderdash," she exclaimed, and she then and there stopped Lady Lillian's self-authorized lessons, saying she cared not whether she became one of the upper orders. A man with blunt would suit her just fine. "I'm thankful the Gypsy hats have furnished money for the come-out, and whatever happens will happen, regardless of whether or not I curtsy just right."

It had been decided that no more hats would be cut and stitched. If Sarah did not make a fine marriage of convenience, then Angeline would pursue the making and selling of hats. And that was that. Beautiful hats had been made for Sarah, for Angeline, and for Lady Lillian. Now the workroom was quiet, but for the pressing and packing of clothes.

The time for departure was growing short, thought Sarah. Mudpacks appeared more often on Lady Lillian's face, and her chin straps were pulled tighter. And she swore that she was regaining her youthful figure by not eating as much as she really liked, but Sarah could see no change in the old woman's eating habits and thought the few pounds her aunt had added were most becoming.

After the rain had stopped, Angeline told Hilda that, while growing up in America, Lady Sarah remembered flowers in the moat. "With the sacrifice she is willing to make to save Merrymount, she deserves flowers to be where she remembers," Angeline said. "There will barely be time to accomplish this before we leave for London."

"John Wesley will help," assured Hilda.

"He's such a dear man," Angeline said, smiling at Hilda. "You are a very fortunate woman, do you know that?"

"Indeed, I do," answered Hilda, and they became quiet while Angeline finished her breakfast. After the meal, the girl left the table and went to the stables to confer with John Wesley.

The old servant was agreeable. Even joyous, Angeline thought. So with the warm spring sun bearing down on their backs, she and John Wesley began clearing the moat and sowing wildflowers. From the manor house Sarah saw them toiling away, and she told Lady Lillian that the two of them most certainly should go help Angeline and John Wesley.

Lady Lillian pulled herself up huffily. "And have our hands looking like a charwoman's? Ladies of quality—"

"Aunt Lillian, if you refer one more time to ladies of quality, I shall tell you to find a rich husband for yourself."

"I would if I could," said Lady Lillian rather pointedly.

Sarah could not help but laugh. The old woman was honest about *why* she was on the shelf. Of course had she not been so bent on marrying a wealthy, titled man, mayhap she would have married years ago, thought Sarah. She looked at her aging aunt, who had recently, since Nathan had furnished the milk cow and the beef, put on weight enough so that she did not look emaciated. The wrinkles in her face no longer reminded Sarah of a plowed field, and were it not for her aquiline nose, she could be called passing handsome. Sarah said to her, "Lady Lillian, you really should use less rouge. And with your new wardrobe, who knows? you might just capture some *ton* gentleman's heart."

Lady Lillian giggled like a young girl. "Do you really think so? Oh, oh! But of course you are funning. Titled men with lots of blunt prefer young, beautiful girls. Like you, Lady Sarah."

"Oh, I would never consider an older man. No, no, no, Lady Lillian. Mayhap I could learn to love a young, handsome man, if he were kind to me, but I could not forbear—"

"Stuff! Girls more beautiful than you have settled for old men with a title and land. 'Tis foolish to consider love a factor."

Sarah could see there was no use in explaining her

feelings to the old woman, whose heart was plainly made of stone. Title and blunt was all that mattered. Sarah said to her, "Lord Chesterson is very handsome, and he is titled. He's kind and caring, a true gentleman. All that is lacking is ready blunt to keep you from debtor's prison."

"He's poor as a church mouse, and I pray that you will not make a fool of yourself over him when we reach London. Every eye of the *ton* will be on you, and every girl will envy your beauty."

Sarah was quiet for long moment before saying, "I know Lord Chesterson's poor as a church mouse. You've told me that before. Many times. But he has other wonderful qualities."

Sarah could hear her own voice catch in her throat. Turning, she quit the room and shut her ears to Lady Lillian's answer, and only a short time later, she was helping plant wildflowers in the moat while wondering why Nathan had stopped telling her he loved her. His missives only spoke of her come-out onto the Marriage Mart.

In London, Lord Chesterson awoke to sunshine streaming across his bedchamber. He was both apprehensive and joyful. Today he would see Sarah. The apprehension was for the uncertain future.

Running his long fingers through his blond curly hair, he pushed himself up and flung his long legs off the side of his high poster bed. The red velvet trappings were always pulled back, for he never used them. They made him feel fenced in.

This day Nathan felt that he had been caught in a trap with a big gaping mouth closing on him. There was no escape. He must needs let his precious Lady Sarah go onto the Marriage Mart. Of late, he had spent all his time, when he was not in Parliament, trying to raise money for the money lenders who were after Lady Lillian. He'd had to be discreet, not letting the banker, even the Duke of Wellington, know *why* he needed the money so desperately. Both had turned him down; the banker wanted collateral; the duke was remodeling his Apsley House and needed his blunt for that. Although neither could help, both wanted to know why Nathan needed the money so badly.

Of course Nathan could not tell them. It must not be spread about that Sarah was fortune-hunting, he reminded himself more than once.

Now his lordship felt his heart breaking inside him. He buried his head in his hands. Invitations had been sent out, announcing the come-out of Lady Sarah Templeton, a distant cousin of the sixth earl of Chesterson. He could not forbear it, and he feared that when a man asked to pay his addresses to Lady Sarah, he would make a fool of himself and call the man out.

What a coil.

But there was no help for it. His lordship was utterly and desperately in love. And since the night in the cabin with his darling Sarah, he had hardly drawn a breath when he did not want her. When he slept, he held her, felt her warm body against his own throbbing desire.

He slammed a fist into a palm. "By God, I am bound she was made for me, not some jackanapes who comes to Town looking for someone to bear his heir."

Again Nathan thought about getting leg-shackled to Lady Arbuthnot for her blunt, but then he would have to perform his marital duties—he could not imagine that woman allowing a marriage in name only—and that would be almost as painful to him as to know his Sarah was in bed with some unworthy jackanapes, the one who would surely lay claim to her during the Season.

Hearing a scratch on the door, his lordship looked up and invited the scratcher to enter. He was not yet accustomed to having servants around the house. He prayed it was not the housekeeper or one of her helpers, for he was naked from the waist up, and only short tights covered his midsection.

Gifford, the recently hired butler, a rather plump man with big jowls that shook, a thin moustache on his upper lip, pushed the door open and entered the room. His long-tailed coat flapped against his short legs as he approached the bed. "A missive for you, your lordship." He held out a silver salver.

Nathan took the missive and ripped it open, his breath coming in ragged spurts. The handwriting was Lady Sarah's. He sought to still his trembling hand as he read the brief message: "Your lordship, would you be so kind as to visit Captain Barksdale in Curzon Street and invite him to my come-out party? He was ever so kind to me and Angeline on our trip over on the *Boston Queen*, and his presence would do wonders for me when I am surrounded by so many strangers." It was signed simply, "Sarah."

"Demme the whole of it," said Nathan, not realizing that Gifford still stood over him. Nathan dismissed him with a curt, "You may go, Gifford."

"I thought you might wish to post a reply, m'lord."

"No. No, I don't. Please go." And then Nathan had another thought. He had servants, he might as well make use of them. He was not in the mood to face Cook or the newly hired footman who stood over the sideboard like a hound guarding his bone. "Bring my breakfast, Gifford. Please. And bring it yourself. I don't want a maid snooping around my quarters."

Gifford bowed from the waist, turned on his heels, and then left hurriedly, as if he were as anxious to be rid of his master as the master was to be rid of him. Nathan scolded himself for being short with a servant. He read Sarah's missive again. Why could she not have given a hint that she would be happy to see him? Why did she not mention the recent rain, about which William had written? Was her demme come-out so important that she had forgotten about their love for each other. Or should he say his love for her?

His lordship rang for Paul, his valet, and asked to be shaved. Until recently the valet had been his only servant, except Cook and a weekly charwoman. His lordship felt quite comfortable with the astute Paul, who was always impeccably dressed and always in fine humor. This day he was smiling like a Cheshire cat.

"What the devil are you grinning about?" asked Nathan.

"You. That scowl on your face would win a prize. I should think you would be quite happy, being your lady is to arrive today. The help is in a dither."

"I hope the help doesn't think she's *my* lady. Lady Sarah's a distant cousin whom I'm helping launch into society. Could I do less for an English girl who grew up in America and who will be surrounded by strangers?"

"You could marry her."

Nathan had not confided in his valet that Lady Sarah was being forced to make a marriage of convenience. He prayed that no one in London knew. That *on-dit* would fly through Mayfair like wildfire.

Mayhap I should let it be known that Lady Sarah is looking for a man with blunt. The kind gentlemen of the ton *would all run the other way. Mayhap then my heart would stop hurting.*

There were times when his lordship wished his Sarah was not so honorable as to want to keep her word to her aunt, and he often thought the old woman would fare rather well in prison for a short time. It just might humble her a smidgen. She had certainly shown how selfish she could be by sending to America for her niece.

The valet wore a grin while he made lather in the soapdish and stropped the razor. "Why don't you marry her?" he asked after a lengthy silence.

Nathan was sitting in his shaving chair, in front of a basin of hot water and a huge gilt-framed mirror, which reflected his image perfectly. His hazel eyes were red-rimmed from the past night of fitful sleep. " 'Tis not my wont to become leg-shackled."

His lordship had barely spat the lie out when the valet slapped a hot towel over his soaped whiskers, covering his mouth.

"That's balderdash, and you know it, my lord. For months you've been talking about needing a helpmeet and a mother for the twins. Tell me the whole of it." He lifted the towel.

"I'm not at liberty—"

"There's something mighty queer about a man who will launch a girl onto the Marriage Mart when he is in love with her himself. I've watched your pain—"

Despite all his effort to stop them, tears suddenly filled Nathan's eyes. He was ashamed, for as close as he felt to his valet and as much as he could trust him not to gossip, he did not want the man to see into his soul. Even so, he found himself pouring the story out to the valet, and when he had finished, his tears had reached his strong chin. The one thing Nathan did not tell him was about the night in the cabin with his beloved Sarah.

"There's nothing to it," said the valet when Nathan had finished baring his soul.

"What do you mean, there's nothing to it? Have you not been listening?"

"Oh, yes, I've been listening, and it hurts me to see your pain. I only meant that there's a simple solution."

Nathan sat forward in his chair. "Fustian, spit it out, the whole of it. I can see nothing simple about—"

"You must needs make the girl yours in every sense. This night slip into her bedchamber and make love to her as if your life depends on it, which, from what I've seen, it does. Give your Lady Sarah yourself, your heart, your soul, and I'll wager she'll forget about marrying for blunt to keep the old woman out of debtor's prison."

Chapter Twenty

The Merriwether crested carriage, pulled by four handsome bays and followed by a lesser carriage transporting boxes of clothes, left the Hyde Park Corner Turnpike shortly after noon and then proceeded along the cobbled street to Nathan's London town house situated next door to Apsley House, the Duke of Wellington's white stone mansion known as No. 1 London. It had been named thus because it was the first large mansion at the beginning of the built-up area beyond the turnpike.

This information came from Angeline, who had read all about the hero of the Battle of Waterloo in the *on-dit* section of *La Belle Assemblée*. "His Grace is spending lots of blunt on the mansion he purchased from his older brother," she said, and then in a lower voice, "He has a mistress because his wife is so tiresome."

"Who has a mistress?" asked Lady Lillian.

"The duke, of course. Did I just not say so?"

"A man will have a mistress," said Lady Lillian, "whether or not their wife is tiresome."

"I don't believe that for one minute," retorted Angeline. "Papa didn't."

"Your father did not live in London. I'm speaking of the gentlemen of the London *ton*. 'Tis the thing to have a beautiful mistress to brag about when he goes to his clubs."

"If that be the case, they are a bunch of heathens and should be horsewhipped."

"If you were English, you would understand," Lady Lillian said haughtily, and Angeline saw the futility of answering and remained quiet.

Half-listening, Sarah sat placidly in the corner of the carriage, her eyes searching not for the town house, but for Chesterson himself. As the carriage pulled under a white portico and stopped, she knew this must be Storm's End. She looked about at the handsome houses and manicured yards. One would think Nathan deep in the pockets, indeed, if one judged him by the neighborhood in which he lived, she thought, wondering why he was not here to meet them. He knew they were to arrive today.

Lady Sarah's heart was in her throat, and she cautioned herself, as Lady Lillian had advised, not to make a fool of herself when she saw his lordship. She set her jaw in an obdurate line and then smiled as civilly as she could. She had been practicing that particular demeanor since leaving Merrymount.

This day, with his lordship in mind, she had dressed carefully, wearing a deep green carriage dress and a straw hat tied under the chin with a green riband.

A liveried footman came to let down the step, but the owner of the house was still not in evidence. Lady Sarah, becoming more angry by the moment, vowed that she would not enquire of him. He had been so adamant about his love for her, and now he was nowhere to be seen. No, she would not make a fool of herself over him, Lady Lillian could rest assured of that.

It was Angeline who did the enquiring. "Where is his lordship?" she asked the footman after he had helped her alight.

He released her hand and bowed from the waist. "I'm certain the butler would be knowing that, m'lady."

By now Lady Lillian was on the cobbled driveway. "Lady Angeline," she said in a stern voice, "it is not *ton*

to converse with the servants. I believe I apprised you of
that earlier."

Angeline gave a deep, courtly curtsy. "I beg your forgiveness, Lady Lillian. Mayhap you can train me to be a
lady of quality, but I doubt that very much."

"You were entirely too familiar with John Wesley and
Hilda. 'Tis against propriety."

"John Wesley and Hilda are my friends," said Angeline. She had removed her bonnet and was twirling it
around by its riband. She noted how proper Lady Lillian
was dressed, a gown with a bustle in the back, black and
red, and a black Gypsy hat with red plumes. Angeline
smiled and admitted to herself that the old woman was
certainly of the upper orders. Her long nose was turned
into the air as if she were worth a million pounds, and she
strutted when she walked. Angeline smothered a giggle
and wondered what the *ton* would think if they knew the
old woman was on her way to debtor's prison.

The butler opened the door, then bowed. "Welcome to
Storm's End."

"Where is his lordship?" Angeline quickly asked.

Sarah wanted to drop through the floor, but she was as
anxious as Angeline to know of his lordship's whereabouts, and she listened intently to the stiff butler's answer. "I believe he left a missive in her ladyship's quarters.
Lady Sarah, that is."

"And where is that?" asked Angeline.

Sarah saw Lady Lillian's eyes roll upward, as if in
supplication for the Higher Being to save them from this
hoyden, and then, inclining her head close to Sarah's ear,
she whispered, "I knew we should have left her in the
country. She will ruin your chances."

Sarah felt herself bristle. "And she might even be my
savior." She had many times scolded her aunt about
speaking disparagingly of Angeline, but it seemed useless.
The old woman just would not listen.

Sarah heard the butler saying. "The housekeeper will

show each of you to your respective quarters, and a footman will deliver your luggage."

"A moment," said Angeline. "I will not have my respective quarters. I'll be sharing with my sister, Lady Sarah."

A horrified look transformed Lady Lillian's face. "Oh, but you must not—"

"Oh, but I shall—"

They had moved to the middle of a great receiving hall, which, Sarah noticed, opened into two huge drawing rooms, with gold scrolled ceilings and silk-covered walls. Across the big hall was a dining room that looked as if it would seat one hundred and fifty *ton* guests She was genuinely impressed until the thought occurred to her that most likely this would be where her come-out party would take place. The feeling of impending doom washed over her.

"Of course Angeline can share my quarters," Sarah said, and that put an end to Lady Lillian's argument, except for a mumbled, " 'Tis not the thing.

The housekeeper came, wearing a stiff black bombazine dress, obviously new, with white collar and cuffs. Her black platter hat atop her gray head was trimmed in white also, Sarah noticed.

The housekeeper dipped into a full curtsy before Sarah. "Welcome to Storm's End. I'm Mrs. Hortense. I will show each of you to your quarters, and if you would like, I will have a repast sent up."

Sarah took the housekeeper's hand and shook it warmly. "I'm Lady Sarah Templeton. This is my sister Lady Angeline, and Lady Lillian Merriwether, my aunt. I think we would all like a repast, if it is not too much trouble. We did not stop after leaving the posting inn at first light, and I, for one, am famished."

Sarah was anxious to reach her quarters to read the missive Lord Chesterson had left. What excuse could he have for not being at Storm's End to welcome her . . . if he had meant it when he said he loved her. She blinked back tears as she vividly remembered sitting on the East India Dock, waiting for someone from Merrymount to come for her and Angeline, and for a moment she felt put upon, sorry for herself, sorry for Angeline, who was walking so close to Sarah that she almost impeded her footsteps as they followed Mrs. Hortense up the long winding stairs.

Reaching to touch her sister's arm, Sarah said, "Don't worry, darling, we will not be separated."

Angeline smiled, and Lady Lillian scowled.

After reaching the landing, they went through huge doors and then entered a long corridor. Soon they came to double doors, which Mrs. Hortense opened. "These are your rooms, Lady Sarah. His lordship picked them because they are done up in green. He said you had green eyes. Is that not strange for a gentleman to notice such things?"

Sarah didn't answer, and she was anxious to be done with the housekeeper. They entered into a very pleasant sitting room with a marble fireplace. The walls were dark green, the window coverings the color of sand. Sarah thought the room very pretty, but her eyes were on a sealed missive on a small table near a plush, pale green sofa. She forced herself to listen to what Mrs. Hortense was saying. ". . . A porcelain tub and basin were added, I understand, when his lordship remodeled the house for his late wife. Only the very finest homes have such amenities. If you will follow me—"

"Thank you, Mrs. Hortense," Sarah said. "I shall explore later. I really am quite hungry, and I'm sure my aunt is anxious to reach her rooms. So will you take her?" And then she added, "Angeline will share these rooms with me."

"Oh, but m'lady, his Lordship assigned very nice rooms to Lady Angeline. The house is very large, one of the largest in London. It will not be necessary to share—"

"We wish to stay together, and that is that," Sarah said, with an attempt to keep the sharpness from her voice. *Why does she not leave so that I can read Nathan's missive?*

Waiting outside the door, Lady Lillian tapped her cane impatiently on the wood floor.

"Please take Lady Lillian to her rooms, and then as quickly as possible have food sent up," Sarah said. "As I told you, I am quite famished, and I am certain Angeline is hungry enough to eat a bear."

Mrs. Hortense left then, and as soon as the door had closed behind her, Sarah ripped the seal from Nathan's missive.

Inside he had written, "Dear Cousin Sarah."

Not "my love," not "my darling with the whiskey curls." Sarah immensely resented the cousin part. She was not his lordship's cousin; she was his love.

Or had he forgotten the night in the cabin?

She read the message, but not aloud.

"What does it say, sister?" asked Angeline. "Why was his lordship not here to welcome us to Storm's End?"

"He's sitting in the House of Lords, and he has ordered Cook to prepare a very special dinner for us, and he prays that his business will allow him to be present."

"Is that all?" asked Angeline, looking flabbergasted.

"He did mention that he had called at Captain Barksdale's residence in Curzon Street, as I had requested, and the good captain is in America and is not expected back in England until the middle of the summer. It seems Captain Barksdale's landlady furnished the information to Lord Chesterson. Now let's not discuss Lord Chesterson further. There's too much to do."

"I think you're too quick to be angry," said Angeline, and Sarah just looked at her hard and went about opening the door for the footman to carry in the boxes of clothes. Soon thereafter a pretty maid came and said she was to be Lady Sarah's maid.

"They call me Peggy, and I'm quite good at dressing hair," she said.

Sarah determined that the young thing was painfully shy, and she tried to make her comfortable by helping unpack the clothes. Peggy insisted the beautiful gowns needed pressing before they were hung in the two huge chiffoniers that lined the wall of the bedchamber.

Angeline announced that she was getting into the porcelain bathtub for a long soak, but only until food had arrived. "Call me the minute it arrives," she said, and Sarah promised that she would. Then she left Peggy to the pressing and sat down and read Nathan's missive again, finding it less comforting on the second read than on the first one. She just did not understand men. She laughed without mirth. What did she know about men? Other than by Nathan, she had never been kissed. Sarah looked at the pretty carriage dress she wore—for his lordship. She decided that before dinner tonight she would bathe, have Peggy press the dress, and then she would put it back on. It was her favorite, and she wanted Nathan to see her wearing it.

Peggy finished the pressing, and Sarah dismissed her, saying that she could return later and press the dress she was wearing. No, she would not need her hair dressed this day, but should the need arise, Angeline knew how she wore her hair and was quite good at pleasing her. The shy girl bobbed and left.

A footman brought the food, then quit the room quickly.

Angeline, wearing a flannel robe, joined Sarah in the small sitting room, saying, "I smell food. Oh, sister, 'tis wonderful to have a long tub for bathing. Hot water spews from the beaks of gold swans perched on the porcelain tub." She sat at the table that held the food and began eating. Between bites, she asked Sarah why she was so quiet, and Sarah told her she was thinking.

"The stew is wonderful," Sarah said, eating as if she were starved.

"Aren't these the most wonderful rooms, sister? One could believe that Lord Chesterson is deep in the pockets, as the English say."

"I know," answered Sarah. "I think in days past that was true, and had it not been so dry—"

"Now that the rains have returned, he will be rich again."

Sarah gave a little laugh. "I fear it will be too late for me. By then I will be married to someone I don't love . . . or Lady Lillian will be in prison—"

A soft knock on the door interrupted the conversation. Sarah called, "Enter," and Peggy came in holding a calling card, which she gave to Sarah.

" 'Tis a handsome lady, wearing the grandest hat, in the receiving room, m'lady," Peggy said as she bobbed. "Says she wants to see you, not Lady Lillian."

"Well, you may tell the handsome lady that it is too soon to have callers, that I have just arrived, and that I am famished." Sarah took another bite of the excellent stew Cook had prepared.

Peggy turned to leave. "Yes, m'lady."

Sarah looked at the card and almost choked on the stew. She said quickly, "Peggy, please tell Lady Arbuthnot that I shall be down directly."

"Lady Arbuthnot!" Angeline dropped her fork and jumped to her feet. "You cannot meet the woman who is trying to steal Lord Chesterson from you looking like that." She took Sarah's arm and began leading her to the bedchamber. "Your hair's a fright."

Sarah resisted, but not overly much. "Oh, Angeline, I'm sure I look presentable enough. And how do you know she's trying to steal Nathan from me . . . if he belongs to me."

"His lordship *does* belong to you. He loves you, and you love him, and you must needs put Lady Arbuthnot in her place. How dare she come calling so soon! I'm sure she's come to tell you that Lord Chesterson belongs to her."

Sarah watched as Angeline brushed her auburn curls with quick strokes and then piled them atop her head, letting feathery wisps frame her face. Long ringlets lay on the back of her neck.

"I cannot imagine anyone possessing Lord Chesterson," Sarah said. "He is a very strong man."

"Nonetheless, you just get ready for her. Shall I go with you? I can tell her—"

"Oh, no. I shall see her alone. I'm certain 'tis a friendly visit."

After another five minutes of Angeline straightening Sarah's deep green gown and giving a final pat to her hair, she figured that Sarah was ready to meet the enemy. "You just remember to hold your own, Sister," she said.

Sarah, although apprehensive, laughed and quit the room, making her way to the end of the corridor, where she started her descent. Looking down, she thought she had never seen a more magnificent house, not even Merrymount. Crystal chandeliers, lighted by gas, which Sarah understood to be another improvement for the better homes in London, swung from an extremely high ceiling, casting circles of light on the black-and-white tile floor of the great hall.

Sarah, walking hurriedly across the hall, looked in each of the drawing rooms and found them empty. Surely her ladyship had not left; the upper orders, according to Lady Lillian, had impeccable manners. For Lady Arbuthnot to leave would be beyond the pale.

Just then Sarah heard a voice and turned to the sound. Standing in an obscure doorway was a woman of considerable height wearing the Gypsy hat Nathan had taken to give to Lady Arbuthnot. As Sarah walked toward her, she saw that she was most attractive, and jealousy once again reared its ugly head inside of Sarah. Steeling herself and forcing a smile, she extended her hand in welcome. "Lady

Arbuthnot, I'm Lady Sarah Templeton. My maid said
you wished to see me."

Lady Arbuthnot took Sarah's hand and held it while
her eyes examined every inch of her, from her pile of
auburn curls on top of her head to the half-boots she wore
on her feet.

Sarah immediately sensed that this was no friendly call
and was tempted to withdraw her hand and turn around
so that the nosy lady could see the other side of her.

"I could not allow Chesterson's dear cousin to come to
Storm's End with no one to meet her. The naughty boy
insisted that he sit in Parliament this day, even though I
told him he should be here when you arrived."

"His lordship left a missive explaining his whereabouts
and apologized for not being here when I arrived. In
truth, I was quite relieved. It was an arduous journey. I
would have welcomed time to rest before seeing anyone,
but my maid said you were quite anxious to see me." *That
should bring an apology.*

No apology was forthcoming. Lady Arbuthnot stepped
back into a small receiving room that held a small settee
and several chairs. A morning receiving room, Sarah
surmised. She had not taken note of the room when she
arrived.

Without being asked to sit, Lady Arbuthnot gracefully
positioned herself on the settee and fluttered her fan. She
was dressed exquisitely, Sarah noted, in a dress of pale
yellow silk and slippers of the same color.

The best money could buy, Sarah thought, noting the
low decolletage and the obstinate woman's ample bosom.
In that instant Sarah wished she had allowed Angeline to
come along, for it was obvious that Lady Arbuthnot had
come to stay until she was ready to leave.

Sarah settled herself into a chair, saying to her unwel-
come visitor, "Your hat is most becoming."

"Isn't it positively divine? 'Tis from a French designer,
and only a limited number are available. I would not be

wearing one had not Chesterson, the dear, dear man that he is, spoken to the company representative. One has to be very deep in the pockets to afford even one. Of course I requested two, but found that it was impossible to buy more than one, due to the limited number being made. I would be most happy to speak to Chesterson about your ordering one if you have the two hundred pounds—"

Sarah smothered her laughter. "That won't be necessary. My dear aunt, Lady Lillian Merriwether, has two of the beautiful creations, and I have several myself."

Lady Arbuthnot's next words made Sarah choke on her laughter. "Since I intend to marry Chesterson, and you are his dear cousin from America, a strange land of savages and heathens, so I hear, I came to Storm's End this day, Lady Sarah, to offer my assistance in your launch into London's *beau mode.*"

Sarah started to speak, but Lady Arbuthnot raised her hand and continued, "I know everyone who is anyone in the *ton,* and I can place you with the right gentleman for a husband. First, you must needs consider position, and then wealth. My late husband had both. He left me unbelievably rich."

Sarah could feel her ladyship's pale gaze searching her countenance. She tried not to blink but knew that she did, and she could not stop herself from asking, "You are promised to Lord Chesterson?"

Lady Arbuthnot's fan of painted silk passed before her face twice before she answered, and then with a little laugh. "Well, not exactly promised—"

"What do you mean, not exactly promised? You are either promised or you're not promised." Sarah scooted back into her chair as she tried to appear nonchalant, knowing she was failing miserably. How could Nathan be engaged to this pompous woman who bragged about her wealth? Even in heathen America one did not do that.

" 'Tis this way, Lady Sarah. I'm sure you are aware of his lordship's present financial difficulty." She shook her head. "Absolutely not his fault. He left no stone unturned in trying to cure his ailing wife. It took all his ready blunt, and then came the dry seasons, three in a row, which gave him no chance to replenish his coffers. So from the goodness of my heart, I have offered to share my good fortune with him."

"Wh . . . what do you mean?"

"I need a husband, and he needs blunt. 'Tis as simple as that."

"And what did he say?"

"He turned me down, but he will come around when he sees the advantage of being leg-shackled to a wealthy widow. Once, when he had had too much wine, he mentioned that he might consider my making him a loan to pay some unscrupulous money lenders. And he said something about keeping someone out of debtor's prison."

"What did you tell him?" asked Sarah, unbelieving.

"I told him absolutely no loan, not without collateral, and he would be the collateral." Lady Arbuthnot, laughing, said, "I hold the ace card. Chesterson needs blunt."

"I think that is disgraceful," retorted Sarah.

"I understand why you feel that way, Lady Sarah. You're young and inexperienced. One learns from what life has dealt one. Chesterson is handsome, erudite, and—"

"I would never consider marrying someone I did not love. Do you love his lordship?"

Lady Arbuthnot tittered. "What a silly question. As I told you, a girl marries for position and wealth. Since I don't need the wealth—"

"I could never do that."

"Of course you can. Then after you've given your husband an heir, take a lover."

"And 'tis your wont to marry Lord Chesterson and be a mistress to someone else?"

"Why not? 'Tis the thing with the *ton*. Of course, should

Chesterson want more children, I would produce a second heir to the Chesterson earldom, though I think it unlikely that he would want more children. At least I should pray not."

Sarah absolutely could not believe her ears. Either this woman was daft, or she was very clever. Sarah was inclined toward the latter, and then a terrible thought raced through her befuddled mind: Nathan was considering this bountiful offer, and that was why his missives had become so distant.

Lady Arbuthnot's next words put Sarah deeper into the desponds. "I thought it wise that we have this little coze, Lady Sarah, as I wished to apprise you of the fact that Lord Chesterson is spoken for."

Sarah rose from her chair and extended her hand, smiling as she did so. "I'm certain his lordship will tell me should it be his wont to marry you, Lady Arbuthnot. We are very close . . . for distant cousins."

Almost instantly Lady Arbuthnot was on her feet, her countenance showing her displeasure in being dismissed by a girl from America who knew nothing of the English ways. She took Sarah's proffered hand and, returning her smile smugly, said, "Surely you don't think his lordship has a *tendre* for you, Lady Sarah. Should that be the case, then why is he helping thrust you onto the Marriage Mart?"

Chapter Twenty-One

Stepping out into the fresh air from the stuffy House of Parliament, Nathan quickly shed his robe and powdered wig, then hurried to his tilbury waiting at the curb. He gave the boy holding the black horse's ribbons a shilling and sprang into the equipage. Within minutes he was tooling over the cobbled streets to Storm's End. He could not stop his heart's pounding. Soon he would see his Sarah. What a respite from the grueling day. For hours he had stood before the august group and argued child labor, most likely to no avail.

It never ceased to amaze his lordship how disinterested the nobility was in what was happening to England's children. Young boys were actually being sold to chimney sweeps for a few pounds, to be used as climbing boys. The demand was ever increasing, for the small lads died young from inhaling the black soot. This day, he had tried hard to get the nobility to listen, but Lords Sefton and Manners had slept through the debate. Sprawled on a bench, they had actually snored while he was speaking. It was disgraceful, and he had told them so.

Knowing he had handled the issue the best that he could, his lordship pushed the day's worry from his mind and thought about Sarah, wondering if she had arrived at Storm's End as expected. He regretted that he could not be there to greet her. But mayhap it was for the best, he told himself, for he was not sure he could have restrained himself from going to her and taking her into his arms in front of Ladies Lillian and Angeline, and the servants. He had thought about what Paul, his valet, had advised him to do, and he was sorely tempted.

That was only half right; the honorable part of him knew it would be wrong, unfair to Lady Sarah, but his heart, his soul, all of his being longed to go to her bed-chamber and make love to her, to feel her warm body against his.

He swore and told himself to stop such thoughts, for the sudden sweet pain that filled his body was excruciating.

Would she turn him out, he wondered, remembering how her missives had only asked favors of him, never mentioning how she felt. "I will go to her this night," he said aloud.

And then it will be harder to let her go to that rich husband she is bound to find.

Nathan swore again and cracked the whip over the black horse's back, even though he was already traveling at a fast pace. The sound of hoofbeats filled his lordship's mind and stilled his heart. To cool his passion, he focused his thoughts on Lady Lillian, hating her but knowing he was being unfair. It was his Sarah's wont not to go back on her word that was keeping them apart. He suspected that had Sarah's father been dead longer and were she not so attached to his memory, things might be different.

His lordship knew that he was indulging in wishful thinking. Lord Templeton had brought his children up in an honorable way, to believe their word was their bond.

Nathan could not fault that. His mind went to Angeline, how plain-spoken she was, how mature at times, the next moment childlike and clinging to her sister, and he realized that he had developed a fondness for the girl. Her forthrightness was refreshing.

There was nothing refreshing about Sarah's old aunt. If the old woman's selfish ways had not run Lord Temple-

ton off all those years ago, she would not be threatened
with debtor's prison, thus claiming his Sarah to exchange
for blunt to save herself.

What a farrago.

By the time the tilbury turned onto the street that led
to Storm's End, Nathan had settled in his mind that he
could do nothing less than help launch Lady Sarah into
society. It was such a painful thought that he prayed that
something, anything, would happen to prevent her from
having to make a convenient marriage. At least he would
see her this day, and if the opportunity presented itself, he
would find out if she still felt for him what she had felt the
night in the cabin. He had not liked this long separation.

Oh, the night in the cabin, he thought, smiling to
himself and feeling overpowering love wash over him. He
would not think of the time when another man would
claim her; he would live for this time when she would be
near him, before her come-out party and her ultimate
marriage to someone else. Was she as beautiful as he
remembered, or was his mind playing tricks on him?

His lordship felt like a young Regency buck of eighteen,
going calling on a chit for the first time, instead of a foolish
old man of thirty. Storm's End came into view, its white
stone glistening in the dying sun. He was glad that his
valet had insisted that this day he wear a Weston-tailored,
blue superfine coat, an embroidered waistcoat, and saddle
tan pantaloons that, as the valet had said, showed his
muscular thighs. His cravat was pristine white, and his
lordship could only pray that it was still creased properly.

Mayhap he should go to his quarters and freshen up a
bit before seeking out Lady Sarah; or mayhap she would
be waiting for him under the portico.

The new groom waited under the portico, no one else,
and for the life of Nathan he could not remember the
groom's name. There were so many new servants.

"Welcome, my lord," the groom said, taking the ribbons from Nathan. "Do yer want him rubbed down?"

"That won't be necessary, ah . . . By the bye, what *is* your name? I apologize for forgetting."

"Walter, m'lord. After me father."

" 'Tis a good name, Walter, and I'll try to remember."

The groom smiled, jumped up into the tilbury, then guided the horse around the side of the house, to the back, where the mews were situated.

Nathan turned to go into the house and was met at the door by Gifford, the butler. "Where is everyone, Gifford?" his lordship asked as his eyes searched for a glimpse of Lady Sarah. "I pray my cousin arrived from the country?"

"Yes, m'lord, indeed they did arrive and are now in the drawing room. I just took a tray up with tea and scones."

" 'Tis late for tea, don't you think?"

"A caller prevented them from having it earlier, m'lord."

Nathan's eyebrows shot up. "A caller? Who?"

"Lady Arbuthnot, m'lord. Her ladyship, Lady Sarah, entertained the caller."

This was an unexpected turn of events, thought Nathan. Since Lady Arbuthnot had laid her cards on the table about her intentions, he had tried to distance himself from her. But she had been persistent, especially after she had learned his cousin from America would be staying at Storm's End for the duration of her come-out.

Nathan felt himself frowning as he made his way across the great hall and up the winding stairs. He wished that he could speak with Lady Sarah alone, for a foreboding feeling had come over him. It was inconsiderate of Lady Arbuthnot to come calling before Lady Sarah was ready to receive her. Poor dear, without a chance to rest she must feel exhausted.

This new turn of events had dampened Nathan's exuberance of seeing his Sarah, but not entirely. His steps were light and quick, and he smiled when he came to the withdrawing room where tea was being served by Lady

illian. He stood unobtrusively in the doorway and
atched.

Sarah and Angeline were sitting with their backs to
m. Lady Lillian faced him, and he was sure that she was
ognizant of his presence. He listened intently. One
ould think the old woman the Queen of England, what
ith the way she presided over the tea table. She poured
om a silver teapot, from which steam curled up from its
out. She tilted her head just so as she handed out
elicate china cups to Sarah, and then to Angeline.

"Watch carefully, Lady Sarah. When you are married
a man of the nobility, you will be expected to serve tea
callers. I'm surprised that you did not offer Lady Ar-
uthnot tea when she called. That was not *ton*. How
oughtful of her to offer her assistance in launching you
to society. One cannot have too many influential
ends."

"Most likely I would have poured the hot tea in her lap,
ould I have served her," Sarah answered. Earlier, when
uestioned about her caller, she had said simply that Lady
rbuthnot had called to offer help in Sarah's come-out.
he would not dare tell the old woman the whole of it.

Sarah could not stop the anger that Lady Arbuthnot
d induced. How dare Nathan not be truthful with her;
ow dare he say he loved her when he was talking matri-
ony with another woman? She could not bear it.

As usual, Angeline was not at a loss for words. "I hear
at English teas are nothing more than scandal broths.
hy would anyone bother serving tea properly if the
rson only came calling to hear the latest *on-dits* about
ciety? And how could one know if the one passing the
-*dit* is telling the truth?"

"I agree with Angeline, why feed someone if they came
ly to gossip?" Nathan said as he strolled across the
om to join the tea drinkers, his burning gaze on Sarah,
ho had turned and was staring at him. Quickly she
mped to her feet and curtsied.

She wore her green dress. Peggy had pressed it whil
Sarah bathed, and even though she was angry with h
lordship, she had donned it again, and she had let Ange
line dress her hair in curls that fell to her shoulder
reminiscent of the night in the cabin. She remembered s
well his saying, "Ah, those whiskey curls, let them f
free."

Nathan took Sarah's hand and lifted her up, the
pressed his mouth to her hand. "Welcome to Storm
End, Lady Sarah," and then he turned to greet Angelin
who had also curtsied to him.

Lady Lillian scowled.

Because he kissed Sarah's hand, his lordship presume
Laughing, for his heart was suddenly light, he bowed fro
the waist and said, "I hope the journey was not too taxin
Lady Lillian."

"Stuff!" she said. "I can hold my own with these your
girls any day. God's truth, I feel younger than I have
years, almost as if *I* were having a Season instead of Lac
Sarah."

"You may take my place," Sarah said, forcing a hollo
laugh. She was as serious as she had ever been in her lif

Lady Lillian instructed everyone to sit down and drir
more tea, and everyone sat. "May I pour for you, Lor
Chesterson?"

"No, I do not want to spoil my appetite. I spoke wi
Cook before I left this morning and ordered a sumptuo
dinner." He slapped his knees with his big hands. "I c
want to hear about the journey. It was my wont to be he
when you arrived, but would you know, the issue of chi
labor was to be argued today. I felt that, since I ha
introduced the bill into the House of Lords, I should l
present."

"Did you wear your powdered wig?" asked Angelin

"Yes, and my robe, but it was terribly hot in the char
ber and I shed them as soon as I left. They are in tl

bury, and I'm sure the groom will deliver them to the
house. If not, I'll send my valet for them."

Suddenly it dawned on Nathan that the conversation
was about nothing of consequence. Sarah was quiet, and
when she smiled, it was obviously forced. He had seen her
chin set in that stubborn line before. He decided to draw
her out. "Lady Sarah, I hear you had a caller this day.
Was the visit pleasant? Lady Arbuthnot is—"

"I know, a very close friend of yours. She is quite nice,
and she is very fond of you. So fond, in truth, that she
means to marry you. When does the wedding take place,
before or after my come-out?"

"I think that a capital idea," said Lady Lillian. "Does
he have blunt?"

"Lady Lillian," chimed in Angeline, "is blunt all you
think about?"

Lady Lillian did not answer, and silence enveloped the
room, his lordship so taken aback that he could not speak.
And he did not want to delve deeper into the subject with
Lady Lillian and Lady Angeline present. "Lady Arbuthnot has a wild imagination at times. When we have a
moment alone, Lady Sarah, I am sure I can explain. I
assure you my intent was honorable."

Honorable! thought Sarah. *He doesn't know the meaning of the
word.*

Nathan rose from his chair. "I think I shall freshen up
a bit before Cook announces dinner ready. She gets quite
agitated if her cuisine is kept waiting until it is cold." He
turned to Sarah. "Would you excuse me?" He almost said
"darling," but caught it with the tip of his tongue.

"Of course. I, too, shall repair to my rooms. Thank
you, Lady Lillian, for a wonderful tea and a most informa-
tive lesson in serving. I shall make good use of it in the
future, when I am a member of the *ton.*"

"There will be more lessons, rest assured of that," said
Lady Lillian. She pushed herself up from her chair, obviously bent on quitting the room with Sarah and Nathan.

And she would have had not Angeline quickly said, '
would like another cup of the delicious tea, Lady Lillia
I'm beginning to take a liking to English ways. And yo
are a master in decorum when you hold that silver pot ju
so. God's truth, I've never seen anything like it. Lac
Sarah will benefit immensely from your instructions."

Nathan, hearing Angeline's false display of flattery fo
the purpose of detaining Lady Lillian, was laughing whe
he and Sarah reached the corridor. Sarah asked, "What
so demme funny? And if you expect me to apologize fo
swearing, I refuse. I'm beginning to believe that all artist
crats talk out of both sides of their mouths—"

"What do you mean, lovely Sarah? What have *I* dor
to displease you?"

He took her arm. She jerked it away.

"Don't play the innocent with me, Nathan Adam
You know perfectly well what I am talking about."

"I swear, darling, 'tis you who is talking out both sid
of your mouth, and I can't make heads nor tails of it.'

By now they were at the door of Sarah's quarters. Sh
reached for the knob only to have Nathan stay her han
With a touch of anger in his voice, he said, "You will te
me what is wrong before you enter that door."

"Unhand me, my lord, or I will slap your face," Sara
said, and instantly Nathan grabbed her free hand to pr
vent that from happening. He turned his back to the do
and pushed with the hopes it was slightly ajar, but t
door held fast. "Demme," he said, and then he held bo
of her small wrists with one of his big hands, turning t
knob with his other.

"What do you think you are doing?" Sarah demande

"I'm going to get you out of this corridor, and when t
door is closed behind us, I am going to kiss you until yo
tell me what I have done to make you so angry with me

Before Sarah could accuse Nathan of talking mat
mony with Lady Arbuthnot, his lips were on hers in su
heated fashion she could not talk. Nor could she thir

d then to further irritate her, he was holding her where
 could not push away and slap him. Even if she had
nted to.

Raising his blond head, he smiled down at her and
ed, "Are you still angry with me, love?"

"Why should I not be——"

"You are not permitted to answer a question with a
estion, and that is what you are doing——"

He kissed her again and then whispered against her lips
t he loved her, that she was the most beautiful woman
he world, that she haunted his dreams. He even men-
ed the handsome dress she was wearing, green to
tch her eyes. "I love you," he whispered before moving
kiss her neck, the white flesh above her low neckline.
 heard the soft moan that escaped Sarah's throat.

All anger drained from Sarah, replaced by the wonder-
 delicious feeling she had experienced the night she
 Nathan were at the cabin. Passion engulfed her
 in, and before she could stop herself, she was telling
 that she loved him, too. She opened her mouth and
 im taste her tongue, and she found her deceitful body
 ing into his, and when he released her arms, instead
 apping his lordship as she had planned, she put them
und his neck, making the kiss much deeper.

Sarah was lost. She allowed her body to lean into his
dship's muscular, throbbing frame, and they melded
ther as if they were one. In truth, she admitted later,
 had forgotten that Lady Arbuthnot had called at
m's End. She certainly did not remember the
nan's insane plan to marry his lordship.

Nor did Sarah remember that she was destined to
ry a man because he was rich. At the moment all that
tered was their love.

 was Nathan who returned Sarah to reality.

He stepped back when he realized that his passion was
e what it had been in the cabin. He hadn't thought

that possible. "I will not allow it," he said in a strangl
voice.

"Allow what?" Sarah asked. The look on his face w
almost frightening. She told her own heart to stop
pounding as she stood staring at him.

"I am bound that I cannot let another man have yo
God made you for me. You are my mate, to love,
honor, and to cherish for the rest of my life."

Tears welled in Sarah's eyes. "You've said that befo
Nathan, but things are the same. I pray each night th
something will happen so that I won't have to make t'
marriage of convenience. Still, the day is drawing no
when I will have my come-out. We must needs acco
God's will."

"Not if 'tis His plan to take you away from me."

"Nathan, you are being sacrilegious."

He reached for her again, to hold her, not passionat
but tenderly. He rested his chin on her whiskey curls a
felt the trembling that shook her body. God, how he lov
her.

"I'll find an answer, Sarah, I swear I will."

He had completely forgotten the advice his valet h
given him, to bed her this night, and his own vow to
on that advice, and he had forgotten that, before the f
kiss, Sarah had been angry with him.

For this moment, he thought, nothing matters. A
Nathan was content just to have his darling Sarah so n
to his heart. Tomorrow . . . tomorrow the answer wo
come.

Chapter Twenty-Two

Sister, Storm's End is the most beautiful house I have
· seen," said Angeline. "Just think, it will be your
1e when you're married to Lord Chesterson—"

Hush, Angeline," cut in Sarah. " 'Tis bad enough to
w that I will never be married to Lord Chesterson,
the truth only becomes more painful when you talk
ut it."

But did he not say that he would find a way to keep
y Lillian out of prison and still marry you?"

It would take a miracle, and Lord Chesterson is not a
icle worker."

No, but God is. Sarah, you must needs have more
·."

hey were in Sarah's bedchamber. Already Peggy had
e to help Sarah with her toilette, but Sarah had told
that she would not need her and that they would be
n for breakfast shortly.

ngeline was still abed, propped up against huge down
ws and doing what she liked best to do—talking
1t when Sarah would be married to Lord Chesterson.
Sarah knew it was only wishful thinking. Last evening
n his lordship talked about how he could not forbear
her man having her and that he would think of some-
g to prevent that from happening, she believed him.
1use she so desperately wanted to believe. But at first

light this day she had awakened to the awful truth: the
was nothing his lordship could do.

Sarah went into the dressing room and splashed c
water on her face, drying it with a soft thick towel th
reminded her of Templeton Hall. She wondered h
Mary Ellen was faring and if her stomach was protrudi
Sarah tried not to think about Hoggie, but thinking of h
sister-in-law made her smile. Mary Ellen would be
happy when the baby came, and she would be the best
mothers.

Standing before the chiffonier, Sarah chose a morni
dress of sprigged muslin, then went into the dressi
room. The dress was plain, with only a small bow un
her bosom, and she felt like a schoolgirl in it. She w
dered if Nathan would like it, that is, if he saw it. At din
last evening, he had mentioned going to the House
Lords, but that he would be home in time to take her
a ride in Hyde Park at five o'clock, saying, "I want v
much to show you off to my peers."

Lady Lillian had objected regally and strenuously, s
ing that would give the wrong impression, that the r
gentlemen of the *ton* would think Lady Sarah spoken
"And since I am responsible for my dear niece's laur
into society, I forbid her to ride in the park with any
until *we* have had a chance to look at the market. 'Two
be ridiculous to spoil her chances."

Tapping her cane on the floor, she had added, "L
Chesterson, you should know that better than I."

Nathan had countered with, "What is wrong with
ing with my cousin from America in Hyde Park? Angel
may chaperon if she would like."

Angeline had quickly refused. Not that she would
dearly love to come along, Sarah thought, but Ange
wanted Sarah and Nathan to be alone.

I'm glad Angeline's not going, thought Sarah. Last even
Nathan had kissed her until she could not think, and
had not asked him about Lady Arbuthnot. During

ride in Hyde Park would be the perfect time to approach the subject. Surely then he would not be kissing her for everyone to see.

Sarah brushed her auburn curls and tied them at the nape with a riband. She added a tiny amount of rouge to her cheeks, for they seemed pale to her, and then, with her smallest finger, she added color to her lips, careful not to overdo. She did not want to look like the silly lampoons of Prinny's wife, Carolyn of Brunswick, whom he was trying to divorce. Finishing her toilette, Sarah then went back to the bedchamber and found Angeline still in bed.

"Angeline, please get up and get dressed," Sarah scolded. "Breakfast will be cold." *And Nathan will have left.*

"I'm waiting," said Angeline.

"Waiting for what?"

"For you to tell me what Lord Chesterson thought about Lady Arbuthnot calling on you when you were too tired to see anyone, and what he had to say about marrying the demi-rep."

"Angeline, you don't have to know everything, and Lady Arbuthnot is *not* a demi-rep. I doubt that you know what the word means."

"A woman who takes a man of the upper orders for her protector."

Sarah laughed. "A protector pays the bills for his mistress. Lady Arbuthnot does not need anyone to pay her bills. She made it very plain that her late husband left her rich. Besides, Lord Chesterson doesn't have a feather to fly with. So, little sister, you are all wrong about that. Now get dressed and let's go downstairs."

"I still want to know what he said——"

"Nothing. I forgot to ask him."

"Well, you should have," declared Angeline as she bounded off the bed like a young colt and dashed into the dressing room.

Sarah tapped her foot impatiently against the carpet. Sitting near the fireplace, she examined the room which would be her bedchamber for the duration of her stay at Storm's End.

The bed hangings were of white silk, as were the window coverings, with deep green tassels to match the walls. Sarah wondered if Nathan's late wife had done the decorating, or had she hired a professional designer such as the architect Holland, who, so *on-dits* had it, was the Prince Regent's favorite architect and interior designer. It seemed strange to Sarah that she felt this extreme jealously of Lady Arbuthnot; yet, she had no such feelings for the woman Nathan had loved and married.

"I'm ready," said Angeline, coming from the dressing room while combing her long hair with her fingers. Seldom did Sarah see her sister when her long black hair was not braided. She asked Angeline about it.

"I didn't have time, your being in such a hurry to see his lordship." Angeline was smiling.

"How did you know?" asked Sarah.

"I have a sixth sense. I can read your mind." Angeline laughed. "Don't be a peagoose, sister, one doesn't have to read your mind, just look at the longing in those beautiful green eyes. Love pours from them. Even yesterday, when you were angry with his lordship about Lady Arbuthnot, your eyes gave you away."

"I didn't know it was so obvious."

"Mayhap only to me. I also know something else. You could have gone downstairs without me, but you stayed because you did not want the selfish old crow berating me at breakfast. You feel that you have to protect me from her sharp tongue. But you needn't worry, I can take care of myself."

Sarah had not doubt of that, and she also knew that Angeline, even though she tried to appear hard-hearted toward the old woman, had sympathy for Lady Lillian. Many times she had said that anyone as selfish as the old crow could not be happy and, therefore, deserved sympathy.

When Sarah and Angeline reached the morning room off the kitchen, where breakfast was being served from a sideboard by a liveried footman, Lady Lillian was alone at the table. There were fresh flowers in the center, which were no doubt, Sarah thought, picked from the garden which could be seen through open windows. The smell of lilacs mingled with the sunshine that cut a swath across the room.

Lady Lillian greeted them pleasantly, and she imparted the information that his lordship had left only moments ago. "He left this missive for you, Lady Sarah. I was tempted not to give it to you. He doesn't seem to understand your purpose in being at Storm's End. 'Tis certainly not to be riding in the park with his lordship, his being poor as a church mouse."

Sarah grimaced but did not reply. She read silently the missive from Nathan, which reminded her that they indeed would ride in the park at five o'clock, regardless of Lady Lillian's objections. He had also added: "Business in Parliament will end at an early hour, and I shall then call on a business acquaintance in regard to what you and I discussed last evening. As I told you, I will not give up. Never, never will I let you go to some jackanapes who could never love you as I do."

The words suddenly filled Sarah with hope, and she began planning on what she would wear for the ride in Hyde Park. The footman served scrambled eggs and ham from the sideboard, after which he held a tray with an assortment of jellies for Sarah and Angeline to choose. Hot bread and coffee were then brought from the sideboard.

Angeline was quiet, but that was not unusual, thought Sarah. Her sister never let anything interfere with her eating, and she would not ask what was in the missive with Lady Lillian present.

"Lady Sarah, are you not going to tell me what was in the letter?" the old woman asked, lifting her lorgnette and peering at Sarah. "Oh, you're smiling, so no doubt 'twas good news."

"Lord Chesterson was only reaffirming his plan to take me to the park," Sarah said, almost giggling when Lady Lillian gave her infamous scowl.

And then something strange happened, at least it seemed strange to Sarah. The butler entered the small dining room and presented Lady Lillian with a silver salver bearing a white envelope. By the surprised look on her ladyship's face, Sarah knew that the old woman was taken off guard. Her hands trembled as she ripped at the seal, and as she read the message, her aging face became ghostly pale.

Sarah pleaded silently, *Oh, please don't go mad again, Aunt Lillian.* Aloud Sarah asked, "Is something wrong, Lady Lillian?"

"No, no, nothing is wrong, but I must needs excuse myself," Lady Lillian answered, her voice not at all strong. She rang the small silver bell that lay near her plate, and when a servant appeared, she asked that the Merriwether crested carriage be brought round front.

The old woman left the table, and when her steps faltered, Angeline went to take her arm. "Do you not feel well, Lady Lillian?" Angeline asked.

"I feel fine. And I can walk by myself." Her ladyship's voice was instantly laced with her usual irascibility. After a few steps, she became more steady on her feet. She shook Angeline's hand from her arm and quit the room, and Angeline returned to the table, saying, "A pox on her. Can you imagine Papa being married to her?"

"Never," Sarah said, hardly cognizant of what Angeline had asked. Deep in thought, she was silent for a long moment. At last, frowning, she said, "I wonder what was in the missive? Something that almost sent her into a spell of the vapors. I suspect it would have had she not wanted to keep the message secret. Did you see how she crumpled it in her hand? But I couldn't tell whether she was happy or sad."

Angeline took a huge gulp of coffee and choked on it. Holding her serviette over her mouth, she sputtered and coughed. When the coughing had subsided, she said, "If you would like, I will find out—"

"How?"

"I'll search her rooms after she leaves. I can see out the window when the carriage leaves. And if the search doesn't produce the missive, I can ask the driver where he took the old crow."

"Oh, Angeline," Sarah said, "you would not dare. That would be beyond the pale."

"Of course, sister, you are right. That would be outside of enough," answered Angeline, smiling inwardly while thinking, *Oh, but I would dare.*

The search revealed nothing, much to Angeline's chagrin, and later she told Sarah that Lady Lillian had, according to her abigail, changed hurriedly into a purple carriage gown, donned a beautiful broad-brimmed hat with purple plumes, and left without hardly a word. "And here it is late afternoon, and she hasn't returned," Angeline said. She stopped and took a deep breath. "The maid also said Lady Lillian crammed an envelope into the reticule she carried when she left. Oh, yes, and she said Lady Lillian forgot her cane. What do you think of that, sister?"

"I don't know what to make of it, and as long as she is all right, I suppose 'tis none of our business. After all, she is no stranger to London. She may be visiting with an old friend."

"You know what I think?" asked Angeline.

Sarah smiled, for Angeline looked as if she kept her thoughts to herself another minute she would explode. "What do you think, little sister?"

It was nearing five o'clock, and still Nathan had not returned to Storm's End. Sarah wondered what was keeping him. After having enjoyed a long soak in the porcelain tub, she was donning a lovely gown of blue-green sarcenet, one of her favorites of her new wardrobe. She hardly had time to worry about Lady Lillian's absence from Storm's End, but still she was curious.

"I think she's gone to the money lenders," Angeline said. "Not the same ones she's already in debt to—I'm sure there's many more in London—and borrowed money for gambling. I can just see her at the whist table—"

"Oh, Angeline, you have such a wild imagination. Surely dear Aunt Lillian has learned her lesson about borrowing money. Besides, what would she use for collateral?"

"I'm sure she would think of something," Angeline retorted.

Sarah turned her back to Angeline and asked that she button the tiny buttons that reached from her neck to below her waist.

"Why do they not make dresses to button in the front?" Angeline wanted to know. " 'Twould be much simpler."

"That's why we have lady's maids. But I prefer that you do it for me. And would you dress my hair? I think down, for I plan to wear my Gypsy hat. I'm sure Lady Arbuthnot will be in the park, and I want the rich lady to see that I can afford a hat as grand as hers."

While Angeline brushed and arranged Sarah's auburn curls to complement her face, the sound of carriage wheels floated through the open window. Dropping the hairbrush as if it burned her hand, Angeline rushed to look out. " 'Tis the carriage Lady Lillian left in, and she's in it, sitting as tall and straight as if she's been to see the King."

"I'm glad she's home. At least we know she's safe."

"But we still don't know where she's been."

"And 'tis still none of our business," Sarah said, as she picked up the big hat and put it atop her head, sucking in her breath when she looked into the looking glass. The hat was absolutely stunning. "Thank you for making this wonderful hat for me, Angeline."

"That's it!" screeched Angeline. "That old woman sold her Gypsy hat for gambling money."

"Oh, Angeline, your imagination is out of control."

But Angeline was not listening. Already she was at the door, vowing, "I will kill her . . ." The slamming of the door drowned out her last words.

Sarah was glad to be left alone, for she had to plan what she would say to Nathan about his special friend Lady Arbuthnot, and Sarah wanted a little time to admire the dress she was wearing. What a wonderful modiste Madame LaCross had turned out to be, and so inexpensive. Sarah turned before the looking glass, then stopped abruptly. A sound came from the door, a soft knock. If it were Angeline, she most certainly would come in without knocking. Mayhap a maid. She called, "Enter." Quitting the dressing room, she made her way through the bedchamber and into the small sitting room.

There, standing just inside the door, tall and gloriously handsome, was Lord Chesterson. She had to restrain herself from running to him, and her voice shook as she said, "My lord, I'm glad to see you."

Nathan's long steps closed the distance between them. "And I to see you. I could have sent up for you, but I was hoping I would find you alone."

"And so you did." Sarah could see in his eyes that something had gone awry. Sadness poured from them, and Sarah felt her happiness of a moment before drain from her body. "Nathan, what's wrong?" she asked.

"I was turned down . . . again. I'm beginning to feel like a beggar."

"Turned down by whom?"

"I went to a banker friend and offered to mortgage this

year's crops. I have over two thousand acres and the rains have assured good harvest, but he reminded me that dry weather could still come."

"That is probably true—"

"I know, my lovely Sarah, but I had to try." He shook his head. "That was my last hope." He reached for her and pulled her to him, only to have the Gypsy hat get in his way of burying his trembling chin in her hair. Patiently he removed it from her head, laid it on a chair, then came back to start over again.

"You were lovely in the hat, but I want nothing to deter me from kissing you."

He kissed her once, long and tenderly, but the passion was not there. The pain in his heart rose up to take precedence over the longing to make love to her. But more than anything he wanted to make her his helpmeet, his wife forever and ever. This day the dream died a horrible death inside of him. Where could he turn? He could not, would not, ask Sarah to go back on her word to her old aunt. With the old woman rotting in prison, what chance did they have for happiness? None, he concluded, for both were too sensitive to each other's pain.

Tears clouded Nathan's eyes, and a sob lodged in his throat. He crushed his lovely Sarah to him and held her tightly, his breath uneven. He felt her body tremble, but she said not a word. For a long time he held her thus, his chin buried in her hair. At last he released her and turned away to look through the window at the small garden below.

He had planted and nurtured the flowers for the time when Sarah would come to Storm's End.

"Sarah," he said, "I'm sorry. I feel that I have let you down. Until today I held the belief that I could keep you from another man's arms."

"I will never let another man hold me," she vowed, knowing she was talking foolishly. If she landed that rich husband, she would be expected to bear his child. The thought made her shudder. Into the silence of the room, she said, "Nathan, let's not let tomorrow ruin today. I would very much like to ride in the park with you. There's something I have been wanting to ask you."

"Of course we shall ride in the park. Your plan to save Lady Lillian must needs go forward. But suddenly I feel that we should steal every moment before your come-out. I beg your forgiveness if I sound morbid."

Sarah didn't answer, and Nathan went to reclaim her Gypsy hat. Sitting it atop her head, he smiled into her eyes. "No girl in the park will rival your beauty."

"Thank you, my lord," Sarah responded. "No one has ever said such lovely things to me before."

"I shall always say them."

Nathan had left the black tilbury under the portico, and they made their way down the winding stairs and across the great hall. "The squeeze is to show off one's traveling equipage and fine horseflesh, and for the girls to show off their newest gowns, but this day I am showing my Lady Sarah to bucks of the *ton*. This day, you are mine."

"Will you introduce me as your cousin from America?" Sarah asked.

"I don't plan to introduce you at all." He chuckled lightly. "Let them think what they will. Already I can feel the young bucks envy."

"What about Lady Arbuthnot? Do you think she will cause a scene since you've been speaking with her about matrimony?"

Sarah breathed a sigh of relief. There, it was out. At last she had introduced the subject that had been worrying her.

Nathan helped Sarah into the tilbury, took his place beside her, and took the ribbons. But the tilbury did not immediately move. He turned to look deep into Sarah's green eyes. "I never spoke with Lady Arbuthnot about marriage. *She* spoke with me about marriage, saying she would share the blunt her late husband left her.

"For an instant, and only for an instant, I entertained her proposal so that I could pay Lady Lillian's debts and you would not be forced to make a marriage of convenience. Now I realize how desperate was my thinking."

The tilbury moved then, and silence held them. As they neared the park, they saw handsome carriages pulled by handsome horses, all going in one direction. Gentlemen, dressed to the nines, were riding fine stallions. Some, Sarah noticed, waved to Nathan. He waved back, but not in a fashion that would invite them to ride alongside the tilbury and chat. He said to Sarah, "You do believe me, don't you, Sarah? I could not see how you and I would be better off with me married to Lady Arbuthnot. And the thought of performing my marital duties with her is most unpleasant."

"The same is true of my being married to a man I don't love," answered Sarah, satisfied with Nathan's answer.

"I will marry her for her blunt if you should want me to, Sarah. Mayhap it would be easier for you . . ."

"Oh, no. You have your children to think of. Lady Arbuthnot did not strike me as the motherly type. She might mistreat the twins." Sarah then added, "Angeline said I didn't have enough faith, that miracles do happen.'

"That's all we have left, darling, is to hope for a miracle," said Nathan. Then, cracking the whip over the horse's back, he reined him in to the long line of elegant carriages entering Hyde Park.

In one of those elegant carriages, a matronly woman quickly raised her lorgnette and peered unabashedly at the woman in the black tilbury pulling in line with the other carriages. The woman said to the man sitting on the opposite squab from her, "Oh, there she is, Anthony! I just knew Lord Chesterson would bring her today. 'Twill be worth the blunt we spent on renting this carriage and horses for you to meet her. *On-dits* have it that she's rich as croesus, which will make it easy to forgive her for being American."

Lord Harrowby yawned and stretched long legs in which he took tremendous narcissistic pride, muscles and bulges in just the right places. It was tomfoolery that he be here to get, as Mum had said, a head-on start at the rich girl from America. Women had always adored him.

Laconically Harrowby said to his mother, "Mum, staring like that will make you appear overly anxious. There's plenty of time for me to woo her. I resent your pulling me away from my games for this silly ride in the park. This day my luck was on my fingertips; I felt it in my bones."

"Your bones have lied to you before," Lady Harrowby retorted, and then she added, "Take a look at her, Anthony, next time she turns around. I don't believe I have ever seen such beauty. And the hat she's wearing must have cost a small fortune. From Paris, no doubt."

Anthony raised his quizzing glass, which was fastened by a black ribbon to the shoulder of his excellently tailored coat. He had always been nearsighted, his only flaw as far as he was concerned. He waited until at last the girl in the tilbury looked back over her shoulder. Quickly leaning forward for a better look, he let out a low whistle. He turned to his mother and smiled. "The girl's a prime article, all right. 'Tis unusual to find such beauty and blunt in the same package. Thank you, Mum, for dragging me to the park this day. I knew that luck would find me—"

"At five and thirty, you should know Mum always knows best. 'Tis fortunate for you that the American is pretty, but it would make no difference if she were ugly. You must needs make a lucrative marriage, and there's no time for dilly-dallying. Your recent losses at the gaming tables, when the tips of your fingers betrayed you, have left us without a feather to fly with."

Chapter Twenty-Three

Lord Chesterson and Lady Sarah agreed that they had
en in the squeeze as long as either desired. As Nathan
d said, "Just enough time for those who had come to
e and be seen to catch a glimpse of the girl from Amer-
.."

"I hate this nonsense about my being your cousin,
athan," Sarah said when she felt eyes boring down on
r. "In truth, our blood connection is so distant that I
uld hardly be called a relative at all. Cousins ten times
noved would be more accurate."

"If the *ton* did not think of you as my cousin, questions
uld be asked about the propriety of your staying at
rm's End. I would not have your reputation sullied."

"Mayhap we should have taken a dwelling. Enough
ney was made from the hats for——"

"I could not endure that. I wanted you close so that
ne scurrilous character would not be asking Lady Lil-
n for permission to pay his addresses. She would not
e as long as the man had blunt to save her. As your
sin, any jackanapes wishing to pay his addresses will
ak to me."

As Nathan broke ranks with the other carriages, the
ll-dressed matron in the carriage directly behind the
ury fluttered a white handkerchief, indicating she
hed to chat.

Nathan nodded, smiled pleasantly, then gave the blac horse office to run, which the horse did, lifting his forefee high.

As if he knew the pinks of the *ton* were watching thought Sarah. Cutting across the huge circle of carriages they were soon at the gate through which they had en tered the park. Laughing and feeling an uplifting of spiri Sarah held onto her Gypsy hat, and when the horse pace slowed, she asked, "Who was the woman waving t you, Nathan, and were you not a little rude?"

"That was Lady Harrowby. The fop sitting across from her was her son, Lord Harrowby. She's been trying to ge him leg-shackled for the past ten years, says she wants a heir to his title. I will not have him near you."

"Why not? If he has money?" asked Sarah, facin honesty straight on. "He was not at all bad-looking. Tha would be better than marrying some old quiz, as Lad Lillian suggested. Nathan, we must needs be practical.

"Harrowby will not do, and that is that."

"Nathan, I need money, lots of it, and quickly. If he ha money—"

"He was left a huge estate." Nathan paused and the shook his head. "No, he will not do. If he asks to pay h addresses, I shall refuse."

Sarah could see there was no use arguing. She let th subject drop. Her come-out was only a few nights from now, and that would be time enough to look the t gentlemen over. She asked, "Nathan, should I tell m future husband right away that he must needs furnis money to pay my aunt's debts? And what about Me rymount? Should I also say that my ancestral home about to be taken over by the Crown for past-due taxes?

Nathan could not help but smile at Lady Sarah's n iveté. "Should you do that, love, the gentleman will r the other way. Every man wants to believe he is irresistib to the lady of his choice, and that it is his attributes she after, not his blunt."

"Oh, it is all so deceitful. I don't like it at all, Nathan."

"Nor do I. I just wish there was another way."

"I could kill Lady Lillian for going to those nasty oney lenders. I could let Merrymount go as long as I uld have Mama's portrait."

They were silent after that, and when Sarah realized e tilbury was headed in the opposite direction of orm's End, she asked Nathan where they were going.

"I want to show you London," he said. "I could not ar some idiot showing you Carlton House for the first ne and King's Theater. 'Tis all a part of England's tory. I want to share it with you."

They drove for hours, so it seemed to Sarah, and she s quite engrossed in what Nathan was saying. It was a nderful respite from worrying about her future. This ;ht, for darkness had gathered, she was by Nathan's e, where, if fate had not deemed otherwise, she wished be forever.

Sarah, at twenty summers, knew that one's past faded one's mind, and she wondered how many years would ss before she could think of this night without her eyes ng with tears. The night in the cabin with Nathan ne to mind so vividly that she heard herself sob, and vowed she would never forget, for should she do so, · life would be as empty as yesterday's dreams.

They were in front of Westminster Abbey and Parlia- nt. "Can you believe we have been gone from Storm's d for three hours?" asked Nathan. "It has been such nderful fun."

'Most likely we have missed dinner. That is, unless geline made Aunt Lillian wait for us."

Nathan laughed. "That would be a battle of wills." He ched to take Sarah's hand. "I pray they have eaten. ner alone with you would be welcome."

Vith the mention of Lady Lillian, Sarah suddenly be- ne worried about her mysterious disappearance from rm's End, and she became quite anxious to go home.

Surely the old woman had not been at the gaming tables as Angeline had suspected.

As they drove toward the town house at a slow pace Sarah talked with Nathan about Lady Lillian's strange behavior, ending with, "What do you think, Nathan Why would she leave like that, and where could she have been for so long?"

"Angeline may be right," Nathan responded. "You haven't known your aunt for a great length of time, Sarah Mayhap she is stricken with the disease, and that is partly the reason she's in the mess she is in."

"But, Nathan, she seemed so disturbed when the missive came, and straight away she asked that the carriage be brought around. I told Angeline that it was none of our business, but I can't help but worry."

"Well, don't, love, for 'twill do no good. We'll hurry home and see what Angeline has found out. Then, if we are lucky, we can dine together. I want to spend every moment that I can with you before the big party." He reached for her hand, kissed the palm, then held it tightly feeling the wonderful sensation of desire wash over him Never in his life had he wanted anything, or anyone, so badly. The gaslights along the streets did magical thing with her whiskey curls when the tilbury passed by them mixing light and dark, making him drunk with desire.

Nathan wanted once again to declare his love for Sarah, but he concluded that would only make it more difficult for him to let her go. He swore under his breath and swallowed the lump in his throat.

"What are you thinking, my lord?" Sarah asked.

"Only that my life is complete when I am with you, my dearest. I'm living for the moment, something I've never done in my life. I've always embraced the future—"

"Even when Naneen was so ill?"

"After I had exhausted all means to save Naneen, I felt that it was God's will to take her. With this . . . this farra of Lady Lillian's, I feel that she has imposed her awful will on you, that God has nothing to do with it."

Lady Sarah did not have an answer. The time was drawing near when she would no longer be this close to his lordship, and, like he, she wanted to think only of the moment. She removed her hat and laid it in the seat beside her, then rested her head on his shoulder and was pleased when he released her hand and put his arm around her, hugging her to him in a most possessive way.

They rode thus for the remainder of the way home, only occasionally conversing, and in the quiet moments, the thought entered Lady Sarah's mind that she could not do this altruistic thing she had set out to do. *If I did not love Nathan . . .*

But she did love Nathan, and she could never let another man touch her in the intimate way he had touched her. Tonight, when they were dining together, she would tell him, and tomorrow, she would tell Lady Lillian.

Lady Sarah's thoughts would not move further into the future.

The butler met them at the door, bowing and saying, "M'lord, m'lady."

"Good evening, Gifford," said Nathan. "Has everyone repaired to their respective rooms for the night? I realize 'tis quite late."

"Only her ladyship, Lady Lillian, my lord. She had her supper sent up, but Lady Angeline has been filling the house with the most wonderful music. I went to the music room and asked that the door be left open . . ."

Just then the sounds of the harpsichord floated down the curving stairs and filled the great hall. Sarah smiled. Angeline was playing a haunting Indian lullaby, one her mother, Wanna, had taught her.

Letting the music wash over them, Nathan and Sarah, hand in hand, silently began climbing the curving stairs, and then suddenly the music stopped, and Angeline was running down the stairs to meet them, her black hair in

ts usual braid, her dark eyes sparkling with her enthusiasm for life. And, as usual, words spilled over words. "I
thought I heard the door open, and I wanted to tell you
that I had cook keep supper warm for you. I waited to eat
so that I could tell you about Lady Lillian."

So much for dining alone with Sarah, thought Nathan. But
he could not be too disappointed, considering how happy
Angeline was to see her sister. He watched as the two
sisters hugged each other affectionately. Angeline then
turned and curtsied to him, saying, "M'lord."

He took her hand, lifted her up, then scolded good-
naturedly, "That is entirely unnecessary, Lady Angeline.
My family does not curtsy to me, and I consider you a part
of my family."

"If only that could be so," answered Angeline, for a
moment looking sadly at him. Then she perked up and
grabbed Sarah's hand. "Sister, I have so much to tell you,
and I want to know what happened in the park. Did you
see Lady Arbuthnot? You've been gone ever so long. Let's
freshen up and then meet Lord Chesterson for supper. As
I said, Cook is keeping the food warm."

"No telling until we are all together," Nathan said,
smiling, "I want to hear all about Aunt Lillian."

They parted then, but only a short time passed before
they were sitting at the table in the small dining room,
being served by a liveried footman. Sarah had splashed
her face with cold water, then brushed her auburn curls,
letting them fall to rest on her shoulders. She felt wonderfully rejuvenated. And ravenous. The smell of hot food
rushed up to assault her taste buds, setting them to watering. Across from her, Nathan was attacking his stewed
kidney as if he were afraid it would get away. His blond
curls were freshly combed, and he was wearing a fresh,
perfectly creased white cravat.

Sarah's gaze moved to Angeline, who looked as if she
would burst. "First," Angeline said, "before I tell you
about Lady Lillian, I want to know what Lady Arbuthnot

thought about *your* Louiezon hat, her thinking that only the very rich could afford one."

"She wasn't in the park," Sarah said.

"Yes, I saw her at a distance," Nathan said. "She was riding in a very elegant carriage, alone. I'm sure she used her spyglass to observe what was going on in the other carriages. That was one of the reasons I left fairly quickly. I did not want an encounter with her, but mostly I did not want you to come under her fast tongue." He was looking at Sarah.

"Well, now she can spread the word that Lady Sarah Templeton is rich, can she not?" asked Angeline. "If only the rich wear the Gypsy hat."

"And I can go about looking for a husband whose riches match my own," Sarah said sarcastically. She still felt that she could not go through with this farce. It was against her nature to be deceitful. She decided to bide her time about telling Nathan and Angeline her decision; she needed more time to think. And to change her mind, if that be that case. Lady Lillian, what would she say? Sarah could only imagine the wailing and gnashing of teeth.

"Now, Angeline, tell us about Lady Lillian. Had she, as you suspected, sold her Gypsy hat for gambling money? Did she win big, freeing me of my promise to her?"

Angeline took a bite of her food, chewed, and swallowed before answering. "I went to her rooms to ask if she had sold her hat for gambling money, but before I could get the words out, I saw the purple plumes sticking up from a chair by the fireplace. So instead I asked her where she had been and why she was acting so strangely."

Sarah smiled. "And what did she tell you?"

"In short, that it was none of my business. But, sister, her eyes were glassy, and she seemed to be enjoying my curiosity. I asked her why she didn't take her cane, and she laughed. Can you imagine that? The old crow just laughed at me."

Sarah looked at Nathan, who obviously was trying to

hide his amusement. He said, "So that just made you more curious, and you went to the driver and asked where he took Lady Lillian and why they had been gone so long."

"How did you know?" exclaimed Angeline. "The driver was just as stubborn as the old crow. He said he delivered her to Gunther's, and that he picked her up there. But 'tis outside of enough to believe she spent the whole day eating sweets at Gunther's."

"And where did the driver spend the day?" Sarah asked.

"He said at a coffee house in Covent Gardens, but the look on his face told me he was up to no good during that time, mayhap hidden away with a light skirt—"

"Angeline!" Sarah's voice was stern, and it brought a roar of laughter from Nathan, who said, "Sarah, the girl is probably right."

He looked at Angeline and asked, "What are your plans now, since you couldn't extract the truth from the driver or from Lady Lillian? Will you let the matter drop?"

Sarah chimed in, "Do you believe now that 'tis none of your business?"

"No," answered Angeline emphatically. "There's something here that does not meet the eye. Lady Lillian looked like she was up to something, and tomorrow, should she leave as she did this day, I plan to follow her."

"I cannot allow that, Angeline," Sarah said. She, too, believed there was more to Lady Lillian's extended absence from Storm's End than met the eye, but she would not have Angeline spying on the old woman. For it was reasonable to believe that Angeline could be putting herself in the way of danger.

And Lady Lillian, in her dotage, could be endangering her own safety, mused Sarah. Although that was less likely to happen with the old woman, who had seen many summers, than with Angeline, who had seen only five and ten, and who had lived in the country all of her life.

It was quite late, and Angeline had excused herself from the table and left them alone. They both had laughed, for it was obvious that she desired to stay but, in her role of matchmaker, had forced herself to leave.

When Sarah was alone with Nathan, she spoke with him about the danger Angeline might be putting herself in by following Lady Lillian, and he encouraged her to speak with Lady Lillian. "She will most certainly be more candid with you than with Angeline," his lordship said.

Now, standing at the door of Lady Sarah's quarters, Nathan reached to draw Sarah to him. He held her for a long moment and then brought his lips to hers, kissing her deeply and with much feeling. And then he said, "I would ask your permission to come in, but I don't trust myself. I have concluded that should we share another time like at the cabin, it would only make the pain worse to part forever. I do not wish to make life difficult for you, lovely Sarah."

"Don't feel that you have, Nathan. I know I will never love anyone as I love you, and I'm glad. I will always be glad for all that has happened."

He left her then, mustering all the will power that his being held. It was demme unfair, he thought, and very painful.

Passion soared through his lordship's body as he made his way to his own rooms and a lonely bed.

Chapter Twenty-Four

Lady Lillian thwarted Angeline's plan to play sleuth by saying to her the next morning at breakfast, "I would not advise your following me, Lady Angeline. I've seen more summers than you've ever dreamed of. I can take care of myself."

Sarah could not help but laugh, and she did not miss the wry grin on the old woman's face.

Angeline, blushing, exclaimed, "How did you know I planned to follow you—just to keep you from harm's way. Are you a mind reader?"

"No, but your curiosity gave you away. With all the questions you asked, I knew that should I leave Storm's End again without explanation, your curiosity would get the better of you."

Sarah looked at the old woman, dressed exquisitely in a gray carriage dress and obviously enjoying herself. Sarah started to speak but was headed off by Angeline's next question. "What will the upper orders think of you going out without an abigail? I'll be glad to go along, giving the appearance of propriety."

Lady Lillian emitted gleeful laughter. "I'm sure that you would, but I shall be just fine. Let the upper orders think what they will."

"Lady Lillian, I can't believe you are saying such a blasphemous thing after all the lessons you've forced on

Lady Sarah about how to go on in society. Even tried to teach me when I don't give a whit—"

Lady Lillian quickly retorted, "Oh, I know when I'm defeated. I gave up on you the first time I laid eyes on you. I said to myself, 'Now there's a girl who has to learn everything the hard way.'"

"Lady Lillian," Sarah said, "if you are going out today, will you please say where you are going. I worry about your safety."

"Well, don't. I'm having more fun than I've ever had in my life."

"Are you—"

Sarah silenced Angeline with a kick on the shin, for she knew that the young girl was going to ask the old woman if she had succumbed to the gaming tables. Sarah watched as Lady Lillian rose to her feet, donned her Gypsy hat with purple plumes, and walked sprightly out to the waiting carriage without so much as a goodbye. This time she carried her cane, but she was not using it to help her along; she was swinging it.

"She's gambling," Angeline said. "There's no other answer."

"If she is gambling, she's winning, for I've never seen the old woman like this."

"I still think I should follow her."

"How? By running along and hiding behind trees?" Sarah laughed. "Best you stay here and worry about my marrying a man I don't love. My come-out is imminent."

"Oh, sister, are you going through with it? I can't bear the hurt that comes from Lord Chesterson's eyes. He's besotted with you."

"Last evening, when I was riding with Lord Chesterson, I concluded that I would not make a convenient marriage, but this day, I cannot help but worry about Lady Lillian. And I can't forget that I gave her my word."

"As I've told you, sister, that old woman will survive prison much better than you will survive marriage to a man you don't love. You are not of the *ton*. They don't expect love in marriage, and husband and wife go their separate ways. Have you seen the Duke of Wellington's wife at Apsley House? No, she stays in the country where, I understand, the duke owns a mansion as grand as Apsley. Sarah, we're from America. We need to be loved by our husbands."

Sarah looked at Angeline, this moment more mature than many women twice her age. Rising from the table, she smiled at Angeline and said, "This day, I plan not to worry. Outside, there's wonderful sunshine. How would you like to go to this place called Gunther's and get a sweet? Lord Chesterson is sitting in the House of Lords."

"That's a capital idea," exclaimed Angeline, jumping up. "Mayhap we will see the old crow and find out what mischief she's up to."

But Gunther's proved nonproductive in finding out Lady Lillian's whereabouts. Mr. Gunther emphatically denied that he had seen a tall thin woman wearing a gray dress and a black hat with purple plumes. Sarah and Angeline ate two sweet tarts each, then walked on Bond Street and Oxford Street until their feet hurt, looking in windows at displays of merchandise while keeping an eye out for Lady Lillian.

"The old crow is just trying to worry us," Angeline said as they made their way back to the carriage that would return them to Storm's End. "I suggest we stop worrying about her."

"Why, Angeline," Sarah said, " 'tis the first time I've heard you admit concern for Lady Lillian."

"Well, somebody has to worry about her; she doesn't have sense enough to come in out of the rain if she were drowning."

"I beg to differ with you. I take her to be a very clever woman," said Sarah.

"And wicked, and manipulative. She proved that when she asked you to come to Merrymount to live."

"What's done is done," said Sarah. "Who knows? I may meet Prince Charming."

"You've already met him. 'Tis Lord Chesterson."

"The Prince Charming I'm speaking of must needs be rich. He'll sweep me off my feet, make me forget why I didn't want to marry him, and we shall live happily ever after." Sarah's voice broke, and Angeline put her arm around her, vowing to kill the old crow when this day she returned to Storm's End.

Lady Lillian did not return that day, and when the day of Sarah's come-out came with still no sign of the old woman, Sarah went to the Bow Street Runners and reported her aunt missing.

Nathan offered to go, but Sarah insisted that Lady Lillian was her aunt and that it was her responsibility to watch after the older woman.

"I should have let you follow her, Angeline," Sarah said, believing that nothing short of foul play would keep Lady Lillian from her come-out. She searched the old woman's room to see if articles of clothing were missing and found nothing amiss. Lady Lillian's personal maid said her ladyship was humming when she quit the room on the morning of her disappearance.

The driver, when questioned, swore that her ladyship did not leave the carriage with anything except her cane which was dangling from her arm as she strutted into Gunther's.

"The old crow is most likely dead in some alley," declared Angeline, and then she added, "Sister, that means you don't have to make a convenient marriage to save her from debtor's prison."

"Angeline, how can you be so cruel-hearted?" Sarah asked, her green eyes swimming in tears.

" 'Tis easy when I think about what she almost did to you. Should we not send drivers out with missives, canceling your come-out?"

"Of course not. We do not know that Aunt Lillian

lead, and I shall certainly do my duty to her until her demise becomes fact. The Bow Street Runners are searching, and we should know something one way or the other by nightfall."

Sarah expected the inconsiderate old woman any moment to walk into Storm's End and get dressed for the party, as if she had been to Gunther's for a sweet instead of gone for three days.

Lady Lillian did not suddenly appear, however, and Sarah readied herself to be launched onto the Marriage Mart. Downstairs, according to Sarah's instructions, the servants were placing flowers and lighting tapers. Two extra chefs had been hired for the kitchen, as well as extra maids to take the ladies' wraps. Sarah had hired extra footmen to let down the carriage steps and extra grooms to take the horses to the mews. Gifford looked smug in his long-tailed black coat and pristine white shirt with high collar points.

And already the orchestra was in place. Dowager and chaperon chairs had been placed on a dais, so they could observe the dancing.

Taking charge in Lady Lillian's absence had been no strain on Sarah, for she had many times taken charge of entertainment at Templeton Hall, most especially after her father had married Wanna, who knew nothing of such things as entertaining.

Worrying about Lady Lillian *had* been a strain on Sarah. She could feel herself frowning, and her mind was in a quandary. Halfheartedly she allowed Peggy to help her dress. She desired greatly to see Nathan, mayhap to seek assurance that the old woman was all right. He had been out all day looking for her.

Leaving Peggy to help Angeline, Sarah quit the room and walked to the other end of the long corridor and knocked on Nathan's door. When he invited her to enter, she pushed the door. It was a very handsome sitting room,

cozy, inviting, masculine; a fire burned in the marble
fireplace.

Through a door, Sarah could see that his lordship's
valet was shaving him. Embarrassed, she turned to leave
but was stopped by his lordship's words. "No, Lady
Sarah, don't leave. I will be out shortly. I want to report
on my day before we go downstairs. Please sit for a few
moments."

And then Sarah heard him say to his valet, "Paul, have
done with the shaving and lay out my clothes. I think the
blue velvet coat and pantaloons."

Not long after that Nathan appeared before Sarah,
dressed impeccably. His white cravat contrasted beauti-
fully with his sun-tanned, freshly shaved face, and the
dark velvet coat set off his hazel eyes. Her gaze moved
down his long frame to his evening slippers, not missing
his well-shaped, muscular thighs.

She sucked in her breath, for Nathan was the most
handsome man she had ever seen. For a moment she
envisioned another woman in his long arms, lying with
him, for surely when she took a husband, he would turn
to someone else. Could this really be happening to her, to
them?

Sarah stood, and Nathan took her small hand, lovingly
clasping it between his two large ones. His eyes were
moist, his voice choked when he whispered, "Lady Sarah,
my love."

"This night I am Lady Sarah, your cousin from America," Sarah said, and Nathan repeated what he had many
times said to Sarah: "You will always be my love."

Sarah knew they were dangerously near to letting her
come-out party go on without them. Never had she felt
such pain in her heart as she struggled to change the
subject. "Aunt Lillian . . . Did . . . did you learn of her the
day?"

"Not even a hint. As you know, private homes are the
only places a woman of the upper orders can go to gam-

e. I enquired and found no trace of a Lady Lillian
Ierriwether. So I went to some of the disreputable places
id, loath to use her name, described her in detail.

"Even though I could not imagine Lady Lillian fre-
ienting such places as the underground at Covent Gar-
:ns, I went there. If she is enjoying herself at these dens
' depravity, she is in a disguise that not even I would
cognize. I then went to the boxing matches, the races at
aymarket, and the cockfights. With no luck."

Sarah listened with a sinking heart. If her Aunt Lillian
:re alive, and Sarah was beginning to doubt that she
is, she would not miss the grand party tonight.

"Do you think we should cancel my come-out?" Sarah
ked. "If she has met with foul play, there's no reason for
e to look for a rich husband."

" 'Tis too late to cancel the party tonight. We shall say
idy Lillian Merriwether, your sponsor for the Season,
s come down with the croup and is abed for the eve-
ng. And we will carry on as if that were the truth.
omorrow, the selfish old woman most likely will strut
to Storm's End as if nothing is awry."

"No, Nathan, that cannot be the truth. Lady Lillian is
ing held against her will. Nothing short of that would
ep her from Storm's End this night."

Sarah started to cry, but Nathan took her into his arms
d comforted her, stroking her back and offering a white
ndkerchief. "Don't cry, Sarah. You must needs put on
rave front until we know what has happened."

Sarah wiped her eyes, then blew her nose into the
ndkerchief before giving it back to Nathan. "Even
ough I resent this business of finding a rich husband, I
s so looking forward to dancing with you at the party."

"I only hope I can keep from monopolizing you," Na-
an said. "My feelings for you, would be obvious to all.
ery eligible bachelor in Town, and some from the
untry, will be vying for your time. Even the Prince
gent. I met up with him this day at the pugilist matches,

and he said he was most anxious to meet my cousin from America."

So there was nothing for it except to go downstairs and put on a cheerful front, thought Sarah. She took Nathan's arm, and they went to the landing above the winding stairs.

Before taking the first step downward, Sarah searched every upturned face. She saw Angeline, so beautiful in her finery, but she was hoping to see Lady Lillian. She was sorely disappointed, and it was with enforced determination that she set her chin and descended the stairs while Gifford stood at the foot of the stairs, announced that the sixth earl of Chesterson was presenting to the *top* his cousin from America, Lady Sarah Templeton, daughter of the late third earl of Chesterson.

Chapter Twenty-Five

When Lord Chesterson swept Lady Sarah across the
nce floor, he felt the jealousy in the eyes of the pinks of
: *ton,* and he knew the highborn ladies were only smiling
hide their envy. His lordship understood, for his Sarah
s as lovely a girl as they had ever set their gaze upon.
r body moved in perfect rhythm with his as they
nced the quadrille. He wanted to stop and kiss her, to
n his fingers through her whiskey curls, to tell all those
king on that she was his.

'or a moment his lordship let himself believe that he
d his Lady Sarah would marry, and his heart soared
.de his chest before plummeting to the bottom of his
1. When the dance was over, he must needs throw this
ely creature, whom he loved more than his own life, to
wolves of London society. They would gobble her up,
oretty was she and so impeccably mannered that one
uld think she had been going on in London society all
life.

Nathan found himself hating Lady Lillian Merriwether
robbing him of his Sarah and for robbing Lady Sarah
happy life, and he stopped just short of wishing the
woman dead. Guilt overtook him for the sinful
ught, and he promised his Supreme Being that on the
rrow he would repent. But not tonight, not tonight. He
ked down at her and, seeing her tremulous smile, felt

her heart breaking. As his was. "Oh, dear God," h
prayed. Then he stopped, for his faith was gone.

Feeling a tap on his shoulder, Nathan knew befor
looking that it was Lord Harrowby. Out of the corner
his eye he had seen Lady Harrowby, who was sitting i
the Dowager's Circle, motioning to her foppish son t
claim the next dance with Lady Sarah.

I have to let her go.

Nathan bent and kissed Lady Sarah on the cheek. A
any good cousin would, he told himself. In a whisper fo
her ears only, he said, "I will always love you."

After that, he turned to Lord Harrowby and made th
proper introduction. Ignoring Lord Chesterson's scathin
look, the intruder bowed, kissed Sarah's hand, made
fancy leg, and then took Lady Sarah into his arms an
bore her away from Nathan.

Each time Harrowby whirled her out, then brought h
back, he bestowed upon her another accolade, speakin
of her utter beauty, her breath-taking smile, her beautif
green eyes, and how happy he was to meet a girl fro
America with such *ton*, such intelligence. "I marvel
your qualifications for becoming one of us," he said.

Sarah wondered how he knew of her intelligence whe
she had not yet spoken a word. She smiled sardonica
while her gaze followed Lord Chesterson. He was heade
toward Angeline, and Sarah was pleased. She wanted h
sister to have a good time.

But Nathan did not make it to Angeline. Sara
watched with disgust as Lady Arbuthnot stepped into h
path, smiling up at him and batting her eyes flirtatiousl
The hussy, thought Sarah, missing a step and causing Lo
Harrowby to step on her foot. She would have cried o
but she was too angry.

"Oh, I beg your forgiveness, madam. I do not oft
miss a step in my dancing. When I was on the Gra
Tour, Mum saw to it that I had lessons with an excelle
French dance instructor, who was noted to be the best

all of Europe. So foolish of me to step on a precious foot when I'm fortunate enough to be dancing with the loveliest—"

"You didn't miss a step, Lord Harrowby," Sarah said crisply. "It was my foot that got in your foot's way."

From where Angeline sat, waiting for someone to ask her to dance, she craned her neck and watched as one of the pinks of the *ton* fawned over Sarah. Angeline could not deny his good looks or his charming smile, which showed beautiful white teeth, but she did not like the way he was looking at Sarah. As if she were already promised to him. And nearby a lady of the upper orders was looking at Lord Chesterson like a dying calf. Something had to be done, and quickly.

Angeline asked the well-dressed gentleman who had suddenly bowed before her, "Is that gentleman dancing with Lady Sarah Templeton rich?"

The gentleman turned and, craning his neck to see over the dancers, said, "As rich as Croesus. If he hasn't lost it in his last gambling bout."

"Well, that does it," said Angeline. "I need a dance partner. Will you dance with me?"

"That was my purpose in coming to you, after I had introduced myself." He bowed again, but only slightly, then continued, "I beg your forgiveness for being so forward, but I have not been able to take my eyes off you since first spying you sitting here alone—"

Angeline cut in with, "I was supposed to have a chaperon, but the old crow got lost somewhere."

"Wha-what do you mean?" Astonishment showed on the stranger's face.

"I mean that Lady Sarah's aunt, Lady Lillian Merriwether, took herself off and didn't make it back in time for this grand ball."

"Oh! I understood that Lady Sarah's aunt is indisposed with a spell of the croup."

"She's indisposed, all right," Angeline said, "but I don't know about a spell of the croup. 'Twould serve her right."

Suddenly Angeline realized she had spoken out of school. Obviously Lord Chesterson had spread the word that Lady Lillian was laid up because of the croup. "What I mean," Angeline said, "is that Lady Lillian got herself out in inclement weather and came down with the croup. She's lost her voice, can't say a word."

Oh, dear me, I'm making it worse.

The gentleman bowed again. "Shall we start over with a proper introduction. I'm George, Prince of Wales."

"Not Prinny!" Angeline sought to keep from squealing. Quickly she jumped to her feet, careful not to stumble, and gave a deep courtly curtsy. Just like Lady Lillian had taught her. Straightening, she looked at Prinny, who looked as if he were about to laugh.

"The Prince Regent himself," he said. "And you are?"

"I'm Lady Angeline Templeton, Lady Sarah's sister."

"But . . . but you can't be. Not with that lovely olive complexion, and her so fair. 'Tis the reason I couldn't take my eyes from you. I thought you might be royalty, mayhap from India."

"I'm part Indian, all right, but from America. I can't claim to be an Indian princess, though, since I've only one-quarter of their blood." In way of explanation, Angeline hurriedly said, "My father was the earl of Templeton. But he's dead. Do you wish to dance with me? You did single me out when there's beautiful girls everywhere."

The Prince Regent was no longer hiding his laughter. He had never met anyone quite like this girl from America. He had thought the girl for whom the party was given, Lord Chesterson's cousin, was quite extraordinarily beautiful, but this olive-skinned girl was intriguing . . . and most curious.

"And who's that woman dancing with Lord Chesterson? She looks as if she's about to have a spell of the vapors."

"I believe 'tis Lady Arbuthnot. Her late husband—"

"I thought so," said Angeline quickly. "Now if you would still like to dance with me, I'm ready."

Anxious to have a go with her, the Prince Regent took Angeline's hand and led her to the dance floor.

But much to Prinny's chagrin, he soon learned that Angeline Templeton from America was not as interested in dancing with him as she was getting in proximity to her sister and Lord Harrowby. "When we get near Lady Sarah Templeton, you may tap her partner's shoulder and ask my sister to dance. I, in turn, will dance with . . . what did you say his name was?"

"I didn't. But 'tis Lord Harrowby."

"Thank you," Angeline said. She thought the Prince of Wales an excellent dancer, his blue eyes most impelling, and she would have enjoyed dancing with him had she not been anxious to dance with Lord Harrowby. And when the Prince Regent danced Angeline close to his lordship, she gave the Prince Regent a pretty smile and inclined her head, indicating that he should now dance with her sister. Which the Prince Regent did, giving Lord Harrowby no choice but to dance with Angeline.

"Are you anxious to marry?" Angeline asked her new partner.

"Every man is anxious to marry when he meets up with the right woman," Lord Harrowby answered. With a deep sigh, he added, "I had begun to think I would never meet the right girl for me, and then tonight I met your lovely sister." He again sighed deeply, twirled Angeline away from him, then brought her back, his nimble feet keeping perfect time with the music.

"Do you mean that you've danced with her once and already you want to become leg-shackled to her? Oh, my dear Lord Harrowby, you do not know what you are in for. You should know her better before you ask Lord Chesteron if you can pay your addresses."

His lordship raised a quizzical brow. "I don't take your meaning. She is lovely, and I understand she is a rich heiress from America. God's truth, that is her attraction."

"What? Being a rich heiress or being from America?"

Lord Harrowby looked over at Lady Sarah, who, Angeline noticed, was dancing with yet another partner. He was old and reminded Angeline of a toad.

"All of her attributes added together make her the perfect wife for me, a perfect mother for my heir," said Lord Harrowby. "Her loveliness is beyond description. I'm afraid I'm acting as a young *ton* buck, for I have fallen helplessly in love."

"Balderdash!" said Angeline. "You hardly know my sister. She's not at all for you. She would never share your bed, and you would not wish her to do so, for she snores something awful and she drools all over her pillow. Sarah has many times confided in me that should she marry, there would never be an heir, that she could not forbear a man to touch her."

When Lord Harrowby did not answer but just kept on dancing and smiling, Angeline asked, "Does that sound like someone you would willingly get yourself leg-shackled to? 'Twould be a terrible alliance."

"If that be the case, I feel compelled to save her from embarrassment. I'm sure you will tell every man who shows interest in your sister of her strange behavior, thus no gentleman of the *ton* will have her. Just think, going through the Season without an offer. Poor, poor dear."

Angeline was thoroughly disgusted. Any jackanapes with brains enough to fill a thimble would not think of paying his addresses to Lady Sarah after what she, Angeline, had just told Lord Harrowby. Obviously the man had windmills in his head.

Angeline asked Lord Harrowby to return her to her chair, where, after due consideration and frantic planning, she decided to tell Lord Chesterson what she had done and ask his advice. Mayhap his lordship could think of something short of breaking Lord Harrowby's legs, thus keeping him away from Storm's End for the Season.

Angeline could not immediately carry out her plan. Lord Chesterson was dancing his second dance with Lady Arbuthnot, who was clinging to him in a shameful way. Angeline was beginning to think that she should have stayed in hiding for the evening, for all the good she was doing. She had come here to prevent Sarah from making the mistake of her life. Her thoughts going to the old crow who had caused this farrago, she vehemently promised herself that should she ever see the old woman again, she would wring her long neck like Hilda had rung the hen's neck at Merrymount.

Standing, so that she could have a better view of the dancers, Angeline waved to Lord Chesterson, but it was obvious that his lordship could not see her hand waving in the air. He just kept on dancing, and Lady Arbuthnot kept on clinging.

Hearing a big sniff come from the woman next to her, Angeline sat down and turned in time to catch a hard glare through the haughty woman's lorgnette. Angeline apologized, saying, "I did not mean to inconvenience you, but I must needs speak to Lord Chesterson, my sister's cousin."

"Your sister is Lady Sarah Templeton? That is not true, surely. Where did your dark skin come from?"

"From my Indian mother. Lady Sarah and I are half sisters."

The woman did not bother to answer. Holding her silk fan in front of her face, she passed, Angeline was sure, this new information to yet another member of the *ton*. Angeline suppressed laughter. Mayhap no one would offer for Sarah, knowing that she had an American savage for a sister. Had not Lady Lillian warned that this might happen?

Angeline's hope in that vein died rather quickly. On the dance floor Sarah was being passed from one handsome buck to another, all smiling at her, making fancy legs, and each trying to outdance the other. At last Lord Chesterson rescued her and danced with her before relinquishing her to a new partner.

Prinny came back to dance with Angeline, and after that, several young men begged to dance with her, one being Lord Chesteron. " 'Tis about time," she told him. "I have something to tell you."

But the dance was a waltz, and propriety did not allow them to touch during the sensuous dance. Lady Lillian had many times apprised them of this bit of *ton* behavior.

Angeline did not want to touch his lordship's body, she thought, she just wanted to speak with him about the awful thing she had done. He might want to kill her for ruining Lady Sarah's chances for a convenient marriage, but in the end, when he and Sarah were married, he would be most appreciative.

Angeline had stopped thinking about what would happen to Lady Lillian should Sarah fail to make a convenient marriage.

When the dance with Lord Nathan ended, he bowed and said to Angeline, "We shall talk later."

A young man appeared and asked Angeline to dance, and they were doing fancy steps to a country dance when the musicians stopped playing, the dancers stopped dancing, and a terrible quiet settled over the huge great hall.

Angeline craned her neck to see, and then she heard herself squealing while running in the direction of the dais. For standing there was Lady Lillian, who wasn't dead at all. Gifford was saying, "Lady Lillian Merriwether has arrived."

"Continue on with your dancing," Lady Lillian said, and the crowd, with the exception of Nathan, Sarah, and Angeline, began dancing when the music started up again.

"Oh, Lady Lillian, you're safe," Angeline said, and then she found herself blubbering as she hugged the old woman, dislodging her Gypsy hat.

"Why, Lady Angeline, I do believe you are happy to see me," said Lady Lillian, her smile wide. With a long bony finger, she wiped the tears from Angeline's face.

"Oh, I am, Lady Lillian," Angeline said. "Truly. We feared you were dead. Where have you been? You look a fright, as if mayhap you've slept in that dress, and your hair is awful. What will the upper orders think, your coming in late like this and . . . and looking so disheveled."

Laughter as Angeline had never heard gurgled up from Lady Lillian's throat. "I care not what the upper orders think."

Angeline could not believe her ears. Lady Lillian not caring what the *ton* thought! Angeline asked, "Did someone kidnap you?"

"More like I kidnapped someone," Lady Lillian answered. She looked at the odd-looking man standing beside her and smiled.

Angeline had not noticed the diminutive man standing beside Lady Lillian, his smile as wide as a three-cow milk stall. Certainly he was not *ton*. He was too oddly dressed, in a coat much too large for him, knee breeches, and white collar points that stuck in his chin. He looked somewhat like a butler to the lower orders, Angeline thought.

Angeline started to enquire but was shushed by Lady Lillian, who was saying, "I must needs speak to Lord Chesterson and Lady Sarah. Will you keep Mr. McGee company for me?" To Mr. McGee Lady Lillian said, "This is Lady Angeline Templeton, my niece's half sister. She refers to me as an old crow."

"Oh, Lady Lillian, I'm so sorry. I should be horse-whipped."

"Most likely I deserved it," her ladyship said, and then she was gone, making her way to Lady Sarah and Nathan, who were standing like statues in the middle of the dance floor.

"I can't believe my eyes," Sarah said, warm tears pushing their way from her eyes to puddle on her cheeks. She had been so worried about the irascible old woman, but until now she had not realized how much she wanted her only aunt to be all right. In Sarah's worst moments, she had feared the money lenders had kidnapped Lady Lillian so they could claim all the treasures Merrymount held. Mayhap they had and, seeing the difficulty in keeping her, had freed her.

Sarah asked Nathan, "Did you see Angeline hugging Aunt Lillian?"

Nathan chuckled. "Your sister has more love in her little finger than all these people put together. Yet, she tries to appear so hard-hearted."

The dancers parted and made way for Lady Lillian as she strode, holding her head high, her Gypsy hat still askew, toward Nathan and Sarah.

"Lord Chesterson," she said when she reached them. "Please follow me, and you, too, Lady Sarah."

Nathan asked, "Where—"

"Abovestairs. And when we reach the landing, I want you to turn and announce for all to hear that you and Lady Sarah are being married as soon as the banns can be read. Tell them to eat their fill and then go home."

"Aunt Lillian, you must needs be drunk as a wheelbarrow," declared Sarah.

"If I'm drunk, 'tis with happiness. Now do as I say. I will make myself clear when we are alone. Let's gather Lady Angeline and Mr. McGee . . ."

Sarah could hear her heart singing, even though she thought her Aunt Lillian drunk, crazy, or both. The old woman had just said that she and Nathan could marry. What about the convenient marriage she, Sarah, was supposed to make to save Lady Lillian from debtor's prison?

The enormity of what was happening slowly washed over Sarah, and she shook with relief as she followed the small entourage up the stairs, and she smiled her happiness when Nathan, stepping onto the landing, turned and announced the engagement of Lord Chesterson and Lady Sarah Templeton, the wedding to take place as soon as the banns could be read.

The crowd was hushed with the exception of one piercing scream. And then the screamer, a dowager wearing a turban, slid slowly to the floor. Immediately Lord Harrowby rushed to bend over her. No doubt his mother, Sarah thought.

"I told him about your snoring," Angeline whispered.

"I don't snore."

"I know, but I had no intention of letting you become leg-shackled to that fop."

Lady Sarah laughed. "He told me that he would marry me even if I did snore, and then I was told that he had recently lost his blunt and was pursuing me because he thought I was a rich heiress."

"That jackanapes," declared Angeline. "He was seeking to save himself from debtor's prison. Little wonder his old mother fell into a spell of the vapors."

Lady Lillian had not lost her bossy ways, and she turned to shush Sarah and Angeline. Nathan had his arm around Sarah, and he gave her a tight squeeze. She saw tears in his wonderful hazel eyes.

Below, the crowd remained silent. They had come for a come-out ball, for another prime article to be cast upon the Marriage Mart; instead, the ball had been an engagement party. Sarah could feel their disappointment, and she was certain that Lord Harrowby was the most disappointed of all. So he had thought he was wooing an heiress. Sarah smiled as she remembered his words: "I would not mind your snoring, precious Sarah. I'm certain 'tis a beautiful sound, coming from your sweet lips."

Gifford announcing that dinner was being served and

the sound of shuffling feet moving in the direction the dining room brought Lady Sarah from her ruminations. She looked to see if Lady Harrowby was still on the floor and was pleased to see that she, along with everyone else, was pushing her way toward the dining room, her foppish son by her side.

Sarah caught a glimpse of a stricken Lady Arbuthnot as she left through the front door, and Sarah, hiding her face behind her fan, gave a quiet laugh. Could this be happening?

"Let's repair to a private place," Nathan said, his arm still around Sarah's shoulders, as if he feared that all he had heard was not true. And in the abovestairs withdrawing room, he, in a stern voice, scolded Lady Lillian: "Madam, I think you should tell the whole of it. You've had your niece and her sister near scared to death. Do you realize the Bow Street Runners are out looking for you?"

Lady Lillian rose to her feet and went quickly to stand in front of the fireplace. For a moment, Sarah thought that in some faint way she resembled Lady Templeton, Sarah's mother.

Sarah could not imagine what her aunt was going to say. Her demeanor was serious, but there was a happiness about her countenance Sarah had never seen before. Her eyes glowed when she looked at the little man still sitting on the sofa she had just left.

"Mr. McGee," Lady Lillian said, "please give Lady Sarah and Lady Angeline that which we spent most of one whole day looking for."

Mr. McGee stood and pulled from his coat pocket two boxes, one of which he handed to Sarah, the other to Angeline. He bowed in front of Sarah, then said, "I'm most happy to return to you your mother's pearls, Lady Sarah." He opened the small box, and there, on a bed of black velvet, was her mother's pearls. Tears rendered her speechless, and her sobs resounded throughout the room.

Nathan, taking a white handkerchief from his pocket

dried the tears from her cheeks, kissing them as he did so. She held the pearls to her heart until she could speak. "Thank you, Mr. McGee. What a kind, thoughtful thing to do." And then, speaking barely above a whisper, she thanked him again.

" 'Twas my pleasure, and Lady Lillian's as well." Turning to Angeline, he said, "And to you, Lady Angeline, the beads that once belonged to your Indian mother. I understand that you hold them when you talk with her Spirit."

Angeline began crying, and she jumped to her feet and hugged and kissed Mr. McGee, making his face flush a bright red.

Lady Lillian laughed, and when Angeline turned to hug her, Lady Lillian hugged Angeline back, saying, "How could I have ever thought you would hold your sister back in society? You are a wonderful sister to her. Forgive me for being so unkind. I hope the beads will make it up to you, Angeline."

"Even if I never got the beads back, I would have had no regrets, for the beads afforded capital for the hat business, which launched Sarah into society."

"After this night, society may very well turn its back on her," said Lady Lillian. "But if I've learned one thing in my long life, 'tis that being loved is more important than anything the upper orders have to offer." She glanced at Mr. McGee and gave him a huge grin, and he smiled back in return.

Nathan watched this with great interest. Sitting on a small settee, holding Sarah's small hand in his own large, trembling hands, he was wondering if he were dreaming. Had the old woman really released Lady Sarah from her promise of making a convenient marriage? Of course she had, for she had told him to announce to all of the *ton* that he and Lady Sarah would be married as soon as the banns could be read. What about debtor's prison, which had frightened the old woman until she escaped into madness?

His lordship's mind raced ahead. The twins and Georgena and William would be sent for straight away. He would ask for a special dispensation to obtain the license.

Nathan shook his head, his mind already accepting what his heart refused to believe. He looked at Sarah, and his tears turned her face to a blur. Could it be true that she would be his forever and ever?

"You have not told the whole of it, Lady Lillian," Nathan at last managed to say. "What about your going to debtor's prison? If I remember correctly, the very thought made you mad—"

"Stuff!" the old woman said. "Mr. McGee took care of it all. He's paid the money lenders and the taxes on Merrymount, which I intend to give to my niece, who was willing to sacrifice her happiness to keep me from debtor's prison."

"You're giving Merrymount away?" screeched Angeline. "But where will you live?"

It was then that Lady Lillian looked her happiest. Placing a long arm around Mr. McGee's narrow shoulders, she said, with considerable pride, "The big house needs youth and children, not an old crow like me. I'm returning with my husband to India where he made all his money—"

Three voices spoke in unison: "Your husband?"

"Yes, we were married three days ago in Paris. Mr. McGee has connections there, and reading banns is not required. Then we crossed back over the Channel and took care of my unfinished business before coming this night to Storm's End. I so wanted to be here for your party, Lady Sarah."

"You came just at the right time," Nathan said.

Angeline followed with, "Surely, Lady Lillian, you did not marry an untitled man."

"I'm afraid she did," said Mr. McGee. "But the first time, many, many years ago, she turned me down because I was not only untitled, but I was as poor as a church mouse. Those were the very words she said to me, that I was as poor as a church mouse. Well, I couldn't do anything about a title, for I'll never be highborn, but I did gain the blunt. Then I came back to claim my Lady Lillian. I never forgot her, not for a moment. I went to Merrymount and was told she was here, at Storm's End."

He paused for a moment, and his face turned red. "By then, when I realized I was getting close to my love, I was afraid to come to Storm's End, afraid she would turn me down. It was Mr. Gunther who insisted I write the missive and ask Lady Lillian to meet me at his sweetshop."

Lady Lillian sailed her Gypsy hat across the room, laughing when it landed squarely on an ottoman. There was a touch of sadness, and much happiness, in her voice when she said, "Years of regret taught me how unimportant a title is to one's heart." And then she gave Mr. McGee a big kiss, right smack on the mouth, and Lady Sarah pinched herself to make sure she was not dreaming.

Chapter Twenty-Six

The crested carriage, pulled by four handsome bays,
mbed to the top of the ridge and stopped, as Garrick,
e driver, had been instructed to do by Lady Chesterson.
side her, settled deep into the squabs, sat her husband
two months.

"Oh, Nathan, look!" she exclaimed, sucking in a deep
eath. "Isn't it beautiful?"

Smiling, Nathan sat forward. "Yes, darling Sarah, 'tis
autiful indeed."

"Just as I envisioned all those years in America, flowers
the moat, lush green grass, sun shining on the many
ndows and on the peaked roof—"

Nathan gave a little laugh and pulled Sarah to him.
Tis good to see you so happy, and 'tis good to see
errymount without the windows boarded up."

"How dreadful that must have been for Lady Lillian,"
rah said, and then Nathan's lips were on hers, cutting
her words. She felt his big hand caressing her thigh.
After a long kiss that sparked every nerve in Sarah's
dy to full passion, Nathan released her and, leaning his
d out the window, gave Garrick office to go. To his
de, he said, "Someday I shall make love to you in the
riage."

Sarah laughed. "Not with a driver on the box, and it
st needs be dark."

The two months since the wedding had been extremel
happy for Sarah. The wedding had been simple, in th
great hall of Storm's End, with only family present. Laur:
had carried flowers, but Larry adamantly refused to "ac
like a girl." He did, however, consent to carry the ring or
a satin pillow.

Angeline had been Lady Sarah's bridesmaid, and Lad
Sarah had laughingly thrown her bridal bouquet to her
"You will be the next bride, dear Angeline," Sarah ha:
said, and, for once, Angeline did not argue. She did say
"Only if I fall in love with someone like Nathan."

Lady Lillian and Mr. McGee had been persuaded t
delay their departure for India until after the wedding
Lady Lillian's only worry being that of her hounds, Cai
and Abel, and she asked Angeline if she would care fc
them, and the girl said she would.

Georgena and William had looked on, smiling like tw
well-fed Cheshire cats as the vicar asked Lord Chesterso
and Lady Sarah Templeton if they would love and chei
ish each other until death parted them. Sarah had criec
and even though Nathan tried to hide his tears, she fe
the dampness on his cheeks when he kissed her as his wif

It had been a joyful occasion, and soon after a grea
wedding dinner had been served and toasts had bee
drunk, Lady Lillian and her new husband departed to th
ship that would take them to India. Other members of th
family, including Angeline, had departed for Copthorn
and Merrymount, leaving the honeymooners to then
selves.

Now they were coming home to Merrymount.

Home, Lady Sarah thought, her heart aching from haj
piness.

It had been decided that Lord and Lady Chesterso:
along with Lady Angeline and the twins, would live .
Merrymount. Georgena and William would stay at Coj
thorne.

"There's Cain and Abel," Sarah said as the carria;

stopped near the bridge over the moat. The dogs were frolicking much like they had that first day when she and Angeline came to Merrymount in a wagon pulled by an oxen, except now the hounds were romping in lush green grass, not over banks of snow.

As Nathan helped her from the carriage, Sarah refused to let thoughts of that awful, cold day enter her head. Nor did she think of the many meals of turnips and the many cups of hot cider. This day, her cup was filled to overflowing. She looked at her husband and thanked God for him.

Inside Merrymount, Angeline joyfully hugged the couple, and then she sat at the tea table, covered with a white cloth, and poured. Just as Lady Lillian had done, Lady Sarah thought, when she was so bent on teaching the ways of the upper orders.

But there was a pensiveness about Angeline which did not escape Sarah's notice. Angeline's usual chatter, words spilling over words, was missing. Sarah studied her sister for a long moment before saying, "Angeline, tell me what's bothering you, and don't start denying it. I know you too well."

"Can't we wait until tomorrow, this being your first day home?"

"No," Lady Chesterson said quickly. "I will not sleep a wink, knowing that something is on your mind—"

"I'm going to America to take care of Mary Ellen when her baby comes," Angeline blurted out. And then she took a white missive from her pocket and handed it to Lady Sarah. "This came soon after I returned to Merrymount, but I refused to let the news ruin your honeymoon. 'Tis from Mary Ellen. Hoggie is dead."

"Oh, my God," said Sarah before blackness engulfed her, and then she felt her husband's comforting arms reach to embrace her. She was not alone.

* * *

Sarah did not mourn her brother the customary year; in truth, had he not been her brother, she would have hardly mourned at all, she told herself. Hoggie, in his short life, had made everyone he touched unhappy. In Mary Ellen's letter, she had said that Hoggie had died fighting an illegal duel over another man's wife. He had, however, done one fair thing: according to the Templeton solicitor, he had willed equal shares of the Templeton land to his wife Mary Ellen and his two sisters, Sarah and Angeline.

So Sarah settled into a very domestic and happy life with her husband. The rains came, and the crops produced blunt enough to revive Merrymount to its former grandeur; servants were hired to help Hilda and John Wesley, who were looking forward to Angeline's return when Mary Ellen no longer needed her.

But it was when Sarah and Nathan learned that Sarah was *enceinte* that their happiness reached its zenith.

"She is the result of our wonderful love," Sarah said in their bedchamber one night, and Nathan countered with, "He is the result of our wonderful love."

Laughing together, he reached to take her into his arms, and she was most willing.

ABOUT THE AUTHOR

IRENE LOYD BLACK is the author of six Regency romances, including *Lady Sarah's Fancy,* and one novella, *The Tattered Valentine. A Husband for the Countess, Charmed Betrothal, The Mischievous Miss, The Duke's Easter Lady,* and *My Sweet Valentine* are available by order wherever books are sold.

Ms. Black was born in Scottsboro, Alabama, but moved to Oklahoma at age five. She now lives in Oklahoma City with her husband, James L. Deatherage, a financial advisor and stockbroker.

ZEBRA'S REGENCY ROMANCES
DAZZLE AND DELIGHT

A BEGUILING INTRIGUE   (4441, $3.99)
by Olivia Sumner

Pretty as a picture Justine Riggs cared nothing for propriety. She dressed as a boy, sat on her horse like a jockey, and pondered the stars like a scientist. But when she tried to best the handsome Quenton Fletcher, Marquess of Devon, by proving that she was the better equestrian, he would try to prove Justine's antics were pure folly. The game he had in mind was seduction — never imagining that he might lose his heart in the process!

AN INCONVENIENT ENGAGEMENT   (4442, $3.99)
by Joy Reed

Rebecca Wentworth was furious when she saw her betrothed waltzing with another. So she decides to make him jealous by flirting with the handsomest man at the ball, John Collinwood, Earl of Stanford. The "wicked" nobleman knew exactly what the enticing miss was up to — and he was only too happy to play along. But as Rebecca gazed into his magnificent eyes, her errant fiancé was soon utterly forgotten!

SCANDAL'S LADY   (4472, $3.99)
by Mary Kingsley

Cassandra was shocked to learn that the new Earl of Lynton was her childhood friend, Nicholas St. John. After years at sea and mixed feelings Nicholas had come home to take the family title. And although Cassandra knew her place as a governess, she could not help the thrill that went through her each time he was near. Nicholas was pleased to find that his old friend Cassandra was his new next door neighbor, but after being near her, he wondered if mere friendship would be enough . . .

HIS LORDSHIP'S REWARD   (4473, $3.99)
by Carola Dunn

As the daughter of a seasoned soldier, Fanny Ingram was accustomed to the vagaries of military life and cared not a whit about matters of rank and social standing. So she certainly never foresaw her *tendre* for handsome Viscount Roworth of Kent with whom she was forced to share lodgings, while he carried out his clandestine activities on behalf of the British Army. And though good sense told Roworth to keep his distance, he couldn't stop from taking Fanny in his arms for a kiss that made all hearts equal!

Available wherever paperbacks are sold, or order direct from the Publisher. Send cover price plus 50¢ per copy for mailing and handling to Penguin USA, P.O. Box 999, c/o Dept. 17109, Bergenfield, NJ 07621. Residents of New York and Tennessee must include sales tax. DO NOT SEND CASH.

ELEGANT LOVE STILL FLOURISHES —
Wrap yourself in a Zebra Regency Romance.

A MATCHMAKER'S MATCH (3783, $3.50/$4.50)
by Nina Porter

To save herself from a loveless marriage, Lady Psyche Veringham pretends to be a bluestocking. Resigned to spinsterhood at twenty-three, Psyche sets her keen mind to snaring a husband for her young charge, Amanda. She sets her cap for long-time bachelor, Justin St. James. This man of the world has had his fill of frothy-headed debutantes and turns the tables on Psyche. Can a bluestocking and a man about town find true love?

FIRES IN THE SNOW (3809, $3.99/$4.99)
by Janis Laden

Because of an unhappy occurrence, Diana Ruskin knew that a secure marriage was not in her future. She was content to assist her physician father and follow in his footsteps . . . until now. After meeting Adam, Duke of Marchmaine, Diana's precise world is shattered. She would simply have to avoid the temptation of his gentle touch and stunning physique — and by doing so break her own heart!

FIRST SEASON (3810, $3.50/$4.50)
by Anne Baldwin

When country heiress Laetitia Biddle arrives in London for the Season, she harbors dreams of triumph and applause. Instead, she becomes the laughingstock of drawing rooms and ballrooms, alike. This headstrong miss blames the rakish Lord Wakeford for her miserable debut, and she vows to rise above her many faux pas. Vowing to become an Original, Letty proves that she's more than a match for this eligible, seasoned Lord.

AN UNCOMMON INTRIGUE (3701, $3.99/$4.99)
by Georgina Devon

Miss Mary Elizabeth Sinclair was rather startled when the British Home Office employed her as a spy. Posing as "Tasha," an exotic fortune-teller, she expected to encounter unforeseen dangers. However, nothing could have prepared her for Lord Eric Stewart, her dashing and infuriating partner. Giving her heart to this haughty rogue would be the most reckless hazard of all.

A MADDENING MINX (3702, $3.50/$4.50)
by Mary Kingsley

After a curricle accident, Miss Sarah Chadwick is literally thrust into the arms of Philip Thornton. While other women shy away from Thornton's eyepatch and aloof exterior, Sarah finds herself drawn to discover why this man is physically and emotionally scarred.

Taylor—made Romance From Zebra Books

TODAY'S HOTTEST READS
ARE TOMORROW'S SUPERSTARS

VICTORY'S WOMAN   **(4484, $4.50)**
by Gretchen Genet
Andrew—the carefree soldier who sought glory on the battlefield,
and returned a shattered man . . . Niall—the legandary frontiers-
man and a former Shawnee captive, tormented by his past . . .
Roger—the troubled youth, who would rise up to claim a shock-
ing legacy . . . and Clarice—the passionate beauty bound by one
man, and hopelessly in love with another. Set against the backdrop of the American revolution, three men fight for their
heritage—and one woman is destined to change all their lives forever!

FORBIDDEN   **(4488, $4.99)**
by Jo Beverley
While fleeing from her brothers, who are attempting to sell her
into a loveless marriage, Serena Riverton accepts a carriage ride
from a stranger—who is the handsomest man she has ever seen.
Lord Middlethorpe, himself, is actually contemplating marriage
to a dull daughter of the aristocracy, when he encounters the
breathtaking Serena. She arouses him as no woman ever has. And
after a night of thrilling intimacy—a forbidden liaison—Serena
must choose between a lady's place and a woman's passion!

WINDS OF DESTINY   **(4489, $4.99)**
by Victoria Thompson
Becky Tate is a half-breed outcast—branded by her Comanche
heritage. Then she meets a rugged stranger who awakens her
heart to the magic and mystery of passion. Hiding a desperate
past, Texas Ranger Clint Masterson has ridden into cattle country
to bring peace to a divided land. But a greater battle rages inside
him when he dares to desire the beautiful Becky!

WILDEST HEART   **(4456, $4.99)**
by Virginia Brown
Maggie Malone had come to cattle country to forge her future as
a healer. Now she was faced by Devon Conrad, an outlaw
wounded body and soul by his shadowy past . . . whose eyes
blazed with fury even as his burning caress sent her spiraling with
desire. They came together in a Texas town about to explode in sin
and scandal. Danger was their destiny—and there was nothing
they wouldn't dare for love!

*Available wherever paperbacks are sold, or order direct from the
Publisher. Send cover price plus 50¢ per copy for mailing and
handling to Penguin USA, P.O. Box 999, c/o Dept. 17109,
Bergenfield, NJ 07621. Residents of New York and Tennessee
must include sales tax. DO NOT SEND CASH.*

DISCOVER DEANA JAMES!

CAPTIVE ANGEL   (2524, $4.50/$5.50)
Abandoned, penniless, and suddenly responsible for the biggest
tobacco plantation in Colleton County, distraught Caroline Gil-
lard had no time to dissolve into tears. By day the willowy red-
head labored to exhaustion beside her slaves . . . but each night
left her restless with longing for her wayward husband. She'd
make the sea captain regret his betrayal until he begged her to
take him back!

MASQUE OF SAPPHIRE   (2885, $4.50/$5.50)
Judith Talbot-Harrow left England with a heavy heart. She was
going to America to join a father she despised and a sister she
distrusted. She was certainly in no mood to put up with the in-
sulting actions of the arrogant Yankee privateer who boarded her
ship, ransacked her things, then "apologized" with an indecent,
brazen kiss! She vowed that someday he'd pay dearly for the liberties he had taken and the desires he had awakened.

SPEAK ONLY LOVE   (3439, $4.95/$5.95)
Long ago, the shock of her mother's death had robbed Vivian
Marleigh of the power of speech. Now she was being forced to
marry a bitter man with brandy on his breath. But she could not
say what was in her heart. It was up to the viscount to spark the
fires that would melt her icy reserve.

WILD TEXAS HEART   (3205, $4.95/$5.95)
Fan Breckenridge was terrified when the stranger found her near-
naked and shivering beneath the Texas stars. Unable to remember
who she was or what had happened, all she had in the world was
the deed to a patch of land that might yield oil . . . and the fierce
loving of this wildcatter who called himself Irons.

*Available wherever paperbacks are sold, or order direct from the
Publisher. Send cover price plus 50¢ per copy for mailing and
handling to Penguin USA, P.O. Box 999, c/o Dept. 17109,
Bergenfield, NJ 07621. Residents of New York and Tennessee
must include sales tax. DO NOT SEND CASH.*